AGAINST THE GRAIN
YA EDITION

A NOVEL

BY

PHIL M. WILLIAMS

Against the Grain
By Phil M. Williams
Copyright © 2018 Phil M. Williams

Printed in the United States of America
First Printing, 2018

Phil W. Books www.philwbooks.com

ISBN: 978-1-943894-36-9

Interior formatting by Tugboat Design

Contents

[1]

The Farm

The boy moves from hive to hive in a tattered gray T-shirt, tan pants, a veil, and bare hands. The fifty hives and three million bees create a collective hum. He works gracefully and efficiently. He's baby-faced, thin, but wiry, short for his age, with sun-bleached light-brown hair, a sharp pointy nose, and tan skin. The hives line the edge of the wood line, overlooking ten acres of wildflower meadows.

Native grasses—and splashes of purple, red, and yellow flowers—dominate the field. Bees fly back and forth, carrying nectar and pollen from the five-foot-tall milkweed flowers, red clovers, and purple chicory blossoms. A shallow pond lies in the depression, dead center. Cattails, pink lotus flowers, and bulrushes cover the waterscape. Ducks submerge their heads, letting the water roll down their backs.

The boy unties his veil and tucks it under his arm. He treks through the well-worn path toward the dilapidated barn and cabin. He steps through the propped-open barn door. Sunlight streaks through the many fissures and imperfections in the structure. He hangs his veil on a rusty hook. A black cat greets him with a meow. He bends down and offers his hand. The cat rubs her head against him.

"How are you doing, Blackie?" the boy asks, as he pets the cat. "That's good. I've got good news and bad news." He sits down on the wooden folding chair in front of the workbench. The cat hops up in his lap, turns around three times, and lies down. "Do you want the good news or the bad news first?" He pauses. "You're just like me. I always choose bad first. Well, I'm concerned about Uncle. I don't mind doing most of the chores. I'm old enough, but he used to be so strong. Now he can't help with the heavy work. I don't even know if he's sick or just old. What do you think?" The boy takes a deep breath and exhales. "I know. You're right. I should talk to him. I just don't think he'll talk about it. He never complains about anything. Do you remember when he cut off the tip of his finger? Not a single complaint. He must be the toughest person on earth. So that's the bad news.

"The good news is the bees are being nice to me. I haven't been stung once this season. We have an agreement. I'm extra careful not to hurt even one bee, and they're extra careful not to sting me. The chickens are doing well too. I gotta tell you what happened last night. We have this new chicken that keeps sleeping in the nesting box. Of course I can't let that happen, because then the eggs get dirty with her manure.

"So at dusk I've been going to the box and picking her up and putting her on the roosting bar with the others. Once I put her there, she stays all night, but she still tries to sleep in the nest the next day. Last night I went to open the nest, and she hurried up and got on the roost before I could put her there. People say that chickens are stupid, but I don't believe it. She's smart enough to know that I don't want her to sleep in the nest, so she just waits to see if I'm gonna kick her out. If I go to kick her out, she pretends like she wasn't in there, but, if I don't get out at dusk, she sleeps there all night. Either way she wins. That's pretty smart, don't you think?"

Blackie purrs as the boy rubs the cat's neck with his finger.

"Oh, come on, Blackie. Don't worry. You're still my best friend … my only friend, if you wanna get technical." The boy gazes at the rafters. "I'd love to sit here and chat with you, but I need to get going, I still have tons to do. I'll bring you some leftovers, if we have anything good tonight."

He grabs two large wicker baskets, the fruit picker from the workbench, and strides for the orchard. He stops alongside the old one-story wooden cabin. Apart from his tiny bedroom, he can see the entire cabin through the dirty window. He sees dust motes in the sun, streaming through the windows, as well as the kitchen, the reading area, and Uncle's bed against the far wall. Uncle is lying on his back on top of his bed, fully dressed in his denim overalls. His stocking feet hang over the end. Uncle is a mountain of a man. He's clean-shaven, his white hair neatly kept. His face is worn from the combined effects of the sun and age. His clothes are loose around his body.

The boy taps the window. Uncle opens his eyes and turns his head, with a little smile. The boy waves and continues to the orchard. The three-acre orchard features rows and rows of fruit in various stages of ripeness. An old orchard ladder is a permanent fixture to access the thirty-foot-tall trees. He finds the peach tree he checked for ripeness yesterday. He props the orchard ladder up against the trunk. He grabs the low-hanging fruit first, then what he can reach with the extending fruit picker. With a flame-red peach inside, the picker looks like the torch on the Statue of Liberty. Finally he gets on the ladder with the picker to get as much as he can. He looks at a ripe cluster, just out of reach. *I'll leave those for the birds.* He fills two bushels and lugs them out of the orchard.

His old wooden cart sits on the porch, partially loaded. He adds the bushels of peaches to his jars of honey, cartons of eggs, and broccoli heads. He pushes his load of produce along the dirt driveway. After a quarter-mile trek on the path through the meadow and the woods, he arrives at the asphalt highway. His senses are overwhelmed. He hears the roar of the motors as cars zoom by. He smells the exhaust fumes from the diesel trucks. White paint is peeling off the fruit stand. The stand is set up in the grass at the end of a concrete sidewalk.

The boy looks over the inventory and adds the produce from his cart to the open compartments. He keys open the lockbox, and stuffs the cash and change into his pocket. He locks the box and places it under the sign that reads Pay What You Think Is Fair. He sits on the plastic lawn chair, grabs a peach and some snap peas to munch on, and cracks open his self-assigned homework, *The Creature from Jekyll Island*, by G. Edward Griffin. He removes his bookmark at the chapter entitled Sink the *Lusitania*.

The boy looks up from his textbook and sees a short, chubby blonde girl with blue eyes, a round face, soft features, and perfect porcelain skin.

"How much are the apples?" she asks.

"The price is whatever they're worth to you."

The girl flashes an instant smile. "So, what if I thought they should be free?"

"Then, for you, they'd be free."

"I could just take all your produce and then what?"

"Well, then I'd be out of business, and you'd have to grow your own produce or go back to buying that awful stuff at the grocery store."

Her nose twitches, and she laughs. "What's your name? Do you go to Jefferson Middle?"

"I'm Matt. I go to school here, at my house."

"You mean, you're homeschooled?"

He nods. "I study with my uncle. What's your name?"

"I'm Emily. I live down the road, over there in Kingstown. You know, the new neighborhood."

"That's a long way," Matt says.

"It's not so far on my bike. I wanted to see what was at the end of the sidewalk, and I found you. Plus I like to bike ride, and my parents tell me I need to exercise. Do you like to ride bikes?"

Matt looks down. "I don't have a bike."

"I have an extra one. It's a ten-speed, not a girl's one either. You could borrow it, if you want to."

Matt looks away. "I never learned to ride."

Emily waves her hand, as if she's swatting a fly. "That's not a big deal. I could teach you. If I can do it, you could definitely do it. I'm bad at everything."

"I'd like—" Matt starts.

Emily turns toward two BMX bikes rapidly approaching. She cringes and braces herself, with slumped shoulders and her chin to her chest.

"Hey, buffalo butt, you better pedal your big ass home, before Mom and Dad get ahold of you," the lead rider says.

The lead rider looks more like a man than a boy. He's tall and muscular, with stubbly facial hair growing densely around his chin and upper lip. His hair is cut short on the sides, with horizontal lines shaved into his scalp and jelled spikes on top. His sleeveless black T-shirt reveals the arms of a bodybuilder.

"You're a jerk, Tyler!" Emily's face is red, and she has tears in her eyes.

"Oh, I see. You're all embarrassed because you like this little Amish homo. I hate to say it, but it ain't gonna work. He prob'ly likes Colton," Tyler says, as he points to his partner in crime.

Colton, still on his bike, wears long black jorts hanging low off his butt, a white tank top, showing off his red skin, and thin developing muscularity. An Oakland Raiders cap sits perched sideways on his head, with the brim stiff as a board. Patchwork facial hair is left to accumulate on his chin and upper lip.

Colton frowns and ticks his tongue off the roof of his mouth. "Whatever, yo. Nigga prolly jonesin' for *yo* ass."

Matt turns his head, wishing he could be invisible.

Colton's self-cultivated suburban caricature of the urban black gangster is rebellious and dangerous in rural Pennsylvania but would hardly pass an authenticity test in downtown Philadelphia.

"Oh, snap, that punk ass be frontin'. You see him look away, yo?" Colton laughs.

"I didn't know you could be Amish and a homo," Tyler says. "I'm pretty sure that's against the rules. I think you can go out with your cow or your goat or whatever, but not a man."

"Stop it. You're being a jerk," Emily says.

Matt turns to Tyler. "I'm not Amish."

Tyler and Colton laugh in unison. "You do this because you're poor?" Tyler says. "It's not even for your religion? I'm sorry. I didn't mean to offend you." Tyler places his hands up in mock surrender. "From now on I won't call you Amish. You'll be the white-trash homo instead."

"White trash and homos don't mix," Colton says. "Homos be rollin' in the Benjamins."

Tyler glares at Colton and exhales. "Fine. ... From now on I'll call him *farmer faggot*."

Colton smiles wide in approval.

Matt's eyes fill up with tears. He wipes them with his sleeve.

"Oh, snap. Nigga's straight-up bawlin' now," Colton says.

"Damn, now I know he's not Amish," Tyler says. "The Amish don't cry like a ball baby."

"Leave him alone!" Emily says.

"Fine. Damn, buffalo butt," Tyler replies. "You need to get your big butt movin' though. Mom and Dad are seriously pissed."

Emily looks at Matt; he looks away. She pedals toward Kingstown. Tyler and Colton grab some apples and throw them toward the highway. Colton holds his pants as he winds up. Apples explode as they hit a passing eighteen-wheeler. They high-five, push each other, and hop on their bikes, racing past Emily.

Matt puts his chin to his chest and lets the tears stream out. His chest heaves, as he sobs. He stands up, still sobbing. He picks out the rotting produce and puts it on his cart. He checks the lockbox to make sure it's secure and starts back for the farm.

Matt yanks open the cabin door, as he enters. Uncle sits at the kitchen table, drinking sage tea, reading Thoreau, his reading glasses hanging off the end of his nose. Matt ignores him and heads for his bedroom. He slams his drawers open and shut. He returns to the living area carrying a clean pair of sweatpants, underpants, and a T-shirt.

"You okay?" Uncle asks, before Matt exits the front door.

"I'm fine," Matt says.

"How'd we do?"

Matt walks over to the table and empties his pocket filled with crumpled bills and change.

"That's not too bad. Why don't you walk down to Tractor Supply and get yourself a new pair of pants tomorrow?"

"No, thank you. I'm gonna take a shower."

Uncle frowns. "Are you sure? Every pair of pants you have has holes in it. You know I'm not much of a seamstress."

Matt nods, his head lowered. He exits the cabin and walks to the rear of the structure. He enters a wooden L-shaped enclosure against the cabin. A black hose connected to a showerhead dangles from the roof. He turns the spigot on full blast but steps back, anticipating the scalding-hot water from the sun-drenched hose atop the roof. He splashes himself with the scorching water. He grabs the soap made from duck fat and lathers up his body and hair. He steps under the now warm water to rinse.

Matt enters the cabin. He inhales the aroma of roasted chicken and rosemary. Uncle looks up from his book, eyebrows arched high.

"You gonna tell me what happened?" Uncle asks.

"It's not a big deal. Some kids from town were mean to me at the stand," Matt says, his eyes searching the floor.

"Being honest is most important when it's the hardest. You might think that it makes you look weak, but nobody's perfect. It's just the strong aren't afraid to admit it."

Matt looks up at his uncle. "They called me an Amish homo, okay? Then when I told them I wasn't Amish, they said I was a white-trash homo, but then they decided, because homosexuals tend to be wealthy and snappy dressers, that they would just call me *farmer faggot.*"

"Do you know what that word means?"

"Dictionary definition or slang?"

"You know which one I'm asking for."

Matt exhales. "It's when people are attracted to their same gender."

"Do you think that's something immoral, something to feel bad about?"

"Everyone else seems to."

"That's lazy thinking, and you know better. It doesn't matter what everyone else thinks. I wanna know what *you* think, based on logic and reason."

"People argue pretty strongly that it's immoral, but I don't understand how it's hurting anyone. If both people want the relationship, and they're old enough to consent, it's moral. If it's forced, then it would be immoral. The same goes for any relationship."

"So, if being homosexual isn't immoral, then why would you be upset if someone called you that?"

Matt bites the inside of his cheek and stares at the ceiling. He looks at Uncle. "I know I shouldn't care what those kids say. I guess I want other kids to like me."

"It's biological and normal. Humans evolved among tribes, and banishment meant certain death. Wanting to fit in is part of our DNA. I'm sorry about what happened today. There will always be people like that. If you stay true to yourself, they will never break you. Why don't you come over here and sit down. You can start your lesson, while dinner's cooking."

Matt purses his lips. "This was a lot easier when you taught *me* everything."

"Yes, but I don't wanna spoon-feed you information. If you wanna master a topic, you *must* be able to teach it to others. If you can teach an old dog like me, then you can teach anyone. Now, where did we leave off last night?"

"We were talking about the Battle at Waterloo between England and France."

"All right then, proceed." Uncle grins. "Teach me, young Professor Moyer. My mind is like a sponge, ready to soak up your wisdom."

"You're not gonna believe this, Uncle. So Nathan Rothschild is this rich, connected banker who has smuggling operations all over Europe. His banking house is literally controlling governments with credit. Everyone knew that they transported goods and, more importantly, information all over the world. During the Battle at Waterloo, Nathan created a panic in English government bonds. He started selling all his bonds, and people thought he knew that England must've lost to France. So then *everyone* started to sell and the price of the bonds plummeted in value. You'll never guess what he did next."

"Go on."

"He buys them all back at bargain-basement prices. Then it turns out that he knew England had won all along, and the value of the bonds skyrocketed. So basically he now owned the English government, the most powerful empire the world had ever known."

"That's quite a story. You don't think England could simply not pay the bonds?"

"They could, but money and credit would dry up, their economy would go through a massive deflationary depression, and people would be seriously upset. The government would then run the risk of being overthrown, without money to pay soldiers. What do they care if they have to pay interest, as long as they stay in power?"

"Then who has the power? The banking house or the English government?"

"They both do. The bank doesn't care about making laws, apart from controlling laws that affect their business. They just care about getting their cut for essentially doing nothing but lending with interest, and creating money and credit out of thin air. The government wants to stay in power, so they can use the people like taxable livestock. So the government and the banks use each other to further their goals."

"Sounds like a match made in hell."

+++

Through his flimsy bedroom door, Matt hears Uncle snoring. Matt's room features a small wooden dresser and a single bed made from locust wood. His pillow is filled with chicken and duck feathers. The eight-by-eight-square closet of a room feels more like a sanctuary than a cell. It's the only private space in the cabin. The walls are cluttered with bookshelves made from old two-by-fours. Books on philosophy and natural farming are prominently displayed.

Lying awake, he stares at the books on the wall beyond the foot of his bed. He thinks he sees them move. He hears a low hum. He gets up and peers through the wooden blinds. There's a light in the distance and the grumble of a diesel engine. He dashes to Uncle's bedside.

"Uncle, wake up," Matt says, as he shakes the old man.

"What, what is it?" Uncle says.

"I think someone's out in the meadow with equipment."

Uncle pops out of bed. He puts on his overalls and boots, grabs his double-barreled shotgun, and the pair move outside toward the commotion. Two hundred meters from the cabin, a green John Deere tractor, pulling a brush cutter, cuts a swath through the five-foot tall wildflower meadow. The tractor headlights illuminate the darkness. The driver has cut a path from one end of the property to the other. They run toward the tractor. Uncle steps in front of the mammoth machine. He fires a shot into the air. The machine stops, but the motor still gurgles. The driver's face is covered by a bandanna. He stares at the business end of Uncle's shotgun levied at his head. He flips on the high beams, blinding Uncle. The driver places the machine in high gear and drives past, narrowly missing the old farmer. Uncle and Matt watch the tractor exit their property, headed for the road at a high rate of speed. Uncle lowers the shotgun, the weight suddenly too much to bear.

"What was that all about?" Matt asks. "Why on earth would someone mow a strip through our field in the middle of the night?"

"I have no idea."

[2]

Meet the Neighbors

Uncle and Matt sit at the round kitchen table, eating chicken sandwiches and apples with honey. A few errant bread crumbs spill from Uncle's mouth. Matt peers out the window in a trance, the early afternoon sun warming his face. An awkward silence hangs in the air.

"Can I ask you something?" Matt says.

"You can ask anything you want, but it doesn't mean I'll answer."

"How come you never got married? Did you ever have a girlfriend?"

"Is this because of your little friend?" A wide grin spreads across Uncle's face.

Matt blushes. "That's not why."

"No need to be embarrassed. She seems like a nice girl. She's been by a lot lately. Is she your girlfriend now?"

"I've only known her a couple of weeks. I know what you're doing. You're changing the subject. You never talk about anything in the past. I don't know anything about your life before here. You don't even have any pictures. I know. … I checked everywhere."

"Sometimes it's best to leave the past in the past."

Matt frowns. "You said that, when I was older, you'd tell me. I'm almost thirteen." He stands from the table and grabs the last bit of chicken from his plate. "I'm tired of guessing. For a while I thought you were a history professor or a philosopher—or maybe a spy on the run from the government. If it's bad, it won't matter to me. I just wanna know." Matt looks at Uncle, waiting for a response. "Fine, I'm gonna go finish my chores." He jerks open the front door.

"It's better you keep your eyes on the future. That's what's important."

Matt turns to Uncle. "Then why do I learn about history? And why in the hell do I learn philosophy from people who lived over two thousand years ago?" He slams the door behind him.

Matt stomps outside. He walks behind the barn, holding out a piece of chicken. "Blackie, Blackie." The cat trots behind him, rubbing his leg. He squats down and holds out the chicken. Blackie rips the meat with her sharp incisors. "He's hiding something, I know it. I'm old enough to know."

"You talk to your cat?" Emily says, as she walks toward the pair.

Matt drops the chicken and stands up, his brow furrowed. Emily strolls toward him, her calf-length sundress flowing gracefully with her gait. Her hair is propped up on top of her head, with wisps framing her sunny face. Matt's ripped T-shirt and pants, with kneeholes, are the perfect disparity.

"She's my friend, okay?"

Emily's smile vanishes. "I'm sorry. I didn't mean anything by that. I talk to animals all the time. I don't think it's weird."

"It's not weird."

"Okay, can we just drop it?"

"Yeah, I'm sorry. I'm just in a bad mood."

"I can go home." Emily looks away.

"No, I want you here. How did you get here so quickly?"

"I cut through the woods. You know, where that tractor cut that trail. After Sunday school I told my parents that I was going to Sophia's."

"I thought she hated you?"

"She does, but my mom wants me to be friends with her, because she's just like my mother ... pretty and popular. When I tell my mom that I'm going over there, she gets all excited. Today when I told her, she clapped her hands and in a really high voice said, 'That's so wonderful.'"

"What about your dad?"

"What about him? He just does whatever my mom says. So, why are you such a crabby Matty today?" Emily puts her hands on her hips.

"My uncle. I wanted to know more about his life, before I came here. As usual I get *nothing*. I feel like he's hiding something. Maybe he's ashamed of something he did."

"Maybe he's just protecting you."

"Maybe."

"No offense, but your uncle looks really old to be an uncle."

"He's actually *my* great-uncle. He's my mother's uncle."

Emily bites the corner of her lower lip. "I wanna ask you something, but, if you don't wanna answer, it's okay. I won't be mad." She pauses. "Where's your mom?"

Matt stares at Emily blank-faced.

She blanches and looks away.

"She died in a car accident with my dad when I was five. That's when I came here."

Emily's eyes moisten; she stares at her feet. "I'm sorry. I didn't know."

"It's fine. I don't remember a single thing about them. How can you feel sad about losing something you don't even remember having?"

"Did your uncle tell you anything about them?"

"He told me that they were never married. He said my dad really wanted to marry my mom, but she was a feminist and didn't need a man's name. He said they loved each other more than any married couple he had ever met. He told me that my mom stayed home with me, and my dad was a civil rights attorney in Philly. My uncle said that I was the center of my mother's universe. He said it was pretty annoying."

"Your parents sound really nice." Emily presses her lips together.

"You probably can't help with chores today, with that dress, but you can keep me company, if you want. You don't have to though."

Emily steps forward, her head down.

His heartbeat accelerates. He places his index finger under her chin, tilting her eyes toward his, her plump lips just inches away. *She is the most beautiful girl in the world.* His stomach is in knots, his heart racing. He presses his lips softly against hers. She reciprocates for a moment, then pulls away blushing.

"I should probably get going," she says, as she strides toward the trail.

"Emily, wait."

She waves without looking back. "I'll see you next weekend."

He does his chores with a perpetual smile plastered on his face. He struts from task to task on autopilot, reliving his first kiss. In the late afternoon he hears the birds peeping near the wood line and the trail. He hears voices. He sees flashes of movement between the trees. He touches the handle of the fixed blade secured in the scabbard attached to his belt. He creeps closer along the edge of the woods, careful not to step on leaves. He sees four people, one woman and three men. One stands out in a blue police uniform. The others are dressed in brand new hiking gear. The police officer takes pictures of the others, smiling and laughing as they walk through the path cut by the tractor.

"What are you doing?" Matt says, stepping in front of them.

The blonde woman jumps back with her hand over her chest. The group stops, startled. They see Matt and exchange smirks. The police officer scowls. The officer has a tight curly blond crew cut, wide flaring nostrils to match his cavernous mouth, eyes almost on the side of his head, and a stocky build. He takes a wide stance, unsnaps his holster, and puts his hand on the butt of his Glock.

"It's none of your damn business." the officer says.

"This is my uncle's property, so I'd say it is my business, and you're trespassing. Didn't you see the signs?"

"There are no posted signs. And this is police business. I noticed you have quite a few code violations. Did you know that you need a permit for that stand out front?"

"If this is about code violations, why are these other people here?"

The police officer stalks toward Matt. He grabs Matt's T-shirt, crumpling it up in his hand, pulling him inches away from his face. Matt turns his head and tries to pull away, to avoid the foul odor emanating from the officer's mouth. The officer clenches his fist like a vise onto Matt's T-shirt.

"Boy, I told you this is police business. It's not your place to question. I do the questioning. You got that?"

"Come on, Dave. Let the boy go. This is unnecessary and terribly premature," the balding man says, as he approaches. The man is tall and fit, sporting a strong chin, high cheekbones, with a short salt-and-pepper half-moon around his shiny dome. Officer Dave relents and steps back. "Name's John. What's yours?" he says with his hand outstretched. Matt straightens out his shirt, the collar now oversize. He disregards John's outstretched hand. "It's not very polite to ignore an olive branch."

"My name's Matt."

"There you go, young fella. It's very nice to meet you. We're just here taking a few pictures for the Kingstown community paper. We're sorry we didn't see any posted signs. We thought we were still on community property. How old are you anyway? Ten, eleven?"

Matt glares at John. "I'm thirteen."

"Oh, then you must go to school with my daughter at Jefferson Middle," the woman says. "I'm Dr. Hansen." She's blonde, forties, short, with large pointed breasts, and a thin waist, with a belt cinched tight around her light blue shirt. Her face is still attractive, even caked in high-end makeup, but she's perilously close to sagging into her age bracket.

"I don't go to the middle school. I'm homeschooled."

She smiles. "Of course you are, dear."

"What's your specialty?" Matt asks.

She takes a step back. "Excuse me?"

"What's your area of expertise?"

She looks dumbfounded.

"You know, are you a plastic surgeon or a brain surgeon or a pediatrician?"

She glares at Matt. "I'm the principal of the high school."

"Okay, it's just you said you were a doctor."

"I *am* a doctor."

Matt nods. "A doctor *and* a principal, you must be really busy."

A tall athletic man with long, wavy brown hair tied in a ponytail whispers in Dr. Hansen's ear. "Honey, I don't think he knows about these things." He turns to Matt and puts his hands on his knees to be closer to his level. His face and neck are clean-shaven. He looks younger than his wife, but probably isn't. He speaks, maintaining a clownlike smile. "My name is Mr. Hansen. It's *so* nice to meet you. We're nice people. We've just lost our way in the woods." His voice is higher at the end of the sentence.

Dr. Hansen shakes her head, scowling at her husband. "Shut up, Chip. He knows exactly what he's saying."

"Let's go, gang. This is counterproductive. We have everything we need." John motions for them to follow, as he walks on the trail toward Kingstown.

"It was *really* nice to meet cha," Mr. Hansen says, as he pats Matt on the back.

[3]

The Giver

Emily bends forward, cutting weeds around an apple tree with a stirrup hoe, sweat droplets forming on her brow, her creamy skin flushed. Matt pushes a wheelbarrow full of wood chips. He stops and glances down her shirt, catching a glimpse of white lace and soft skin. She looks up; he looks away. She adjusts her clothing to make sure nothing pinches. He dumps half of the wood chips and rakes them around the tree. In just a year, she's grown like a weed, shedding some of her baby fat. The rising ninth grader is growing into her body.

"This goes a lot faster with you," Matt says.

"Where'd you get the mulch?" Emily asks.

"Reggie's Tree Service. He brought it early this morning. He gives us all the wood chips we need, and we give him produce." Matt sets down his rake and wipes the sweat from his face with the bottom of his T-shirt, exposing his muscular stomach. Emily's staring goes unnoticed. "He tells me every time that I don't need to give him anything, but his wood chips have really increased yields and cut down on the weeding. I feel like it would be wrong not to give him something."

"Is that it?" Emily asks.

Matt nods. "We should probably get to the stand. The lunchtime crowd will be there soon."

Emily looks away. "I should go home."

Matt furrows his brow. "Did I do something wrong?"

"No, I just feel sticky and sweaty, and my clothes feel too tight. You must think I look disgusting." Emily looks down.

Matt steps into her personal space and lifts up her chin. He presses his lips to hers. She tugs on the sides of his T-shirt. He pulls her tight to his chest. She opens her mouth just enough to allow tongues to touch. She steps back with a smile on her face.

"I wish you could see what I see," he says.

"So do I."

Matt pushes the overflowing cart down the dirt driveway, with Emily strolling alongside. They pass the wildflower meadow and the small stretch of woods to the roadside stand. A middle-eastern woman in a *hijab* peruses the produce. Matt grabs two large baskets of cut herbs from the cart.

"Hello, Mrs. Ahmed," Matt says.

The woman smiles. "Hello, Matthew." She eyes Emily.

Matt motions. "This is my, um ... Emily."

Emily blushes and waves. "Hi."

"Hello," Mrs. Ahmed says.

"I picked a bushel of basil and coriander a couple of hours ago," Matt says. "I cut them at the base of their stem, so you can hang them up and dry whatever you can't use fresh."

Mrs. Ahmed's eyes bulge. "The plants look wonderful."

"Emily picked the apricots you were looking for."

Matt and Emily load the produce into her minivan. She hands Matt a fifty-dollar bill. They wave as she drives away.

Matt glances at Emily, then to the ground. "Hey, I'm sorry I didn't introduce you before as my girlfriend. I'm not sure how Mrs. Ahmed views young people dating, but it shouldn't matter. It was wrong of me to lie."

"I'm glad you didn't tell her. It would've been weird," Emily says.

"I just don't want you to think anything bad."

"I don't. I'd prefer we didn't make a big production out of us. At school I see kids with the scented notes, the hand-holding, and the kissing between every class. It's just … embarrassing. I like that we're not in anyone's face."

Matt bites the inside of his cheek. "Your parents still don't know, do they?"

"If I tell them, I can never untell them. What if they don't want me coming over here all the time?"

"You said they're so wrapped up in themselves to even notice or care what you do."

"They *are* oblivious, but if they find out, my mom will wanna know all the details, and my dad will try to act cool. He'll probably make you a mix tape of some obscure reggae. And then my brother, … he'll be a nightmare. He'll make fun of me constantly. And he'll harass *you* even worse. He said something at dinner last night that kinda worries me."

"What did he say?"

"He made this big production of asking me where I've been going all summer. He usually wants nothing to do with me. It's like he wanted to watch me squirm in front of our parents."

"What did you say?"

"I told him that I don't answer to him and that he's not the only one who has friends."

Emily sits down on a plastic chair under the shade of the fruit stand. Matt grabs a small basket and gathers apricots, cherry tomatoes, bell peppers, carrots, and raspberries. He sits down in the empty chair next to her. He scoots over so the chairs touch.

"Are you hungry?" he asks.

"I'm starved," she replies.

He hands the basket to Emily. She takes a carrot, an apricot, and some cherry tomatoes. She hands the basket back and flashes a grin. They eat in silence, watching the cars motor by.

Emily turns to Matt. "I finished *The Giver* last night."

"What did you think?" he asks.

"It was pretty unrealistic, but I liked it. It was a really easy read. Some of the stuff you give me is so complicated."

"But even the complicated stuff, you understand."

"I know, but sometimes it's nice just to relax and read, not have to think so much. You're worse than my honors English teacher. I did like the concept of sameness. Jonas lives in this community that is totally safe and secure without any pain and sickness, but the flip side is that there isn't any real joy or love. I think there is a lot of truth in that concept. How do we ever truly appreciate love, if we don't know what it's like to have a broken heart? How do we really know and appreciate health, if we've never been sick? I think that's why you see people, who have narrowly escaped death, living their lives with such joy."

"What about the allegory to government?"

"I knew you'd bring that up. I hate politics. But, yes, I got that the elders are like the government, and they control everything and keep secrets and commit murder, but they call it *release*."

"If you or I killed someone, we'd go to jail, but if we kill someone in war with a uniform on, then we might get a medal."

"In *The Giver*, the people don't know what they're doing."

"But the elders do. Just like soldiers go to war and people think they're fighting for freedom or justice or some threat. From the books I've read, they always say that they were just protecting their buddies, hoping to get out in one piece. I don't know what makes the other side any different."

Emily sighs.

"I know, I know, politics isn't your thing. What do you wanna talk about?"

Emily smiles. "Something fun."

"Did you find out any more about where your mom's been going all summer?"

"This topic's not exactly a barrel of laughs either."

Matt frowns. "Sorry."

"No, it's fine. It is on my mind. I should talk about it. I just wish I could drive. I'd follow her."

"Let's go through the evidence again."

"Okay," Emily says. "She leaves relatively early, dressed like she's going to work, and she says that she's going to work, and she probably is, but I think she's going somewhere else too."

"And what evidence do you have?"

"Last week, when I went to the mall with my dad for school clothes, we passed by the school. Her car wasn't there, and it wasn't there on the way back either."

"And you asked your dad about it?"

"Yeah, that was the really weird part. I thought he'd be suspicious, but he totally wasn't. He told me that she had a budget meeting at the district office."

"That sounds plausible to me."

"Yeah, but it took him like five minutes to come up with that. At first he said that she told him where she was, but he forgot what she told him. Then he remembered, out of the blue, like he finally came up with a good lie."

"Suspicious, yes, but still not conclusive. I think your most damning evidence is her clothes."

"Yeah, me too. She comes home every day in a good mood, with her scarf thing undone and the top two buttons of her blouse undone too. And this one time, I swear, she left in panty hose and came back with bare legs."

"But during the school year, it's not like that, right?"

"Exactly, she's usually stressed and bitchy, and her clothes are still crisp and perfect, just like when she left in the morning."

Matt bites his lower lip and shrugs. "Could be that it's just less stressful and less formal in the summer."

"You and I both know you don't believe that."

"I'm sorry, Em. I really hope we're both wrong about our theory."

"I wanna know who it is," she says.

"Maybe it's best you don't."

"That's crap, and you know it. I thought you always wanna know the truth, no matter how painful? Didn't you say that you can never truly be free without the truth?"

Matt nods. "You're right. I'm sorry. I just don't want you to be sad."

"You have to experience sadness to know true happiness, right?"

Matt nods and puts his hand on top of hers. He leans over and kisses her plump cheek.

"On the plus side, she isn't hassling me about my weight," she says.

"I don't know why she would. You look beautiful."

Emily frowns. "I look so gross *all the time*. I'm just so … heavy. Aren't you embarrassed that we weigh the same?"

Matt shakes his head. "You weigh almost the same as last year, right?" She nods.

"But you're three inches taller and more muscular. Muscle weighs more than fat. I bet you're in better shape than most of the girls at school."

"I still feel so fleshy and wide."

"You're not. You just have a distorted view of yourself."

"I'm just being honest with myself."

"No, you're not. I don't know how you could be."

"What do you mean?"

"Your mother cooks low-calorie meals for you, while your brother and your dad eat whatever they want. She locks up the snack cabinet, and you're the only one in the house without a key. I think that's cruel, and the way people have treated you has given you a distorted view of your body." Matt squeezes her hand. "I'm sorry that happened to you."

Emily shrugs and looks down. "Well, she doesn't seem to care what I eat now. You know what's messed up?" She looks at Matt.

He looks at her.

"I actually think I look a lot better than last year, but nobody notices, and I still get made fun of."

"I'm sorry, Em."

"Yeah, me too."

Matt turns toward the sound of approaching bicycles.

Emily shrinks in her chair.

Tyler and Colton pedal their BMX bikes toward the stand. Emily tucks her chin to her chest that has spontaneously erupted in red blotches.

Colton hangs on to the studded belt that holds his black jorts halfway down his butt, as he steps off his bike. His nipples and tan lines are visible through his tight white tank top. Tyler drops his bike. He looks like a white Incredible Hulk, with spiky hair and acne.

Tyler cackles as he saunters up to the stand. "I knew it. I just had to see it for myself. I knew you weren't hangin' out with Sophia and Megan."

"*Whaaaatttt*, farmer faggot tryin' to be a playa." Colton says.

Tyler glares at Colton. "More like bein' a chubby chaser."

"Oh, snap, he be liking them big ole booties."

Emily buries her head under her arms. Matt marches around the stand, placing himself between Emily and the teenagers.

"It's fine if you wanna be mean to me," Matt says, "but I don't understand why you have to be such a jerk to your sister."

"Damn, farmer faggot standin' up for his ho," Colton says.

"You two are not welcome on my property. I'd like for you to leave," Matt says.

Tyler chuckles. "You gonna make us leave?"

Matt thinks about the knife attached to his belt, under his T-shirt, but decides that the escalation is too violent.

"I'll do the best I can to make you leave," Matt says.

With the speed of a viper strike, Tyler has his hands around Matt's neck. He lifts him up off the ground with ease. Matt's face turns red; he can't breathe. He grips Tyler's wrist, trying to pry him off. Tyler grins at Matt and drops him on the ground. Matt wheezes.

"You ain't gonna do nothin'," Tyler says and struts over to Emily. "You better say good-bye to your little boyfriend, because I'm tellin' Mom and Dad."

Emily looks up, her chubby face red and tear streaked. "Please don't," she says. "I'll do anything."

"How much money you got?"

She reaches into the front pocket of her tan shorts and presents a five-dollar bill.

Tyler shakes his head. "That it? You think I work this cheap?"

Matt stands up, rubbing his neck. He staggers toward Tyler.

"You want some more?" Tyler says, his fists clenched.

Matt reaches into his pocket and hands him the fifty-dollar bill. Tyler and Colton's eyes widen. Tyler snatches the bill and shoves it in the pocket of his jean shorts.

"*Damnnnn*," Colton says.

"That's more like it," Tyler says as he turns around and gets on his bike. "Farmer faggot and buffalo butt, such a cute couple."

"Later, bitchez," Colton says.

[4]

Guess Who's Coming to Dinner

Matt rearranges produce on the stand, prominently displaying his fall fare of apples, winter squash, spinach, lettuce, pawpaws, sweet corn, and peas. He hears ten-speed bike brakes squeaking behind him. He turns to see Emily. She puts down her kickstand and steps off her bike. She has her book bag tight around her shoulders. Her feminine curves are prominent in her designer jeans. Her face is round and symmetrical, but no longer chubby. Her mouth is turned down.

"How was the first day of tenth grade?"

Emily slams her book bag on the ground behind the fruit stand. "I am so sick of everybody at that stupid school."

"Are you okay?"

She purses her lips and takes a deep breath. "Yeah, I'm fine. I'm just so tired of how cruel and immature people are."

"What happened?"

"At lunch, these tenth grade boys were throwing rolls at this girl. I got in their faces and told them that they were immature. And then they were like, 'Relax, buffalo butt.' I could've wrung their little necks. I told them to shut the F up, and one of the lunch monitors heard and sent me to the office."

"What did your mom say?"

Emily shakes her head. "It's so ridiculous that she gets to discipline me at school. Isn't that like a conflict of interest or something? She gave

25

me Saturday detention, and those boys …" Emily clenches her fists and tightens her jaw. "Nothing, they got nothing. My mom said she didn't want it to seem like she was favoring me. It's such bullshit." She exhales and plops down in a plastic chair. "So I can't hang out on Saturday."

A rusty Ford F-150 stops at the end of the driveway. A thin elderly man with a full head of white hair steps out, with the speed of a tortoise.

"I wish you could just study with me," Matt says, watching the old man.

"Me too. I learn more here than I do at school anyway."

The old man shuffles toward the stand, bent over with his head down.

"Good afternoon, Mr. Miller," Matt says.

"Matt, how are you?" he says.

"I'm good." Matt grabs a box of produce from behind the stand. "I put the best stuff in here for you."

"They don't grow good food like this no more," he says. "In my day farmers grew food, not a bunch a corn to feed a damn animal that eats grass." He glances at Emily. "And who's this pretty young lady?"

"This is my girlfriend, Emily," Matt says with a smile.

Emily blushes and shakes the old man's hand.

"Much obliged," Mr. Miller says.

Matt carries the old man's box of mixed produce, and Emily carries the box of sweet corn to his pickup truck. He opens the tailgate and slides the box inside. Emily does the same. Mr. Miller reaches into his pocket and pulls out a thick wad of cash. He licks his thumb and flicks out two twenties.

"Thank you, young man," he says, as he hands Matt the cash. "It was very nice to meet you, young lady."

"Thanks, Mr. Miller," Matt says.

They watch with bated breath, as he slowly merges onto the busy highway.

"I'm not sure he should be driving," Matt says. "If we had a truck, I could do deliveries."

"You need a license first. One more year."

"For you maybe. No sense in me getting a license. We'll never get a truck."

As they walk back toward the stand, Matt grabs Emily by the arm. He points to a small hole in front of them near the driveway's edge.

"Careful," he says, "yellow jackets."

Emily looks down. The wasps fly in and out of their ground nest, the flight path coming from the wood line. They step around the nest.

"It doesn't look like that many of them," Emily says. "I mean, the honeybees have a lot more bees coming in and out of their hives."

"The honeybees have about eighty thousand bees in a hive. Yellow jackets usually have only five thousand, but they're far more dangerous, because they're so aggressive, and they can sting over and over again. I should probably put up a barrier so people don't walk on it."

"What would happen if you stepped on the nest?"

"A couple of years ago, I was cutting some grain with a scythe, and I hit a small stump, and yellow jackets poured from the nest. It was fall, so I had on gloves and a sweatshirt, but they stung me right through my sweatshirt. I ran like crazy, but they chased me, and they wouldn't stop stinging me. I had to crush them with my fingers to get them to stop. I must've been stung twenty times."

"Maybe we could put up some temporary fencing."

Matt nods. "That's a good idea. I'll bring the fencing up tomorrow."

They plop down in their plastic chairs. Emily opens her backpack, and pulls out a notebook and a purple pen. Matt grabs the tattered text from the edge of the fruit stand.

"What are you working on?" he asks.

"I'm taking a creative writing class. The teacher, Ms. Pierce, wants us to keep a journal. She says we can write anything we want—no judgment. I really like her. She's funny and pretty and so smart. My brother and his stupid friends drool over her. It's so gross. I don't know what she's doing in this hick town." She glances at the book in his lap. "What about you?"

"I'm reading *Anatomy of the State* by Murray Rothbard. This guy tells some serious truth."

Emily groans. "Sounds like more boring government stuff."

"It is, but can I read you this one passage? It won't be boring, I promise."

"Do I have a choice?" she asks, grinning.

Matt smiles and flips to a bookmarked page. He glances at Emily to make sure she's paying attention.

> The State is that organization in society which attempts to maintain a monopoly of the use of force and violence in a given territorial area; in particular, it is the only organization in society that obtains its revenue not by voluntary contribution or payment for services rendered but by coercion.

"What do you think about that?" Matt asks. "The idea that government is forced upon us."

Emily shrugs. "I'm not sure it's forced. We do get to vote. Well, *we* don't. But, when we turn eighteen, we do."

"But what do we get to vote for?"

"Politicians who try to do what's best for everyone. Not that they ever do exactly, but the majority decides. That seems fair to me."

"What if there were two wolves and a sheep voting on what's for dinner? Would voting be fair then?"

Emily frowns. "That's kind of an extreme example, don't you think?"

"Fair enough. How about you have a Democrat and a Republican, and they both believe in taxation and using your money to finance the military. But you don't want taxation or the military. But they are the only choices. You can't simply opt out and say, 'I'll keep my money, because I don't like what you're doing.' That's never an option."

"So you don't think voting is fair?"

"I think it's—"

They hear the thump of bass in the air. Matt frowns; Emily clenches her fists. A red lifted Jeep hops the curb and drives onto the grass, stopping within a few feet of the stand. Gangster rap blares from the speakers. Colton bobs his head to the beat, and Tyler grins from the driver's seat. He cuts the engine and hops out.

"What up, bitchez," Colton says, as he walks up to the stand.

Tyler saunters toward them, his arms bent, as if his muscles are too big for them to hang normally. He puts his hands on the apples and leans forward. His nose is filled with blackheads, and his cheeks are a mass of puss-filled lesions.

"I need a twenty," Tyler says.

"Go to hell," Emily says. "I told you last time, we weren't doing this anymore."

"I guess I'll just tell Mom about your little boyfriend."

"I really don't care what you do anymore. Just stay away from us."

"Damn, buffalo butt's pissed off," Colton says.

"Shut up, Colton. Your ghetto act is so lame. Your dad's the chief of police. You're the whitest person I know."

"It ain't my fault Pop's in the popo."

Emily frowns and shakes her head.

"You just gonna let your girl fight your battles for you, farmer faggot?" Tyler says.

"She's doing a pretty good job," Matt says with a smile.

Emily crosses her arms. "We're not giving you any more money."

"I think twenty bucks is a small price to pay," Tyler says with a smirk. "I could tell Mom and Dad that I saw you two havin' sex or doin' drugs. You'd never see each other again."

"We can't keep doing this," Emily says to Matt.

"You're right," Matt replies.

"So which one of you is gonna gimme my twenty dollars?"

"No more," Emily says. "Go away."

Tyler shakes his head. "Don't make me beat his little ass again, like I did last year. Open the box and give me a twenty, or I'll just take the whole thing."

Matt and Emily sit silent. Tyler reaches for the box, but Emily grabs it and tosses it to Matt. He sprints toward the driveway. Tyler and Colton give chase. Matt stops at the edge and turns around. Tyler and Colton slow to a strut.

"I'm gonna open it, give you your money," Matt says, walking toward the pair.

Matt stops and looks down at the hole between his feet. He holds out the box. Tyler and Colton move closer. Tyler reaches for the box, but Matt slams the heavy box on the ground, and sprints for the woods. He watches from a safe distance as pissed-off yellow jackets pour out of the ground nest, looking for the invader. Tyler and Colton look at each other in confusion, with their hands held out. Tyler bends over to grab the box, and three yellow jackets sting him repeatedly on his hand and arm. Colton is stung repeatedly on the exposed area of his calves below his baggy jean shorts.

After the initial stings, the yellow jackets have formally marked their targets, and hundreds of wasps attack. Tyler drops the box, and he and Colton sprint toward the Jeep, flailing their arms, smacking themselves, trying to stop the onslaught of venom. They jump in the open Jeep, but the wasps still attack. Tyler fumbles with his keys.

"Go, hurry up!" Colton says, still smacking himself.

Tyler starts the Jeep and guns the vehicle into the street. An SUV swerves to avoid them, the driver leaning on the horn in the process. Matt stands in the woods, watching the chaos. Emily walks over. She kisses him on the lips. Matt furrows his brow and steps back.

"What's wrong?" she asks.

"Do you know if Tyler or Colton are allergic to bees?'

Emily shrugs. "I don't know."

Matt bends over, with his hands on his knees. "I hope not, because if one of them is, I might have killed someone." Matt shakes his head, his eyes glassy. "I shouldn't have done that. I should've just given him the money."

Emily puts her hand on his back. "You didn't do anything wrong. You were defending yourself."

Matt stands up. "Do you have your cell?"

"Yeah."

"Can you call him? We have to make sure they don't have any allergic symptoms."

Emily frowns. "It's in my bag."

They jog back to the stand. She removes her cell from her bag.

"Do you wanna talk?" she asks.

"It would probably go over better coming from you. I'll tell you what to say."

Emily nods and dials her brother. She waits as the phone rings.

"What the hell do you want?" Tyler says loud enough that Matt can hear.

"Ask him if he or Colton have any hives or swelling in areas where they were *not* stung," Matt says.

Emily asks.

"What do you care? Tell that little bitch, I'm gonna kick his—"

"Because you could die, dumbass!" Emily says, cutting him off. After a pause Emily looks at Matt. "He says no."

"Ask him if either of them have swelling of the face or throat or tongue."

Emily asks. "He says no."

"What about trouble breathing or dizziness?"

Emily asks. "He says no."

"How about stomach cramps, nausea, or diarrhea?"

Emily asks, listens, then replies. "I don't care what you say to Mom. You act like you're so tough, and then you get a few bee stings, and you go crying to Mommy. You got what you deserved, Tyler." She closes her phone with a grin. "He said, if he shits himself, he's gonna kill you."

Matt laughs. "I shouldn't be laughing. He might actually kill me."

"He won't. He's such a bully. He doesn't pick on people who fight back. We will have to deal with my parents though."

+++

Matt puts on his newest and cleanest pair of canvas pants. He tucks in Uncle's oversized button-down shirt. He runs his hand through his sun-bleached light-brown hair. He looks at his face in the small mirror attached to his wall-mounted bookshelf. His tan skin is even, healthy, and smooth, minimizing his pointy nose. He steps from his bedroom and strides to the kitchen.

Uncle sits at the kitchen table with his reading glasses perched on the end of his nose. He sets down his book on the table, next to a wine bottle, and smiles wide.

"You look like quite the gentleman."

"Thanks."

"That shirt doesn't look half bad on you." He stands with a groan and hands the wine bottle to Matt. "This is for Emily's parents. It's elderberry wine. It's the last of the stuff I made a few years ago. You should always show up for dinner with a gift for the host."

Matt hikes through the wooded trail to Kingstown, holding his unlabeled wine bottle. The sun is waning, but it's still humid from the warm September day. He's thankful for the tree canopy, keeping him cool.

The trail ends at a concrete sidewalk and an empty basketball court. He walks through the court to the community of sameness. The luxury homes sit on tiny plots barely adequate for their girth. Like makeup hiding the ugliness beneath, every home's face is covered in faux brick or faux stone, with vinyl siding on the sides and back. In front of each are lawns that comply with their rules for sameness. Each is deep green, chemically treated, clipped and edged to perfection, and eradicated of anything, but Kentucky bluegrass. Matt strides past two SUVs in the driveway—one shiny, the other dirty. He follows the front walkway to the door. He runs his free hand through his hair and straightens his shirt. He takes a deep breath and presses the doorbell. The door swings open.

"I said, 'I got it,'" Emily says to someone behind her. She looks around and steps outside, shutting the door. She smiles and gives Matt a quick kiss on the lips. "You ready for this?"

Matt shakes his head. "Probably not." He stares at her. "You look really pretty."

Emily frowns and wipes her blond hair from her eyes. "It's like I still have baby hair. It refuses to do anything but lay straight."

"I like it."

She smiles. "Remember what we talked about. My parents ask a lot of questions. When in doubt, don't say anything."

"Got it."

She opens the door and motions for him to come inside. "Are you hungry?"

Matt nods and steps inside. "There was a lot to do today, so much to preserve."

Emily starts toward the kitchen. Matt stands still in the foyer, looking up at the churchlike ceiling. He gazes at the mural of a vineyard on the wall.

Emily stops and looks back. "You coming?"

Matt breaks from his trance and follows Emily to the kitchen, trying to avoid staring at the curve of her hips moving under her knee-length cotton dress. The kitchen is open and airy, with a center island of granite, and glistening pots and pans hanging overhead. Stainless steel appliances and oak cabinetry line the back wall. An electric guitar solo strums in the background. Dr. Hansen stands behind the center island with a glass of red wine in her hand. Her blond hair is held on top of her head, with wisps framing her face. Her makeup is thick and flawless. She's much taller than Matt remembers. She smiles wide at Matt, but her eyes remain vapid. She steps gracefully around the center island with six-inch heels and a little black dress. Her limbs are bony, devoid of shape.

"Hello, Matt," she says, with her veiny hand held out. Matt smiles and shakes her delicate hand. "It's been a long time."

Emily frowns.

"Two years to be exact. Thank you for inviting me to your home. This is for you," Matt says, handing Dr. Hansen the bottle of wine. "It's elderberry wine that my uncle made."

Dr. Hansen frowns at the bottle and sets it on the center island. "Thank you."

The back door opens, and Mr. Hansen and the smell of steak enter the kitchen. His brown ponytail is pulled tight, and his button-down shirt is untucked. He grins at Matt and sets the plate of steaks on the center island.

"You've really grown since I last saw you," he says and holds out his hand. Matt shakes it. "I hope you like steak."

"I'll eat just about anything," Matt says.

"When you're a young boy, you can do that," Dr. Hansen says and glances at Emily. "Us ladies have to really watch what we eat. Don't we, Emily?"

Emily glares at her mother.

Mr. Hansen looks at Matt. "You like The Grateful Dead?"

Matt shrugs.

"The guitar solo on the stereo, that's The Dead. Good stuff, huh?"

Matt shrugs. "We don't have a stereo."

Mr. Hansen's eyes widen. "What do you do for music?"

"My uncle plays a harmonica, and Emily brings her radio to the stand sometimes, but mostly I just listen to the birds."

"I couldn't live without music," he says. "I'd take the Dead over anything."

"Not if you were starving."

Mr. Hansen laughs. "I suppose not, but that was just a saying, I wasn't being literal. Do you understand what *literal* means?"

Matt nods.

"You probably miss out on things like that, being homeschooled, huh?"

Matt bites the inside of his cheek. "Things like what?"

"Oh, you know, social things that make people fit in, little intricacies."

"He's not missing out on anything," Emily says with her hands on her hips.

"That's not what I'm saying," Mr. Hansen says to Emily. "I'm just trying to help. I know it must be hard to fit in, when you aren't around other kids your age."

"It's okay," Matt says. "I understand. Apart from Emily, kids my age are very confusing."

"I really wish Emily would have told us you two were friends much sooner." Dr. Hansen says.

"Do you meet all her friends?" Matt asks.

"Absolutely, we are very good friends with Sophia's family."

Emily rolls her eyes.

"Why don't we all fill our plates and make our way to the dining room," Mr. Hansen says.

They each put a steak, mashed potatoes, and asparagus on their plates. Mr. Hansen grabs a beer bottle from the refrigerator.

"I put water out for everyone," Mr. Hansen says. "Does anybody want anything else to drink? Matt, you want a beer?"

Dr. Hansen shakes her head. "Chip, not funny."

"Water is fine for me," Matt says.

"I found this new microbrewery that's very good," Mr. Hansen says, holding up his beer.

They take their plates to the dimly lit dining room. Matt and Emily sit on one side, her parents on the other.

"Where's Tyler?" Emily asks.

"He's out with Colton," Mr. Hansen says.

"Are you gonna make him give Matt's money back?"

Matt shifts in his seat but keeps focused on his food.

"I don't think this is polite dinner conversation, young lady," Dr. Hansen says.

Emily narrows her eyes. "I knew it. You let him get away with everything."

"You're not innocent in this. You lied to us for two years, and Tyler and Colton could have been seriously injured the other day."

Matt looks up. "That was my fault. I'm sorry about the yellow jackets."

"I can appreciate that you're sorry," Dr. Hansen says, "but that doesn't undo what you did. You do realize that people die from bee stings, don't you?"

"Yes, I do know that," Matt says.

"What if one of those boys were allergic or what if they got into an accident trying to get away from the bees?"

"They're wasps."

"What?"

"Yellow jackets are wasps, not bees."

"Does that really matter?"

Matt looks down. "I guess not."

"You keep bees, don't you?"

"Yes."

"Then you were very well aware of what would happen if you disturbed that nest, weren't you?"

"Yes, I was. It was wrong. I wish I could take it back."

Emily stands up. "They were gonna beat him up and take his money!"

"Sit down," Dr. Hansen says.

Emily crosses her arms.

"We haven't yet decided whether or not we're going to let you see Matt anymore, so you better sit down, or my decision will be easy."

Emily bites her lip and sinks into her seat.

"I won't do anything like that ever again," Matt says. "It was my fault."

"Maybe we should talk about this *after* we eat," Mr. Hansen says, before taking a bite of steak.

"It's not fair," Emily says. "Matt is way nicer than Sophia or Megan or anybody at school. And, by the way, those girls are total bitches. They're not my friends. They've been mean to me since elementary school."

"Sophia and Megan didn't almost get your brother and Colton killed," Dr. Hansen says.

"You've already made up your mind, haven't you?" Emily says. "You're just *acting* like you'll give him a chance."

"You've never lied to us before, and you've never been so angry at your brother before you started spending time with Matt."

Emily grits her teeth and clenches her jaw. "You can't stop me from seeing him."

"We're your parents. We can do whatever is best for you. You may not see that now, but we have the experience that you don't."

"Your mother's right," Mr. Hansen says.

"She's right, Emily," Matt says. "She *can* force you not to see me, but I don't think force is a good option for creating loving relationships. Parents choose force out of convenience or because that's what their parents did. It's easier to force someone than to look at your own hypocrisy."

Dr. Hansen drops her fork on her plate with a clang. She glares at Matt. "Excuse me, young man? Do you have any idea how unbelievably rude it is to call an adult a hypocrite? Especially when it is completely erroneous."

"I'm not trying to be rude. It's just that children live in involuntary relationships that are kind of like slavery, in that kids have to obey their parents. They can't simply trade them in for new parents, if they don't like how their parents are treating them."

Emily reaches over and squeezes his hand under the table. She turns and mouths *Stop.*

Matt smiles at Emily. "It's fine. I'm just explaining that I think, when you have involuntary relationships, it's easier to act badly, because you know the other person isn't going anywhere, no matter how badly you act."

"Who's teaching you this nonsense?" Dr. Hansen says.

Matt shrugs. "It's common sense, don't you think?"

"No, I don't."

"Imagine if, instead of choosing to marry Mr. Hansen you were forced to marry someone else against your will, and the guy knew that you could never leave. Do you think he'd try really hard to please you, to be a good husband?"

"This is a ridiculous argument."

"This is how it is for kids. We're slaves to our parents. Hopefully our parents are nice, benevolent plantation owners who allow us to grow up to be free independent people. But for a lot of kids, that's not the case."

Dr. Hansen smirks. "I've worked with thousands and thousands of children. I can tell you that the vast majority of their parents would do anything for them, myself included." She looks at Emily and back to Matt. "This is where you really need experience and *proper* education. I don't know how you could possibly understand the parent-child dynamic when you've never been married, had children, or even had much socialization. You should really be careful about espousing these ideas you obviously know *nothing* about."

Matt nods. "It just seems to me that a lot of kids in the neighborhood enjoy sadistic, dysfunctional behavior. I can't imagine that their parents don't have any blame for that."

"Kids make mistakes," Mr. Hansen says. "You yourself admitted to a very big one tonight."

"I am sorry for that," Matt says.

"Our concern," Dr. Hansen says, looking at Chip and back to Matt, "is that you and Emily lied and concealed your relationship to begin with, and your inadequate socialization makes you a magnet for dangerous behavior. Now our daughter is in danger because of it. Mr. Hansen and I have a duty to protect our children at all costs."

"I'll do my best to never put her in any danger ever again," Matt says.

"I'm sorry, Matt, but that's not a risk we can take."

Emily clenches her fists, her eyes glassy. "I knew you were gonna say no."

"That's not true," Dr. Hansen says. "Matt has shown to me that he has no interest in changing."

"I'm not sure how you want me to change," Matt says.

"Have you ever even been to church or a formal school?"

Matt looks down. "No."

"Church would be a good start. We can let you see Emily at church and then see if you get better."

"I don't understand what you mean by *get better*. I wasn't aware that there's something wrong with me."

Emily turns to Matt. "There's nothing wrong with you, nothing at all."

"If there is one thing my twenty years as an educator has taught me is that, where there's smoke, there's fire. Before you, I had a perfect daughter. Now she's lying, she's mouthy, she's disrespectful. I had to give her detention at school for heaven's sake. Do you know how incredibly embarrassing that is for me?"

Emily slams her fists on the table. "This is bullshit, Mom!"

Dr. Hansen frowns and shakes her head. "This proves my point exactly. Just remember, Emily, I gave you both a chance."

Matt stands up, his eyes wet. He looks at Dr. Hansen. "Thank you for dinner." He turns to Emily. "I'm really sorry. I'm gonna go home now."

He marches through the living room, out the front door, into the darkness.

[5]

What About Your Parents?

Matt enters the front door of the cabin. Letters are laid out in organized piles on the kitchen table. Matt turns to the lump along the far wall. Uncle lies in his bed, in the fetal position.

"Uncle, I'm going swimming with Emily. Do you need anything?" He's unresponsive. Matt walks to the back of the cabin where Uncle's bed is pushed up against the wall. The open interior is sparse, except for the overflowing bookshelves. Books are stacked up on the floor against the walls, piled as high as a man. "Uncle, are you okay?" He touches the old man's back. He feels bony and cold to the touch. "Uncle, are you okay?" Uncle's eyes flutter. He groans.

"I'm fine. I just need to rest," he says.

"Are you hungry? I could heat up that soup I made."

"No, I'll eat later. Is Emily with you?"

"I'm meeting her at the pond."

"You go have a good time."

Matt exits the cabin. He sees Emily, sitting on the dock with her feet dangling in the water. Her skin is creamy white with sun-kissed strawberry hints. No longer the chubby short kid, she's tall and fit, with full breasts, rounded hips, and a thin waist. Her blue T-shirt covers her blue bikini top that's tied behind her head.

Matt's bare-chested, wearing the blue board shorts that Emily gave him yesterday for his sixteenth birthday. She couldn't stand him wearing old cutoff farming pants to swim in. He still has a baby face, but with his short haircut, his straight light-brown hair is wavier and not so childish. He'd love to be taller. Emily passed him by an inch earlier this year. He's short for a boy, at five feet seven inches, and thin, but his muscles are well developed from farmwork.

The sun beats down on him from directly overhead. He walks down the well-worn path with a smile he can't suppress. The wildflowers reach for the sun, flowering, desperately trying to spread their seed. The flowers cover the color spectrum from white to dark purple, with honeybees collecting nectar and pollen in exchange for pollination. Lining the path, Matt planted gigantic sunflowers, with twelve-foot-tall stalks that stand straight and proud, guarding the promenade like soldiers in patriotic propaganda. Throughout the day, the cartoonish soccer-ball-size flower heads track the sun in perfect unison.

"Lookin' good, farm boy," Emily says, as she stands.

"What did you tell them?" he says with a grin as he approaches.

"The truth."

Matt stops, his eyes widen.

Emily smiles. "Well, not the whole truth. I said I was going swimming."

Matt purses his lips and closes the gap between them. "We have to be careful."

Emily smirks. "You worry too much. We've gotten away with it for a year now. As long as I don't go to the stand, nobody even knows I'm here. And my parents are even less interested than they used to be."

She puts her hands on his hips, turning him toward the water. She kisses him; he loses himself in the moment. Emily lets go and shoves him off the deck. Matt's arms and legs flail on the short drop, ending in a splash.

He surfaces, smiling, and splashes Emily on the dock. "I can't believe you did that. It's freezing."

Emily laughs. "Someone had to. I didn't wanna wait the half hour it takes you to get used to the water." She unbuttons her shorts and slides them down her long toned legs, revealing her blue bikini. She slips her

T-shirt over her head and drops it on the dock. Her stomach is flat but feminine, and her chest is well restrained by the top. She smiles at Matt and dives in headfirst. She surfaces, and they swim closer to shore, where they can stand with their heads peeking above the waterline.

He places his hands on her hips and pulls her closer. She hops up on him, weightless from the water, her legs wrapped around him. They kiss, mouths open slightly, tongues exploring. He moves, with Emily attached, to their secret place. Bulrushes dominate the pond up to four-feet deep. Inside the sea of thick green grasses is a phone-booth-size area of five-foot depth without vegetation, surrounded by the giant grasses. In their hiding place, they feel lost and safe at the same time, like they're the only people on earth. From the shore, it's impossible to see inside their nook. Here they feel free to express their lascivious desires.

After their make-out session, they return to the dock, climbing up the makeshift rope ladder.

"You really do look beautiful," he says.

She frowns. "I feel fat. I had lunch not too long ago, and now I just look so bloated." She shakes her head. "I don't want you to look at me out of the water, okay?" She covers her bikini with her beach towel and sits down on the dock, dangling her legs in the water.

"You're in great shape. I know. I've *been* looking." Matt sits down next to Emily, hands touching, feet swirling in the water. He kisses her cheek and feels it tighten as her smile develops.

"You see me through rose-colored glasses."

"That's not true. If you needed to lose a few, that's what I'd say ... tactfully of course."

"This is one area where I know you lie."

Matt places his thumb and index finger on her chin, turning her face toward him. He leans in, pressing his lips against hers. After a moment, they uncouple, but he still holds her chin. "I thought you were the most beautiful girl in the world when we first met. Time with you has only made me more certain."

Emily blushes and turns away, trying to suppress a smile. "You say these things to me, and I know you mean them, but I still think I'm that fat, chubby kid to everyone else."

"I don't know how they can't see what's so obvious. What about your family? Or Sophia and her bitchy friends? Do you think they've noticed any changes?"

"My mom's been working all summer." She throws up air quotes as she says *working*. "I'm not sure I even care if she's having an affair anymore. My dad's totally oblivious. He spends all his time working out, getting high, and burning CDs for his stupid Kingstown parties. I swear the adults in my neighborhood are more immature than the kids. I've been avoiding everyone from school and the neighborhood. After the year I had, I never wanna see them again. I can't believe this is the last day of summer vacation."

"I wish you could homeschool with me."

"Me too. I don't wanna go back. The summer's gone, and it makes me feel sick to my stomach just to think about it. It's the same feeling I got every day at school, just waiting for someone to make some stupid comment about my body. You know, as much as I hate my brother and all his stupid friends for calling me buffalo butt, that was better than the girls calling me *bubbles*. Do you know why?" She looks away. Her face reddens; a single tear slides down.

"Buffalo butt is just ignorant and sophomoric. If you videoed them saying that and replayed it twenty years from now, they'd be horrified. It's obvious whose being the idiot in that exchange. These girls who call you *bubbles* are cruel and calculating. You're in a terrible position, because they can call you what they want, then claim that it means that you have a nice 'bubbly' personality. Meanwhile they can laugh behind your back, knowing that what they're really doing is criticizing your body, insinuating it's shaped like a bubble. The worst part about it is the insult to your intelligence. They think they can have this inside joke, where they can make fun of you, but you won't understand it." Matt pauses. "Em, these kids are stupid."

Tears stream down her face. "Goddamn it, Matt. I can't do it again.

I won't. I don't have to be popular. I just don't wanna be harassed. You know, I didn't eat lunch the whole year."

She puts her head in her hands, tears forming small puddles. Matt scoots closer, putting his arms around her and pulling her toward him. She pulls her feet from the water and curls up in his lap like a child. She buries her head in his neck. He feels her body convulse as she sobs. The weeping slows. She swallows, sits up, moves out of his lap, and wipes her eyes on her towel.

"I'm sorry," she says. "It's our last summer day together. I don't wanna ruin it. I wish we could go back in time and redo this whole summer."

"I love you. You're my best friend. If you can't talk to me, who can you talk to?"

"Technically I'm your only friend." She forces a smile.

Matt smiles. "You forgot about Blackie. It wasn't easy to beat her out for best friend honors. She's a great listener, especially when you have chicken. She's always happy to see you, and she never says anything rude."

"You know what I don't understand?"

"What?"

"I know I've lost weight this summer, but I wasn't really fat before. There are plenty of other girls who are heavier than me. Why do they have to pick on *me*? Is it something I'm doing?"

Matt grasps Emily's hand and squeezes. "I'm not exactly the best person to ask that. It's like a rite of passage to harass farmer faggot at the fruit stand."

"I know you know the answer. You're just trying to save my feelings."

"I guess I have some insights, but I'm not always right, and I don't wanna say something that might have some consequences and then turn out to be wrong."

Emily pulls away her hand. "You can't say that and then not tell me. I need to know. I won't be mad if you end up being wrong."

"I'm not a psychologist, just because I read a lot of books."

She rolls her eyes. "I'm aware that you're not a sixteen-year-old psychologist."

"Okay, ... kids who get picked on are more likely to have been abused by their families in some way, whether it's emotional, physical, sexual, or just plain neglect. It's almost like the bullies can smell the abuse on them. That abuse makes kids self-conscious—or lack confidence or self-esteem. These bullies are predators who simply prey on the weak. It's actually really sad, if you think about it. These kids suffer abuse from their parents and then suffer more abuse from their peers, and eventually spouses and bosses. By abusing, these parents ensure their kids will have a lifetime of abuse to navigate."

Emily stands up, her hands on her hips. Matt rises, trying to hug her. She pushes away his hands. "But what does that have to do with me? My parents never hit me or even spanked me. They don't believe in it. And I was certainly never sexually abused or neglected. My parents are gonna pay for my college and even buy me a car, when I get my license. How could any of this be *their* fault?"

"Maybe this wasn't such a good idea."

"No, answer the question. You can't open this door, then shut it, before I can even look in the room."

"When your brother calls you buffalo butt or punches you in the stomach so he can see you gasp for air, that's abuse. It's emotional and physical abuse."

Emily crosses her arms and leans away from Matt. "That's my stupid brother. Everyone fights with their siblings. He's not always like that. He's nice when he's not showing off around his friends. Besides, that's not my parents' fault."

"Maybe, but why don't they ever put a stop to it? From what you told me, he does whatever he wants, and your parents worship him. Why would he feel like he could abuse you without consequence? And whose fault is it when your mother gives you a hard time about your weight or what you eat?"

Emily drops her arms and hangs her head.

"In your mother's shallow world, being fat is the worst thing you could possibly be. Then you always feel fat, which is the most hated thing in the world by *your* mother. She fills the cupboards with junk food that she pukes up. Then she shames you for eating the junk food that she herself can't resist. Then your dad is partying and acting like a child, so passive that he doesn't stand for anything. Letting you do whatever you want isn't being a cool dad, it's being neglectful."

She looks up, her eyes glassy, tear streaks developing. "What about you? You don't even go to school, and you get picked on by the whole neighborhood. Who abused you? Don't you ever wonder why you can't remember *your* parents? Maybe they did something terrible to you! How can you say these things about my parents, when you don't even know what it's like to have parents?"

Matt turns and strides away.

"Matt, I'm sorry." Emily runs after him. "I'm sorry. I was just mad, I shouldn't have said that."

"Go home, Emily. I've got work to do. I'm done with this."

"So we're breaking up?"

"Whatever you want," Matt says, as he walks away.

He marches to the garden to pick some carrots and turnips to beef up the soup for dinner. Out of frustration he yanks far more root vegetables than he needs. He feels tightness in his chest; he has trouble breathing. He drops the vegetables and runs to the woody path.

"Emily, wait. Emily, wait!" He doesn't see her. He sprints through the woods for five minutes. He sees her at the end of the path, where the woods meet the Kingstown sidewalk, just in front of the basketball court. She's talking to her brother who has a basketball wedged in the crook of his muscular arm. Matt stops; fear overcomes his urge to continue, as if a force field exists between the two properties. He puts his hands on his knees, trying to catch his breath, still looking at the siblings. Tyler glares at Matt over Emily's shoulder. He puts his arm around her and leads her away. Matt hangs his head. He replays the argument over and over again on the trek home.

He opens the cabin door. Uncle is finally up, but his skin looks translucent. He's sitting at the kitchen table, looking over a pile of letters.

He used to seem larger than life; now he looks frail, teetering between life and death. *One day he's gonna be gone, and I'll have nobody.*

Uncle looks up, eyes peering out above his reading glasses. "You okay, Matt? You look like you've seen a ghost."

"I'm fine. I don't really wanna talk about it."

"Okay, but did you pick up the cash from the stand today? We need some money."

Matt washes the root vegetables in the sink, Uncle behind him. "I'm sorry, Uncle. I didn't get there today. I'll go first thing in the morning."

"It's been quite a few days since you replenished the stand and pulled the cash. I know you've been having a great time with Emily, so I haven't said anything. I just can't make that walk anymore. There's probably three or four hundred dollars in that box."

Matt's shoulders slump. He looks at his reflection in the window over the sink. "I know. I'm sorry. It won't happen again. Emily's gone anyway. I can go back to being your slave."

"I hope you know that I don't think of you that way. You're right though. You've been carrying me for a long time now, and I'm sorry for that. I wish I could've given you the life you deserve. You deserve better than this broke old man."

A single tear blazes a trail down Matt's face, followed by another. "I'm sorry, Uncle." He wipes his face with his T-shirt. "You've given me a great life. I shouldn't have said that."

"Do you wanna tell me what happened?"

Matt turns around and slumps in the chair opposite Uncle. "We had a fight, and I said some things I shouldn't have, and so did she. She tried to apologize, but I shut her out."

Uncle exhales. "The first one's always the hardest. Give it some time. It'll blow over. What'd you do, criticize that crazy mother of hers?"

Matt's eyes widen. "How'd you know that?"

"Emily's had enough lunches with us this past summer that I know a few things about her. She's a kind person. She sees the good in those closest to her and rationalizes the bad. She's not a pushover, so, if you did something awful to her, she'd probably give you your walking papers. I know you wouldn't do anything on purpose to hurt her. That leads me to my conclusion that you pointed out something her family did that threw her for a bit of a loop."

Matt shakes his head. "I don't understand why she got so upset. She hates her mother."

"You need to understand the parent-child relationship. Emily's been under that woman's care her whole life. A lot of parents brainwash their kids into believing they're doing right, when they're not. Not that parents plot this out, mind you, but they do it because it's easier than doing the right thing. They may not be able to verbalize it exactly, but kids start to rebel when they become aware of it on some level. That usually starts when they're teenagers. Emily's torn between the love she has for her family and the abuse they've inflicted on her."

"I should've kept my big mouth shut."

"We're all learning as we go. You two have been thick as thieves for three years. You can't ruin that with one fight. It'll work out. You'll see."

"I hope so."

Uncle takes a deep breath. "I've been putting this off, but we need to have a discussion about this property. I've tried to keep all this ugliness from you, because I wanted you to have fun this summer. I don't know what's gonna happen with the mess I'm in with the township. Things are coming to a head now, and we need to make some hard choices."

"I thought you said it was fine, that you were handling it? We've been getting this crap for three years, and they haven't been able to do anything to us."

Uncle exhales, looks down at the table, then back up at Matt. "They haven't been able to do anything to us *yet*. Before that community was built, nobody cared what we did back here, and the property taxes were low. Now the township police are enforcing every damn code down to the letter, and they keep raising the taxes. They want us to get rid of the livestock, the bees, and cut the meadow like it's a goddamn suburban lawn. If we do that, we can't afford to live here and pay the taxes. If we don't do what they want, we can't afford the citations. We're stuck between the proverbial rock and a hard place. On the positive side, the codes are so vague, that I can argue in court that our use is permitted."

Matt breathes a sigh of relief. "Okay, then what's the problem? We go to court with good legal arguments, and we win."

"The problem is that the rules are so vague that we *are* breaking them. That's how they getcha. They keep adding rules, bureaucrats, police, code inspectors, and before you know it, everyone's breaking the rules. It gets so damn oppressive that you can't live without breaking the law. Then the state has all the power to enforce against any undesirables."

"Undesirables?"

"Anybody opposed to the state in general, or anybody opposed to individuals working for the state. So if a cop or a township official has it out for you, or a connected neighbor doesn't like what you're doing, then they can make your life miserable. Everybody's breaking the rules, but they get to choose who to crack down on. That's the power of the state."

Matt hangs his head and rubs his temples. "What do we do now?"

Uncle removes his reading glasses and wipes them off with his handkerchief. "I requested an appeal to the citations, and we have a hearing next week. If we lose, ... well, ... we have to win."

[6]

Memory Lane Is Filled with Regret

A polite beep emanates from the yellow sedan. Matt opens the front door to the cabin and pokes his head inside. "Uncle, the cab's here. Are you ready?"

Uncle places his pertinent papers and handwritten arguments into a manila folder. His hands are shaky and sluggish; his old suit, quite a few sizes too large. If it wasn't for his peaked face and normal-size shoes, you might think he was a wearing a clown costume.

"As ready as I'll ever be," he says.

"Are you sure you don't want my help?" Matt asks with a furrowed brow.

"I may be old, but my marbles still work just fine. I can handle it. I need you to harvest the fruit and get to the stand. No sense in both of us wasting the workday."

Matt opens the passenger door of the taxi. Uncle groans as he contorts his lanky body into the cab. He gives a confident wave, then buries his nose in his arguments.

Matt tries to concentrate on the tasks at hand, but he can't shake the sick feeling deep in the pit of his stomach. After harvesting as many apples, pears, and quinces as he can carry on his cart, he pushes toward the stand. He thinks about Uncle struggling to ascend the courthouse steps. As he approaches the fruit stand, his heart sinks; he feels woozy. The old wooden stand is obliterated, with pieces of wood fifty yards from

50

the original site. Flies buzz around the crushed produce strewn about the ground. Glass and honey litter the asphalt shoulder in front of the site. It appears the initial run-through had left quite a few jars of honey intact. A quick toss to the asphalt solved that problem.

The old roof is propped up, facing the road, and staged with spray-painted signs. If not for the messages and the honey, he would have thought it the accidental work of a drunk driver. The makeshift sign is spray painted with black letters. There are two messages, with two distinct handwriting styles. The first one is neatly written: Farmer faggot. The second is messier but still legible, in all capitals, FAKE-ASS AMISH.

The lockbox sits neatly in front of the signage. Fear courses through his veins, as he stares at the innocuous wooden box. The lock is attached unbroken, but the latch has been pried out, leaving the lock impotent. His heart pounds as he opens the lid and peers inside. A small folded purple note sits like a ticking time bomb at the bottom where his daily pay once gathered. His hands shake as he unfolds the stationary. At the top is preprinted cursive text: From the Desk of Emily Hansen. The note reads in large loopy cursive handwriting:

I never want to see you again.
I was only nice to you because I felt sorry for you.
Emily

He's overcome with dizziness. He drops clumsily to one knee. His head and shoulders slump; his eyes shut. His mind flashes blurry images. He sees an enormous form, tall and wide, from a low vantage point. The image comes into focus. He sees the back of a colossal man, wearing an oversize green jacket with Eagles written across the back. Beyond him, is a young blonde woman sitting on the couch, with her knees pulled to her chest. Her eyes are puffy and red, her face pale and washed out.

The woman speaks in sad whispers, "He never wants to see me again." She buries her face in her hands. The large man plops down beside her.

Matt's mind flashes back to the purple note. He blinks, his breath labored. He swallows the lump in his throat. "Stop your crying. Think this through," he says, his voice bringing him back to reality.

He flips the handmade sign down and sets the produce from his cart on it. He moves wood with his cart and makes piles to separate the usable pieces. The good pile for the rebuild, the bad pile to burn in the wood stove. He gives the damaged produce to the chickens and saves the sellable. He uses his cart as a temporary stand and neatly arranges the produce. He finds the piece of wood that states Pay What You Think Is Fair and sets it up behind the broken lockbox. *With forty or fifty dollars in lumber and a few days, I can fix it.*

A few hours later, the yellow cab flies down the grassy driveway, dust spewing in its wake. Uncle struggles to exit. Matt props the fruit picker against an apple tree and runs toward the cabin.

"Matt!" Uncle says.

"I'm right here," Matt answers, as he jogs closer.

Uncle grabs the railing along the front steps to steady himself, breathing a sigh of relief. "Are you okay? I just saw the stand, and then I didn't see you. I was so damn focused on my papers, I didn't see it when I left."

"I'm fine. I think it was just a drunk driver. I can have it fixed by next week. We may have to wait to paint it until we have more money. I haven't spent the forty dollars you gave me for clothes. We could use that."

Uncle shakes his head. He looks at Matt with a solemn expression. "I don't think that'll be necessary. We lost. We have three business days to get rid of the bees, chickens, ducks, and cut the meadow."

"But we can still sell the produce."

"I'm sorry, Matt. We can't have the stand either."

"There's no way we can get that done in three days. It'll take weeks to sell the hives, and probably at least a month for someone to get a rig in here to transport them. I doubt we could even *give* the livestock away in three days."

"You're right. There's not an easy way to do this."

"Can't we ask for an extension?" Matt asks with his hands held out, begging.

"It's over." Uncle looks past him.

"What the hell does that mean?"

"It means, if we don't comply, the fines run into the thousands per *day*. We could lose this property. If we comply, we can put the property up for sale. The going rate for land that can be subdivided is $25,000 per acre, so we should net a bit over half a million."

Matt shrugs. "I still don't know how we could possibly comply."

Uncle strokes his chin and takes a deep breath. "The farmer we used to get trees from could cut the field. We'd have to harvest the chickens and ducks and burn the hives."

Matt balls his fists tight, his fingers going white. "*We*? You can barely stand up. That means me! No, I won't do it!"

"Matt, this money is for you. I'm not gonna be around too much longer. If we don't do this, they win, and we get nothing."

"I won't do it!" Matt stalks toward the barn.

He enters the barn and kicks the piece of wood propping the door. The wooden door slams shut. Light filters in through the ramshackle structure. He climbs up on a straw bale and lies on his side with his knees pulled to his chest. Tears slide across his nose and down one side of his face. He hears a meow, and Blackie hops down from the mountain of straw bales. She does her customary three turns and settles next to him. He shuts his eyes and tries to think of a better time. He tries to think about the summer with Emily, but he keeps seeing that note. He drifts off to sleep.

Matt's eyes flicker. He sees big amber eyes staring back at him—Blackie still by his side. He straightens his legs and groans as he sits up, his body stiff, and his jaw sore from grinding his teeth. "You're a good friend, you know that?" He gives his cat a pat on the head.

Matt feels nauseated, as he marches to the chicken pen. Laying hens quietly peck at the weeds and scratch the earth in search of bugs. The chickens scurry toward him, as he approaches. They begin peeping, and pacing back and forth along the fence, anticipating a treat. He reaches down for the largest chicken. She braces herself but is comfortable in his arms. He stands up, and she surveys her new vantage point. Her feathers are soft to the touch. She purrs and lightly peeps, as he pets her.

He walks to the side of the barn, out of view of the others. The stainless steel cone is attached to a tree, with a bucket filled with straw underneath. Matt gently turns her upside down. He can feel her heart beat faster. She struggles and peeps louder now. He places her headfirst into the steel cone. He takes his razor-sharp knife from the scabbard attached to his belt. He grabs her head, peeking out of the bottom of the cone, and pulls it down, so her neck is exposed. He lines the knife up under her ear, and makes a long deep cut on one side of her neck and another on the opposite side, severing her carotid artery. Warm blood pours onto Matt's left hand. She's quiet at first, but then begins to squawk, a shrill noise. After twenty seconds or so, her body starts to convulse. A few minutes later, she's limp, her blood and life exsanguinated.

By noon the bodies are piled in his cart twenty-five high. He cut out the breast meat, but did not have time to fully process the birds. He pushes the carcasses out to the woods and dumps them for the coyotes. He looks down at the lifeless bodies and empty expressions. He closes his eyes. He can still hear the squawking. He can still see the blood gushing from their necks. He can feel the warmth running down his hand. He remembers the hopeful peeping, as he picks them up one by one. His chest and throat tighten.

Matt retrieves the rusty gas can from the barn. The can is three-quarters full with stale gasoline. He shoves matches in his back pocket. He pulls the garden hose within striking distance of the beehives. He puts on his one-piece bee suit with attached veil and elbow-length gloves. He tightens the cuffs at the wrists and the ankles. He moves with robotic precision. He opens the top of every hive. Bees circle the air above their homes in mass. The buzzing is deafening.

He splashes a little fuel on the bottom of each hive, using every last drop. He lights a match and tosses it at the first target. The hive is engulfed in flames. There's a popping sound from the bees being cooked. More bees exit the hive, as the smoke and heat force them out the top. He lights another match and throws it at the next hive, then another, then another, then another. The survivors are confused. Matt stands back, watching them burn, hearing the pops and crackles. The fires are almost beautiful, if it weren't for the three million homeless or dead honeybees. He drops to his knees.

"I'm sorry. I didn't know what else to do," he says.

Matt enters the cabin. His eyes are puffy, his face worn, and his head hangs. The smell of baked chicken and apples stimulates his stomach that's been neglected for more than a day. Uncle moves in front; Matt sidesteps him, headed for his bedroom.

"Matt, talk to me, please," Uncle says.

Matt slams his door.

Half an hour later, Uncle taps on the bedroom door. "Your dinner's ready. I know you haven't eaten in almost two days. You need to eat something."

Matt is lying in his bed, facing the wall, unresponsive.

Uncle knocks again. "I'm leaving your plate by the door. You don't have to talk to me, but I want you to eat. I'm sorry that you had to do that."

In the dawn hours Matt places his empty plate in the sink and exits for the outdoor shower with fresh clothes in hand. Upon reentry, Uncle is cooking eggs and heating the teakettle on the wood stove.

"Matt, sit down please," Uncle says, as he motions toward the table.

Matt stands firm. "I'd rather not."

"Bill's gonna cut the field today, so we should be in compliance for the inspection tomorrow."

"Great, we can kill more wildlife. I doubt anything lives in ten acres of mature meadows."

Uncle takes the scrambled eggs off the burner. He looks at Matt, pleading. "I know I messed this up, and I made you clean it up for me. I don't know what to say, but, if there's anything I can do to make it up to you, I'll do it."

Matt looks up toward the ceiling, and pauses for a moment. "I want you to answer my questions with total honesty."

"Let's be reasonable."

"The truth isn't reasonable? It's the only thing that's reasonable." Matt starts for his room.

"All right," Uncle says. Matt stops in his tracks. "What do you wanna know?"

Matt takes a seat at the table, crossing his arms. "I wanna know what you did before coming here."

Uncle rubs his chin. "I was a hotshot Wall Street stockbroker, back in the sixties and seventies. Well, maybe not such a hotshot, but I was fairly successful for a while."

Matt uncrosses his arms, his eyes wide open. "What happened? Why'd you leave New York?"

Uncle places two mismatched plates on the table and plops a helping of eggs on each with his spatula. "I was a commodities trader, mostly precious metals. I actually worked in the pit, right there on the trading floor. Anyway I wasn't just a metals trader. I learned everything I could possibly learn related to precious metals that might give me an edge. I had some connections that went pretty deep into the Treasury Department and the Federal Reserve.

"Through the sixties with the Great Society programs and the Vietnam War, our government was overspending. At that point we were still on the gold standard, but France was concerned because they thought our deficit spending would devalue the dollars they were holding. So they cashed in their dollars for gold. Quite a bit of gold was draining from our vaults, so Nixon stopped dollar convertibility. Our government no longer had to limit their spending. In 1971, when Nixon took us off the gold standard, I knew what was coming, and I knew what it meant for our money."

"So you went out and bought gold, right?"

"Actually I mostly bought silver. I had started to stockpile it in 1964, the last year our coins had silver in them. At the time it was just common sense."

"You must've done pretty well through the seventies?"

"It was a whirlwind, but I didn't handle the money or myself appropriately. I thought I was invincible, and, for almost twenty years, it seemed that way. I spent the early seventies blowing the money I earned on heroin and women. The more money I made, the more I spent."

Matt frowns. "So you blew everything on drugs and women?"

"No, not exactly. By the midseventies I finally settled down. I met a good woman, and she helped me get clean. Anne ..." Uncle closes his eyes, savoring a thought. "We met at a trendy bar that her friends had dragged her to. She was smart as a whip and the most unselfish person I had ever met. Most of her friends were big-time lawyers or worked on Wall Street, but she just wanted to help people. She was a social worker. Worked in places that I was afraid to go to."

Matt smiles. "Did you guys get married?"

Uncle hangs his head and shakes it slowly. "We had been dating for a few years, and I did ask her to marry me. I asked her in Central Park. She said yes and jumped into my arms. We were so happy. This was the late seventies now, and things were getting out of control with inflation and the stability of our monetary system. Some people pretty high up thought our system was gonna collapse to the point where a dollar was worthless, and you couldn't get money out of the banks. Mathematically I knew it was gonna happen sooner or later. In 1979, when silver rocketed from six dollars to forty-nine, I thought, 'This thing is going down.' I had made some seriously leveraged bets all the way up to forty-nine. At this point I was a multimillionaire a couple times over."

"I guess this is the part where it goes bad?" Matt asks.

Uncle nods his head solemnly. "Oh, it certainly did. I purchased this property in '78, because I wanted to be able to get away from the impending chaos. I had this crazy idea that Anne and I could live off the land, while the rest of the country burned. Plus I was banking on ten tons of silver to ride out the apocalypse.

"Then in early 1980, the Commodity Exchange placed some heavy restrictions on buying silver on margin. The Feds actually halted all buying in silver, so people could only sell. I had leveraged long bets that went sour pretty quick. I had to use a lot of cash to cover them, but I was so confident that I simply doubled down. Then on March 27, 1980—I'll never forget that day—silver crashed from $20 an ounce down to around $10.

"I was beyond broke at this point. My broker called in my margin, and I didn't have the cash. The Feds busted the Hunt brothers for cornering the silver market, and I was fired because my bosses thought I was trying to ride their coattails. The rub was that the Hunts weren't trying to corner the market. They were billionaires who were worried about their money, same as me. They bought up as much silver as they could, because they thought it was the best way to protect their wealth. Hell, they even sent jumbo jets to Switzerland, loaded down with silver, protected by the fastest gunslingers in the West."

Matt laughs. "Come on, Uncle. That's ridiculous. Gunslingers and jumbo jets going to Switzerland?"

Uncle smiles wide and leans back in his chair. "That's the truth. They even had tryouts to find the best shots. These guys were professional gunfighters. The problem that the Hunts and I didn't foresee was that the US government would step in and manipulate the market. Silver and gold are the proverbial canaries in the coal mine of the monetary system. They simply took the canary out, so it no longer served its purpose. Most people couldn't care less, because they don't understand how money works. It's like what Henry Ford said, about how if people understood our banking and monetary system, there would be a revolution tomorrow. I tell you what, Matt, one day, maybe not in my lifetime, but definitely in yours, this thing is gonna blow up in our faces."

"Wow, that's quite the story. I would've never guessed that you were a commodities broker." Matt's face turns serious. "What happened to Anne?"

Uncle adjusts himself in his chair and takes a deep breath. "As you can imagine, I was upset at the time. I thought I was pretty smart, and it was quite a blow to my ego. There was nothing left for me in New York, except for Anne. I wanted us to move here together, but she couldn't leave her job. She felt it was life and death for some of her clients. She had to be there for them. I tried to stay with her, and I did for a couple months, but I was lost. I wasn't used to depending on someone for support, and it's not like Anne made much money. I was miserable, and I made *her* miserable.

"One night I slipped out and came down here. I never set up a phone, and she didn't know where this place was, not that she should try to contact me after what I did. It didn't take that long to get over losing my wealth. I love this piece of land. It's the simple things that make me happy. But not a day goes by that I don't regret walking out on her. It is one of the two biggest mistakes …" Uncle trails off.

Matt sits silently, wheels turning in his mind. "What was the other mistake?"

Uncle shakes his head. "Let's leave it at that. It's hard to go down memory lane, when it's filled with regret."

[7]

There Goes the Neighborhood

At 10:00 a.m. on the dot, four police cruisers zoom down the grassy driveway, vomiting dust behind them. The old meadow, cut yesterday, is like a once thriving city burned in a day, without warning the inhabitants. Most of the flora and fauna is dead or homeless. Vegetation is piled haphazardly. Charred ground exists where bees once hummed. Matt and Uncle wait for them in front of the cabin. Matt cringes when the stocky crew-cut blond exits the lead car, with Kevlar under his short sleeves. The other officers stand just out of polite introduction range, with arms crossed and eyes obscured by mirrored sunglasses.

"Jack, we're here to do an inspection," the blond says, blank-faced.

"This is horseshit, and you know it, Dave," Uncle says.

"You can address me as Chief or Chief Campbell." The cop crosses his arms. "My officers and I are gonna take a look around. If we find any new code violations, I'm gonna issue a warning. If you haven't adequately addressed the adjudicated citations, we will fine you. If you cannot or will not pay, we will place a lien on your property. Is that clear?" The chief smirks.

"We are within our rights to accompany you on this inspection," Uncle says.

"Knock yourself out, old man."

They walk into the wasteland; only the pond stands as an oasis of life in a desert of death. A family of ducks bobs and swims happily in the cool water. Immense bulrushes provide shade and protection. Pink water lotuses float on the surface. The chief stares at the pond. He nods to himself, with a slight grin on his face. His officers are close behind, still speechless drones, providing "needed" backup.

"I'm gonna have to fine you for the tall vegetation in the pond and the livestock," Chief Campbell says.

"You might have a problem with the Department of Environmental Protection," Uncle says. "That pond and its inhabitants are a protected waterway. I wanted to fill it in years ago. It just takes up field space and grows mosquitoes. DEP said it was illegal to fill in an established wetland."

The chief grunts. He looks over at the barn and the cabin. "That barn's gonna need to be torn down. Safety hazard and all. You can't have an outhouse either. You need to be hooked up to the public sewer. That's gonna cost you a pretty penny." The chief strides toward his car; Uncle hobbles behind.

"These rules didn't even exist when I moved here," Uncle says.

Chief Campbell turns around at his cruiser, a slight grin on his wide face. "They do now." He drives away, with his entourage in tow.

Matt closes his eyes, takes a deep breath, and turns to Uncle. "Do you know the chief?"

"We had a run-in many years ago, but it wasn't a big deal."

"Well, this *is* a big deal. We can destroy the barn, but there is no way we can afford running the pipe to hook up to the sewer."

Uncle pats Matt on the back. "Don't worry so much. We'll sell the property well before we have to do anything about the sewer. Remember, it took them three years to make us comply. I'm just glad we passed the inspection of the *old* violations."

+++

Matt sits on Uncle's wooden rocking chair on the front porch, his hazel eyes intent on finishing *Walden* by Henry David Thoreau. A lazy breeze with a slight hint of fall replaces the afternoon heat. He pushes the planks on the porch deck with his boots, rhythmically rocking, engrossed in the multilayered classic. A black SUV, trimmed with shiny chrome, moves "drive-by" slow down the driveway. *What now?*

The truck idles in front of the cabin, tinted windows concealing the driver. The engine is cut, and a tall balding man emerges. Despite his bare, sun-beaten dome, he's handsome. His strong chin, high cheekbones, active blue eyes, athletic build, and confident stride tell the story of a man who's used to getting what he wants. His black polo shirt is neatly pressed and tucked into his pleated khaki pants.

Matt sets *Walden* on the chair and meets the man at the bottom of the porch. "Can I help you?"

The man smiles wide. "It's Matt, right? It's been a couple years. Do you remember me?"

"No." Matt stands, with his arms crossed, blocking his path.

"I'm John Jacobs. I need to speak with Jack Moyer. Is he here?"

Matt ascends the porch steps two at a time. He opens the door and says, "Uncle, there's a John Jacobs here to see you." He whispers, "He's one of the ones from the trail."

Uncle invites John inside. They sit at the table. Matt pretends to return to his book, while eavesdropping from the window over his shoulder.

"Mr. Moyer, I know you've had your troubles with the township," John says, "and, lord knows, they've cost me a fortune over the years, but I think we can work something out that'll be good for everyone."

"I'm listening," Uncle replies.

"I'm prepared to offer you ten thousand dollars an acre. I'll take care of the legal issues. You and your boy can walk away free and clear."

"You must think I was born yesterday. Seth Kreiser got $25,000 an acre just a few months ago."

"I figured you knew the comps, but you may not know how precarious your legal issues are."

"I passed my inspection today."

"Mr. Moyer, I'm a business man, I'm happy to come in and buy a distressed asset for a fair price, but I won't overpay for one that'll probably end up in bankruptcy. You may not realize it, but I'm trying to help you, because, if you don't sell to me now, you may end up with nothing."

"Are you threatening me in my own home?"

"It's not a threat. I know how these things go. I really don't wanna see you and your boy on the street with nothing. If the township wants you gone, they'll figure out a way. If you change your mind, here's my card."

John Jacobs exits the cabin and turns to Matt. "You should talk some sense into him. This is gonna go from bad to worse."

+++

Matt pushes his cart alongside the three sisters' garden. With his black hooded sweatshirt and raggedy tan pants, he could pass for homeless in Philadelphia. He vanishes when he steps inside the twelve-foot high corn stalks. Bean stalks snake up every corn plant with brown bursting bean pods. He steps carefully among the dense squash groundcover. He cuts the stem of a ten-pound winter squash, then two more, and hauls them, cradling them in his arms, to his cart. Its inflated wheels are bulging. He pushes the cart toward the cabin, stopping at the steps where two buckets await. He places forty pounds of squash in each and lugs them inside. Matt opens a trap door in the floor of the cabin. An old ventilated refrigerator lies on its back. He opens the door and places the heavy fruits inside. *Will we even be here to eat these? It's only been a month, but we haven't had a single offer.* Uncle sits on his bed in a trance, a piece of paper on the floor in front of him, and a thick legal textbook in his lap.

"A lot of squash this year," Matt says, as he looks over at Uncle. "You doin' research?"

He's unresponsive.

"Uncle, did you hear me?"

"That man was right. They're gonna take everything." Uncle is robotic in his speech and movements.

Matt walks to the bed and picks up the paper from the floor. He reads the paper, stating that the Kingstown Homeowner's Association is now the legal owner of fifteen of the twenty-one acres formerly owned by Jack Moyer. Kingstown Homeowner's Association satisfied the state's requirements under adverse possession and is thereby awarded land use and title. The title transfer is signed by Dr. Jennifer Hansen, Kingstown Homeowner's Association President.

"This is crazy," Matt says. "They can't just take land like that, can they?"

Uncle shakes his head in disbelief.

"Is this real?" Matt waits for a response. "Uncle, what's going on?"

"Adverse possession is like squatters' rights. It's that damn trail they cut. Kingstown must've shown they've been using this property to walk through. I just don't know how they could've shown that they've been using our land for twenty-one years."

"That community was just built. If you count when they started construction, that might have been six years ago, maybe. How would we not be notified ahead of time that they were claiming this?"

"I don't know. I don't know how they got around the twenty-one years. I don't know why we weren't notified. I don't know how they did this!"

"All right, don't yell at *me*."

"Where does Emily live?"

"It's the model home near the basketball court at the end of the trail."

Uncle grabs Matt's wrist. "Take me there ... now!"

"I'd have to walk to the pay phone to call for a cab. That might take an hour or so." Matt yanks away his arm.

"No, take me through that goddamn trail they made to steal my land." Uncle is shaking, his fists clenched.

"It's a mile at least. You can barely walk to the mailbox."

With bloodshot eyes and shaky hands Uncle grabs his jacket, fedora, and homemade walking stick. He stops at the front door and turns back to Matt. "Let's go."

Uncle's breathing is labored. He's bent at the waist, leaning forcefully into the locust walking stick. He looks straight ahead through the forest path, the afternoon sunlight waning. Shredded mulch covers the pathway, creating a soft, spongy surface. The freshly mulched path silences their footsteps, further emphasizing Uncle's wheezing.

"You need to stop and rest," Matt says.

"No."

The pair trudges along silently at a snail's pace, Uncle's wild eyes fixed on his goal, with Matt using his peripheral vision to monitor the old man. He listens to the desperate wheezing, trying to decipher the point of danger and thinking they passed it long ago.

"Uncle, please."

"No."

They reach the end of the trail. Uncle stops on the sidewalk; he leans on his walking stick, gasping. The stick starts to wobble. The old man's legs sway. Matt embraces his uncle as his legs give way, and the walking stick falls. Uncle turns and puts his arm over Matt's shoulder, allowing his grandnephew to support half his weight. Matt walks him to the bench by the basketball court. The old man grunts and slumps down on the metal bench. Matt retrieves the walking stick.

"I gotta get up," Uncle says, groaning, as he tries to push up from the bench.

"Please sit down. Just for a minute," Matt says, as he guides the old man back to his seat.

Uncle's labored breathing subsides. They look past the basketball court to the neighborhood of nearly identical single-family homes on plots of land barely big enough for the extravagant monstrosities. The homes are covered in faux brick facing and vinyl siding. In front of each are squared hedges and rounded shrubs growing in a sea of fresh brown mulch with dark green grass, chemically treated, clipped and edged to perfection, and bordered by concrete sidewalks. Beyond the enormous vinyl boxes are endless rows of townhomes, only slightly smaller in footprint. Each three-story townhome has a micropatch of grass with a sad solitary six-foot-tall twig of a tree. The sun is low in the sky, casting rays of orange-yellow light on the neighborhood. Lights are on; a late model SUV drives into a garage, but not a single person walks the streets.

Uncle sighs; his eyes water. "Gimme my stick, will ya?" He groans as Matt helps the old man to his feet. "That's why I didn't wanna sit down. I wasn't sure I could get back up." Uncle offers a pained smile. "Now which one is it?"

"It's at the end of the cul-de-sac, the model home," Matt says.

"They all look the damn same to me."

"What exactly are we gonna do? Shouldn't we make a plan?"

"I wanna look that bitch in the eye and see what she's made of."

"That doesn't sound like a plan."

"It's not."

Uncle staggers up the concrete driveway and walkway with Matt close behind. The walkway looks like an airport runway with short lights illuminating the path. Matt's heart beats rapidly, his palms sweaty. Uncle appears calm and focused. A doorbell invites visitors to press the button, but Uncle jabs on the front door with the end of his walking stick. He waits for a moment, then thumps the door harder. He continues to pound on the door, until it jerks open. Chip Hansen stands blank-faced, with khaki shorts, Teva sandals, and a purple music festival T-shirt. Hair grows on the tops of his toes, but his muscular calves are clean-shaven.

Chip smiles stiffly. "Hello, Matt. This must be your uncle." He holds out his hand to Uncle. "I'm Chip Hansen."

"Cut the crap and get your wife out here," Uncle says.

Chip's eyes narrow; he crosses his arms. "What's this regarding?"

"It's HOA business."

"We don't conduct HOA business here. We have meetings once a month at the community center, … if you have a grievance."

"Listen here, shit for brains. Unless you want me to go door to door telling people what your wife did, I suggest you bring her out here, right now."

"Excuse me," Chip says, holding up one finger and closing the door behind him.

Matt puts his ear to the door. He hears hushed, urgent tones.

"Who is it?" Dr. Hansen says.

"It's Matt and his uncle," Chip replies.

"Dave said this might happen. Call him and let him know. I'll take care of them."

The door flings open. Matt catches himself, almost falling over the threshold. Dr. Jennifer Hansen appears with a wide smile and dead eyes. Her blond hair is tied up in a ponytail, the sides darker from sweat and exposed roots, but her makeup is intact. Her breasts are mashed together in a tight blue sports bra that's visible through her sweaty white tank top. Her thin legs and narrow hips are showcased by her black spandex shorts.

"Mr. Moyer, Matt, how can I help you?" she says.

"I'd like to know how you can live with yourself after stealing my land," Uncle says.

"I assure you that the land was seized legally. I am the HOA president, but I don't control the business affairs of the association. I'm mostly just a figurehead to organize block parties and such." The corners of Dr. Hansen's mouth turn up ever-so-slightly.

"Oh, bullshit! You think I fell off the turnip truck yesterday, missy? You think I can't put the pieces together. The developer, Mr. Jacobs, Police Chief Campbell, and you, the HOA president, make quite the team."

Dr. Hansen scowls and taps her foot, occasionally checking over Uncle's shoulder, as he reads her the riot act.

"I bet I could find some irregularities in the books at the HOA and your personal finances. I wonder what kind of kickbacks you've been getting from Mr. Jacobs."

"If you think I've wronged you, I encourage you to call the police, let them sort it out. The homeowners association has always followed laws and protocols to the letter. If you obeyed the law, you wouldn't be in this situation."

"Just because you think you followed some law doesn't make it right.

The law and morality aren't the same things. Hell, slavery was legal 140 years ago. In 1865, when the Thirteenth Amendment was passed outlawing slavery, do you think slavery was moral in 1864, then immoral in 1865?"

"Mr. Moyer, you're not making any sense whatsoever."

Uncle sighs. "I guess not, for someone like you."

Dr. Hansen puts her hands on her hips. "What's that supposed to mean?"

"It means, you're a sorry excuse for a human being," Uncle says, as he points a thick finger at the good doctor.

"Mom, what's going on?" Emily asks.

"Emily, go to your room," Dr. Hansen says.

Emily looks over her mom's shoulder at Matt. "What are you doing here?" Emily asks.

"We're here because *your* mom stole *our* land," Matt says.

"Mom?" Emily asks.

"Of course not. These gentlemen simply don't understand how to abide by the laws of polite society," Dr. Hansen replies.

"There has to be a misunderstanding," Emily says, her eyes wet.

"Don't act like you care. It's pathetic," Matt says. "You never wanna see me again, remember?"

Dr. Hansen glares at Matt.

Emily turns and streaks up the stairs.

A single police siren blares in the distance; blue and red lights cut through the night sky. Tires screech as the cruiser stops in the driveway, creating black marks on the clean concrete. Chief Dave Campbell emerges from the cruiser, his hand on his belt, striding toward the action. His wide nostrils flare; his face is red, and his jaw set firm. Dr. Hansen steps inside, shuts the front door, and turns the deadbolt. Two more police cruisers park in the driveway, lights turning, without sirens.

"We've had calls of a disturbance," Chief Campbell says, eyeballing Uncle and Matt.

"I bet you did," Uncle says.

AGAINST THE GRAIN

"Watch it old man. Let me see some ID."

"You know damn well who I am. Is this why you became a cop? To satisfy your sick craving to have power over others?" Uncle spits on the ground in front of Chief Campbell.

Chief Campbell shoves Uncle against the door, his bulky forearm lodged in the old man's throat. Uncle's eyes bulge, his face turns beet red, then purple. The chief is focused and intense, looking at the fear in Uncle's eyes. He's unaware as Matt takes the nightstick off his belt. Matt winds up and smashes the side of Chief Campbell's face, knocking him out cold. Uncle falls like a ton of bricks, his legs useless, as his head bounces off the sidewalk.

Matt takes one step toward his uncle, and he feels a bite on his back. His body stiffens like a board. He loses all motor function and falls awkwardly, facing his uncle. The pain from the 55,000 volts coursing through Matt's veins is breathtaking. Uncle's mouth and nose are filled with foam; his blue eyes are lifeless. Matt tries to reach for Uncle, but he can't move. He focuses on the old man's eyes, hoping they blink, hoping they show life. Matt is overcome with déjà vu. His eyes flutter and shut. He sees the face of a pale, gaunt young woman, her blue eyes lifeless. He touches her face; she's cold.

69

[8]

God?

Matt peers through the bars on the van window, watching the early harbingers of spring. The edge of the wooded roadside is filled with rose-colored redbud flowers and clusters of white on the chokecherries. Deeper, beyond the edge, serviceberries bloom white, under the oak trees. He feels the social worker look over at him periodically, hoping to spark a conversation. He closes his eyes and pictures his bees dancing from flower to flower, covered in orange and yellow pollen specks. He imagines the bees returning to their hive, only to find it engulfed in flames. He opens his eyes.

The forest gives way to freshly planted cornfields, then strip malls filled with fast-food joints, dollar stores, and superstores selling all manner of consumer crap. Sprawling suburban developments of vinyl sameness surround the shopping meccas. The van drives past Kingstown. He sees the sign that reads Luxury Single-Family Homes Starting in the 200s. His stomach churns and his heart aches as he catches a glimpse of his home, or what's left of it. The property looks naked and desolate. Much of the forest that once surrounded the property was logged, only stumps remain. The old cabin and barn are gone, erased as if his uncle had never existed. It's only been seven months since Uncle took his last breath, but, to Matt, it feels like a lifetime ago. A mound of fill dirt is piled up where the pond and ducks once thrived. A gravel road cuts through the property. Wooden stakes dot the landscape, denoting property lines and homesites. He wonders if Blackie is still alive after a homeless winter.

The van turns down a road just beyond Kingstown into a middle-class community of homes built in the fifties and sixties. A hodgepodge of spilt-level, ranch, and colonial homes line the streets in no particular order or sequence. Some homes are neatly kept with Buicks and Cadillacs in the driveways, the occasional American flag out front. Others are ragtag—bikes, motorized miniature cars, and plastic houses laid out chaotically, with minivans and pickup trucks parked in front. Their garages are always full of everything but their cars.

The van pulls into the driveway of a colonial with white vinyl siding and black shutters. A porch covers the front of the house, with a swing swaying in the breeze. Closely mowed green grass dominates the quarter-acre lot, with boxwood hedges in front of the porch pruned in neat squares à la Edward Scissorhands.

"Are you ready, Matt?" the social worker asks.

Matt nods. His baby face is a bit more haggard, with a scar under his right eye and another above his left eyebrow. He grabs his duffel bag, containing all his belongings, from underneath the bench seat with ease. His build is still sinewy, but it's bulkier and chiseled now. His light brown hair is cut short, military short. Matt steps from the van and throws his duffel bag over his shoulder. He wears a plain gray T-shirt from the Juvenile Detention Centers Association of Pennsylvania, with the letters JDCAP across the back, and generic blue jeans. A short, pudgy woman—with rosy cheeks, short red hair, and a jean jumper with buttons decorating the straps—bounds toward Matt and the social worker.

"Regina, it's so good to see you," the pudgy woman says, as she hugs the social worker. Regina's tall, slim build and smooth black skin are a perfect contrast to the woman in her embrace.

"How are things with you, Ms. Grace?" Regina replies, as the pair disengages.

Grace smiles and shakes her head. "You know me. I always take on too much."

"You better slow down, girl. Lord knows these kids need you." Regina smiles; Grace touches the golden cross dangling around her neck.

"This must be Matt." Grace motions toward Matt, with a wide, toothy grin. "I've really been looking forward to meeting you. You know I prayed for God to help me with my garden, and now I've got a bona fide farming expert right in front of me."

"I don't farm anymore," Matt says, his head lowered.

"Well, that's all right, sweetheart. I'm still happy to meet you. I just know you're gonna do great here."

"Matt, Ms. Grace here is one in a million. Everyone just loves it here with her," Regina says.

Matt extends his hand. Grace pushes through and gives Matt a warm hug, her pins and large breasts pressing against his chest. Matt's body stiffens; his arms go limp. Grace gives Regina a pouty look after the awkward hug.

Matt zones out, reading the pins as Grace and Regina talk: Kids First. It's a LIFE not a Choice. Children are the Future. And a heart-shaped pin that reads Teaching Is a Work of Heart, plus another that states To Teach Is to Touch a Life Forever.

"Matt, are you ready to see your room?" Grace asks.

He nods.

"Good luck, Matt. I know you'll do just great," Regina says, as she holds out her hand, smiling, exposing bright white teeth.

Matt shakes her hand and manages a brief grin. He trails Grace into the house, following her into the immaculate kitchen. Pots and pans hang neatly over a center island of granite, with a spotless indoor grill. Stainless steel appliances fit neatly between cherry cabinetry.

"Now, Matt, you're allowed to eat anything you like. I don't have any restrictions on your diet. You're old enough to make good decisions." Grace opens the side-by-side refrigerator with a built-in ice-maker.

Matt peers inside at the stocked fridge with loaves of bread, seven different colored sports drinks and juices, milk, cheese, eggs, rotting fruits and vegetables, an aluminum pan of lasagna, rolls, condiments, ground beef, stacks of Lunchables, bologna, and cheesecake. Matt's eyes bulge at the mini–grocery store in the kitchen. Grace opens the freezer side, exposing a plethora of frozen treats and microwavable Weight Watchers, Healthy Choice, and Lean Cuisine meals. The walk-in pantry reveals twelve different types of sugary cereals, one of which is essentially cookies, value-size bags of potato chips, cookies that aren't pretending to be cereal, oatmeal, candy bars, and cases of soda stacked as high as a man.

Grace leads Matt around the corner to the TV room where Fox News shouts at a thick, pasty, balding man with a bushy mustache, glasses, and small squinty eyes. He sits mesmerized in his recliner, with a bag of chips in his lap.

"Matt, this is my fiancé, Dwight."

Dwight sits motionless, in a trance.

"Dwight, dear, why don't you say hello to Matt?" Grace says, as she taps the top of his expanding forehead.

Dwight snaps to reality and smiles with his mouth shut tight. He stands, bits of chips falling to the floor. "I'm sorry, Matt. I get so focused on those darn Democrats. It's really nice to meet cha," he says, as he extends his hand.

Matt shakes his hand. Afterward Matt nonchalantly reaches behind his jeans and wipes off the grease.

"Let me show you the basement, where the boys play their games," Grace says. "George and Ryan are probably down there."

Matt follows Grace down the winding white-carpeted steps. He hears taunting and laughing with coarse rock music in the background. A fifty-inch television sits inside a wooden entertainment center, its glass doors shielding various boxes with tiny red and green lights, one flashing 12:00. Two boys sit on a couch, their hands holding identical game controllers, but their faces telling conflicting stories.

The younger boy is borderline obese, with red chubby cheeks, straight brown hair over his eyebrows, puffy eyes, a runny nose, and tears on his face. His clothes are oversize, the blue T-shirt reaching his knees and his nylon pants bunching around his ankles. The older boy, thin and handsome, with wavy blond hair, wears a winner's grin, designer jeans, and an untucked blue polo shirt.

Grace rushes to the younger boy, putting her arms around him. "Ryan, what happened, sweetheart? What's wrong?" Ryan's crying intensifies in the warm embrace. Grace glares at the older boy. "What did you do, George?"

George smirks. "Don't look at me. It's not my fault he's such a baby. He starts bawlin' every time he loses."

"It's … because … he … laughs," Ryan says between sobs.

George throws his hands up in the air. "What? I can't laugh when I win?" George glances at Matt, lingering on the staircase. "Farmer boy's not bunkin' with me."

"Matt, come on down and meet your foster brothers," Grace says.

Ryan takes a deep breath and wipes his tears on his sleeve.

"This here's Ryan. He's in the fourth grade, and he loves his games. Can you say hi to Matt?"

"Hi, Matt," Ryan says, barely looking up.

"Ryan has agreed to give up half his room for you," Grace says.

"Thanks, Ryan. I appreciate it," Matt replies.

"And our oldest here is George. He'll be graduating in a couple months."

"What up, bumpkin. I heard about you," George says. He grins and leans back on the couch.

"We don't need to be gossiping," Grace says.

"Whatever, I just thought the boy might wanna know what he's gonna be dealin' with at school. I sure as shit would wanna know."

"Language!"

George chuckles at Grace. "I'm just jokin'. No need to get your granny panties in a bunch. Don't worry. I'll show the boy around. Keep him out of trouble."

Grace and Matt hold on to the bannister as they walk up the wooden stairs to the second floor.

"My bedroom's down the hall on the first floor, but all the kids' rooms are up here," Grace says.

They walk to the end of the second floor hall. A crucifix, complete with Jesus bleeding from his hands and feet, adorns the wall. An embroidered picture of a house with Bless this House stitched on the roof hangs crooked. Grace pushes open the door at the end of the hall, revealing a bathroom. Towels hang neatly, the sink wiped clean. The toilet seat is lifted, revealing a sparkling bowl and rim. A hint of bleach and Windex lingers in the air.

"This is the boys' bathroom," Grace says. "George is fanatical about keeping it clean, so I suggest you do your best not to make a mess."

Grace leads Matt away from the bathroom. She grabs hold of the first door handle and tries to turn it.

"I forgot. George keeps his room locked. Don't go in there, unless he invites you in. He can be a bit territorial. He's almost eighteen, so I try to give him his own space. It's hard being the oldest."

Grace waddles to the next door and pushes it open. "Heavens to Betsy, would you look at this mess."

Two single beds, one made, one unmade, line opposite walls. A dresser sits against the far wall. Clothes haphazardly litter the floor, hang on bedposts, and spill from the dresser drawers. Action figures, with every color represented, all holding weapons ranging from a samurai sword to a death-ray gun, are set up as opposing gangs. Size is the only common denominator among the two forces, with large action figures on one side and small ones on the other. David and Goliath are being played out in gangland style.

Posters and pennants cover the walls, with the Philadelphia Eagles and Phillies represented. A small TV, with a built-in VCR, sits on stacked crates at the foot of the unmade bed. Cookie crumbs litter the sheets, with VHS tapes and their cases on top of the television, on the dresser, and on the floor. An empty toy box sits at the foot of the made bed. Grace gestures toward it.

"You can leave your bag on the bed," Grace says. "That one's yours.

I told Ryan to clean up for you, but he's just so unmotivated these days. Maybe you can help him."

Matt tosses his duffel bag on the bed. "It's really not a problem. I can clean it."

They walk to the last door, decorated with a sign shaped like a pom-pom that reads Abigail Arnold cheers for Jefferson High. Angelic male voices, coming from the room, sing in the background.

Grace taps on the door, her fatty triceps jiggling with each rap. "Girls, open up."

The door cracks open, an attractive blonde blocking entry. "What do you want, Grace?"

"Abby, open up and meet your new brother."

Abby peers around the door at Matt. She rolls her eyes and puts one hand on her hip, still holding on to the door handle. Her hair is blonde, almost white, creating a stark contrast to her orangey-tan skin. She's thin, shapely, wearing tight white shorts, exposing muscular thighs, with a braless pink tank top, revealing bouncy breasts. Her teeth are straight and white, and her facial features are rounded and buttonlike.

"Why?" Abby says.

"Abby, would you please be polite?" Grace says.

Abby exhales and throws her hands up. "Fine."

Grace pushes in. The humongous room is dominated by pastels. A white canopy bed with lace hanging elegantly, pink walls, a lavender bedspread, and a white vanity and dresser covers the majority of the space. Posters of quartets of young men garnish the walls. In the corner, a dark, defiant blemish exists, like MLK swimming in the Grand Wizard's pool. A thick teen girl sits upright on a simple wooden bed covered with dark flannel. She leans back against the headrest, headphones atop her head, scribbling furiously in a black marble composition book. Her hair is as unnaturally black as Abby's is white. A ring grows out of her eyebrow, another from her nostril, and six studs follow the curve of each earlobe. Her face is full and round, with a wide nose, plump lips, and a wide mouth. Her makeup is powdery white, with black eyeliner and lipstick. Grace touches her black lace-up combat boots.

She glares.

Grace snatches back her hand, as if she touched a hot burner. Matt is still in the doorway, standing on the threshold, not sure whether to enter or stay out. Abby sits Indian style on her bed, leafing through a fashion magazine.

"Our resident writer here is Madison. She's just a year behind you, Matt. We'll have to let her be while she's writing. She's so focused." Grace forces a smile; then motions to Abby. "And over here is Abby."

Abby ignores Grace.

"Abby, why don't you try to make your new brother feel welcome? George was nice to you when you first got here, remember? Matt here is your age actually. I bet you two have a lot in common."

Abby smacks her magazine shut. "I doubt that."

Grace smiles at Matt. "She's just being a teenager. I'm gonna leave you to get settled into your room. We eat dinner at six, and we leave for church tomorrow morning at 8:30 on the dot." Grace leaves the room.

Matt stands, looking from faux sister to faux sister, his eyes settling for a moment on the nipples poking through Abby's braless top. Abby looks up from her magazine, glares at Matt, and covers her chest with her arms.

"Pervert," Abby says.

Matt stares at her, stunned.

"Get out of here!" Matt exits the room; the door slams behind him.

He returns to his room and chucks action figures into the toy box. He makes Ryan's bed and brushes the crumbs into the trash can. He throws the clothes from the floor into the hamper, folds the clothes hanging out of the drawers, and resets the dresser. He grabs the toy box to push it out of the way. When he feels something sticky on the back of the wooden box, he yanks his hand back. He peers at the back of the toy box and gags. He sees a collage of mostly dry, but some wet, yellow, green, and brownish boogers covering the entire backside of the box. He pushes the box to the far corner, the boogers facing the wall. He sits on his bed and takes off his boots, pushing himself back. He closes his eyes, shutting them tight.

+++

Matt trudges to the kitchen, where morning light floods in. Grace sits at the table with a cup of coffee and a blueberry muffin the size of a softball. She's wearing a short-sleeved pantsuit, with a white blouse. Her bright-white, meaty arms and calves are exposed.

"Good morning. Did you sleep well?" Grace says to Matt.

Matt nods. He's still wearing his jeans and gray T-shirt from the day before.

"Feel free to have whatever you want for breakfast. Most of the kids have cereal or Pop-Tarts."

"Would it be okay if I made myself eggs and some fruit?"

"Be my guest. I'm not sure if we have eggs though."

"You do. I saw them yesterday."

Matt cracks the eggs and scrambles them in a bowl. He puts a pan on with a little butter and cooks his eggs. He fishes some strawberries out of the crisper. The bottom berries are moldy. He washes the good berries and puts them on a plate with his eggs and grabs a glass of milk.

"Do you compost these?" Matt asks, showing Grace the container of moldy berries.

Grace crinkles her face. "Oh, heavens no. Throw that away."

Matt sits opposite Grace, eating his breakfast. Abigail hops down the stairs in a low-cut floral sundress, her whitish-blond hair tickling her shoulders. She opens the pantry and grabs a chocolate Pop-Tart, then plops down next to Grace.

"Good morning, sunshine," Grace says.

"Morning, Grace," Abby replies, her eyes and hands fixated on the chocolate pastry.

Ryan and Madison slog down the stairs, bleary-eyed. Ryan's dressed in oversize khakis and an oversize, untucked button-down shirt to hide his girth. Madison wears her typical all-black gothic gear. She grabs the box of Cookie Crisp and the milk. She prepares a bowl for herself and Ryan.

"You two look like you stayed up too late last night," Grace says.

"It's too early. I wanna stay here," Ryan says.

"You say that every Sunday," Abby says.

"Because every Sunday it's early."

"You'll be fine once we get there," Grace says. She stares at Madison, narrowing her eyes. "Would it kill you to wear something nice for church, instead of those darn devil clothes?"

"Well, I'm not going out dressed like the Christian slut over there, I can tell you that," Madison says.

"Madison, don't talk about your sister that way."

"She's not my sister. I barely know the girl."

"With that attitude, what do you expect, young lady?" Grace turns to Abby. "Madison's being very rude. I think you look just darling."

Abby whispers to Grace; they laugh.

Dwight stomps down the hall from the master bedroom. His thinning hair and mustache are neatly combed; his pleated khakis are pressed, and his large ass fills the rear tightly. His pants are pulled up high, exposing a bit of blue sock. His blue short-sleeved, button-down shirt is tucked in tight with a Pittsburgh Steelers tie.

Grace smiles, revealing coffee-stained teeth. "Uh-oh, Dwighty bear. You're gonna be in trouble today with that tie."

Dwight laughs, mostly keeping his teeth covered. Matt catches a glimpse of bright yellow. "I can always start talkin' about Super Bowls, if they give me a hard time. That shuts up those Eagle fans pretty darn quick."

Grace glances at the clock on the microwave. "Matt, it's almost time to go. You need to hurry up and get changed."

"I won't be going to church. I'm not religious," Matt says.

"Well, that doesn't stop us with Madison," Grace says. "You may not know it, but you need God more than ever now."

"I'd still rather not. Besides, I don't have anything nice to wear."

"Oh, nonsense. Dwight can give you anything you need. Can't you, Dwight?"

"I've got tons of church clothes. I'll go get you a few things." Dwight exits the kitchen.

"I'd still prefer not to go, even with church clothes," Matt says.

"Heavens to Betsy, you have to go," Grace says.

"George doesn't have to go," Madison says.

"He's older, and he has to work anyway."

"Bullshit," Madison mutters under her breath.

Dwight returns. "Here ya go, Matt. I've got the works for ya. Pants, a shirt, *and* a tie."

Matt takes the clothes to his room. He takes off his jeans and puts on the pleated khakis. He runs his belt through the loops. The pants are baggy and a few inches long. He tightens his belt to make the generous waist fit. He puts on his boots, and the pant legs gather at his feet. He shrugs into the short-sleeved button-down shirt. It's quite a few sizes too large, so he tucks it into his pants. He clips on the brown paisley necktie. He looks at himself in the mirror over the dresser and frowns. He thinks about Uncle toward the end in his oversize clothes. Matt treks back to the kitchen.

"Oh, my God, he's dressed like Dwight." Abby laughs with her right hand over her heart.

At church Matt is sandwiched between Ryan and Madison. Madison scribbles in her notebook; Ryan plays with his Game Boy. Abby stares, fixated on the young pastor. Pastor Roberts is bearded, with long, wavy brown hair and large brown eyes, not unlike the life-size Jesus nailed to the cross behind him.

"Nine thousand years ago, when God created this bright blue planet in six short days, it was a miracle," Pastor Roberts says. "Nonbelievers often ask me how He did it. Truth be told, I don't know how He did it, but I have faith that He did, because I look around and I see miracles every day. Is a newborn baby not a miracle? How about the Rocky Mountains?

80

Or Niagara Falls? Is it not a miracle that all of us are here today, full of faith in a world gone mad? I see all of you, and my heart swells with love for each and every one. Where does that love come from? Where does all love come from, if not from God? The love I feel for all of you is as strong and real as the heat I feel when I put my hand over an open flame."

Matt and his foster family pile out of the pew and work their way down the crowded aisle. Grace and Dwight shake hands and bless their neighbors on the way. Matt freezes; his stomach plummets. He recognizes the face, but not the expression. The wide nose, big mouth, curly blond hair, and eyes almost on the side of his head like a hammerhead shark, are unmistakably Chief Campbell's, but his smile and gregarious affectations are wholly unfamiliar to Matt.

The chief holds onto the hand of a dark-haired, blue-eyed, fair-skinned woman, reminiscent of Snow White. A younger version of the woman is close behind, followed by a familiar face in a blue suit that Matt can't quite place. As the line starts to move, the athletically built boy struts with a hitch in his step. Matt's mind flashes back to the gangster wannabe, Colton. Matt feels like he's at a reunion filled with fire and brimstone. The Campbell family stops near the door to talk to the Hansens.

Chip Hansen holds Dr. Hansen's purse, while she smiles and exchanges pleasantries with the chief. Tyler and Colton walk out together. Emily stands, eyeing the exit, in a sundress with a white sweater and flats. She is more beautiful than Matt remembers. He feels weak. He grabs on to a pew and sits down, camouflaged by the crowd. He peers around churchgoers to keep her in his line of sight. His heart beats quickly. She's gone.

The church is mostly vacant. Matt trudges toward the exit, his pant legs scraping the ground and his short sleeves touching the middle of his forearms. Grace stands in front, flirting with Pastor Roberts. She flips her hair, laughs, and touches his arm in one fluid motion.

"I was wondering what happened to you," Grace says to Matt. "Come over here and meet Pastor Roberts."

"Hello, Matt. I've heard so much about you," the pastor says, as he holds out his hand. "What did you think of the sermon?"

"It was good … for what it was intended," Matt replies, as he lets go of the pastor's hand.

The young pastor chuckles. "I'm not really sure how to take that, but I'll just chalk it up as a compliment."

"You're gonna be late, if you don't get your little bee-hind moving," Grace says to Matt.

"Late?"

"Sunday school, silly. Follow those boys across the parking lot."

Matt stands, like his feet are set in concrete.

"I'll take him," the pastor says. "I've got the high school kids today."

Matt follows the pastor into the classroom. A collective roar of laughter from twenty teenagers fills the room upon Matt's entry. His eyes meet Emily's, and she looks away. Colton and Tyler laugh and pound on their desks. Madison sits in the back corner, her desk moved away from the others, looking out the window. Matt takes the only available seat, dead center in front.

"All right, that's enough everyone. Settle down," Pastor Roberts says. "Let's start with a verse from Mark 10:25. 'It is easier for a camel to go through the eye of a needle than for a rich person to enter the kingdom of God.' Anyone wanna try to explain this verse?"

Abby's hand shoots up.

"Go ahead, Abby."

"I think it means that poor people are more likely to get into heaven, and the rich are probably going to hell. You know, like 'the meek will inherit the earth.'"

"Thank you, Abby. Anyone else?"

Colton raises his hand, leaning back, slouched in his desk.

"Colton?"

"I think it means ballers be goin' to heaven, knowamean?" A smirk spreads across Colton's face.

Pastor Roberts suppresses a smile. "Anyone else? Anyone?"

Matt raises his hand, his jaw set tight.

"Matt, go ahead."

Tyler and Colton cough into their hands. "Farmer." Cough. "Faggot." Cough.

"I think it's simply a propaganda piece to make the downtrodden feel as though they don't need wealth in this life," Matt says. "That it's okay to let those in charge in the church and in government take their money through donation and taxation, because they'll receive their reward in a nonexistent afterlife."

The room is silent, the kids motionless. Pastor Roberts paces, stroking his beard.

"Now, Matt, you seem like a smart kid, so I don't wanna embarrass you, but you do know that Jesus was destitute. He gave everything he had to us, including his life. Now I can't speak for the government, but I do know that the church does a tremendous amount to help the … downtrodden, as you say. We certainly do nothing to keep them down."

"When you propagandize children, making them suspend disbelief, it confuses them and makes them more gullible for the rest of their lives," Matt says. "It's child abuse to send kids to church."

The teenagers in the room erupt in a collective revulsion that manifests in groaning and random shouts of "Bullshit" and "Homo."

"Hold on, everyone. Matt is entitled to his opinion," Pastor Roberts says. "It's up to *us* to show grace and help him find his way."

Tyler stands up. "Hold on, hold on. Is this little dirt ball saying that our parents are abusing us by taking us to church? And he thinks Jesus is a lie? That's bullshit, because I saw on the History channel that He existed."

"Let's be respectful, Tyler. I don't think that's what he's saying," Pastor Roberts says.

"That's exactly what I'm saying," Matt says.

The room erupts with taunts. Someone kicks the back of Matt's chair.

"That's enough!" Pastor Roberts says. "How can we survive tests of faith, if we can't debate a young man in crisis?"

The room settles down.

"My heart goes out to Matt," Pastor Roberts says. "I'll never give up on him, but he has some pretty strong opinions and myths we need to dispel, for us and for Matt. Now, tell us how you could possibly know Jesus is a lie."

"Jesus Christ may have existed as a man, but he was not the Son of God, because God doesn't exist."

The pastor chuckles to himself. "Just because you can't see Him, doesn't mean He's not there. In fact He's everywhere. How could you possibly explain the Rocky Mountains or Niagara Falls?"

"Niagara was formed by glaciers receding and the great lakes cutting through the Niagara escarpment. The Rocky Mountains were formed by tectonic plates shifting."

"Matt, you're missing the point. Who do you think *caused* the plates to shift or the glacier to recede?"

"Well, it certainly wasn't your god, because you said today that the world was created nine thousand years ago. The Rocky Mountains were created three hundred million years ago." Matt crosses his arms.

"I think you need to check your facts on that. I've studied religion my entire life. I can assure you, we know what we're doing."

"*That*, I can agree with," Matt says, glaring at the pastor.

"Let's take your other assertion that the church is abusing children. This is awfully inflammatory, don't you think? Would you like to take a trip to our day-care center or watch as we help out at the children's hospital? Have you ever been to a pediatric burn unit?"

"It's not the charity work, it's what you teach. If I had kids, and I made them go to church in my basement and taught them about a unicorn god that craps out rainbows but would send them to a fiery place for all eternity if they didn't follow the unicorn rules plus give the unicorn 10 percent of their salary, then people would say that was child abuse or more likely that it was a crazy unicorn cult, and I'd probably have my kids taken from me by the state. That is no different than teaching kids about a god who heals the sick, walks on water, makes water out of wine, and scaring them with tales of hell, if they don't do what the church tells them to."

"We need to step outside," Pastor Roberts says.

The teenagers let out a collective "*Oooooo*" and "Busted."

The pastor guides Matt outside. "Now, I know you've had it rough, with your uncle passing, but this is not the way to handle it. I can't let you poison the well here. Your uncle would not want you acting out in this way. He's looking down on you *right now*, hoping you'll make the right decision. Now what do you think he'd say?"

Matt stands silent for a moment. "I know exactly what my uncle would say."

The pastor's face softens.

"He'd tell you to stick it where the sun don't shine."

[9]

School Daze

"You're not gonna wear that *again*, are you?" Grace asks.

"It's clean," Matt says.

Matt stands by the front door, dressed in generic jeans and his gray JDCAP T-shirt, with his duffel bag slung over his shoulder. Grace wears her blue ankle-length nightgown.

"That's not the point," she says. "You don't want everyone to know that you were in juvie. It's a bad first impression. And, after yesterday, you need to make a *good* impression."

"I appreciate your concern, but it doesn't matter to me."

"It should, mister. Pastor Roberts banned you from church."

The corners of Matt's mouth turn up for a split second. "For how long?"

"I really don't know." Grace throws her hands up. "You're not gonna lie around here on Sundays, when we all go to church. You're gonna have chores to do, mister."

"I think I can handle the chores."

"Well, you're gonna need to get a job too. I expect you home today at three o'clock sharp. I'm gonna take you over to the Hardee's. Dwight will set you up with an after-school job."

Matt exits the front door. A sparkling black Ford Mustang with tinted windows idles in the driveway. Through the front windshield, Matt sees George and Abby kissing. George's hand is up her shirt.

Matt passes the Mustang and meanders on the concrete sidewalk. He searches for honeybees in the close-cropped, chemical-laden lawns. He sees none. Matt hears the pounding of boots and the shuffling of shoes not tied. He looks over his shoulder to see Madison and Ryan.

"Hey, Matt," Ryan says, his hair wet in the back and front to keep his cowlicks down.

Matt stops, waiting for his foster brother and sister. "Hey, Ryan, Madison."

Madison lifts her chin in acknowledgment. She walks next to Matt in silence for a block. Ryan follows closely behind.

"I liked what you said in church," Madison says, looking away, her jet-black hair covering one eye.

"I don't think anyone else did," Matt replies.

"I really hope you don't care what they think." Madison's one eye is focused on Matt's face.

"Of course I care. Don't you?"

Madison recoils, as if opening a package of spoiled fish. "Then why did you say that crap about church being all about brainwashing and manipulation? Everybody who's anybody in this town goes to church. You can't be that dense to not know what you're doing. You could just go along with it, and your life would be much easier. The way you look, you could get yourself some decent clothes, and, with an attitude adjustment, you'd fit right in."

Matt doesn't respond.

The throaty roar of a V-8 engine interrupts the silence. "Bitches," Abby says, with two middle fingers hanging out the passenger window of the Mustang.

Madison glowers at the greeting. Matt's unfazed.

"I said that stuff about the church because it's true," Matt says. "The truth is more important than fitting in."

"Really? That's what you care about?"

"More than anything."

Madison laughs. "Good luck with that."

The trio arrives at Jefferson Elementary. Buses line the curb at the main entrance. Cars creep along, jockeying for a closer spot to drop off their precious cargo. Ryan hides behind Madison, his chin tucked into his chest.

"Let's go, Ryan. We'll do this together," Madison says.

"Maddy, no, I can't," Ryan says, his voice trembling and unsteady.

"It's gonna be fine. We'll do it together."

"Matt too?"

Madison and Ryan look at Matt.

"Sure, why not," Matt says.

The trio walks toward the elementary-school entrance. Matt leans toward Madison.

"What are we doing exactly?" Matt whispers.

"Just helping the little man get to class." Madison flashes a wicked grin.

Children bustle up and down the hallways. A few girls lock arms and skip down the corridor. A group of boys trade football cards like riverboat gamblers. The hallway is decorated with finger paintings, sketches, and papier-mâché art projects. Teachers sit at their desks, oblivious to the chaos outside their classrooms. The card-trading boys glare at Ryan. Matt and Madison stop at a classroom doorway.

"Thanks, Maddy," Ryan says, before entering his classroom and finding his seat toward the back.

The card-trading boys head for the classroom. A spiky-haired boy, with an Eagles number five jersey, only a few inches shorter than Matt but head to head with Madison, saunters behind the other card-traders. Madison steps in front of the boy, just before he enters. The bell rings. Madison grabs his upper arms, her nails digging in. She leans forward and whispers in his ear. She pulls back and smiles wide, showing her white teeth.

The boy shrinks and sidesteps her into class. He turns back to look at the doorway.

Madison's still smiling, with black lips and powdery white cheeks.

She puts her hand up and slowly bends her fingers up and down, giving the kid a case of coulrophobia.

Matt and Madison trudge down the concrete sidewalk. Students pass them on the grassy median strip, frantic, carrying mountains of books on their back. Just beyond their development, they see the sprawling two-story campus, with a rotunda and a football stadium.

"What did you say to that kid?" Matt asks.

"I told him how easy it is to poison a black lab, how stupid they are, how they'll eat anything."

"I'm assuming that kid is the reason Ryan didn't wanna go to school?"

Madison frowns. "You're quite the detective. Did you also notice that I like to wear black?"

Matt looks down.

"Don't be a baby. I'm just messing with you. That little douche was making Ryan do the Truffle Shuffle at recess."

Matt stares at Madison, blank-faced.

"You know, like in *The Goonies*?"

"What's a goonie?"

"Are you serious? You never saw *The Goonies*?"

"No TV."

"Even my messed-up mom had a VHS and a television. I stole that movie from Erol's. I wore that tape out. The Truffle Shuffle is from the movie, where this little fat kid, Chunk, lifts up his shirt and jiggles his fat."

Matt winces.

"Yeah, I know. Messed up, huh?"

"What happened to his parents?"

"Ryan's a lifer, probably the only white lifer in America. I overheard Grace one time say his mom was a junkie, gave him up for adoption when he was born. As a baby, he looked like he had Down's, so nobody wanted him. He was always behind. You know, crapping his pants until he was five. People want that perfect child. They don't want the fat kid who looks retarded and craps his pants. Now he's just too old, like the rest of us."

Matt and Madison cross the street and step onto the campus of Jefferson High School. Muscle cars and pickup trucks spit head-crunching bass from their subwoofers. He recognizes Tyler and Colton in the lifted Jeep, heads bobbing to gangster rap. Girls in tight short skirts with chunky heels and dyed hair travel in packs. Athletic white boys with baggy jeans, white baseball caps pulled down low, flannel shirts, and worn construction boots dominate the male, socially enforced dress code.

Madison stops at the main entrance.

"Welcome to the jungle. This is where we part ways." Madison smiles and motions to the main entrance. "The main office is just inside."

+++

Matt walks from the main office into the cavernous linoleum-floored hallway. It's quiet, only a few kids scurrying to class. He looks down at his schedule. "First Period, Journalism, Mrs. Campbell, A132."

He strolls down the corridor glancing at the room numbers. He stops when he reaches the door labeled A132. He twists the handle, but it's locked. A woman lectures inside. He knocks on the door. He waits for a moment, then knocks harder. The door jerks open. A curvaceous dark-haired woman with creamy white skin, round blue eyes, and a scowl stands on the threshold. He recognizes her from church. *Chief Campbell's wife.*

"What do you think you're doing, young man?" Mrs. Campbell asks.

Matt hands her his schedule.

She waves it off, as if it were an unpleasant odor. "This isn't middle school. That's *your* responsibility, and it's *your* responsibility to be on time. You can stand here, until I'm done." She slams the door.

Matt rubs his temples. He leans against a nearby locker, listening through the door.

"This is journalism, people. You need facts and sources, not opinions. I don't care what you think. I want the news. That is *your* job. Remember, your freedom project oral reports are due four weeks from today, the day after Memorial Day. I know that sounds like a lot of time, but every year someone fails this class, because they wait too long to find an interviewee. This project is about freedom. You need to find someone who serves and protects our freedom and our way of life. Most students find a soldier or a police officer to interview about their job, their life, and why we should be grateful for their service. I've had quite a few students interview an influential teacher as well. If you have trouble finding someone to interview, let me know, and I can put you in touch with a police officer."

The door opens, and Mrs. Campbell motions for Matt to enter. The classroom is drab, with only newspaper clippings on the walls. The desks are arranged in neat angular rows, facing the front, where a podium stands for Mrs. Campbell to pontificate. Matt follows her to the front. His face brightens when he sees Madison seated in the back, giving him a middle finger and a smile.

Mrs. Campbell looks at Matt's schedule, then hands it back to him. "Class, this is Matt Moyer. He'll be with us for the rest of the year." She turns to Matt, handing him a sheet of paper. "You'll be responsible for the final project. Just follow the instructions on the sheet. You're not going to come in here and mess around, just because the year's almost over. Now find a seat."

They spend the rest of class dissecting interview techniques from old *60 Minutes* clips.

The bell rings; the kids file out. Madison waits at the door, next to a squat guy with black hair, brown skin, and a goatee, wearing a black T-shirt and jeans.

"Hey," Madison says. She motions toward the guy. "I want you to meet my friend Tariq. Tariq, this is my new foster brother, Matt."

"Nice to meet you, Matt," Tariq says, as he extends his hand.

"Likewise," Matt says.

"We have the school paper at three. You should join us," Madison says. "I'm sure we could get you working on a story, if you want one."

"I'm supposed to get a job today ... Hardee's."

"Screw that. What are they gonna do if you just don't show up?" Madison says.

"Fast food's the worst," Tariq says. "I used to work at Wendy's, and cleaning the grill smelled like puke. It was nasty. Never again."

"Thanks, guys. I'll think about it," Matt says. "I should get going. I have American History with Mr. Dalton in C building."

"Better hurry up, mind that bell, be a good little rule follower," Madison says with a smirk.

Matt enters C224, as soon as the bell rings. Pictures of heads of old men form a ring around the room like decorative wallpaper. A young athletically built man, with a short-trimmed beard, stands at the podium in front. He wears black pants with a red shirt and a black tie, not unlike what you might picture the devil wearing if he were a teacher. The front row is filled with teenage girls, sitting, enchanted with the beast. Matt walks up to the man and hands him his schedule.

"Ah, fresh meat," Mr. Dalton says. The front row giggles in approval. "Think fast." The teacher tosses Matt a five-pound textbook, which he drops.

Matt bends over and picks up the book.

"Oh, come on, butterfingers Moyer. Ya gotta catch that." The front row continues to giggle.

Matt takes his seat.

"*Yins* knew it was coming, so here it is—the pretest for your final," Mr. Dalton says. "This won't count toward your grade, but do your best, because it'll help you prepare for the final. Put away your books, and only have out your writing utensil. The questions are open-ended."

The class groans.

"But do not write me a book. You won't get more points just because you write more." Mr. Dalton passes out the test papers. He turns to Matt. "You should've been studying this at your old school, so I want you to take this awhile. I know you just got here, but you're gonna have to pass the final to pass my class, so this is good practice."

Matt opens the test booklet.

1. Why did the United States enter World War I? The House of Morgan, acting as partners to the Rothschilds, made a fortune selling war bonds for England and France, as well as dealing in munitions, submarines, blankets, shoes, and thousands of other items needed for war. Unfortunately investors and the House of Morgan and the Rothschilds stood to lose a fortune if England and France lost the war. And they would have lost if the United States had stayed neutral. The bonds they had purchased would default, and the gravy train of business would halt.

Colonel Edward House was the top advisor to Woodrow Wilson. Colonel House was linked to the House of Morgan and the Rothschilds. Ten months after Wilson was elected, because he kept the United States out of WWI, Colonel House negotiated a backdoor agreement with England and France to intervene in the war.

The only problem was they had to sell the American people on the idea. They started with the top newspapers, making sure they were prowar. This was easy because the House of Morgan already controlled the top newspapers.

Then they loaded the *Lusitania* with munitions. The German Embassy made a formal complaint with the US government, because it was a violation of neutrality agreements. The Germans tried to take out ads in newspapers to warn Americans not to get on the boat, but all but one of the ads were stopped. Winston Churchill set the stage where the *Lusitania* was supposed to meet a British destroyer off the coast of Ireland where U-boats had been sinking vessels. The boat was ordered to cut back on coal use, thereby slowing down the craft. The destroyer was also called away, so the *Lusitania* was a slow-moving, unprotected sitting duck in U-boat waters. The Germans sunk the boat, as they said they would. This angered enough Americans, fanned by propaganda, to accept and embrace the entry of the United States into WWI.

I'm sorry for the long-winded answer. It's a complicated question.

2. What was the nature of the warfare in World War I? I can only imagine the hell that was trench warfare. I couldn't know the true nature, because I wasn't there. I can say that, like all government wars, it was deadly. There were seven million civilian deaths and ten million military deaths. Civilian deaths are typically underreported, so I don't trust that figure, and it doesn't include the deaths of civilians who lost their homes and subsequently froze or starved or died from disease.

3. What did Franklin Roosevelt's New Deal accomplish? It prolonged the Great Depression and increased state-sanctioned theft through taxation and government programs.

4. What was Social Security designed to accomplish? It was and is a pyramid scheme designed to take far more in contributions than would ever be paid out in benefits, thus allowing the US government to steal more from their citizens, yet call it a benefit.

5. What event or events brought the United States into World War II? The seeds of WWII were sowed with the crippling economic sanctions against Germany at the end of WWI. Again the United States was neutral to its citizens but clearly not neutral to other nations. Refusing to send oil to Japan, while at the same time sending oil to Britain, was a clear message. This poking of Japan and the withheld intelligence about the incoming attack on Pearl Harbor ended in disaster, but that was exactly what the US government wanted. They now had the public support they needed to enter the war. Without the power to tax by governments worldwide—and the power to hide the true cost of war by creating money through central banks, thereby obscuring the cost through inflation—none of the major wars throughout history would have ever been fought.

6. What was the duty of the Navajo Code Talkers? They transmitted encrypted messages to the US military.

7. During WWII, Japanese Americans on the West Coast were considered security risks. What happened to them? They were illegally placed in internment camps without due process.

8. What was the purpose of the Manhattan Project? To develop and build nuclear weapons to further the power and control of the state.

The bell rings; the students exit. Matt scribbles in his test booklet.

"All right, that's enough," Mr. Dalton says to Matt.

Matt closes his booklet. "Sorry, I was enjoying the questions, very thought provoking. I would've liked more time to write."

Mr. Dalton's face reddens. "Do you think that's funny?"

"The questions made me think, but I didn't find them comical." Matt stares, blank-faced.

"That's how it's gonna be, huh? Your first day and you gotta be a smart-ass. There's no point, you know. None of your classmates are here to see how cool you are."

"Okay?"

Mr. Dalton erupts like a volcano. "Get out of my face! Go on. Get out of my classroom, before I write you up for insubordination."

Matt heads to the lunchroom for his designated lunch period. Kids are fast-walking around him like soccer moms exercising away their baby fat. The hall is empty by the time he strolls to the lunchroom. He enters the propped-open double doors, and his eardrums are inundated with a cacophony of voices: quiet and loud, deep and high, and soft and shrill. Students bustle about holding trays, standing in line, sitting and milling around in groups of like appearance. Long rectangular steel-and-plastic-laminate tables are arranged like burial plots at a cemetery.

He sees a line winding out of an open doorway, zigzagging around a few ropes like a popular carnival ride. The line moves slower than molasses in January. After fifteen minutes he crosses the open doorway. The smell of fried chicken, green beans, and BO permeates the air. A neglected cart stands with heaps of iceberg lettuce, cherry tomatoes, shredded carrots, diced bell peppers, and creamy dressings. Styrofoam bowls are stacked on the side. He grabs a bowl and fills it to the brim with everything except the dressing. He grabs a tray and places it on the counter, pushing it as the line trudges along. The wrinkled hair-netted lunch lady slops mashed potatoes, green beans, fried chicken, and a red Jell-O–like substance onto a sectioned Styrofoam tray and hands it to Matt. He's one customer away from the mythical cash register, when a corn-fed white boy with jeans and cowboy boots steps in front, brandishing a Hostess apple pie.

"No cutting," the cashier says.

"He doesn't care," the boy says. He turns to Matt, glaring. "Do you?"

"I guess not," Matt says.

Matt removes a voucher card from his pocket and hands it to the cashier. She clips the card with a hole puncher and hands it back to him.

"Honey, you do know that the salad bar isn't part of the free and reduced lunch?" the cashier says.

Matt shakes his head.

"It's two-fifty."

Matt takes it off his tray.

"I'm sorry, honey. You should hurry up and eat. Lunch is almost over."

Matt smiles with his mouth shut. He slogs to the lunchroom. Kids dump Styrofoam trays, soda cans, plastic bottles, and salty snack wrappers into the fifty-gallon rubber trash cans strategically placed around the room. Students line up at the exits, mock shoving each other and jockeying for position, like the start of the Boston Marathon. He finds a lonely seat in the corner, away from the fray. His stomach grumbles. The bell rings, and, within seconds, the cafeteria is empty. Matt sits casually eating his lunch.

"What do you think you're doing, young man?"

Matt looks up from his food to see a stocky middle-aged woman sporting a cane, with salty, short curly hair and thick ankles.

"Finishing my lunch," he says.

"I see that, smart aleck. You need to get to class. You already had your lunchtime," she says.

Matt puts down his fried chicken breast, wipes his fingers with his napkin, and glares at the lunchroom monitor. "Does it look like I've finished my food?"

"My next step is to call one of the School Resource Officers to deal with you."

Matt picks up his chicken and takes a bite.

"Have it your way." She grabs the walkie-talkie from her belt. "I have an unruly student who won't leave the cafeteria. Please send an SRO for assistance."

Matt inhales his lunch.

Two police officers—one female, one male, both serious—march into the lunchroom. The male has Popeye-like forearms, a dark crew cut, a weathered face, a burly build, tight blue pants stretched across his expansive ass and a name tag that reads Blackman. The female has curly red hair, thick pasty arms, and hefty thighs and hips. Her skin is dotted with freckles. She looks like she could be little orphan Annie, grown up and blown up. Her name tag, Mullen, says otherwise.

"We can do this the hard way or the easy way," Officer Blackman says. Officer Mullen taps the Taser attached to her belt.

"I prefer the easy way," Matt says. He picks up his tray.

"Leave it," Officer Blackman says.

The officers escort Matt to the main office. Blackman guards Matt, while Mullen marches to the corner office. After a moment she returns.

"I can take him back now," she says.

She leads Matt to the corner office. The placard on the door reads Principal, Dr. Jennifer Hansen. Officer Mullen knocks once, opens the door, and escorts Matt inside.

"Thank you, Sally. I can handle it from here," Dr. Hansen says.

The officer nods and shuts the door behind her.

Dr. Hansen stands behind her desk, motioning to the seats on the other side. Her shoulder-length hair is dirty blond with light highlights, formed into a perfect hair-sprayed helmet. She looks trim in her brown pencil skirt with patterned tights, a white button-down blouse, and a red scarf.

"Why don't you have a seat, Matt."

Matt stands still.

"That wasn't a question," she says.

Matt sits, his heart thumping in his chest, his mouth dry.

Dr. Hansen sits behind her desk. "Now I know you're used to a more laissez-faire style of life. Do you know what that means, laissez-faire?"

Matt nods his head.

"Well, it's good to know you've learned something over the years. What I'm trying to say is that we do things a little more structured than how you grew up. You'll just have to try a little harder to do what all the other kids are doing. They all find a way to eat their lunch and get to class on time, so I know you can too." She smiles.

"Okay," he says.

"I can't hear you. Speak up."

"I just said, 'Okay.'"

"You've made some bad decisions. I hope you're going to start making good decisions. I'm going to let you off with a warning today but don't let it happen again."

"Okay," Matt says, with his head bowed.

Matt staggers to class, his stomach in knots and his head pounding. He passes a boys' bathroom. He rushes inside and dumps his textbook-laden bag on the floor. He falls to his knees in front of a porcelain bowl and heaves. Nothing comes at first. He retches powerfully and chunks of red partially digested pieces of chicken plop into the water. He heaves again, and a hot reddish-yellow liquid pours out, burning his throat. He vomits over and over again, until only warm bile spews from his mouth. Bits of bile dribble down his chin.

The toilet smells of hot sickness. He collapses on his side breathless, the cold tile floor soothing against his body. After a few minutes he sits up, then stands, flushes the toilet, and spits in the bowl as the sickness is vanquished. He wobbles to the sink and turns on the faucet. He looks in the mirror. His face is pale; his eyes are red. He splashes cold water on his face and rinses out his mouth. He reaches for a paper towel, but the dispenser is empty. He lifts his T-shirt and dries his face. He cups his hands under the water and rinses his mouth out again, then dries his hands on the back of his jeans. He staggers back into the stall and locks the door. He kicks the seat cover down, sits, and places his head in his hands, using his thumbs to rub his temples.

The bell rings. He pushes from the stall and collects his bag on the way out of the bathroom. He shuffles down the hall, his head lowered, like an old man in a retirement home. He stops at his locker and pulls a tiny piece of paper from his back pocket with three numbers. He follows the instructions, and the combination lock releases. He shoves his bag, filled with textbooks, inside. He grabs his notebook and pencil, and slams shut the locker. He catches a glimpse of a familiar face down the hall. Emily's designer jeans hug her waist and highlight her shapely figure. Her blond hair bounces, as she laughs and smiles at her partner. A chestnut-haired cowboy with broad shoulders and a strong jaw, smiles back with white teeth. They kiss briefly, before going their separate ways. Matt feels his gag reflex quiver. He swallows a little bile. He walks behind her.

He enters C102, English with Ms. Pierce, behind Emily. The chairs are set up in a U shape. Colorful posters, with quotes from famous and not-so-famous authors, cover the walls. At the rear of the classroom are bookshelves and colorful bins, overflowing with books. A cluster of purple beanbag chairs is arranged in a circle next to the library. Ms. Pierce stands near her desk, dressed in black velvet pants and a thick white sweater. She's tall, youthful, and energetic. Her blond hair is pulled up in a bun, with a few strands hanging along her cheeks. Her skin is creamy. Her smile is perpetual and infectious.

"Good afternoon, Jared," Ms. Pierce says.

"Hi, Ms. Pierce," Jared says, as he saunters past, a pick sticking from his afro.

"Good afternoon, Emily. I like those jeans on you."

"Thanks, Ms. Pierce," Emily replies.

"Dan, always a pleasure to see you, kind sir."

"Hey, Ms. Pierce," Dan replies, his green eyes shielded by a white PSU hat.

"And who do we have here?" Ms. Pierce says, stroking her chin. "Are you not a vagabond trying to secure passage on this grand ship?" She falls out of character with a bright smile.

Matt looks around confused.

"I'm sorry. I get a little goofy toward the end of the day. Too much tea and all. I'm guessing you'd be my brand-new, shiny student."

"I'm Matt." He hands his schedule to the teacher.

She glances at the paper. "Welcome, Matt. I'm Ms. Pierce, and I am very happy to make your acquaintance. We have one rule in this class, and you will be severely punished if you do not abide by it. You must, absolutely must, … have fun."

Matt smiles.

"There you go. You're already having fun. Claim a seat for yourself, any one you like." Ms. Pierce looks around at her students. "Let's go, lovelies. Find a seat in the U." She waits until everyone's settled. "Now that we're all comfortable, I'm going to … make everyone get up. Let's take the chairs at the base of the U and put them in the middle, so we have two lines of chairs, and a small cluster in the middle."

"I love philosophical chairs," Jared says.

"Me too," Emily replies.

Ms. Pierce walks around, cradling an empty fishbowl. "You guys know the drill. Everyone dump your philosophical quandaries into the fishbowl." Students drop folded pieces of paper in the bowl. She turns to Matt. "This is philosophical chairs, which is simply a framework we use for debating current events. I'll pick a topic from the fishbowl, and you choose a side, for or against. If you're unsure, you stand in the middle. If someone makes a good argument, you can switch sides at any time." Ms. Pierce reaches into the bowl and retrieves a folded piece of paper. "The first topic was brought to us by someone who apparently really liked the movie *Gladiator*."

"Isn't it supposed to be something recent? That movie's about Roman times," Jared says.

Jared's short, but powerfully built, dressed in baggy black jeans and a tucked-in vertically striped shirt.

"You're right, Jared, but whoever wrote this was clever. They found a loophole. Russell Crowe recently won an Academy Award, so it qualifies. We should make a rule that Russell Crowe should *always* qualify for philosophical chairs." The boys groan, and the girls giggle. "It says, 'In the movie *Gladiator*, vicious games are displayed that people love, not totally unlike football or boxing today. Do you think these games are good for people or not?' Okay, people, if you think they're good, mush on over to the right, with bad to the left, and unsure in the middle."

Matt moves to the middle of the room. Jared, Dan, and the boys go to the right. The girls, including Emily, go to the left.

"This is really interesting. We're split across the gender lines with the ladies not liking the violent games, but the guys liking them, except for my shiny new student, Matt, who's in the middle. Anyone from the boys' side want to speak up?"

"That's just how we are," Jared says. "We like to fight and play violent games. I think it's the testosterone."

"That's a good point, Jared, but I don't see anyone moving with that argument. Anyone from the ladies?"

"I don't think we should have violent games, because of concussions causing problems with brain function or kids getting paralyzed," Emily says. "Don't you guys remember Robert from last year? He was paralyzed on our own football field."

Two boys switch sides.

"Sellouts," the remaining crowd of boys says.

"Very good, Emily. You moved two students to your side, using emotional appeal. Emotional appeal is the most effective argument that we have, because most people will respond to emotions before they respond to facts and figures. Matt, you're still the man in the middle all by yourself. Can you tell us why?"

"Well, I'm against the type of gladiator games from the Roman times," Matt says. "They slaughtered slaves and defenseless animals for fun. But a game like football or boxing today is harder for me to decide. I think, if adults wanna play a violent game, and they are informed of the risks, then it's okay with me, but I don't like it when sports teams use tax money from cities to build their stadiums or when colleges won't allow athletes to make money. So I guess I think the NCAA and college sports are immoral for using players like a free farm system, where they control it like a monopoly that uses these players as slaves. But, on the other hand, pro teams are okay with me, if they don't take taxpayer money."

A handful of boys and girls move to the middle.

"Very good, Matt. I like the way you reason. All right, let's pick another topic." Ms. Pierce fishes out another quandary. "This is a good one. It says, 'The Netherlands made same-sex marriage legal, the first country in the world to do so. Do you think same-sex marriage should be legal in the United States?' Everyone who thinks yes on same-sex marriage to the left, no to the right, and, as usual, unsure in the middle."

Every student, except three, packs in on the right side of the room. Matt, Emily, and Jared stand on the left. Emily flashes Matt a fleeting smile; he looks away.

"Wow, guys. You're almost in total agreement. Anyone against same-sex marriage want to speak up on the topic?"

"Everybody here knows Leviticus 20:13," Dan says. "'If a man also lie with mankind, as he lie with a woman, both of them have committed an abomination: they shall surely be put to death; their blood shall be upon them.' So according to the Bible, it's not just a sin, but it's punishable by death."

"Now, Dan, I respect your opinion and your knowledge of scripture, but just so we're all clear about one thing," Ms. Pierce says, "if someone kills a homosexual, because it's in the Old Testament of the Bible, they deserve to go to jail … forever."

Dan's face reddens.

"Jared, Emily, and Matt, you guys are all alone over here. Tell us why you think same-sex marriage should be legal."

Emily's red-faced and scowling; her eyes are narrowed. "I get so sick of how close-minded this town is. We need to learn to think for ourselves. We're supposed to be Christians. Jesus was accepting of everybody."

"Not fags," Dan says.

Ms. Pierce's friendly demeanor vanishes, and she marches up to Dan. "I will not have that kind of talk in my classroom. If I hear that word again, I will write you up. Do you understand?"

Dan nods.

"See, this is what I'm talking about," Emily says. "Do you really think someone would choose to be gay, when your life ends up being so much harder? Why can't we leave them alone and let them be happy?"

Two girls and a boy change sides.

"They choose to be gay," Dan says. "God doesn't make mistakes."

"He made you, didn't He?" Emily says.

"Emily, stick to the argument," Ms. Pierce says.

"Sorry."

"Jared, you look like you have something to add," Ms. Pierce says.

"I don't understand why this town's always trippin' over this," Jared says. "In Philly, they're everywhere. It's not a big deal. The way I see it, it's *more* ladies for me." A wide toothy grin spreads across his face.

"It's not more ladies for you, because the lesbians go with other ladies," Dan says with a smirk.

Jared laughs. "See, now I know you've been stuck in this town your whole life. The lesbians I've seen look more like a man than you do. On the real, they don't look like they do in the porn you've been stealin' from your daddy's collection."

The class erupts in laughter. Several more students change sides.

"All right, all right, settle down," Ms. Pierce says. "For the record, lesbians are every bit as beautiful as straight women. We should probably move on. We've already pushed past the boundary of what Dr. Hansen would deem acceptable. We do have time for one more topic though." Ms. Pierce retrieves a folded piece of paper from the bowl. "This one says, 'Vice President Cheney is calling for increased use of domestic fossil-fuel supplies and nuclear power to meet America's energy demand.' What this means is that the vice president would like for the United States to use more oil, gas, coal, and nuclear energy to power our country. If you're for increased use of these energy sources, go to the right, against to the left."

Emily moves to the middle; Matt stays on the left. Everyone else goes to the right.

"Emily and Matt out on an island again," Ms. Pierce says. "Let's start with you, Matt."

"The fossil fuels are nonrenewable, so why would we wanna use more of them? We should be using a lot less, because, without fossil fuels, our entire way of life doesn't work. Without diesel fuel, coal, and gas there is no food or electricity. Even nuclear energy is nonrenewable, because uranium is depleted. The United States is already using 24 percent of the world's energy with only 4 percent of the population. We should be doing everything we can to conserve what we have, because, eventually, it will run out."

Emily moves to Matt's side along with a handful of girls.

"So why did you ladies move?" Ms. Pierce says.

"I don't know. It just made sense to me, that we shouldn't waste things," a girl says.

"Anyone from the right?"

"My grandfather was a coal miner, and, when the mine went under, it hit my whole family real hard," a boy says. "So, if we use more domestic energy, it will create good jobs for Americans."

"Me too," Dan says. "My grandfather lives with us. He never got another job, after the mine closed."

Two girls move back to the right; Emily stays.

"That's a good point, guys. We are talking about jobs and people's lives," Ms. Pierce says.

"But those mines were abandoned when the coal ran out," Matt says. "The mining towns rusted and fell apart, because nobody had money anymore. If we use more fossil fuels, yes, we will have more jobs today, but we'll have less in the future."

The bell rings. The class groans.

"Okay, lovelies, go home. What are you going to do tonight?" Ms. Pierce asks.

"Read," the class says in unison.

Emily races from the room with her classmates. Matt lingers, feeling faint, his face drained of color. He grabs his notebook and shuffles toward the door. He hears Ms. Pierce in the background like an echo.

"Are you okay?" she asks.

Matt leans on her desk, the room spinning. Ms. Pierce pushes her chair behind him.

"Just sit back, right here."

Matt slumps into the chair. After a moment he regains his faculties.

"Here, drink this." Ms. Pierce hands him a miniature carton of orange juice with a straw.

Matt sips the juice. He gains some color in his face.

"Did you eat lunch today?" she asks.

"Yeah, but I threw it up."

Ms. Pierce touches his arm. "Should I get the nurse?"

"No, I just ate lunch too fast, and I was stressed, plus the food was awful."

"I'm sorry, Matt. Sounds like a rough first day. Do you want to talk about it?"

"I was last in line at lunch, so I only had a few minutes to eat. I was so hungry. Then the lunchroom monitor lady tried to throw me out before I was finished, so I ate as fast as I could. Did I say that the food was terrible?"

"You mentioned that."

"Well, I told the lady that I wouldn't leave, then she called the police, and they took me to Dr. Hansen's. After that I was stressed and nauseated. Anyway that's it."

"Who wouldn't be nauseated after that?"

"Do you eat the school lunch?"

"Oh, God no. I wouldn't eat that. I did pressure the school board into getting a salad bar. Of course they keep threatening to get rid of it, because they say the students don't eat salad. What lunch period do you have?"

"B."

"If you want, you're welcome to bring a lunch and eat here. I have my planning period during that time."

"Hey, blondie," a male voice says from the hallway.

Matt and Ms. Pierce turn toward the hall. Mr. Dalton stands in the doorway wearing Jefferson High football shorts and a T-shirt, with dense dark hair covering his bulging muscles. He grins wide, his eyes trained on Ms. Pierce's chest. She stands and strides over to Mr. Dalton.

"What can I do for you, Mr. Dalton?" she asks.

He eyes Matt in the background. "I thought we could work out, then have a couple drinks afterward," he says in a hushed tone.

She crosses her arms over her chest. "I already made myself clear."

"Come on, Liv."

"I should get back to work."

Mr. Dalton motions to Matt by lifting his chin. "Kid's a dirt ball. Watch yourself," he whispers.

Ms. Pierce frowns. She walks back to her desk; Mr. Dalton follows the sway of her hips with his eyes. She sits on the edge of her desk, next to Matt. Mr. Dalton leaves. "I'm sorry about that."

"That's okay," Matt says. "I should probably get moving, I have to be somewhere at three." Matt pushes off the chair, as he stands up. "Thank you for the juice."

"You have to take a book with you. I have the perfect one. Just give me a second." She marches to the bookshelf, scanning titles. "I really liked hearing your point of view in philosophical chairs today. This school could use a little divergent thinking. I bet you and Emily would really hit it off. Oh, here it is. I knew I still had it. Nobody ever checks this out." She grabs a worn copy of a book with the Earth on the cover entitled *Limits to Growth*. "Don't let the raggedy look fool you. There's truth in here."

"Thanks, Ms. Pierce. I appreciate it. I *would* like to eat here, if that's okay?"

"Of course. See you tomorrow?"

Matt nods.

Matt ventures down the empty hallway, clutching Ms. Pierce's book recommendation. He passes his locker, leaving his textbooks and homework stranded. He passes the school media room. The door's propped open.

"Matt, Matt," Madison says.

He turns to see his gothic foster sister standing in the doorway.

"Are you all right? Didn't you hear me yelling for you?"

"I'm sorry. I'm a bit out of it," Matt says.

"I'll say. You look horrible. Come in and meet the newspaper crew."

Matt follows Madison into the media room. Televisions are on carts. VCRs, digital cameras, and computers line the back of the room. Two boys sit at a round table, staring at Matt.

"You remember Tariq," Madison says. "He covers all the social events. It's boring as hell, but somebody's gotta do it. And this is Jared, our sports editor and reporter."

"Hey, Tariq. Nice to see you again, Jared," Matt says.

Madison looks at Jared, with raised eyebrows.

"He's in my English class," Jared says.

"So, I'm the editor and chief here—the first sophomore to ever hold the honor, I'm proud to say." Madison does a curtsy with an imaginary skirt.

"It's just you guys for the whole paper?" Matt asks.

"Mrs. Campbell is our advisor, but she doesn't really help us," Madison says. "She's such a bitch. So, that's kind of the problem."

"That Campbell's a bitch?"

"No, dumbass, that we need help."

"I don't know anything about this school. Besides, I've been here one day, and I already hate it."

"Then you're perfect for the position," Madison says. Jared and Tariq glance at each other and nod.

"Position?"

"We need an investigative journalist. Someone who's not afraid to go after the juicy story. With your background, I thought you'd jump at the assignment."

"My background? What does that have to do with anything?"

"Listen, Matt," Jared says, "it's cool. We know about how you smacked the chief upside the head. That was gangster."

"We wanna do some real journalism," Tariq says. "We're tired of reporting on proms and school lunch menus and who scored all the touchdowns in the football game. Sorry, Jared, no offense."

"It ain't no thang. Football's just a vehicle to get me out of this backward-ass place. I do love runnin' over cracker-ass white boys though."

"We wanna do a piece on Dr. Hansen, but a real piece," Madison says. "We need someone willing to do a little semilegal spying. That bitch has some skeletons buried somewhere. We just need to start digging."

Matt frowns and shakes his head. "What makes you think I'd do this? As bad as it is here, juvie was worse."

"Do you remember my mom coming to your produce stand?" Tariq asks Matt. "She always wore a colorful *hijab*, only her face showing."

Matt smiles. "Mrs. Ahmed. I didn't know she was your mom. I grew all the basil and coriander I could, because I knew she'd buy it. She was one of my favorite customers."

"And she loved those apricots. We used to spend half a weekend drying them at the end of the season. My mom actually cried when she saw your stand was destroyed. And then, just like that, you were gone, and Kingstown was moving in." Tariq pauses and looks at Matt. "I'm sorry about what happened. We just figured you might want a chance at …"

"Revenge?" Matt asks.

"Yeah."

"You guys think I haven't thought about getting back at her? It's a great fantasy, but it's not reality. You know what was the most important lesson I learned in all this?" Matt pauses. "If you're different in any way, you better not make waves, because you will be put firmly in your place. I just wanna finish my time here and get out."

"Come on, Matt. Don't be a sellout," Madison says.

"That's bullshit, and you know it, Madison. And even if I found whatever it is you wanna find, Mrs. Campbell would never print it, and we'd all get busted anyway. So what's the point?"

"Mrs. Campbell doesn't even check the proofs," Tariq says. "I left her last week's proof, and the memory stick didn't move a millimeter from where I put it on her desk."

"Besides, we don't have to print it in this dinky-ass paper," Jared says. "We can put it on the Internet. Nobody can censor that."

"If what we dig up is bad enough, she might get fired, which means she wouldn't be able to discipline us for exposing her," Madison says with a crooked grin.

"If you wanna do this so bad, why don't *you* do it?" Matt says. "What do you need me for?"

"Come on. Why are you being such a bitch about it?" Madison says.

"I'm not the one acting like I'm so antiestablishment, then trying to get someone else to do the dangerous stuff. This is bullshit. I'm outta here."

[10]

Revenge

Matt opens the door to Grace's foster home. She's standing in the foyer, her flabby arms crossed, and her foot tapping the floor. She's dressed in jeans pulled high above her protruding stomach.

"Do you have any idea what time it is, young man?" Grace says.

"I'm not gonna work at Hardee's," Matt says, blank-faced.

"Dwight went to a lotta trouble to help you. He started with no experience, just like you, you know? He manages the whole restaurant now."

"That comparison is not enticing. I'm gonna go lie down."

Matt slogs past Grace, his eyes trained on the stairs.

"You won't get a dime of spending money from me. Everybody works here."

Matt continues up the steps, unfettered. He opens his bedroom door. Ryan is weeping, curled up in the fetal position, his comforter pulled over him, facing the wall. A pair of jeans lays on the floor, the crotch area covered in crusty white stuff.

"What's up, Ryan? You okay?" Matt asks.

"No."

"Do you wanna talk about it?"

"No."

"All right, I'll be on my bed reading, if you need anything."

Matt sets *Limits to Growth* on his bed and kicks off his boots. He lies down on his back, props his head up with his pillow, and opens the tattered text.

"She's mean, that's what she is," Ryan says between sobs.

Matt puts his book down and sits up. "A girl in class?"

"No."

"Madison?"

"No."

"Teacher?"

Ryan sobs.

"Ryan, seriously, I'd like to help you, but you gotta give me more than that. I just don't have the patience for twenty questions right now."

"It's too embarrassing."

"I'm sure it's not near as bad as you think."

Ryan rolls over, and wipes his eyes and nose on his sleeve. He looks at Matt through glassy eyes. "You have to promise not to tell anyone, not even Madison."

"All right, you have my word."

"You have to swear to God."

"My word actually means more to me." Ryan stares at Matt. "Okay, I swear to God." Matt provides air quotes when he says the word *God*.

Ryan's eyes narrow, his mouth turns down. "You can't do that thing with your hands when you say *God*. That means, you don't mean it."

Matt exhales and puts his hands together in mock prayer. "I swear to God, Yahweh, Jesus, Allah, Buddha, Vishnu, Zeus, and L. Ron Hubbard that I will not tell *anyone*."

"We were doing art, and I was putting glue on my hands and peeling it off when it dried, but it wasn't even that much."

"Okay, so what's the problem?"

Ryan sniffles. "Mrs. Jennings saw that I was playing with the glue, and she got really mad. ... She made me hold out my hands, and she squeezed two bottles on my hands and made me sit there. She said that I should be happy, because now I got lotsa glue, but I wasn't."

Matt walks over to Ryan's bed and sits down. He smells urine. He pats him on the shoulder. "It's really nothing to be ashamed of. Your teacher's a bitch. I know it's really upsetting, but you didn't do anything wrong. She did. Some people like to be teachers, just so they can have power over others."

Ryan looks at Matt. Tears streak down his face. "That's … not … the … bad … part," he says between sobs.

"All right, whatever it is, we'll figure it out. Did anyone die or get permanently injured?"

Ryan stops wailing. "No."

"Okay then, it can't be *that* bad."

"She made me get up and do stupid stands, still holding all the glue."

"Stupid stands?"

"It's called *stoop and stand*, but we call 'em *stupid stands*. You have to squat down and stand up, but you have to do it over and over again, until she tells you to stop. I was getting really tired, so I stopped, just for a little bit." Ryan lowers his head and starts to cry.

Matt puts his arm around him. Ryan's bawling intensifies. "You didn't do anything wrong. I promise."

Ryan calms down. "That's when she came over and started yelling at me really loud. Then I peed. I couldn't help it. It just happened. I didn't want the other kids to notice, so I put all the glue on my pants. Mrs. Jennings was so mad. She made me do stupid stands in the hallway for the rest of the day. I stopped doing them, because she wasn't looking."

"I'm sorry, Ryan. You know what? You don't have to do anything humiliating like that ever again."

"I don't?"

"Nope. Next time Mrs. Jennings orders you to do stupid stands or to put out your hands or anything else you don't wanna do, just say no."

"She'll get really mad."

"So what? What's the worst thing she can do? She can't hit you. She'll just send you to the principal. It doesn't matter how mad they get, they don't have the power to really hurt you, so they try to scare and intimidate you."

"Really?"

"Yep."

"Thanks, Matt."

"No problem."

"Can I ask you something?"

"Yeah, sure."

"What does it mean if someone says I came in my pants? On the way home, these middle-school boys were laughing and pointing, saying that I came in my pants. I told them it was glue."

Matt stifles a grin. "We should probably leave that one alone for the time being. We do need to get your clothes down to the laundry though."

+++

Matt lies back on his bed reading *Limits to Growth*. There's a knock on the door. He pulls his bookmark from the back, places it in the middle, and slams the book shut. He opens the door to find Madison with a greasy Hardee's bag and a camera case slung over her shoulder.

"I thought you might be hungry," she says. "Dwight brought everyone Hardee's roast beef and fries. I brought you a bottled water too." She lifts up the fast-food bag in one hand and the water in the other.

"Thanks, I'm hungry enough to eat even this crap." Matt flashes a grin.

"I'm sorry I came on a bit strong earlier today."

"It's okay. I should've been nicer about it," Matt says, sitting on the edge of his bed.

"I really appreciate what you did for Ryan," Madison says, still standing.

Matt raises his eyebrows.

"He told me at dinner that you helped him, although he wouldn't tell me exactly what happened. He's a nice kid, deep down, you know?"

"Yeah, I do."

Matt grabs a few fries from the bag; Madison lingers.

"I checked out a camera for you from school." Madison sets the camera case on Matt's bed. "You can just take pictures if you want, then give it back at the end of the year."

"You can take it back. I have no idea how to use one of those things."

"Will you at least consider it? Please?" Madison looks down.

"Why?"

"Because I can't, okay?"

"That's not an argument, Madison. I'd like to help you out, but I barely know you, so why should I take the risk?"

Madison exhales and looks at Matt. "I just can't. Can we please leave it at that?"

"Sure, but I won't get involved—"

"Because I'm scared, okay?" Madison's eyes are red.

Matt puts down his food. "It's not a big deal. I'm scared every day."

"I can't go back to juvie. It was really bad."

"I know."

"I don't think you do. You'd be different."

"What happened?"

Madison shakes her head, squeezing her eyes shut. A few tears escape and race down her cheeks. "I can't."

"You need to show me how to work this stupid thing," Matt says, holding up the digital camera.

+++

Matt stares at the white ceiling, eyes wide open, wondering if Ryan has sleep apnea. He hears a distant door shut and light footsteps getting louder. Another door opens and closes, then giggling. Whispering comes from George's room next door, then soft music, moans, and a squeaky box spring. Matt sits up, pulls on his jeans, and puts on his black hooded sweatshirt. He pulls the hood over his head, straps on the camera case, grabs his boots, and an old pair of leather gardening gloves. He tiptoes from his room in his socks, holding the doorknob to prevent the clicking sound when he shuts the door. He feels a surge of adrenaline, as he descends the stairs. The downstairs smells like fast food and Clorox. He creeps to the front door and slips out.

Standing on the front stoop, he puts on his boots and his worn leather gloves. He walks alongside the house to the backyard. The night air is crisp; the moon is full, and the grass is wet. He inhales, smelling the sweet aromas of spring. He moves into the forest, just beyond the back lawn. Brambles tug at his jeans, as he makes his way through the forest edge. Once past the brambles, the forest floor opens up. Within minutes he's swept away to the past, when his life was in harmony with nature. He hikes nimbly, the moon supplying dim light through the canopy.

He sees the land of humongous houses on tiny lots. Streetlights buzz and illuminate the neighborhood. Most houses are dark, except for the lampposts and porch lights. He walks perpendicular to the McMansions, staying concealed by the brush and brambles along the forest edge, until he reaches Dr. Hansen's home.

He pushes through the brush into the Hansens' backyard. The windows are dark, with light curtains covering only the edges. An irregular flagstone patio connects to the house and a sliding glass door. A stainless steel grill with two propane tanks sits near the glass door, with grilling utensils hanging from the handle. A square hot tub, with a lattice privacy fence, sits at the far end of the patio, with steam coming from the circulating water.

As he walks toward the sliding glass door, a spotlight illuminates the backyard. Matt runs behind the hot tub. He crouches down, listening, his heartbeat pounding. The house remains silent, the windows still dark. The spotlight clicks and turns off. He creeps around to the front, squeezing behind the hedges to provide concealment. He peers into the windows. The living room is filled with white furniture and carpeting, with black accents. The white couch has black pillows and black end tables. The patterned white carpet is trimmed in black. Beyond the living room, he catches a glimpse of the shiny stainless steel appliances in the kitchen.

He crouches next to the illuminated front stoop. There's a faint silver-dollar-size bloodstain, unnoticeable to others, but Matt remembers the exact location. He stares at the stain embedded in the cold concrete. *If I didn't hit Chief Campbell, Uncle wouldn't have fallen, wouldn't have hit his head, wouldn't have ... died. I'm so stupid.* Matt wipes his eyes with his thumb and index finger.

He sneaks toward the garage, avoiding the illumination from the porch lights. He peers into the garage window. A vintage white Mercedes convertible with a red leather interior fills one space. The rest of the garage is filled with covered furniture and boxes stacked to the ceiling. A silver Mercedes SUV and a blue Toyota 4Runner sit side by side in the concrete driveway. Tyler's red lifted Jeep is parked along the curb, next to a blue trash can on wheels.

Matt slips down the driveway, tightening his gardening gloves. He opens the lid on the trash can and winces at the fishy smell therein. He removes the offending white trash bag, with his head held back. He removes another one, smelling of rotting produce. A small tied-up white plastic grocery bag sits at the bottom. Matt sticks his head and arm deep into the bin to retrieve the bag. It's lightweight, filled with papers. *Office trash.* He returns the rank trash bags, shuts the lid, but holds on to the office trash.

A large leather duffel bag sits in the back of Tyler's Jeep. A notch at the end of the bag sticks out, allowing for long items. Matt unzips the black bag, emblazoned with Mizuno in white letters. Inside are two pairs of baseball cleats, batting gloves, and a few baseballs. He opens the compartment for long items, where two aluminum baseball bats reside. He pulls one out, like a knight removing a sword from his scabbard. He walks up the driveway, looking at the back end of the Mercedes and the 4Runner. The Toyota is dirty, with a finger-written Wash Me sign on the back hatch. There's a bumper sticker that states Coexist and another with five colorful dancing bears. The Mercedes SUV is spotless and glistening in the ambient light from the porch and the moon.

He stands in the Hansens' driveway, staring at the Mercedes, the bat in his left hand, the small trash bag in his right, the camera bag strapped to his shoulder, and his black hood up. The neighborhood is silent, except for the hum of the streetlights. He looks at the front stoop again, then closes his eyes. He opens his eyes, and tears fall out. He tosses the trash bag and the camera case to the lawn area next to the driveway. He puts both hands on the bat and takes a few practice swings.

Matt feels a cocktail of rage, adrenaline, sadness, guilt, and regret surge through his veins. He moves to the side of the Mercedes SUV and lines up the bat with the rear-tinted window. He winds up and swings with every ounce of his strength. He connects dead center, and it shatters the window into tiny shards of glass. The alarm blares, the horn honks, and the lights flash. Matt takes a few more steps and smashes the driver's side window. He takes a couple of swipes at the side-view mirror. The mirror dangles, only wires holding it to the Mercedes.

He strides to the front of the vehicle. He takes a few swings at the headlights, plastic cracking and lightbulbs smashing. Plastic and glass litter the driveway. He overhead chops the hood, creating several large dents. He climbs up on the hood, the alarm still screaming. He winds up and swings at the windshield. Some glass shatters, and a divot of broken glass appears, but the windshield is still intact. He takes another swing, again resulting in another hole, but the windshield still stands. He swings faster now, over and over and over again. Finally the holes coalesce into a gaping hole. Shards of glass litter the black leather interior.

"Stop it!"

Matt jolts from his trance, the car alarm finally piercing his eardrums. He turns upward toward the voice, toward the bedroom window over the garage. Emily stands in her plaid pajama top, her arms crossed, her blond hair disheveled, and a frown on her face. He throws the bat in the front seat of the Benz. He runs and jumps off the side of the hood into the grass. He lands next to the plastic trash bag and the camera case. He picks them up and hustles to the woods, his adrenaline surging and his heart beating a mile a minute.

He jumps over the brambles, some scratching his jeans. Everything's a blur. He sprints through the woods, deftly avoiding low branches, tree roots, rocks, and stumps. The car alarm shrieks in the background. Sirens compete with the alarm. When he reaches Grace's backyard, he doubles over; his breathing's heavy. He no longer hears the alarm or the police sirens. At the front stoop, he unlaces his boots and slides them off his feet, carrying them inside. He slips back into his room, hiding the trash bag under his bed. He removes his sweatshirt and jeans, and creeps under his comforter. Ryan still snores. Matt lays awake, his adrenaline still pumping.

[11]

The Hunt

Matt leans forward in his seat, his elbow on his desk, and his head propped up against his palm. Mr. Dalton drones on about the Allies and the Axis, the good and the bad, how "we" saved the world, how "we" would be speaking German right now if not for the brave men who fought in World War II. Matt blinks. He blinks again, this time holding his eyes shut for just a second. He opens to Mr. Dalton waving and flexing to make a point. The girls in the front row are impressed. Matt blinks, holding his eyes shut for ten seconds. He opens to more of Mr. Dalton's theatrics. He closes his eyes again. Everything melts away.

"Bam!" Matt's textbook is dropped on his desk.

Matt pops up from his slumber, his eyes blurry. He looks up to see the bearded warrior, Mr. Dalton, standing in front of him. His face is visibly red through his facial hair. His eyes are narrowed, and his arms are crossed, further accentuating his ripped biceps.

"Is my class boring you?" Mr. Dalton says.

Matt rubs his eyes. "I'm sorry. It's just that …"

"It's just what?"

"Nothing. I'm sorry."

"Spit it out, Mr. Moyer."

"It's really not you. I just don't find state-sanctioned propaganda very interesting, apart from why everybody actually believes it."

The teacher's face reddens further. He shakes his head with a smirk on his face. "I'm talking about the single most important war in history, where we saved the world from disaster. That's propaganda? You wouldn't be here today if it weren't for our brave military who fought and died, so little punks like you can sit here and spout off about things you know nothing about."

"Yes, that's propaganda," Matt says. "The winners get to write the history books and force their citizens to learn this crap."

"Are you some kinda Nazi-sympathizer?" Mr. Dalton chuckles and walks back to the front of the class. "We did have Americans who left the United States to fight for Germany. Can you imagine that, class? Someone leaving the land of the free and the home of the brave to fight for the Nazis? The same Nazis who killed millions of Jews."

"I do sympathize with the German people of that time," Matt says. "They were propagandized and brainwashed, like we are. If we suffered through the same reparations they did, and then had a charismatic leader like Hitler rise to power, we'd probably commit similar atrocities."

Mr. Dalton stares at Matt, then smiles at the class, stroking his beard. "So whaddaya think, class? Do you think, under the right circumstances, we could kill millions in concentration camps?"

A brown-haired girl in braces raises her hand from the front row. "That's why we learn history, so we don't repeat the mistakes of the past," she says.

"That's a great point, Ashley," Mr. Dalton says. "Anyone else?"

A ruddy-complexioned blonde raises her hand. Mr. Dalton points at her.

"This country was founded on freedom," the blonde says. "People came here to get away from the bad places, because we have so much freedom. I don't think we could ever be like that."

"Stanley Milgram would disagree with you," Matt says. "He proved that most Americans will kill someone, simply because someone in authority tells them to do so."

"You need to raise your hand, Mr. Moyer," Dalton says. "My grandfather was an engineer in World War II. He repaired bridges so our infantry could free Europe. He was there. He saw the concentration camps. He saw the malnourished children. He lived the real history. Matt doesn't know the intimate details of the war that my grandfather told me, when I was just a kid." A thin boy appears at the classroom door's window. Mr. Dalton makes eye contact and waves him in. "There's a real human side to the story. It's not simply facts and figures from a book. I'm not saying our government's perfect, but we have done some spectacular things throughout history." The boy hands Mr. Dalton a note. "It must be my lucky day. Mr. Moyer, you're being called to the main office. Take your stuff with you."

Matt's stomach churns. His eyes open wide; his mouth turns down. He thought he was in the clear after his first few classes came and went without incident.

Mr. Dalton grins. "Don't worry. We don't have gas chambers here."

Matt walks slowly with his frail escort, like a dead man walking. He glances at the exits next to the office, then through the office windows. The waiting area is clustered with the school's malcontents. His stomach settles, and his face brightens.

The office waiting area looks like a who's who of disaffected youths. The gothic kids are represented, with Madison at the center; the stoners; the dirt balls; the only male Latino; and the heavy metal kids. Most adults can't tell the difference between the gothic kids and the heavy metal kids. To adults, they are simply the devil worshippers. Matt finds an empty space in the corner. Madison paces over.

"What the hell?" she whispers.

"What do you mean?" he replies.

"What do you mean, *what do I mean*? Someone destroyed Principal Hansen's car. Please tell me it's just a coincidence that this happened on the same night you agreed to help."

"You shouldn't be concerned. *You* didn't do anything."

Madison crosses her arms and glares at Matt. "Do you think it's gonna be easier to do what we planned or harder now?"

"Relax. If she knew anything, she wouldn't have all these people here."

"Madison Elliot," Officer Mullen says.

Madison's eyes widen. She frowns at Matt and stomps toward the officer, her lace-up Doc Martens reverberating through the floor. Matt surveys the room, deciding how and why each person might be a suspect.

"Matt Moyer," Officer Mullen says. Her voice is husky and authoritative, the perfect contrast to her middle-aged, little orphan Annie appearance.

Matt passes Madison in the hallway. Her eyes are red. She looks away. Officer Mullen opens the door and follows Matt inside. Dr. Hansen sits behind her expansive cherry desk. Officer Blackman stands to the side, his hands behind his back, like a bouncer at a strip club ready to pounce on a patron who gets handsy with a dancer.

"Stop right there," Officer Mullen says to Matt. "Show me your palms. Hold your arms out." Matt shows his palms and holds his arms out. She frisks him and reaches in the front pocket of his black hooded sweatshirt. "Take off your shoes." Matt unlaces his boots and steps out of them. "Hand me the right shoe." The officer looks it over. Dr. Hansen cranes her neck to catch a glimpse. "Now the left." The officer grabs the boot from Matt. "I think we got somethin' shiny." She holds the boot over the desk for Dr. Hansen to see.

Dr. Hansen frowns. "It's a rock," she says.

Officer Mullen hands Matt his boots. He steps into them, leaving the laces undone. The redheaded officer takes her place alongside Dr. Hansen's desk, opposite Blackman. They stand like toy soldiers.

"Sit," Dr. Hansen says.

Matt sits and crosses his arms over his chest.

"Long night? You look awfully tired." Her makeup is flawless; her blue pantsuit is pressed, and her blond hair is coiffed, but, under the caked foundation, puffiness resides under her eyes. "I *know* you have quite a bit to hide. When you cross your arms like that, your subconscious is trying to keep a secret, like you're trying to keep the secret from literally spilling off your chest."

Matt keeps his arms crossed.

"Is there something you would like to get off your chest, Matt?" she asks.

"No."

"Are you sure? I'm going to give you this one chance to help yourself. We already know everything, but a confession dramatically reduces your punishment. Officer Blackman, can you please tell me again what you found at my home."

"We found fingerprints, ma'am. The lab's processing them now," Blackman says.

"We have a source that identified you as the perpetrator," Dr. Hansen says. "This is your last chance to help yourself. I hate to see you continue to make mistake after mistake. It really is sad. Your uncle would have been disappointed."

Matt clenches his fists under his biceps. He unclenches, places his hands on the armrests, and leans back, blank-faced.

"So? What's it going to be?" she says.

"I'd like to make the right decision, but I have no idea what you're talking about," Matt says.

Dr. Hansen smiles and shakes her head. "You have no idea? Dents, smashed in windows, headlights, and a side-view mirror?"

Matt shakes his head.

"It really is sad to see you throw your life away. Don't say I didn't give you a chance for mercy. You'll be back where you belong at least until you're eighteen. Who knows, maybe long enough to do a stint in prison with the sodomites. What do you think, Officer Blackman? You used to work upstate. How do you think he'd do?"

"His smooth white ass would be used up in a week," Blackman says.

"Do you normally discuss student's butts with Officer Blackman?" Matt asks.

Dr. Hansen's face reddens. "You just bought yourself a month of Saturday detentions. Get him out of my face."

The two officers converge on Matt, pushing and prodding him out of the office.

"I can walk on my own," Matt says.

Matt spends the next few classes pretending to pay attention. The bell rings for lunch. He strolls against traffic. He appears at Ms. Pierce's open door. She sits, working on her computer with her lunch in front of her. He stands in the doorway and knocks. Ms. Pierce, still chewing, waves him in. She wears brown corduroys and a maroon sweater. Her shoulder-length blond hair is shiny and straight, except for the wavy ends.

"Take any seat you like," Ms. Pierce says with her hand covering her mouth.

"Your lunch smells good," he says, as he walks past.

She swallows. "I try to eat healthy. I go to the Whole Organics Grocery."

"That's good." Matt purses his lips.

She smiles. "You say that like you have something to add."

"No, I think it's great that you eat healthy."

"But?"

"I'm just not a big fan of the organic label."

"Oh, yeah?" Ms. Pierce raises an eyebrow at Matt.

"I only know because my uncle and I researched it for our farm. The organic farms are still done in a monoculture, and they still spray—"

"Monoculture?"

"Yeah, where they grow the same things in rows, making it like grocery-store aisles for pests."

"How should they be grown?"

"Like in nature, in plant communities. Certain plants grow better with other plants, than by themselves. For example, carrots, tomatoes, basil, garlic, and onions grow really well together. In gardening, usually the stuff that tastes good together, grows good together."

"The plants are cooperating instead of competing."

"Exactly."

"I wish people could be like that. I'm sorry. I cut you off. You were talking about how they spray."

"I was just gonna say, they use approved sprays, which are usually botanical pesticides, so they're better, but not as much as people probably think, especially for how much more money it is."

"It is expensive. I guess that's why they call it 'whole paycheck.' Plus I have to drive forty-five minutes to get to one."

"You could grow everything you're eating. It's really easy, and the quality of the food would be better than anything you could buy at Whole Organics."

"For you maybe, but I'm not much of an outdoor girl. I'd love to have a garden at my little cottage, but I can barely keep the grass cut, much less tend a garden."

Matt places his duffel bag on the desk near the window a few seats away from Ms. Pierce. He pulls out a few Ziploc bags filled with nuts, cheese, apples, and carrots.

"That's probably the healthiest student lunch I've ever seen," she says.

"It's the best I could do. Luckily nobody where I live eats the good stuff." Matt grabs *Limits to Growth* from his bag. "Thank you for lending me this. I thought it was fascinating." Matt places the book in the return bin.

Her eyes widen. "You read it in one day?"

He nods.

Matt sits down at the desk, facing away from Ms. Pierce, who's immersed in her computer screen. He stares out the window, watching a robin steal straw from a freshly seeded area. The bird takes the building materials piece by piece to a nearby tree.

After lunch Matt fakes his way through the rest of his classes, daydreaming about last summer. *I always worried about losing Uncle, losing Emily, losing the farm. I thought things people worry about rarely ever happen. I guess the silver lining is that I have nothing left to worry about.*

After school Matt strides down the empty hallway, toward the media room. His duffel bag is slung over his shoulder. He hears the newspaper crew whispering. He shuts the door behind him. Madison, Jared, and Tariq sit at the round table, mouths open, staring at Matt. He opens his duffel bag and tosses the plastic bag filled with office trash onto the center of the table.

"I'm out. Do what you want with this," Matt says.

"What the hell?" Madison says.

Tariq and Jared pull out pieces of paper from the plastic bag. "Holy shit, this is her mail," Tariq says.

"Are you insane?" Madison says. "They searched our lockers today."

"Relax," Matt says. "I asked Ms. Pierce to let me keep my duffel bag in her closet this morning."

"We can't do this, if you're gonna be so reckless."

"That's why I'm out."

"Hold on a minute," Tariq says. "Matt put *himself* in danger, not us. And he brought us some serious intel. Come on, Matt. You must be dying to see what's in this. Unless you looked already?"

"I haven't. I was too tired last night."

Jared undoes the knot, widening the opening on the bag. "I gotta see this," he says.

"Sit, Matt. You know you want to," Tariq says. He smiles, exposing straight white teeth under his goatee.

Matt sits opposite Madison.

She glares. "What did Hansen say to you this morning?"

"She said I should confess, that they had a witness," Matt says.

"Do they?"

Matt shrugs. "I don't care if they do."

Madison shakes her head. "You're crazy."

"Chill, Madison. Player knocked out a *cop*. You think he wasn't gonna mess some shit up?" Jared says, with a toothy grin.

"Fine, whatever. All three of you are stupid," Madison says. "We need to be more careful. She's gonna be more guarded now."

"Fine, we'll be more careful," Jared says.

"I agree. Matt may have ruined the sneak attack. But, damn, that took some balls," Tariq says, laughing.

The trio looks at Matt.

"Fine. I'll be more careful," Matt says.

The news team sorts the papers, reading and separating the important from the unimportant.

"Damn, this bitch spends some money," Jared says. "Between Banana Republic, The Limited, and J.Crew, she spent almost two grand last month."

"All that for nothing," Madison says, shaking her head. "A bunch of credit card bills and junk mail."

"Hold on a second," Tariq says, his dark eyes moving back and forth. "I think I got something. She's got this place, The Coffee Ground, all over her bills. She must go there almost every day."

"So what? The bitch drinks coffee," Madison says.

"Have you ever been there?" Tariq asks.

"No."

"I have, and it's pretty far from here, about thirty minutes. My cousin lives near there."

"Why would she drive thirty minutes for coffee?" Jared asks.

"Exactly," Madison and Tariq say in unison.

"We should go now," Tariq says. "Who's with me?"

"I'm already late for track practice," Jared says.

"I'll go," Matt says.

Tariq looks at Madison.

"I should get rid of this mail," she says.

Tariq and Matt strut to the school parking lot. Tariq's short, squat build is accentuated by his baggy jeans and untucked polo shirt. Matt still wears his hooded sweatshirt and the camera case from the night before. Tariq's white Nissan Sentra sits lonely on eighteen-inch chrome wheels and low-profile tires. Matt stares at the wheels.

"Pretty badass, huh?" Tariq says. "I bought 'em from a guy in Philly for two hundred."

"Shiny," Matt says.

Tariq drives with his left hand and fiddles with the stereo using his right, while holding his lit clove cigarette. He looks at the road, then back to the stereo, then back to the road. He settles on Dr. Dre.

They pull up to The Coffee Ground with the bass pumping. The white brick building has a flat roof, with large overhangs and semitinted windows. A large coffee cup sits on the roof with the store's namesake written on the mug in Times New Roman. The rear of the building has a drive-through and a Dumpster. Matt turns down the stereo, his head pounding.

Tariq frowns.

"Low profile, remember?" Matt says.

The parking lot is three-quarters full, with late-model Hondas, Toyotas, BMWs, and Mercedes. Tariq circles the lot.

"Her car's not here," Tariq says, as he parks near the Dumpster.

"I doubt *her* car is drivable." Matt smiles at Tariq. "Her husband's is though."

"Is it here?"

"That dirty 4Runner behind us with the bears on the bumper sticker."

Tariq grins. "You should stay here. I'll do some recon."

"You want me to stay?"

"If she sees me, no problem. If she sees you, we've got problems. I'll be right back."

"Take the camera."

Matt puts up his hood and watches Tariq from the side-view mirror. Tariq creeps around the building. Matt loses sight of him. He watches the mirror. After a minute, he sees Tariq swaggering toward the car.

"She's in there all right," Tariq says.

"Did she see you?" Matt asks.

"Nah, I was smooth. She's sittin' by herself."

A hefty black SUV trimmed in shiny chrome, with tinted windows, turns into the parking lot. Matt's body stiffens. He grips the armrest, exposing the whites of his knuckles.

"Look at this baller," Tariq says.

A tall balding man emerges from the Cadillac SUV. He looks like an ex-NFL quarterback or the movie star who's a bit too old to be the leading man. He has a confident gait to accompany his protruding chin, high cheekbones, and active blue eyes. His white long-sleeve, button-down shirt is neatly pressed and tucked into his black slacks, with his sleeves rolled up.

"That's who she's waiting for," Matt says. "You should get a picture."

The man enters the coffeehouse. Tariq sneaks around the building. The man exits the coffeehouse alone. He hops into his SUV and rumbles off.

"Damn it." Matt says.

Matt turns around, scanning the building and the parking lot. Dr. Hansen hustles to the 4Runner, with her hands in her purse. She opens the blue SUV, cranks the engine, and exits the lot.

Tariq yanks open the driver-side door.

"Hurry, Tariq. They're getting away!" Matt says.

Tariq starts the engine and peels out of the parking lot.

"I know," Tariq says. "By the time I got to the building, they were leaving, but I was still searching inside."

"They went right."

Tariq turns right from the parking lot and floors his four banger.

"Watch the road ahead. I'll check the side streets," Matt says.

Tariq weaves in and out of traffic, eliciting a few honks. "They're gone."

They pass a three-story Days Inn on the right-hand side. The blue 4Runner is parked in front.

"Turn right at this light!" Matt says.

Tariq cuts off a minivan to get over. The van slams on its brakes, no horn. Matt looks back at the driver as Tariq makes the turn. The soccer mom presents her middle finger.

"The Days Inn, pull in the back," Matt says.

Tariq parks behind the building. His breathing is labored; his hands are shaky.

"Are they here?" Tariq asks.

"I think so."

Matt and Tariq creep along the building to the front. They peer through the automatic sliding doors. The balding man is at the front desk. He looks over. They jerk their heads back from the door.

"I'm gonna go check the 4Runner. Keep an eye on him," Matt says.

Matt crouches along a row of cars, until he's behind a Dodge Durango, next to the 4Runner. He slips along the Dodge to its passenger window. He peers through the front windows of the Durango into Dr. Hansen's car. She gazes at herself in a handheld mirror, spritzing hair spray. Matt runs across the lot to Tariq, who crouches between two cars near the double-door entry.

"She's still in the car," Matt says.

"He went to the room," Tariq says.

"Please tell me that he didn't get on the elevator."

"Nope, he went down the hall to the right."

"We gotta find the room before she gets there."

"Who is this guy?"

"John Jacobs, the developer of Kingstown."

Matt and Tariq skulk along the building, glancing into rooms with open curtains. Matt catches a glimpse of a man kicking off his shoes. Matt puts his arm up to stop Tariq from walking in front of the window.

"He's here," Matt says. They see Dr. Hansen scurry across the parking lot. "I'm assuming we only have a few seconds to get some shots of them together before he closes those curtains. Would you take the pictures?"

"I gotcha," Tariq says, pulling out the camera.

John Jacobs sits on the bed and flips on the television. MSNBC stock tickers slide across the screen. Matt and Tariq hide behind a squared holly hedge, primed like the paparazzi. John stands up and saunters toward the door, letting in Dr. Hansen.

A bead of sweat falls to Tariq's eyebrow. Dr. Hansen kicks off her high heels and hops into John's arms. Tariq shoots as the embrace ensues. They turn around, Dr. Hansen's legs still latched around John, her skirt hiked. She rubs her pelvis against him, like a cat in heat. They kiss. Tariq continues to shoot. John tosses her on the bed, Dr. Hansen smiling in midair. She glances out the window, scowls, and points. Tariq and Matt hit the dirt in front of the hedge, like they're taking enemy fire. Matt sees John looking out, shaking his head. John draws the shades.

[12]

Gotta Play the Game

Matt strolls to Ms. Pierce's classroom, going opposite the lunch traffic, like a subway commuter traveling toward the city in the afternoon. Students give him a wide berth, with the occasional, "Hey, Matt." Matt waves or nods, trying to vary his greeting, but feels awkward that he doesn't know their names.

"Hey, Ms. Pierce. Same lunch?" Matt asks.

"I make my lunch in a big vat on Sunday, because I don't have time to cook during the week, so pretty much the same thing all week."

Matt places his duffel bag on the windowsill. He removes a sheet of paper from his notebook.

"Can you look at this and tell me what you think?"

Ms. Pierce speed-reads the history pretest. She grins and hands it back.

"Your responses remind me of a boyfriend I had a number of years ago. He was like this drifter." She shakes her head, with a smirk.

Matt raises his eyebrows. "You went out with a drifter?"

Ms. Pierce laughs. "Well, sort of. He was probably the smartest guy I've ever known. I actually thought we might get married, but he had some real problems. He was a pretty paranoid guy. He used to rail on about how much he hated the government. He always called the government, 'the state.' You used similar terminology on your test. Anyway he used to tell me all these outrageous stories about how governments try to start wars on purpose to increase their power over their citizens."

"For example?"

"Oh, let me think." She taps her index finger to her lips. "He once told me that the Gulf of Tonkin never happened, that we were led into Vietnam on a lie. He told me some of the same stuff you wrote too."

"What happened to him?"

"It actually went really well for a while. We got along great. I learned a ton about history, the real history. He shared all his sources, and it really opened my mind. It was pretty shocking stuff. I felt like I was dropped into a rabbit hole that just went deeper and deeper, the more I uncovered. It really made me question my profession. Then he got really focused on the idea that the very nature of government is immoral, that it was impossible to have a moral government, because all their power originates from the barrel of a gun." Ms. Pierce takes a deep breath, looking through Matt. "So anyway I think I can understand what you're up against."

"Where is he now?" Matt sits at the edge of his seat.

"I probably shouldn't talk about ex-boyfriends with you." Her face flushes; she looks away.

"So, what should *I* do?"

"You and I both know that you know the answers that Mr. Dalton's looking for. You could easily ace that final in a fraction of the time it takes to get deep into the truth. My ex-boyfriend, he always chose the truth, no matter what the consequences, and it really cost him. Sometimes you have to go along to get along. Our system is pretty flawed, but it's all we have. If you constantly go against the grain, it can wear you down. Do you understand?"

"I think so." Matt unpacks his lunch. "I have another thing I wanted to run by you. I have a business proposition for you."

"Oh, yeah?" Ms. Pierce raises an eyebrow.

"I wanted to see if you'd be interested in hiring me as a sharecropper."

She laughs. "Sharecropper? Are we in Mississippi at the turn of the century?"

"I'm serious. It doesn't have to be exploitive. You want good produce, and you already pay a lot for it, *and* you have land that you can't take care of. But I don't have any land or money. I can only offer my labor. So, I do all the work, you provide the land and materials, and we split the harvest."

"It sounds like a great idea, but it doesn't sound very fair."

"How about a sixty-forty split of the harvest?"

"That's not what I meant, honey. I don't think it's a good deal for *you*. You end up doing a lot without getting paid. I'm not exactly rich, but I could pay you forty dollars a week on top of the harvest."

"Deal."

Emily stands in the doorway, her gaze on Matt, then to Ms. Pierce, then back to Matt. Her head's cocked, and her hands are on her hips.

"Emily, don't linger. Come in, honey," Ms. Pierce says and motions with her arms.

"I'll come in on Monday. I didn't know you had *someone* here," Emily says.

"Matt may be here on Monday. I'm sure he'd give us some privacy, if you need to talk."

"I can go to the lunchroom," Matt says, packing his lunch and stuffing it into his bag.

"That's not necessary," Emily says. "I'll go."

"No, I'd be happy to leave *this* time."

"Good, *go*. That's what you're good at."

"Guys, *what* is going on here?" Ms. Pierce asks, standing from her desk.

"Nothing," Emily says.

"That's what I am to you—nothing," Matt says, as he zips up his bag and swings it over his shoulder.

"Then why did I cover for you?"

Ms. Pierce slips out of her classroom, with her lunch in hand.

"Did you? Your mom says she has a witness." Matt crosses his arms.

"Come on. I know you're smarter than that. If she knew it was you, you'd be done."

Matt drops his arms, sets his bag on the floor and sits in his desk chair, facing Emily. He stares at her feet. "Why'd you do it? You could've just let it go. They destroyed my stand. Your note was the beginning of the end for me." Matt blinks; a tear beads on his lower eyelid.

Emily walks closer, standing one desk away. "What note?"

Matt wipes his eyes with his shirt sleeve. "Let's not do this."

"I wanna know. What note?"

"It's funny you don't remember, because I remember like it was yesterday. It said, 'I never want to see you again. I was only nice to you because I felt sorry for you.'"

Emily sits in the desk across from Matt, dazed. She closes her eyes and exhales. "I didn't write that, I swear. And I didn't know your stand was destroyed. I saw that it was gone, but I thought it was from the police. I'm sorry." Emily looks away.

"Why didn't you ever come back? I needed you." Matt's voice is soft, like he might break if he speaks too loud.

Emily turns toward Matt. Her neck and upper chest are blotchy; her eyes are glassy. "I didn't know what to do. I thought you hated me after our fight. Then when you came to my house with your uncle …" Tears streak down her face. "I'm so sorry."

Matt stands and approaches Emily's desk. She gazes up. He leans over and wraps his arms around her upper back. She tugs at Matt's hips and sinks her head into his chest, tears pouring out, her weeping reverberating through his body like seismic activity. She calms; the storm passes. Matt lets go.

"So what now?" she asks.

"I don't know. Can we go back to where we were before?"

"Can we be friends?"

"You don't want things like they were?" Matt asks.

"It's just …"

"It's just what? Your boyfriend?"

"Well, … yeah. I'm sorry. I want you in my life. I do."

"Just not like I want."

"I don't know. It was really hard when you went away, and now you're back, but I've moved on."

"I get it. I do." Matt grabs his duffel bag.

"You guys okay?" Ms. Pierce asks, standing in the doorway.

"We're fine," Matt says. "I'm gonna eat in the media room. I forgot I had some stuff to do for the newspaper."

Matt trudges to the lunchroom instead. His head pounds; he's overloaded by the sights, sounds, and smells of a thousand kids trying to eat lunch in twenty minutes. He finds a sparsely populated back corner table, slumps into his seat, and unpacks his lunch. He's inundated with greetings and offers of good tidings across cliques and genders.

"Hey, Matt."

"What up, Matt."

"Maaaattt, wuzzzz uuuup."

"Um, hi, Matt."

"Hey, do you mind if I sit?"

"What's up? This seat taken?"

Matt feels a tap on his shoulder. He looks up to see a busty brunette with high cheekbones biting the corner of her lip, flanked by two leggy blondes. "I'm Megan. Can we sit?" she asks.

+++

Matt sits at the round table in the media room, opposite Madison and Tariq.

"Where's Jared?" Matt asks.

"Spring football meeting," Tariq says. "He should be here in a few minutes. Madison doesn't think we can use the pictures of Dr. Hansen bonin' that Jacobs guy."

Jared saunters in. "What up, party people."

"Jared, we're just talkin' about whether we can use the Dr. Hansen photos," Tariq says.

Jared dumps his backpack on the table. "Why not? That shit is scandalous."

"I'm not saying we can't use it, just that we need more," Madison says. "That might get her fired in our Jesus-freak town, but it might not. If it doesn't get her fired, we're screwed. I think we need to start looking at Mrs. Campbell too."

"Where are you going with this?" Matt asks Madison.

"You remember when all those kids were in her office because *someone*, who shall remain nameless, destroyed her car?"

"Yeah?"

"You know what all those kids have in common?"

"They get into trouble?"

Madison grins, her nose ring flaring with her nostrils. "Nope, they all did a stint in juvie because of that bitch."

"*Damn*," Tariq says.

"Damn," Jared says.

"Indeed," Matt says.

"We need to find Hansen's jailhouse connection," Madison says. "At first I thought maybe we should look closely into the SROs, but I think this might be over their heads. That's why I was thinking of Mrs. Campbell."

"Chief Campbell's wife," Matt says.

"Bingo."

[13]

The Connect

The neighborhood's quiet, with dew on the grass. Matt treks along the sidewalk, *Civil Disobedience* in the back pocket of his jeans. He hears the roar of George's Mustang. George pulls over to the curb with a screech of his tires. The passenger window motors down. Abby looks forward, like a horse with blinders.

"Where the hell are *you* goin'?" George asks across Abby.

Matt walks over to the shiny black coupe.

"Saturday detention," Matt says.

"Get in."

"I can't. I really have to be there."

"You think I'd wake up this early for no reason? Pull up the seat, Abby. Let him in back."

Abby sighs and shakes her head, avoiding eye contact with Matt. She steps from the car and pulls the seat forward. Matt squeezes into the backseat. Abby sits in the front seat and slams the door. George mashes on the accelerator, leaving rubber tire tracks in the street.

They park close to the school, in spaces normally taken by the early birds. George and Matt walk together. Abby follows, pouting with her arms folded.

"What are you in for?" George asks.

"I pissed off Dr. Hansen. You?"

"Skipping."

"That would be hard to get away with," Matt says. "You're either here or not."

"I miss at least one day a week, sometimes two. I get Grace to gimme a note. I always say I got allergies in the spring. That's like back pain. You can't prove or disprove a sinus headache. I had some stuff to do last week, so I took the week. Freaking Grace hung me out to dry."

"That sucks."

"Don't I know it. You know, a lotta people been talkin' about you. You've got some serious juice, my man."

"Juice?"

"You know, like power. You're not quite in *my* league, but you got potential." George nods his head.

George and Matt, followed by Abby, stroll into the lunchroom. Three teenagers, two boys and a girl, sit on top of a table, their feet on the seats. Matt's body tightens when he sees Colton lounging back, using his hands for support. Colton pops up at the sight of the trio.

"Oh, snap, look at this baller," Colton says. "I thought you dropped out. You make enough duckets." He stands and slaps hands with George, eyeing Matt from the corner of his eye, under his rigid New York Yankees cap. "This punk-ass ain't wich *you*, is he?"

"Don't be talkin' about my brother like that, bitch," George says.

Colton puts up his hands. "Ah-ite, my bad. Don't start trippin'."

Matt notices a black eye and a bruise on the side of Colton's face. Abby and the girl, another fake blonde with orange skin, jabber to each other. The other boy hops off the lunch table. The table creaks as the three-hundred-pound black teen pushes off. He's a mountain of a man, with tight cornrows, gigantic facial features, and ears punctured with diamond studs.

"My man, George, it's a sad day, when you get stuck in here," the humongous teen says.

"Tony, what's up? I could say the same thing to you," George says.

"I'm black and three hundred pounds. What's your excuse?"

"You gotta know your limits. I pushed too far."

"Who's your boy?"

"This is my foster brother, Matt."

Tony nods his head, with a gargantuan grin. "This is the playa the youngins be talkin' about, bitch-slapped that cop." Tony chuckles. "I hear you be stirrin' some *shit*, pissin' of *er body*. Teachers be mad as hell. Like Bob Marley said, 'a real revolutionary.'"

Matt extends his hand. Tony's mitt swallows his hand past his wrist. "Nice to meet you, Tony," Matt says.

"Listen to this white boy, all polite and shit." Tony laughs.

"Tony's gonna be playin' defensive tackle for Rutgers in the fall," George says.

Matt shrugs. "I don't know much about football."

A lanky, wrinkled white-haired janitor, with Herb written on his name tag, treks toward the teens in Timberland boots.

"Damn, Herb, you straight up *pimpin'* in those Timberlands," Tony says.

"I don't wanna be doin' dis anymore 'an you do, believe you me," Herb says.

"Hey, Herb, my friend Matt here is interested in pursuing a career in the custodial arts. Maybe you could keep that in mind when you're assigning work today," George says, grinning.

"Watch yaself, ya li'l smart-ass. If *yins* don't mess around, we can get outta here early."

"I thought you got in trouble for lettin' us out early?" Abby asks.

"Shut up," George whispers.

"Ya think I give a damn," Herb says. "I'm seventy-five years old."

The kids laugh.

Matt and George walk from class to class, emptying trash cans into a large plastic bag. They enter Mr. Dalton's history classroom with the master key Herb provided. George holds the bag open, while Matt dumps the trash inside. Matt scans the room.

"What are you doin'? Let's go," George says.

"Go ahead, I'm looking for something," Matt says.

Matt opens the drawers of Mr. Dalton's metal desk.

George laughs. "You ain't gonna find any dirt in there."

Matt looks at George, blank-faced.

"You got balls, I'll give you that, but you don't know what the hell you're doin'. You want the dirt, you gotta go to the computer. I know your country ass doesn't know jack about computers."

Matt shakes his head. George pushes the button on the monitor and the hard drive. He walks over to the printer on the windowsill and pushes that button. The printer starts to move and whiz. The hard drive beeps and boots up. George sits down at Mr. Dalton's desk. Matt pulls up a chair. George cracks his knuckles and runs a hand through his wavy blond hair. His hazel eyes stare at the password prompt.

"Let's see how dumb he is," George says, cracking his knuckles.

George types in "password." The computer sends an error message, which states Incorrect Password in red letters. He tries "123456," which gives him another error message, then "password1."

The screen flashes, the Microsoft startup music sings, and the icons appear.

"What a dumbass," George says.

"So we're in his computer now?" Matt asks.

"*Yes*, we're in. So what do you want me to look for?"

"Anything that might be particularly embarrassing or inappropriate."

"Damn, you are hateful."

Matt frowns and looks at the floor. "Do you think this is wrong?"

George chuckles. "You're asking me? I think Dalton's a dick."

George searches Dalton's documents, videos, and e-mails, doing a word search for the seven dirty words.

George's eyes widen. "Jackpot."

A string of e-mails addressed to Olivia Pierce show up on the screen.

"We should shut this off," Matt says.

"Hell no. Ms. Pierce is hot. Maybe she sent him a naked picture."

George opens the first e-mail containing one of the seven dirty words.

From: Chris Dalton
To: Olivia Pierce
Subject: Get Together

Olivia,

You look great today. I love it when you where that turtleneck. We need to get together this weekend. I know you think I come on strong but I know we have a connection don't deni it. I know you think I'm an asshole sometimes but deep down I'm not. Lets get together I'll make it worth your wild.

Chris

George cackles, his body convulsing in the chair as he doubles over. "That's the funniest thing I've ever seen. What a tool." George scrolls down. "Her response is underneath."

From: Olivia Pierce
To: Chris Dalton
Subject: Re: Get Together

Chris,

First of all, I don't *where* a turtleneck, I *wear* a turtleneck. Second of all, it's *worth your while*, not *wild*. If you're going to ask out an English teacher, use proper grammar. I already told you nicely that I was seeing someone.

Ms. Olivia Pierce
Eleventh Grade English
Jefferson High

PS: Please learn to use a comma.

George has another laughing fit. Matt joins in. George opens the next e-mail in the string.

From: Chris Dalton
To: Olivia Pierce
Subject: Re: Re: Get Together

Olivia,

Your reply was so funny. I guess that's why I teach history and not English. For you I will work on my English skills. I could use a tutor though. Know anybody good? Please consider my offer, it's a good one.

Chris

"Let's print this whole string out. There's like ten of 'em," George says.

He sends the documents to the printer. The printer spits out the pages. George and Matt read through them as they come, hot off the press. George picks up the second-to-last page and turns it over, a stifled grin on his face.

"Hey, Matt, check this one out."

Matt looks over, and George shoves a picture in Matt's face of a man's penis hanging from a jungle of dark curly hair. George falls to one knee, cackling. His face is red, and his eyes are watery.

"He sent her a dick pic!" George says, before convulsing back into hysterics.

Matt drops the picture in disgust. George regains his composure.

"Goddamn, this is fun," George says. "I'm surprised Ms. Pierce didn't get his dumb ass fired."

Matt reads the final e-mail in the string. "She's threatening to go to the administration, if he doesn't stop. He deserves to be fired."

"What was the date on that last one?"

"It's from two days ago."

"If he can't stop himself from sending dick pics at school, I wonder what else he can't stop himself from doin'. Let's check his Internet history."

"Internet history?"

"It's exactly what it sounds like, homeboy. The history, if he didn't delete it, will tell us what he's been looking up at school." George clicks around, opening up Dalton's history folders. "This douchebag is all over porn sites. Is this cliché or what? He's on *naughtyschoolgirls.com* almost every day." George chuckles.

Matt frowns and shakes his head.

"Now, Matt, we gotta analyze this. Let's think about how this happens. So he's checkin' out these teenage girls all day, in the halls, in class, checkin' out their asses in those tight little shorts, lookin' down their shirts as he stands over 'em teachin' history. He's so worked up by the end of the day that he gets on *naughtyschoolgirls.com*, imagining all the hot chicks in school. This dumbass can't even wait till he gets home."

"Can we print the history too?"

"I'm sendin' it to the printer now." George turns to Matt, his jaw set tight. "Just so we're clear—this is on you. I did not help you. Do you understand me?"

"Of course. I appreciate you helping."

George glares at Matt.

"I mean, not helping me. What do you think I should do with this?"

"Get the fool fired, what else? It'll be a public service."

"One thing I don't get. If we can find this stuff, why doesn't the school? Don't they check?"

George shrugs. "I guess that depends on the tech guy." George grins and nods his head.

"What?"

"The tech guy is Mr. Richardson."

Matt shrugs.

"He coaches with Mr. Dalton, so he probably doesn't even check his history, or, if he does, he wouldn't narc on him."

The boys stop off at Matt's locker to deposit the evidence. They continue with their rounds, until they reach Mrs. Campbell's classroom. They open the door with the master key. Old newspaper clippings of heroic tales of police glory hang on the walls, some framed, some not. Her metal desk sits in the back of the room, with a tubby computer monitor on top and a hard drive underneath.

An old framed picture of Chief Campbell, Mrs. Campbell, and their two kids, Colton and Sophia, sits on the desk. Everyone's smiling, with crinkles at the corners of their eyes, except Colton, who looks to be about ten. He forces a smile, but his eyes tell the truth. Everyone's dressed in khakis and white polo shirts, with the ocean in the background.

"So what's your beef with Mrs. Campbell?" George asks, as he sits down at her desk and boots up her computer.

"I don't know yet," Matt says.

George types in common passwords. "I don't know what this could be," George says.

"Try 'police.'"

"Nope."

"How about 'ColtonandSophia'?" Matt asks.

"Nope. Lemme try with an ampersand." George beams. "Look at that. I'm a hacker now."

George searches for the seven dirty words. No results. They scan through her e-mails.

"Damn, she's boring," George says. "No personal e-mails at all."

Matt frowns. "Can you check to see if she has any e-mails to or from Dr. Hansen?"

"She has a bunch, but those are part of the mass e-mails Hansen sends out to the whole staff. I'll bring up any e-mails just between the two of them." George does the search. "Nope, nothin'."

George shuts down the computer, and they lock up Mrs. Campbell's classroom. Matt drags the bulging plastic bag along the linoleum hallway toward the lunchroom. George strolls beside him. Matt stares at the main office.

"I think Dr. Hansen needs her trash can emptied," Matt says.

"I bet she does," George says, grinning.

The pair walks down the corridor to the principal's office. Matt reaches for the handle, but the door is locked. He slides the master key into the lock, but it won't turn. He jiggles it, but no movement. He flips the key over, but still no dice.

"Whadda *yins* think yer doin' down dare," Herb says.

Matt and George return from the corridor, to the office waiting area. Herb stands, eyes narrowed, with his hands on his hips.

"Takin' the trash," George says.

"Uh-huh, I bet. Classrooms only. Take dat dare bag out to da Dumpster. And don't drag it. It gonna split."

+++

The six teens push through the front doors, their faces awash in sunlight, and their moods light with the completion of their penance. George, Matt, and Tony walk together with Colton close behind. Abby and the other blonde walk together.

"You got my order tomorrow?" Tony asks.

"Yeah, I'll drop it by your place," George says.

"Ah-ite. Layta, playa."

George turns to Matt. "I have some business in Philly. Ever been?"

"When I was a baby, but I don't remember it," Matt replies.

"Well, then ya gadda come."

"Yo, can I come?" Colton asks.

"Listen, Colton, I don't wanna be a dick, but you can't go to Philly with that wigger shit you got goin' on."

"Come on, George. I can talk regular. I gotta get outta this town."

"All right, but I want twenty dollars for gas, and you gotta wait in the car."

"Ah-ite."

George glares at Colton.

146

"I mean, all right."

"Abby, you comin'?" George asks.

"I guess, but I'm sittin' in front," Abby says.

George guides the black Mustang onto I-76, stopping at the toll booth to grab a ticket, before mashing the accelerator, the V-8 roaring to life. Matt's head pushes back into the headrest. Abby raises her arms like she's on a roller coaster. George bangs through the gears like a NASCAR driver. The two-hour ride to Philly is short on conversation but long on blasted rock ballads from Def Leppard and Guns N' Roses.

George drives into a neighborhood with endless brick row homes. Air conditioners and fans stick out of the upper windows, bars protect the lower. Satellite dishes are the most common upgrade. Reddish brick colors vary just enough to make each house in the row clash with the others. Cars line the curbs in front.

"Parking sucks here," George says, as he circles the block. George slams the stick into Reverse and parallel parks. "You two stay in the car. Keep the door locked. Matt, let's go."

"Come on, George. I'll be cool," Colton says.

"Shut up and stay in the car," George replies.

George and Matt stride down the sidewalk. Other than the odd tuft of grass or dandelions growing in the cracks of the sidewalk, no greenery exists. A few neighborhood stoop-sitters give the two boys the evil eye. George stops at a brownish-redbrick row home, with black bars protecting the windows and the door. This row home is the only one with a sickly small tree quarantined by concrete. George reaches his hand between the vertical bars and knocks on the door. A scantily clad black woman with wide hips opens the wooden door, with the barred door still shut.

"What the hell y'all want?" she says, her eyes narrowing at George's backpack straps.

"We're here to see Jimbo. I'm George."

"Oh snap, you're George? I'm sorry, honey. I was expecting you to be … older. Come on in." She opens the barred door and steps aside for the boys. "Now who's your friend?"

"This is my brother, Matt."

"Okay, I can see the family resemblance. I know some young girls that'd be real interested in you two. I could get you an employee discount." She giggles; her cleavage shakes. "Why don't y'all wait here in the TV room. I'll get Jimbo." She saunters to the stairs. "Jimbo, George is here."

An L-shaped couch, with a plastic covering on it, sits along the wall and in front of a big-screen TV standing on built-in speakers. The number *227* appears on the screen, with intro music, followed by two black women arguing: one dressed in a tight-fitting leotard; the other, older, with a perpetual scowl.

"I love this old show," she says. "It reminds me of *my* neighborhood back in the day." She laughs and puts her hand on her chest. "I don't know why I'm telling y'all. Prolly never hearda *227*."

"Marla Gibbs, Jackee Harry, Hal Williams—I remember it," George says.

She giggles. "You so crazy. What are you doin' watchin' these old shows?"

"That's all I did as a kid."

Heavy footsteps descend the stairs. Chubby ankles and thick calves appear, followed by a bear of a man who looks like a white-trash version of Santa Claus, the day *after* Christmas, one who wouldn't get pelted with snowballs by Eagles fans.

"George, my boy," Jimbo says.

"Hey, Jimbo. How's it hangin'?" George says.

"Low and to the left." Jimbo smacks George on the back. George stumbles forward. "You know how I feel about new people." Jimbo motions with his chin toward Matt.

"It's just my little brother, Matt."

"Well, why didn't you say so? Nice to meet ya, li'l brother." Jimbo holds out his thick, sun-spotted hand.

"It's nice to meet you," Matt says, shaking the man's hand.

"Good manners, I like that," Jimbo says. "Nobody has manners anymore."

"Don't you think they look alike?" the woman says.

Jimbo strokes his long white-and-gray beard. "I can see a little family resemblance. Of course all white people look alike, right?"

She makes a ticking noise with her tongue directed toward Jimbo. "You know I didn't mean it like that." She struts to the couch.

"Whaddaya got for me?" Jimbo asks George.

George takes off his backpack and unzips the pocket. He removes a thick white envelope and hands it over. Jimbo holds it up, bouncing it in his hand.

"Feels about right to me," he says.

"You can count it. It's all there," George says.

"Have you ever cheated me?"

"No."

"That's why I trust you, and I don't trust easy, been burned too many times, but I like to do business with people I can trust. You can't have any type of relationship without trust. Give me a minute. I'll grab your order."

Jimbo walks toward the kitchen in oversize gray cutoff sweats and a XXXL green Eagles T-shirt that barely covers his gut. Matt sees an eagle tattoo flying on his left calf. He's overcome with a sense of déjà vu. His head sags; his eyes flutter and shut. He sees the tattoo walking past him at eye level. He hears a woman sobbing. His eyes jolt open with the slamming of a cabinet door. Jimbo appears with a brown paper bag. He hands the bag to George.

"Thanks," George says, placing the paper bag into his backpack. "I might need more in a week or so. I can barely keep inventory these days."

"Be careful, young buck. It's a marathon, not a sprint," Jimbo says.

"I gotta save up for my own place. I'll be eighteen in a few months."

"Another reason to be careful. You're runnin' with the big dogs now. Speakin' of bein' careful, you get rid of that cop magnet, like I told ya?"

"Aw, come on, Jimbo. You worry too much."

"No, I've just seen a lotta shit in my life. You don't see me livin' it up like Scarface. You oughta get a minivan or one of those new ugly-ass Azztecs? *That* could be the ugliest plastic piece of shit I've ever seen. That's what I'd be drivin'."

"I'll think about it." George rolls his eyes.

"Don't think about it. Do it. And drive slow on the way home but not too slow. Stay in the right-hand lane and go with the flow of traffic."

George straps on his backpack. Matt and George stride to the car. George's eyes dart back and forth. He occasionally looks over his shoulder. He pounds on the car door. Abby hits the automatic unlock.

"Get in back, Abby," George says.

"What, why?" she says.

"Matt's sittin' up front."

Abby crosses her arms. "This is bullshit."

"Fine, you wanna hold on to the stash?"

Abby climbs in back. Matt opens the passenger door and settles into the front seat. George places the backpack in Matt's lap.

"Hang on to this," George says.

George hops on I-76, flying down the left lane at a blistering pace.

"What's the rush?" Matt asks.

"I gotta couple parties to get to. I can probably sell half my product tonight. If I'm late, they might go elsewhere. You know, customer satisfaction and all. It's always harder to get a new customer than to keep a good one."

"Remember what Jimbo said about driving in the right lane, with the flow of traffic."

"I got eagle eyes, plus I know where all the cop spots are. I've made this drive a hundred times."

George pulls off I-76 and stops at the toll booth on their exit. After the toll, he drives his Mustang into Kingstown. He speeds by rows of townhomes. He gives his brakes a quick pump, then blows through a stop sign. George guns the engine, as he scoots down the road. Matt's stomach drops when he catches a glimpse of blue and red lights out of the corner of his eye.

"Damn it!" George says, as he hits the steering wheel with the palm of his hand. He turns to Matt. "Shove that shit under your seat."

Matt pushes the backpack under his seat. George pulls over and cuts the engine. He grabs his registration and insurance card from the center console, and removes his license from his wallet.

"Ohmigod, we are so busted," Abby says.

"Be cool, everybody. Act natural. It's just a ticket," George says.

George motors the window down. The police officer approaches. He's medium height, with a muscular build, mirrored sunglasses, and a dark mustache.

"License, registration, and proof of insurance," the cop says. Georges hands him his documentation. "Do you know why I pulled you over?"

"No, sir," George replies.

"You ran a stop sign, and you were going forty-five in a twenty-five-mile-per-hour zone. That's reckless driving, son. Do you know what the penalty is for reckless driving?"

"No, sir."

"It's a two-hundred-dollar fine and a six-month license suspension. Is there anyone with you who has a license?"

"No, sir."

"If there isn't, we have to tow the car." The officer peers into the backseat of the Mustang. "Colton, is that you?"

"Uncle James," Colton says.

"What are you doin' with this clown? Your dad would be pretty pissed, if he knew about this."

"I know. I'm sorry. Please don't tell him."

The cop clenches his jaw. "This is your one pass. You don't get another from me, got it?"

"Yes, sir."

The officer turns to George. "If I ever catch you drivin' like that, I'll make sure you never drive again. You got me? You better thank your lucky stars that you got Colton in the backseat, because you woulda been in a world a hurt. Now get outta here."

[14]

The Nuclear Option

George pulls up to the stately McMansion at the end of the cul-de-sac. The driveway's empty, but Tyler's lifted Jeep, a pickup, and a sedan are parked along the curb.

"Gimme that bag," George says.

George, Colton, and Abby walk toward the house. Matt stands by the car. George stops.

"What are you doin'?" George says.

"I'm gonna stay here," Matt says.

"What's the problem?"

"I don't think I'm welcome here."

"Bitch is outta town. Let's go."

Matt shuts the car door. The brothers stride across the lawn to the front stoop. Matt eyes the bloodstain on the concrete. George opens the door and waltzes in. The foyer is bare and churchlike, with black and white marble under their feet. A hand-painted mural of a vineyard resides on the wall to the right, a spiral staircase with a wrought iron railing to the left. Stainless steel appliances and hanging pots and pans glisten in the distance. George marches past the mural and opens a door. Gangster rap and raucous voices spill out. They descend the white carpeted staircase. The rap lyrics and animated voices get louder. A black leather sectional couch surrounds a wooden entertainment center, featuring a fifty-inch television and Kenwood speakers.

A movie plays to the empty couches, with no sound. Matt and George stop and watch. A young man with a goatee holds a white mouse by the tail, with little mouse feet touching his lips. He slowly lowers the mouse into his mouth, while an attractive young blonde looks on in horror, and the tail still sticks out of his mouth. The young man rests his hand on the nearby aquarium. The boa constrictor strikes, swallowing his hand whole. Chaos ensues, with the man swinging his arms, the snake still clamped on his wrist, destroying furniture in the dorm room. Matt watches mesmerized, with a painted grin.

"I love this movie," George says. "Have you seen it?"

Matt shakes his head; his neck cranes to catch a few more seconds as they walk through the open double doors. Inside, a pool table dominates the room. A dark wooden bar and six bar stools with black cushions sit along the far wall, with a television hung behind the barkeep. Three-hundred-pound Tony stands, grinning, with a towel over his shoulder, pouring shots for his patrons. Colton, Abby, Tyler, Sophia, and Megan sit on the bar stools. They clink their shot glasses together and swallow the light brown liquid in single gulps. The girls scrunch up their faces and press lime wedges between their glossed lips. Tyler calls for another.

"What up, playas?" Tony says to George and Matt.

"Anybody wanna get high?" George says.

The teens turn on their bar stools. Tyler hops off, glaring at Matt. Tyler's face is puffy and acne-riddled. His tank top accentuates his arms that hang out from his body, his barrel chest preventing them from hanging normally. His brown hair's shaved on the sides, with a gelled flattop. Bass pumps in the background. Tyler marches toward Matt. He stands in front of Matt, looking him up and down, his eyes narrowed, his fists clenched, contempt on his face. The teens freeze; the room is quiet, save the music. Matt concentrates on Tyler's hands. Tyler reaches back and swings. Matt ducks, Tyler's fist glancing off the top of his head. Tyler rears back again. Tony swallows him up from behind, pinning his arms behind his back.

"Calm down, ... damn," Tony says.

"You bring this little bitch to *my* house," Tyler says, struggling to break free. "Let me go!"

Tony lets go. Matt's hands are up, his fists clenched. Tyler lunges at Matt. He hears *clack, clack, clack, clack, clack,* in rapid succession. George presses a black box into Tyler's side.

"*Ah, ah,*" Tyler says, as he falls to the ground, contorting his body away from the electrical current.

George continues to electrocute Tyler with his black box pressed firmly against his side. The box is still emitting a *clack, clack, clack, clack, clack.*

George relents but holds the black box with a current of electricity streaming between two electrodes over Tyler's fetal-positioned body.

"That hurt, George! What the hell?" Tyler says.

"I can't have clients attacking my employees," George says. "You gotta complaint about Matt, you can voice it to me, and I'll take care of it."

Tyler staggers to his feet, giving George and his stun gun a wide berth. "This piece of shit used to mess around with my sister."

"My boy, Matt, be straight-up pimpin'," Tony says with a chuckle. "Emily's fine too. She must like them farmer boys."

"Shut up, Tony," Tyler says.

"Okay, I can see why you might be mad, so I'll let you get one punch in," George says. "Not to the face though, then it's over, you leave him alone."

"Fine," Tyler says.

"What?" Matt says.

"It's one and done, Matt. Just get it over with, so we can get down to business," George says.

Matt walks over to Tyler, his arms held out, and his body unprotected. Tyler winds up and plunges his fist into Matt's stomach. Matt doubles over, falling to one knee, coughing.

"*Damn,* home skillet got jacked *up,*" Colton says.

Tony laughs; the girls giggle. Matt stands up straight.

"Look at this soldier," Tony says.

"This shit squashed now?" George asks.

Tyler nods.

"All right then. Is there a place where we can conduct our business?"

George, Tyler, and Tony go upstairs. Matt sits on the couch, watching the movie. Megan saunters out to the leather sectional. She taps Matt on the shoulder, bending down, her wavy brown hair tickling his face and her deep V-neck exposing full breasts.

"Why don't you come to the bar and hang out?" she whispers. Megan kisses Matt's earlobe, lightly tugging with her teeth. She struts to the bar; Matt's gaze follows.

Matt steps around the pool table toward the bar. Colton stands behind the bar, playing Tom Cruise in *Cocktail*. Abby, Sophia, and Megan giggle as Colton flips a bottle of tequila from one hand to the other. As Matt approaches, Colton mishandles the catch in his left hand, the bottle bouncing off his leg and landing on the floor.

"Saved it," Colton says, picking up the unbroken bottle.

"Come sit next to me," Megan says, patting the bar stool next to her. "Do you know everyone here?"

Matt shakes his head.

"We haven't met formally. I'm Sophia," Sophia says with a wave.

Sophia's skin is creamy white and flawless. Her hair is dark and her eyes blue. Her facial features are proportional, with bright red lips. Her waist is thin, but her chest and hips are well developed. It wouldn't be a hyperbole to call her beautiful.

"Nice to meet you, Sophia," Matt says.

"You best step off," Colton says, playing the protective brother.

"Shut up, Colton," Sophia says. "He can talk to me if he wants. Matt can probably kick your ass anyway."

"Why you trippin'? You shouldn't even be here anyway."

"Why you trippin'?" Megan says, mocking.

"Why y'all have to be such bitches?" Colton says, shaking his head.

"Why do you have to be such a c-blocker?" Abby says. "Let your sister have some fun. She ain't crushin' on Matt anyway."

The girls giggle.

"Whatever," Colton says.

"So, Matt, you wanna go someplace private?" Megan says loud enough for the others to hear. The girls giggle.

"You go, girl." Abby high-fives Megan.

"You betta watch yaself," Colton says. "Tyler's gettin' with that tonight."

"Says who?" Megan says.

Megan reaches over and puts her hand on Matt's crotch. She leans over and presses her lips against his, opening her mouth and shoving her tongue inside. Tyler, George, and Tony walk into the room.

"Megan, what are you doin'?" Tyler says.

"Relax, I'm just warmin' up for you," she says.

"Get the hell outta here, farmer faggot!"

Matt hops off the bar stool. He strides over to George and Tony.

"Catcha layta, playa," Tony says to George. "Appreciate the free bud with my package. Reminds me of my mom's Mary Kay lady."

George frowns.

"No disrespect. She be givin' my moms free lipstick and shit. That works too. She got that pink Mary Kay Cadillac, makin' mad paper."

George chuckles. "Later, Tony. Hit me up when you need a resupply. Hey, Abby, we're leavin'."

"Can you pick me up later?" Abby asks.

"No."

"I can take you home," Megan says.

"Suit yourself," George says.

Matt and George exit the room; Colton bounds after them.

"George, I gotta axe you somethin'," Colton says.

"We gotta get going," George says.

"I helped you today."

George frowns.

"You know, with the cop and all. I was thinkin' that I could move some product for you. I could be one of your soldiers."

"I'll think about it."

"Ah-ite."

George and Matt exit the basement, returning to the first floor. Matt gazes up at the spiral staircase. He starts up the stairs.

"Matt, let's go. I got business to attend to," George says.

"Then go," Matt says. "I can walk from here."

George exhales and follows Matt up the stairs. At the top of the stairs is a hallway, with a cluster of doors to the left and one door at the end of the hall to the right. They go to the left, opening the first door, revealing a bathroom. They open the next door, the room smelling like BO and bleach. Dirty clothes are strewn about, pictures of half-naked women line the walls, and one fully nude on the ceiling over the bed.

They open the final door, the room light and airy. The walls are painted yellow, the bedspread white. Light wooden furniture lines the walls. Matt and George walk in. Matt breathes in, smelling Emily's perfume. He moves to the window, peering out at the driveway below, then to the vanity. A few pictures stick to the corners of the mirror, another propped up in a frame. He picks up the framed picture of Dr. Hansen, Mr. Hansen, Tyler, and Emily, smiling in front of their fireplace. Tyler looks smaller and Emily looks happy. Another picture of a young man on one knee, holding a football, is wedged into the corner of the mirror. Matt recognizes him as Emily's boyfriend.

"Don't be a stalker." George grins. "Let's check out the master bedroom."

George and Matt walk down the hallway to the master bedroom. Matt opens the door; they step inside. George lets out a low whistle. A king-size four-poster bed sits in the middle. Dark cherry dressers, bedside tables, an armoire housing a television, and a full-length mirror fill the room. Paintings of country houses overlooking colorful meadows, babbling brooks, or sprawling lakes decorate the light green walls. They hear a splash from outside, followed by laughter.

Beyond the bedroom is a wide corridor, with a couch, vanity, bookshelves, walk-in closets, and a gas fireplace. Toward the end of the corridor, open double doors lead to a large bathroom. The floor is tiled in white, with a Jacuzzi tub, his and her sinks, a water closet, and a marble shower with four showerheads.

"Damn, can you believe this?" George says.

"This bathroom is bigger than my whole house at the farm," Matt says.

They walk out of the bathroom, following the corridor to the end, where a closed door blocks their entry.

"Another closet?" George asks.

Matt shrugs and opens the door. A sprawling dollhouse the size of a dining room table fills the space. The miniature mansion sits off the ground on twelve built-in legs. Framed pictures of the dollhouse hang from the walls. The exterior of the mansion is faced in stone, with four stone chimneys on the slate roof. Matt touches the roof.

"This is real stone," Matt says.

They peer through the windows, looking at the stunning detail of the interior.

"How did they get all that stuff inside?" George asks.

Matt looks at the dollhouse legs. At the bottom, swiveling wheels are attached. He runs his fingers along the sides of the house. He feels a latch. It's painted slate gray. He undoes the latch. He finds another one near the bottom of the house. He pulls the house apart, revealing the lavish interior.

"This is crazy," George says. "Probably cost more than my car."

The inside is equipped with winding staircases, seven bathrooms, six bedrooms, a movie theater, a gym, a library, two kitchens, a formal dining room, a sitting area, a family room, a game room, an indoor pool, and a six-car garage filled with a gullwing Mercedes, a Ferrari, a Porsche, a Bentley, a Range Rover, and a BMW. Each room is decorated with the appropriate furniture, and every wall is covered with the appropriate adornment. Matt reaches into the library and removes a miniature book from the shelf.

The binding reads *Adventures of Huckleberry Finn* by Mark Twain.

Matt slides the book back on the miniature shelf using the tips of his two fingers. He picks up the desk from the tiny library. He opens the top drawer. Miniature stationary, pencils, and a stapler sit inside.

"This is really creepy," Matt says.

"Let's get outta here."

"Hold on a second."

"What? You wanna get out the tea set?"

"Check this room out."

"Whoa, this *is* really creepy."

Matt and George study the identical representation of the master bedroom they're standing in.

"They even have this room across from the bathroom, with a miniature of *this* dollhouse. A dollhouse in the dollhouse," Matt says.

"What are you looking for?" George asks.

"I don't know, but I feel like the answer is in *here*." Matt points to the master bedroom in the dollhouse. "It's the only room in the dollhouse that looks like a room in their real house."

Matt looks in the miniature walk-in closets, one with women's clothing and the other with men's. The woman's closet has tiny pencil skirts, blouses, and pantsuits that hang on wire hangers made from paper clips. He spies the corner of something obscured by the clothes. He sees a tiny square seam on the wall behind the clothes the size of his thumb. He runs his fingertip along the seam. He tries to stick his fingernail in to pry it open, but it won't budge. He pushes the middle of the square, and a hidden compartment opens. Inside, a miniature leather mask and miniature VHS tapes sit on two shelves built into the wall.

Matt grins and shakes his head.

"What the hell?" George says.

Matt and George rush to Dr. Hansen's walk-in closet. They run their hands along the walls, searching for a seam.

"It should be right here," Matt says, looking at a return duct. "I can see the duct. It's not fake." Matt stands on his tiptoes to get a better look down the return duct. "It looks like it just ends."

Matt feels around the edges of the metal grate covering the duct. He finds a latch on the right-hand side. He turns the latch, the metal digging into his fingertip. The metal grate opens out on a hinge, with the small bit of nonfunctional ductwork attached to it. Behind it are two small shelves: the top one filled with VHS tapes labeled by date only, and the bottom containing a solitary leather mask that zips from the back.

"Jackpot," George says. "Grab one of those tapes."

Matt puts his hand on the most recent, only two weeks old, starts to pull it off the shelf, then pushes it back. He works his way back and removes a tape from last fall, the day after everything changed. George flips on the thirty-six-inch television and powers on the VCR. He pops in the tape that's labeled October 23, 2000. A blank screen gives way to the four-poster bed. The room appears empty.

"Let's fast forward," George says, pressing the Fast Forward button. "Oh, here we go." George and Matt watch in silence. "Wow, I've seen some shit in my day, but, wow, this is messed up."

"Why is ... ? Never mind," Matt says. "This is really disgusting."

"He's not gonna ... aww, that's sick," George says. They turn their heads.

"Turn it off."

George presses Eject on the VCR and hands Matt the tape.

"You got yourself a nuclear warhead right there," George says.

"I should shut the compartment and put the dollhouse back together," Matt says.

"I gotta take a leak."

Matt pushes the tapes together, so a space between no longer exists. He notices a small wooden dowel on the corner of the bottom shelf. He reaches for it, pushing, then pulling. The bottom shelf moves. Underneath is a secret compartment filled with stacks of bound one-hundred-dollar bills. He shuts the compartment, then closes the faux grate. He walks to the dollhouse, pushes the house back together, and resets the latches. He hears splashing.

"Ya gotta see this," George says from the bathroom. George looks through the bathroom window at the backyard, his jaw set tight. Matt joins him. "Check out the hot tub."

Sophia's on Tony's lap, their lips locked together. At the opposite corner of the hot tub, Tyler's back riddled with acne, tan legs and arms wrapped around his body, kissing, touching, and Abby's face in ecstasy. Matt turns away.

"I'm sorry, George."

George looks down. "Let's get outta here."

[15]

People Don't Want Truth

Matt runs on gravel, his lungs burning and the chirping birds barely audible above his breathing. He slows at the one-story stone cottage. The forest edge creeps close to the structure, only the front offers any open space. Two mountains sit on the driveway, one of rich black compost, the other of wood chips. A sparkling wheelbarrow, pitchfork, shovel, rake, and a stack of cardboard sit off to the side. An old Jeep Cherokee, with faux wood paneling, is parked along the gravel road. Matt walks across the lawn, and climbs three steps to the porch, where two wooden rocking chairs and a hanging swing reside.

Ms. Pierce opens the door, smiling, her hair pulled back, wearing light blue running shorts and a T-shirt. "Good morning. Come on in." She looks down the road. "Did someone drop you off?"

"No, I ran."

"In pants and boots?"

"I walked some too."

She frowns. "Next time I'll come pick you up. When you said you could get to my house, I thought you meant you had a ride. It must be five miles from your neighborhood."

"There's a shortcut through the woods. It's not too far. I really needed to get out this morning anyway."

Matt steps inside and wipes his feet on the mat. He looks around at the country decor. The walls are yellow, the windows bright, with sheer white curtains. A large lump of anthracite coal sits on the mantel over the stone fireplace. It's shiny and black with jagged edges. A plaid couch and a recliner face a rustic armoire. Matt stares at the antique classroom desk.

"This was an old schoolhouse," Ms. Pierce says. "That desk was actually used by students here a hundred years ago."

"Your house is really nice," Matt says.

"I love old homes. I just wish they didn't come with repairs. Would you like some breakfast before we get started? I could make you some eggs."

"I ate before I left."

Matt and Ms. Pierce walk outside, surveying the piles on the driveway and the new tools.

"Do we have everything?" she asks.

Matt nods. "I think we're gonna have a really good garden."

Matt places the cardboard to the left of the driveway, where the ground is flat and sun-drenched.

"What can I do?" she asks.

"You don't have to do anything. The agreement was that I'd do the labor."

"That's no fun. I'd like to learn. What if I need to do this myself one day?"

"You can get the hose and drench the cardboard, as I put it down."

"We don't have to remove the grass first?"

"Nope, it'll die and provide organic material to the soil life."

"What about tilling?"

"If we till, it just kills the soil life, destroys the soil structure, unearths weed seeds, and creates a hard pan just beneath the tiller tines."

"Then why does everyone do it?"

Matt shrugs. "I don't know. It took me forever to convince my uncle to stop tilling. We just started covering the garden with wood chips, and everything did so much better, not to mention all the time I saved weeding. He was so concerned about buying wood chips, but Reggie was happy to give us all we wanted."

"Reggie was really nice by the way. He asked about you. He seemed concerned when he dropped off the chips. He wanted me to tell you that, if you need a job, he has one for you."

Matt smiles at the pile of wood chips. "Reggie's a nice guy. Did he haul the compost?"

Ms. Pierce nods. "I can't believe we got all this for sixty dollars."

"Yeah, and, if I hadn't gotten Saturday detention, I'd probably be Dumpster-diving for cardboard today."

Ms. Pierce flicks some water on Matt with the hose. "You need to stay out of trouble. Detention is never a good thing, although it was very nice of Herb to save all this cardboard."

With the cardboard laid and drenched, Matt dumps wheelbarrow load after wheelbarrow load of compost onto the cardboard, while Ms. Pierce spreads it with a rake. Matt works efficiently, falling into a familiar rhythm. Once the compost is laid, he moves the wood chips. Ms. Pierce, now experienced in the art of raking, pushes the chips around with ease. After three hours of focused work, Matt dumps the final load of wood chips over the last corner of exposed compost with a wide grin.

"That's it. Garden's ready to plant," he says.

"You shoveled both those huge piles so quickly."

"Reggie made it easy. He put the piles right next to the site. Do you wanna plant the seeds now?"

Ms. Pierce glances at her sport watch. "It's almost noon. How 'bout lunch?"

Matt unlaces his boots and leaves them at the door. Ms. Pierce unlaces her neon running shoes and smacks them together over the railing of the porch. Compost clods fall out.

"I really need to get some gardening gear," she says.

Matt sits at the kitchen table, while Ms. Pierce rifles through the refrigerator and the cupboards. The wooden table for two sits in the middle of the white-tiled kitchen.

"How about a turkey sandwich with some veggies on the side? It's free-range turkey meat," she says.

"That sounds great. Can I help?"

"Yes, you can sit there and talk to me."

Matt grins.

"What would you like on your sandwich? I've got mayo, tomatoes, mustard, honey mustard, lettuce, pickles."

"I don't care. However you normally make it."

"The Olivia Pierce special it is." Ms. Pierce slathers on mayo and slices fresh organic tomatoes. "So, how do you like Jefferson High so far?"

"It's okay, I guess. I don't know."

"Well, that's not much of an answer." She turns from the counter and mock frowns at him.

"I liked learning with my uncle better. I guess I just miss it."

"I'm sorry, honey."

Matt looks away for a moment.

Ms. Pierce turns around and sets his plate in front of him, hers opposite. Her plate has only one half of a sandwich, Matt has a full sandwich, plus another half. Cut up carrots, bell peppers, and celery sticks fill the plates. She grabs two glasses from the cupboard and holds them up.

"Do you want water, milk, juice? Sorry, I don't have soda. I used to be addicted to diet soda, but, after learning about aspartame, I try to stay away from it."

"Water's fine. This looks really good. Thank you."

"You're very welcome." She places two waters on the table and sits down. "It must be hard."

"What do you mean?"

"Well, a new school and all."

"It's okay. I'm making some friends. I never really had any on the farm, except Blackie."

"I assume Blackie's a pet?"

"She was … or is this old barn cat. I don't really know what happened to her."

"I'm sorry."

"When I got to Grace's—you know the foster house?"

Ms. Pierce nods her head.

"I went out a few nights and searched for her at the old farm site. If she's still alive, I doubt she stayed, because they destroyed the barn and the meadow where she caught mice and voles. I know it's just a cat, but I guess I just wanted *something* to live."

"Emily told me a little bit about the farm."

Matt looks up, his eyebrows raised.

"It sounded like a beautiful place."

"It was." Matt takes a bite out of his sandwich. "This is really good," he says, after swallowing. "Since we're not at school, may I ask you something?"

Ms. Pierce grins. "You can ask."

"But you may not answer. I know. My uncle used to say I ask too many questions."

"I bet he was a good father to you."

"He was." Matt looks away. After a moment he looks at Ms. Pierce. "Can you tell me what happened to your boyfriend, you know, the anarchist? You told me the other day that it wasn't appropriate for school, but we're not at school."

Ms. Pierce smiles and shakes her head. "I never said he was an anarchist."

"You didn't have to."

"It's just … that word tends to freak people out. You know, it's kind of a long story."

"I love long stories."

"Well, Derrick had no regard for people's perception of anarchy. He was better when we first started dating. When we would meet some of my friends and their husbands, he'd complain about how they were all asleep, that they were advocating for his death by supporting the state. He had some pretty deep philosophical arguments on why my friends were advocating murder, rape, and theft, simply by supporting the state. I didn't mind it so much when he just told *me* those things. It was actually very intellectually stimulating. After some time though, he got much more radical. I couldn't take him anywhere. We were at a dinner party at my best friend's house. Well, we used to be best friends. Victoria never talked to me again after what happened. We were all sitting at the dinner table, several couples, and some polite arguing was going on between my friend's husband, Dave, who's actually the chief of police, and the wife of a local developer. I think her name's Jill.

"Do you remember the name of the developer?"

"John I think. I don't remember his last name, but he's apparently pretty successful for around here. They were Dave and Victoria's friends. Derrick and I had just met them that night."

Matt nods.

"Anyway, Jill and Dave were arguing over politics. She was a Democrat, and he's a pretty staunch Republican. Jill was talking about how the government needed to spend more money on education and helping the poor, and Dave was talking about how, without defense, we'd be like some third-world country in Africa. Anyway I could tell Derrick was annoyed. I actually grabbed his hand and squeezed it, to sorta say, 'I know, just leave it alone.'

"He just went off. He said they were both supporting immoral institutions. This, of course, stunned everyone at the table. You could hear a pin drop. He went on to explain how taxation is theft, and both Democrats and Republicans are responsible for theft through taxation, murder through wars, and rape through our legal system. He cited some statistic about how governments have killed a quarter of a billion people over the past hundred years. My friend, Victoria, kicked me under the table, to kinda tell me to get Derrick under control, but what could I say?"

"Was he telling the truth?"

Ms. Pierce nods her head and rubs her temples. "He certainly thought he was, but he wasn't using any tact. He was beating everyone over the head with a sledgehammer of truth. Most people aren't ready for any real truth."

"How did Jill and Dave react?"

"Jill was mortified, but she kept quiet. Her husband tried to get a word in, but Derrick called him a fascist and he told Jill how he was hitting on me earlier. Dave turned red, like a teapot ready to blow. He got up, and Dave can be kind of an intense guy, you know? He told Derrick that he'd better leave, before he kicked his ass. Then Derrick called Dave a rapist. He said something about it being immoral to imprison nonviolent offenders, where male rape is commonplace."

"It was crazy—I mean, Derrick saying this stuff to the chief of police. That's when it got really ugly. I stood up and grabbed Derrick by the arm. I was worried that Dave was gonna hurt him. I think at that point Derrick knew he'd gone too far, and he was ready to leave. So we started to leave the table, and Victoria smacked him *really* hard across the face."

"What did Derrick do?"

"He was stunned, but he ignored it and kept walking toward the door."

"I don't understand why Victoria would hate you for what Derrick did."

"It's not what Derrick did—it's what *I* did. Derrick was a gentle person. He was troubled though. He was abused pretty badly as a kid, and he still had bouts of depression from it. It was really awful. Derrick and I were really close. I was the only one who knew what he had been through, and, when Victoria put her hands on him, I didn't see Derrick—the man who had just insulted all these guests. I saw Derrick—the little kid who was being hit again. I lost it. I punched Victoria in the face. I used to take that Tae Bo stuff, but I had never actually punched a person before. She dropped like a sack of potatoes."

"Wow, … Ms. Pierce," Matt says, laughing.

"It's really nothing to laugh at," Ms. Pierce says. The corners of her mouth turn up just a little, then she starts to laugh. "It's still nothing to laugh at."

"So what happened to Derrick after that?"

"A few weeks later he was arrested for tax evasion. He did odd jobs under the table, but, before that, he was actually a lawyer for a while, and I guess he stopped paying his taxes. He said it was immoral to support the state."

"How long ago was that?"

"Almost five years."

Matt frowns. "That seems like a long time for tax evasion."

Ms. Pierce nods. "It is. The judge gave him the maximum jail sentence of five years, because he was so belligerent. Instead of trying to defend himself, he spent the whole time arguing that taxation is theft. The judge was *not* amused."

"So he should be out soon. Are you looking forward to seeing him?"

Ms. Pierce shakes her head, her eyes cast down. "He could've gotten out after a year, but he was just as belligerent at his parole hearing. I begged him to tell them what they wanted to hear, but he wouldn't do it. Dave even tried to help him, but Derrick wouldn't listen. We had a huge argument after the hearing. He wanted me to quit my job. He said that he didn't want me working for the state. We haven't spoken since."

Matt bites the inside of his cheek. "I'm really sorry, Ms. Pierce."

Ms. Pierce wipes her eyes with the back of her hand, then waves it off, as if she's erasing a blackboard. "Ancient history now. We should probably get back to work."

+++

Matt leans his head against the window of the old Jeep Wagoneer. His eyes are closed. The Jeep stops, the soothing rhythm of the passing road grinds to a halt. Matt's eyes pop open; he looks around disoriented. Ms. Pierce stares at him with the warm smile of a proud mother.

"We're here, sleepyhead," she says.

Matt rubs his eyes and blinks life into focus. The late-day sky is orange. "I think rain's coming tomorrow. It'll be good for our seeds."

Ms. Pierce nods and smiles.

"Thank you," Matt says. "Today was the most fun I've had since …"

"Me too." She hands him an envelope. "This is for you."

Matt shakes his head. "Ms. Pierce, it's not necessary. The agreement was for payment once the harvest starts. That won't be for six weeks or so."

"I want to. You worked so hard today." A brief smile flashes across her face.

Matt takes the envelope. "See you at school tomorrow. Thanks again." Matt exits the Jeep. He turns and gives a quick wave, before walking toward Grace's white colonial. He unlaces and removes his boots at the door. He looks back toward the curb. Ms. Pierce drives away. He steps inside; the smell of pizza wafts from the kitchen. Matt climbs the stairs, his boots in hand, and the envelope in his back pocket. He enters his bedroom.

Ryan lies in bed, his head propped up with his pillow, watching *Goosebumps*, and surrounded by Tootsie Roll wrappers.

"Hey, Ryan," Matt says.

"Hi, Matt," Ryan says, without breaking his television trance. "George was looking for you. He's kinda mad."

Matt grabs his towel and a change of clothes. He treads down the hall toward the bathroom. He passes George's room. The door swings open. A gladiator decapitates a massive man with two swords on the big screen television in the background. Endless DVDs and CDs line the walls. George stands in gray Baltimore Ravens sweats.

"Where the hell have you been?" George says.

"I was working," Matt says.

"You work for me."

"I appreciate it George, but I can't."

"You can't? After everything I did for you?"

"I do appreciate your help yesterday, but I don't wanna do that type of work."

"This comin' from the dude who stole homemade porn from the principal."

"I'm not questioning the ethics of the drug trade. It should be legal as far as I'm concerned. Cigarettes and alcohol kill far more than drugs."

"You need to shut your mouth. I don't have anything to do with drugs. Do you understand me?" George's jaw is set tight.

"Yes, I do."

George laughs. "I'm just messin' with ya. Colton's been buggin' me for a job, that's all. I've been holdin' it for you. You shoulda told me earlier."

"I'm sorry, George."

"Whatever."

"I still need your help with the computers on Saturdays."

"You're a pushy little bastard, ain't ya?" George holds up his index finger. "But I like that. I like that."

Matt looks at George dumbfounded.

George grins. "You never saw *Karate Kid*?"

Matt shrugs.

"Jesus Christ. Come by my room later, and I'll play it for ya. And don't make a mess of my bathroom. There was water on the floor yesterday."

[16]

Forgiveness

Matt follows Emily down the congested corridor. She doesn't stop in her normal spot for a kiss from her cowboy. She shuffles, her head held low, and her fingertips barely hanging on to her mini lunch cooler. She cuts across traffic to Ms. Pierce's sanctuary. Matt enters shortly afterward.

"Good afternoon, lovelies," Ms. Pierce says. "I hope you two don't mind, but I'm gonna be antisocial today. I need to work through lunch."

Emily turns a desk toward the window and sits down. Matt sits next to her.

"I'm sorry about last week," he says.

Emily shrugs. "It's totally understandable."

"I'll settle for being friends. It's a lot better than nothing."

Emily turns toward Matt and flashes a brief half smile. "I'd like that."

"You okay?"

Emily shrugs. "You don't wanna know. Trust me."

"If we're gonna be friends …"

"Boy trouble."

"Oh."

"Didn't think so."

"You can tell me."

"It'll be weird."

"So what? I'm pretty weird." Matt grins.

"Lucas wants to have sex."

"Your boyfriend?"

"No, the mailman." Emily frowns. "Part of me wants to."

Matt gags; Emily doesn't notice.

"Part of me is terrified. I guess I just don't fully trust him."

"I think the second part of you is the smart one, the one you should follow."

"Seriously, Matt, you can't just give me advice for what *you* want."

Matt puts up his hands. "You're right. So what's the dilemma? You say no, and he breaks up with you? You say yes, and he allows you to grace his presence?"

"Sometimes I really hate you." Emily looks away.

"I'm sorry. Too blunt?"

Emily turns to Matt, her eyes glassy. "No, it's just you hit the nail on the head with me so easily, like I'm so … uncomplicated. Then you present the problem in a way that the answer seems so simple."

"Simple, yes. Easy? Absolutely not. You're not uncomplicated. It's just, I think about you a lot. I do hope I know you really well. I hope that you can say the same about me."

"He's actually been really patient with me. We've been going out for a month, and we've only really kissed. He did touch my chest once—"

"Get to the point, Emily. You can leave out the details."

"Sorry, anyway he's been patient, but I'm just not ready."

"Well, that's your answer then. If he really cares, he'll stick around. If he doesn't, he'll move on."

"Just like that?"

"Pretty much."

+++

Matt treads into the media room. Madison, Tariq, and Jared sit at the round table. Madison taps her bare wrist with a scowl. Jared and Tariq flick paper footballs to each other through finger uprights.

"I'm sorry, guys. I got caught up," Matt says.

"Uh-huh," Madison says.

"So whaddaya got, Matt?" Jared asks.

"I'm not sure I have anything," Matt says. "It doesn't really help us with this whole juvie thing anyway. I think we should just leave it alone."

"On Sunday you told me you had something huge," Madison says. "Then today you say it's not important? I saw you eating lunch with little Ms. Bright Eyes. I thought you were all about the truth."

"Without truth, it's just propaganda," Tariq says.

"I'll show it to you on one condition," Matt says. "We only use it if we absolutely have to, and, if we do use it, we try to use it in a way that Emily doesn't get hurt. So we might use it as a bargaining chip, with no intention of releasing it. Do you guys agree? Otherwise I'm destroying it."

"All right, fine," Madison says.

"Okay," Jared and Tariq say in unison.

Matt places his duffel bag on the table. He grabs the VHS tape labeled October 23, 2000. He hands it to Tariq.

"Are there any teachers left in the building?" Matt asks.

"A couple, but they never come in here," Jared says.

"It's pretty bad. I'm warning you."

Jared shuts and locks the media room. Tariq turns on the cart-mounted television, and pops the tape into the VCR. A black screen arises.

"You need to fast forward a little," Matt says.

Tariq presses Fast Forward on the remote. He hits Play, when he sees the four-poster bed.

"A little more," Matt says.

Again Tariq presses Fast Forward. He stops when he sees two naked figures on the screen. Matt turns a chair around and sits down.

"You not gonna watch?" Jared asks.

"No, and you'll wish you didn't too," Matt replies.

"Oh, damn. That's Dr. Hansen. She's fine too."

Madison glares at Jared.

"What? … She is fine. You gotta give her props for that. Wait, who's that dude under her?"

"It's her husband," Matt says in monotone.

"This is some serious shit," Madison says to Matt. "Where did you *get* this? No, don't answer that. I don't wanna know."

"Oh, snap, another dude," Jared says. "He's got a mask on. It's about to get freaky!"

"Do you know the guy in the mask?" Madison asks.

"He looks like the same height and build of that Jacobs guy that Matt and I got pictures of," Tariq says. "Matt?"

"I think you're right," Matt says, his back still turned.

"I guess this renders our pictures obsolete," Tariq says. "It doesn't appear Mr. Hansen has much of a problem with infidelity."

"This is foul," Jared says.

"It gets worse," Matt says to the wall.

"That is seriously sick," Tariq says.

"*Ewww,* that's gross," Madison says.

"Oh, damn, that is triflin'," Jared says.

Tariq hits the Stop button on the VCR. Matt turns around.

"That's the type a shit you can never unsee," Jared says, as he shakes his head.

"I told you," Matt says.

"She is *done,*" Madison says. "All we have to do is make a few copies and send them to the school board anonymously. She'll be fired so fast."

"What about the juvie thing? I mean, in the video, what she's doing is gross, but it isn't immoral. They're all consenting adults. Me taking the video and showing it to you guys is the only immoral part."

"This is gold, Matt. You don't wanna use it?" Tariq asks.

"It's not right." Matt presses Eject on the VCR. He shoves the cassette in his bag. "I don't wanna get her like this. I think we should keep working the juvie angle."

"It's a dead end," Madison says. "I can't find any evidence. I interviewed all the juvie kids I know from here, and they all have similar stories. They get busted by the SROs, usually for drugs, then they get sent to juvie. Some of them just had some weed, but, because it was on school grounds, they get punished worse than any adult would. It's messed up for sure, but not illegal."

"Don't you think she might be getting a cut from the JDC for sending all these kids their way?"

"I do, but I can't prove it. I called the JDC upstate, posing as a reporter. I did find out that the more kids they get, the more funding they get. I'd bet my life that she's getting kickbacks, but how do you prove that? I'd have to find someone willing to talk. That's not gonna happen. This tape is all we have."

"Do you remember what I said earlier about Mr. Hansen not caring about infidelity?" Tariq says, with a wide smile.

Matt grins. "You're a genius, Tariq."

"What?" Madison asks.

"*Mrs.* Jacobs might care," Tariq says. "Provided there is a Mrs. Jacobs?"

"Oh there is," Matt says. "I could go see Jacobs and use the tape as leverage for info on Dr. Hansen."

"Wait a second," Madison says, her eyes wide. "I was talking about sending some anonymous tapes, not much risk. You're talking about *extortion* and meeting this guy face-to-face. He could literally kill you."

Jared laughs.

Madison glowers at Jared. "I'm not joking, Jared. This guy's pretty rich, right? A divorce would cost him millions. People kill for a lot less. I don't like it. It's too dangerous."

"The alternative is to release a private consensual tape that's gonna hurt innocent people," Matt says.

"You mean, *Emily.*"

Matt nods. "I'm not saying that I go see this guy with no plan. We'd have to figure out a safe way to do it."

"We shouldn't rush into anything," Tariq says. "Let's at least take a few days to think about it. Agreed?"

"Agreed," they say.

Matt stands and throws his duffel bag over his shoulder, the precious tape inside.

"I'll see you guys tomorrow," Matt says.

"Where are you going?" Madison asks.

Matt shrugs. "I don't know. It's a nice day. Maybe I'll go for a walk."

Jared laughs. "A walk? What are you, like ninety?"

Matt smirks. "I'll see you guys."

He strolls out of the media room, through the empty linoleum halls, and exits the main entrance. Emily sits on a concrete bench, gazing into the distance. He approaches her.

"What are you doing?" Matt asks.

She looks up at Matt, her face blurred by the sun's rays. "I thought he'd surprise me. I thought, if he passed the test …"

Matt squints down at her. "Lucas?"

She nods.

"What surprise? What test?" Matt sits next to Emily on the bench.

She shakes her head, looking at the ground. "It's stupid. … I'm stupid."

"You and I both know that's not true. You're the smartest person I know. Have you ever even gotten an A-minus?"

She turns to Matt, her face paved with tear streaks. "Getting good grades doesn't make me smart."

"It certainly doesn't make you stupid."

"No, I make me stupid." She holds her head in her hands.

Matt puts his arm around her and pulls her toward him. She doesn't resist. After a moment, she pulls away, sits up straight, and wipes her face with the sleeve of her T-shirt.

"I'm stupid, because it's so obvious to me now. And I was gonna sleep with him. If he wasn't such a dumbass, he could've easily convinced me."

"What happened?" he asks.

"I told him the truth—that I wasn't ready, that I needed more time."

Matt nods.

"All he had to say was that he'd wait for me. It was like he was a different person. He told me about all these girls who supposedly like him and how he passed up so many opportunities to hook up, because he was with me. Then he told me how he has needs that have to be satisfied." She looks at Matt. "Who the hell says that anyway? *Needs that have to be satisfied?* Does he think he's R. Kelly? I told him to try his hand, that it wasn't my responsibility. Then he said that was the whole point of having a girlfriend. Otherwise, why bother?"

"I'm sorry."

Emily frowns. "No, you're not. You're probably ecstatic."

Matt smiles. "*Ecstatic* might be a bit strong. How about *glad* or *content*? *Content* seems to be honest enough without being totally insensitive to you."

Emily laughs. "You're such a dork."

Matt grabs her hand and squeezes.

+++

Matt sits silently in Tariq's Nissan Sentra, watching the corn and soybean fields flash by, the occasional new development marking some farmer's retirement package. Tariq parks on the shoulder, next to a small stretch of woods. The occasional car whooshes past. Tariq looks over at Matt.

"You ready?" Tariq asks.

"Probably not," Matt replies.

"We can abort this whole thing, you know. You got some brass balls even considering this."

"No, I can't." Matt takes a deep breath and opens the car door.

"I'll be waiting right here."

Matt disappears into the woods. The crunch of the leaves and the sounds of the birds comfort and center him. He looks carefully at the landmarks, mapping the most efficient return trip in his mind. After a quarter mile walk, he sees the pond beyond the wood line. A pump shoots water into the air, creating a fountain and aerating the otherwise stagnant water. Ducks paddle themselves with their orange webbed feet.

A gaggle of geese eats grass along the edge. An asphalt sidewalk wraps around the acre pond, with a few empty benches for rest. On the hill above the pond sits the backside of a single-story redbrick building, with a gray metal roof. With the woods and the hill for cover, the pond is secluded. Matt walks along the asphalt sidewalk and up the hill to the building. He creeps along the side, to the front corner of the structure. He scans the parking lot. It's normally empty on Sundays, but today one car sits in the lot, a black SUV, trimmed in chrome. Jacobs Land Development is featured prominently on the building in gold lettering.

Matt opens the front door and slips inside. Wall-to-wall gray carpeting extends to the empty front desk. Framed color photos of houses, interiors, and entire communities hang on the walls.

Mr. Jacobs strides toward the front desk from the right-hand hallway. He's casual in his dress, with jeans and a polo shirt. He takes long strides, like he's trying to stretch his legs. His expression is open and unworried, with an air of hubris. A Mr. Jacobs can be found in successful circles of all types. Matt pictures him as the military general who soldiers willingly die for or the ex-football-player-turned-coach who his players love or the titan of business who approaches now.

"Matt, how have you been?" Mr. Jacobs says, smiling, his hand held out.

Matt shakes his hand, with a firm grip, that's returned a bit firmer. "Mr. Jacobs."

"What can I do for you? I normally reserve Sundays for family time, but it sounded urgent."

"I need you to lift up your shirt."

Mr. Jacobs smiles and looks around. "Excuse me?"

"I need you to lift up your shirt. I have something important to tell you, and I don't wanna be recorded."

Mr. Jacobs chuckles. "You've been watching too much TV, kid."

"Please do it, or I can't continue."

He lifts his shirt, exposing a muscular physique of a man decades his junior.

"Now empty your pockets, and leave everything on the front desk," Matt says.

Mr. Jacobs shakes his head and frowns. He puts some change, his wallet, a folded piece of paper, and his cell phone on the front desk.

"Happy?" he asks.

"Let's take a walk."

Matt exits the building and paces toward the pond, with Mr. Jacobs matching him stride for stride.

"What's this about?"

"I like your pond. You wouldn't need that aerator, if you didn't kill all the aquatic plants with herbicide."

"The pond people take care of it. Matt, stop. What is going on here?" Mr. Jacobs stops.

Matt continues to the asphalt path.

"I'm done with this game."

"Just a little farther."

Mr. Jacobs breaks into a trot. He catches up, as Matt reaches the bench near the woods.

"I need you to sit down here and sit on your hands," Matt says.

"I don't understand what you're trying to do," Mr. Jacobs says. "Why don't you just tell me what this is about?"

"Sorry, I can't do that. Please sit on your hands. This is my last request."

Mr. Jacobs exhales, sits down, and shoves his hands under his legs. Matt stands off to the side, close to the woods.

Mr. Jacobs has to crane his neck to see Matt. "I'm not playing any more of these goddamn games. I've got better things to do. Now why am I here?"

"These are the rules. We talk this out, but, if I see those hands move an inch, I'm gone. Understand?"

Mr. Jacobs is red-faced. "Let's move this along. You're really trying my patience."

Matt stares at Mr. Jacobs's hands. "Here's the thing," Matt says. "You're a pretty successful guy—"

"Let me stop you right there. If this is about money, whatever scheme you think you got cooked up, my lawyers will bury you."

"I don't want a dime from you."

Mr. Jacobs's body relaxes.

"It's your wife who wants money and lots of it too."

"What the hell is this about?" His hands twitch. His muscles flex.

"Watch those hands, if you wanna know what this is about."

He pushes his hands back to their original position. "I don't know what you think you know."

"I know your wife, *Jill*, has suspected you of having affairs. She's never actually caught you, because you're pretty slippery. I'm sure you tell her how crazy she is to think something like that. You've probably given the poor woman a complex. I'm gonna give her a new lease on life, a golden parachute if you will."

"I know we have some history, but I don't think you understand the danger you're in right now."

"Here's the thing. I have evidence of your affair with Dr. Hansen that I plan to share with your wife, if you don't give me what I need. I really don't wanna burn your sham of a marriage to the ground. That's not something I wanna be involved in."

Mr. Jacobs cackles. "That's funny, Matt. You actually think my wife gives a shit what I do? You think she doesn't do the same? We have an arrangement. I'm sorry for laughing, I know you're just a kid, but, believe it or not, married people can agree to see other people."

"Nice try, John. Can I call you John? You call me Matt, so I should be able to call you John. I am swimming in the deep end now, right? If you don't care that I expose your affair, go ahead, stand up, and I'll be gone."

John sits still, his face reddening.

"That's what I thought. What I really want is evidence of the unlawful imprisonments of teenagers by Dr. Hansen and also, I suspect, Chief Campbell."

"I have no idea what you're talking about."

"Dr. Hansen and Chief Campbell get kickbacks for arresting kids and sending them to juvenile detention on trumped-up charges. Judge Toomey presides over these cases, so I'm sure he's involved too."

"If I knew about this stuff, I'd gladly turn them in for nothing, but I don't. Maybe your judgment's clouded. I know you got a raw deal with your land and what happened with your uncle. So maybe you want some revenge, but you're wrong, and you're gonna end up in prison, if you're not careful. I could go to the police right now and tell them how you're extorting me for money. Extortion is a *felony.*"

"Information, not money. And good luck proving that."

"I'm actually trying to help you, Matt. Remember when I tried to buy your land and I told you it was the best thing for you. It was, wasn't it? I told you the township was gonna come down on you. If your uncle had taken my offer, he'd be alive, and you'd be living in a nice house right now. I know you think your uncle's death was your fault."

Matt's eyes are glassy. "That's none of your business."

"I felt really bad about what happened."

Matt clenches his fists. "What *exactly* do you feel bad about?"

"Listen, I never did like adverse-possession seizures. They're about as un-American as you can get. The HOA took the land. I just built on it. I really did want you and your uncle to walk away with a pile of money. Hell, I would've made a lot more money if your uncle would've just sold the land to me."

"So Dr. Hansen and Chief Campbell must've done quite well?"

"I can't speak for them. Business is pretty nasty these days. You can't just be a good businessman anymore. Local governments, with their permits and zoning laws, you really gotta work with these slimy bureaucrats. I don't make the rules."

Matt glares at John. "You just benefit from them."

"Maybe." John looks at the pond, then back to Matt. "I do feel bad about what happened to your uncle. Believe it or not, you remind me of myself once upon a time. I grew up in Pottsville, dirt poor. I used to believe in right and wrong, the good guys always win."

"So there's no right and wrong? Is that the bullshit you tell yourself to sleep at night?"

John exhales and shakes his head. "That's not what I mean. When I started my construction business thirty years ago, I was gonna take care of my clients and outwork my competition. That was my business plan. I really struggled, and I couldn't figure out what I was doing wrong.

"Then you take an inspector out to lunch, and, before you know it, the guy's collecting a consulting check and your jobs don't get delayed. You get to know the township board. You take 'em golfing and donate money. Before you know it, you're dropping off envelopes filled with cash, and then projects—that others couldn't get approved—start to go through. Residents don't care either. Everyone's so apathetic. We're lucky if we get five people at our township meeting."

Matt rolls his eyes. "I don't see what this has to do with me."

"My point is, you can't go through life thinking in terms of black and white, good and bad. People are gray. Everyone in your life will disappoint you, if you can't accept that."

"Are you gonna give me what I need?"

"You're not listening. I told you. I don't have that information. I might have money and some power, but not that kind of power. I do have a counteroffer for you."

"I'm listening."

John leans forward. "Can I put my hands in my lap?"

"No."

John frowns. "I have a copy of the original coroner's report of your uncle's death."

Matt's heart beats rapidly. "How did you get that?"

"Let's just say I'm friendly with the doc."

"You knew I was gonna do this." Matt exhales and shakes his head.

"This isn't my first backdoor deal. In fairness, I thought you were gonna try to shake me down for money. I wanted to have a bargaining chip. The deal is, I show you the report, and you hand over the evidence you have."

"How do you know that I don't have copies?"

"I'm sure you do, but I'm fairly certain that, if you make this deal, you won't feel compelled to ruin my life."

"I can't make that deal, until after I see the report."

"Fair enough, but I won't show you the report, until I see what you have."

Matt grabs six photos from his back pocket and steps toward John. He holds out the photos.

"Can I use my hands now?"

Matt nods. John opens and closes his fists several times, his fingers going from white to tan. He flips through the pictures with a small grin. He shakes his head and chuckles.

"That's pretty definitive," John says. "You'd make a good P.I."

"I have one more request," Matt says.

"Okay."

"You can't tell Hansen I took these."

"Okay, fair enough, but, if you do contact my wife, I'll tell Hansen."

"That's fair." Matt and John stare at each other. "So, let's see it," Matt says.

"We're gonna have to go back to the office."

Matt scowls.

"You made me empty my pockets, remember?"

John walks toward his office. Matt follows five paces behind. They walk silently. The air is still, only the occasional goose honk to break the monotony. John disappears around the front corner of the building. Matt takes the turn wide, in case danger lurks. John holds the glass door open. Matt hesitates at the threshold. John lets the door go and strides to the front desk. Matt catches the door with his foot and enters. John holds out a folded piece of paper, his arm stretched from his body, revealing a basketball player's wingspan.

"Before you read this, I want you to know that, if anyone finds out you have this, it could be dangerous for you," John says. "Do you understand what I'm trying to tell you?"

"I do," Matt says.

"This is only for your peace of mind. You cannot go to the police with this. Do you understand me?"

Matt nods, reaches out, snatches the paper, and takes few steps back. John sits down on a chair against the wall, looking up at Matt. Matt unfolds the paper.

Jefferson County Coroner
101 Anthracite Ave.
Jefferson, PA 17880

Case No. 10-272
Date of death 10/22/2000
White male, age 78.

Moyer, Jack M.
12 Church Road
Jefferson, Pennsylvania 17880

On October 22, 2000, Jefferson County Hospital reported Jack Moyer dead on arrival at 8:48 p.m. The Jefferson County Police investigated and reported that the deceased died of blunt force trauma to the head. After reviewing the evidence and completing the autopsy, it is the finding of this office that Mr. Moyer died from asphyxiation caused by strangulation and pulmonary edema. Mr. Moyer had bruising around his neck, subconjunctival hemorrhages, and an accumulation of fluid within the parenchyma and air spaces of the lungs.

Patricia Davis, M.D.
Acting Coroner, Jefferson County, Pennsylvania

Matt stares at the carpet in a daze, his head sagging. Tears spill down Matt's face. He staggers to a chair along the wall. He sits, drops the paper and buries his head in his hands. His body shakes; tears slip between his fingers.

"It wasn't your fault," John says.

+++

Matt lays awake, his eyes open, listening to Ryan snore. Whenever Matt closes his eyes, he sees Chief Campbell, with his thick hands around Uncle's frail neck. Matt removes the covers and slides out of bed. He dresses, grabs his boots, and slips into the dark hallway. He tiptoes downstairs and opens the front door, holding the doorknob under control to avoid the loud click, as he allows the latch bolt to seat in the doorjamb.

On the front porch he steps into his boots and laces them up. He strides to the backyard and into the woods. He's guided by the occasional moonlight, peeking through the forest canopy, as he hikes toward Kingstown.

He comes to a familiar clearing. He avoids the motion-activated light along the back of the vinyl-sided McMansion. He creeps under the deck, next to the hot tub. He grabs a handful of pea gravel and shoves the rocks into his pocket. He hugs the side of the house to the front. The windows are dark. He sprints to the garage, and crouches between the garage and the repaired Mercedes SUV. He glances at Tyler's lifted Jeep parked along the curb. *I wonder if he still keeps his baseball bats in there?* He shakes his head. *It's just stuff. They can always fix stuff. I can never fix Uncle.*

He wipes his eyes with his thumb and index finger. He steps back, standing between the Mercedes and Mr. Hansen's Toyota 4 Runner. He looks up at her window over the garage. He grabs a few pebbles from his pocket. He throws one. It misses, landing short on the asphalt shingles. He throws another, hitting the window dead center. He stops, watching the window. No movement inside. He continues to toss pebbles. After five minutes of consistent plinking, the bedroom light clicks on.

The window opens, and Emily sticks out her head. Her face is radiant and glowing white in the moonlight. Her blond hair is tied back in a ponytail. Her lips are full and pink, without lipstick. Her features are round and soft, no hard edges. Matt motions for her to come down.

She puts up one finger and mouths *Hold on.*

After a few minutes, she opens the window wide. She steps onto the garage roof in hiking boots, light blue pajama bottoms and a sweatshirt. She shuts her window and inches to the edge of the garage, looking down at Matt. She sits on the edge and dangles her feet. Eight feet of air stand between her dangling feet and the concrete driveway below.

"I'm gonna jump," she whispers.

"I'll catch you."

Matt positions himself underneath her, his arms held up. She pushes off, her body in free fall, her arms flapping like she's trying to fly. Matt braces himself for impact. He positions his arms under her armpits. Her boots slam onto the pavement, her knees bend, and Matt gives some support. She stands with a smile, Matt's arms around her in an embrace. She tries to pull away, but he doesn't let go. She stays, letting him hold on to her. He holds tighter, burying his face into her neck. Her skin is soft and smells like vanilla. Her smile turns down.

"What's wrong?" she whispers.

He doesn't answer.

"Let's go to the trail," she says. "We're gonna get caught out here."

He lets go; they walk through the woods to the mulch trail that used to connect Kingstown to his farm. Now it's advertised as a nature walk, a welcome respite from hectic workdays. Once in the woods, she stops.

"Are you okay?" she asks.

"Yes. No. ... I don't know." He shakes his head. "I want you to go home with me, to the farm."

"You're scaring me. You do know it's gone."

He smirks. "I know, but I need you to see. You're the only one who knows it like I did. Nobody cares about what happened. It's just progress. I need someone else to justify ..."

She grabs his hand. "I care. What happened was wrong."

"You didn't see what I had to do. I want you to see."

"Okay, show me."

They walk hand in hand through the forest, their steps softened by the mulch. He points to a clearing off to the right.

"That's where I dumped the chickens," he says.

She looks at him with her eyebrows raised.

"We were gonna lose the farm with all the code violations, so I had to kill the chickens. I didn't even have enough time to harvest all the meat. I just cut the breasts out and dumped the carcasses over there. They were still laying, and I killed them for nothing."

She squeezes his hand. "You had to, or you were gonna lose the farm."

He looks at her, his eyes glassy. "We lost the farm anyway ... and Uncle. This happened because I compromised what I believe in. I thought I'd make one concession, and then it would be over, but it wasn't. I can't lie to myself anymore. I didn't have to do it. I should've said no. If I can't stand up and do what's right when things are hard, what's the point? Someone will always be able to push me around, if they apply the right pressure." Matt looks down.

They stop walking. She lifts his chin and presses her lips to his. "You're way too hard on yourself. It's too much to deal with, for *anyone*."

They continue to the end of the trail. Emily gasps at the construction site. Moonlight reflects off the vinyl siding and concrete curbing. Matt points to the wood line.

"I burned the bees." He shakes his head. "I put gasoline on the hives and torched every one of them. I did that."

"They would've done the same thing."

"Maybe, I don't know. At least I could've made it difficult for someone, make someone else carry this. I didn't have to do their dirty work for them."

"At the time you thought you had to do it."

Matt frowns. They walk past pallets of particle board and skeleton homes built with two-by-fours, awaiting their skin. They stop in the middle of the not-yet-paved gravel road.

"Do you know where we're standing?" he asks.

She looks beyond the half-built homes at what's left of the woods, trying to orient herself. A tear slides down her cheek. She wipes it with the back of her hand.

"Our pond," she says.

He nods.

"I'm sorry."

He looks down. "Don't be."

"We need to talk about my parents."

He looks at Emily. "There's nothing to talk about."

"You'll talk about anything, but you avoid this topic. Why?"

Matt shrugs.

"And you have an answer for everything except this."

"I lost you before, because I talked about your parents. I'm not doing it again."

"We can't avoid them forever. I hate lying to see you."

"I won't make the same mistake twice," he says.

Matt retrieves a folded piece of paper from his back pocket. He hands it to Emily.

"What's this?" she asks.

"Read it."

She unfolds the paper, her eyes scroll back and forth, as she digests the coroner's report. She looks up, her eyes red.

"Jesus," Emily says. "Where'd you get this?"

"John Jacobs, the developer. I met with him earlier today. ... Well, I guess technically yesterday."

Emily crosses her arms over her chest. "Why would he give this to you?"

"He said he felt bad about what happened with the farm and Uncle."

"Just like that, out of the blue?"

Matt looks down.

Emily narrows her eyes. "What did you do?"

Matt spends the next fifteen minutes explaining how he had followed

John Jacobs with Tariq and how they took illicit pictures of him with another woman at the Days Inn and blackmailed him with the photos. He left out the other woman's identity.

Emily frowns with her arms crossed. "Jesus Christ, Matt, this isn't a Hardy Boys novel. This is really dangerous. Please don't ever do anything like that again."

"I'll try not to."

She smirks and shakes her head. "Try, huh?"

He nods.

"What now? Do you take this to the police?"

Matt frowns. "I'm not sure it makes sense to take it to the same people who made a false coroner's report. We are talking about murder here. I doubt Chief Campbell would have an issue murdering again to stay out of jail. I could find myself at the bottom of a river with concrete shoes. I just wanted you to know. Please don't tell anyone about this."

Emily nods. "This is really scary. Do you think he knows that you know?"

"I was there, remember? But it doesn't matter what I know, if nobody believes me."

+++

Matt shuffles, bleary-eyed, to his locker, as kids rush to their buses. He shoves a textbook inside and slams shut his locker. He catches a glimpse of Emily down the hall, her straight blond hair a little messier than usual, but her face is bright and radiant, as if she didn't skimp on beauty sleep. She sends a smile his way through the crowd. His pulse quickens. He waits, leaning against his locker, feeling like he could hibernate. She saunters over, her hips moving side to side.

"You look like you're about to die," Emily says with a grin. "Did you sleep at all?"

"Maybe an hour or two," he says.

"You should take a nap. Do you still wanna meet up later?"

"Of course. What time?"

"My parents are usually asleep by ten, so how about eleven at the mulch trail?"

"I'll be there."

"I should get going. I have physics club." Emily glances around and gives Matt a quick peck on the lips. "Get some sleep."

"See you tonight," he says.

Matt staggers to the media room, his head sagging, and his eyes bloodshot. Madison, Tariq, and Jared stop talking, as he enters the room. They sit at the round wooden table.

"I can't stay today," Matt says. "I didn't sleep much last night."

Madison glares through heavy black eyeliner. "We need to talk," she says.

Matt slumps into the empty seat at the table.

"We've been talking." Madison looks around at Jared and Tariq. "And, we think you're letting Emily affect your judgment, and not in a good way."

Matt rubs his temples and sits up. "I'm gonna tell you guys this once. I've known Emily for a long time. She's my best friend. I've been racking my brain for a way to do this without hurting her. I'd rather not do it, if it's going to."

Madison frowns. "We don't even know what *it* is yet. All we have is a bunch of hypotheticals, and Tariq told us that you let Jacobs off the hook."

"That's not true. I've given you guys tons of information. George and I hacked about every computer in this school. We have enough dirt to get a third of the staff and administrators fired. And I didn't let Jacobs off the hook. He and his wife have an open marriage. She already knows."

Madison purses her lips. "But we don't have enough to get rid of Dr. Hansen. Not without using the tape."

"She's right," Tariq says.

"I agree," Jared says.

"I don't think we need to use it," Matt says. "Once the media gets ahold of how corrupt and poorly run this place is, she'll get fired. She's ultimately responsible."

Madison rolls her eyes. "See? This is what we're talking about."

"You can do it without me and without the tape then."

"Hold on," Tariq says. "Matt did risk his ass to get that tape, so he should decide."

Madison glares at Tariq.

"If we do what we talked about last time, he'll be the one who takes the heat anyway."

"Tariq's got a point," Jared says.

"Whatever," Madison says.

"Are you in?" Tariq asks Matt.

"As long as Emily doesn't get hurt."

"She's gonna get hurt either way," Madison says. "If her mom gets fired, then her perfect little suburban existence will be turned upside down."

"That's enough," Matt says. "If you want me here, I won't listen to you bad-mouth her. You don't know anything about her. If her mother gets fired for doing a poor job, *that* Emily can handle. If that tape gets out, I'm not so sure. How would you like to see your parents like that?"

Madison glares at Matt. "I don't have parents."

Matt exhales. "Neither do I. It's called *empathy*."

"Relax, Madison," Tariq says. "Why don't we continue planning and making preparations, and, if we can't come to an agreement, we'll abort."

"I agree," Jared says.

"Me too," Matt says.

"Fine," Madison says.

[17]

The Calm before the Swarm

"Later, dude," George says.

Matt shuts the door on the black Mustang. The car kicks up gravel, the back end fishtailing as George drives away.

Ms. Pierce's blond ponytail bounces as she strides toward Matt in her jeans and hiking boots. Her face is riddled with concern. "I'm not sure we can work today. I need to call an exterminator. You're not allergic to bees, are you?"

"No."

Ms. Pierce walks around the house to the backyard.

There's a strong hum of buzzing. A stone shed sits under an old honey locust tree. She points halfway up the tree at a football-size cluster of honeybees, hanging off a branch. Matt smiles wide and walks toward the bees.

Ms. Pierce grabs his arm. "Not too close," she says.

"They're honeybees. They're swarming. They're just getting together, waiting for a scout to find a new home. They usually only sting when they're protecting their hive. Since they don't have a hive yet, they're really docile. We could make a hive for them. They're great for pollination, plus you can stop buying those twenty-dollar jars of honey."

"Will I have bees swarming everywhere? I don't want to be afraid to go outside."

"They won't bother you, I guarantee it. Bees are really nice. I can take care of the hive. We'll split the honey like the produce. These bees will make a great colony. They've already adapted to the local environment."

"How do you catch a swarm?"

"It's simple. First we need to build the hive. Do you have any wood?"

"Derrick kept some stuff in the shed. There might be some odds and ends in there."

Matt marches to the shed, underneath the swarm. Ms. Pierce keeps her distance. He undoes the latch and opens the wooden door. The smell of mold and dirt wafts through the air. Rusted shovels, rakes, and a wooden stepladder hang from the east wall. A workbench, with hand tools hanging from a Peg-Board, sits along the north wall. Two-by-fours and a few sheets of plywood lean against the west wall. Matt inspects the hanging tools. A cabinet with tiny drawers sits on the workbench. He opens a drawer filled with nails, another with screws, and another with smaller nails.

Matt emerges from the shed, grinning. Bees buzz in and out of the swarm over his head.

"We have almost everything we need," Matt says, as he strides toward Ms. Pierce. "I do need to hurry, if I'm gonna catch 'em. They could leave at any time. Do you know anyone who would lend us some power tools?"

"Mr. Clemens, our old shop teacher, he lives up the road. I see him working on his farm all the time, now that he's retired. I'm sure he'd lend us whatever we need."

+++

Mr. Clemens stares at the wooden box sitting on a four-post wooden stand. His face is worn, with a white beard absent hair on his upper lip. He wears black trousers, a short-sleeved button-down shirt, and suspenders.

"That's a mighty fine box, Matthew," Mr. Clemens says.

Matt nods his head. "Thank you. There's no way I could've done this without your help."

"Thank you, Elam," Ms. Pierce says.

"It was my pleasure. It's the most fun I've had in quite some time. Now I wanna see you catch those bees." The old man grins and strokes his beard.

Matt sets up the ten-foot-tall wooden stepladder next to the swarm. He steps up to the top rung of the ladder, holding a handsaw. He saws off the end of the limb to make it lighter. The buzzing of the swarm intensifies as the branch end drops twelve feet to the ground. Matt repositions the ladder and saws the branch between the swarm and the trunk of the tree. He saws with one hand and braces the branch with the other. Bees circle Matt's head, buzzing his ears.

The branch cracks. Matt holds tight and keeps sawing. The branch comes free. He sets the saw on top of the ladder and steps down, holding on to the branch of swarming bees. Mr. Clemens watches with a grin. Ms. Pierce winces, waiting for Matt to get stung. Matt treads to the open wooden box. He places the swarm inside the hive, still holding on to the branch. He lifts up and slams the branch end down on the bottom of the box. The swarm falls off the branch into their new hive. Matt removes the bee-less branch. Mr. Clemens sets the roof on top of the hive. A few stragglers linger on the branch. Matt sets it near the hive entrance.

"As long as we got the queen in there, the others will follow," Matt says.

"Do you think they'll stay?" Ms. Pierce asks.

"It's a good home. They'll stay."

"Fine work, young man. ... I'm gonna head on back awhile," Mr. Clemens says. "I gotta couple chores to finish. You let me know if you need anything, Olivia. Matthew, it was mighty fine to meet you."

Ms. Pierce and Matt wave as Mr. Clemens drives away in his old diesel pickup truck.

"Wow, where did the day go?" Ms. Pierce says. "It's a bit late for lunch. How about an early dinner?"

"I'm sorry. I have plans. It's Emily's birthday. She's gonna pick me up soon. Her parents bought her a car."

Ms. Pierce smiles. "She must be excited."

"They gave it to her last week, so the shock has worn off, but she's pretty happy."

Ms. Pierce frowns. "Are you gonna go like that?"

Matt looks down at his dirt-stained tan pants and holey T-shirt, and shrugs. "I guess so."

She shakes her head. "Not a great idea."

"Emily doesn't care. I'm actually pretty clean. I didn't sweat much. We were working in the shade."

"Emily's a nice girl, so she might not say anything, but she's still a girl. She'll want you to be clean and somewhat presentable. It *is* her birthday. You can shower here. Derrick left his clothes, so you can borrow whatever you want. You're about his size."

Ms. Pierce leads Matt to the guest bedroom and shows him Derrick's clothes. She gives him a fresh towel and a washcloth, and leaves him to clean up.

+++

Matt strolls to the kitchen in jeans and a black T-shirt with a red A on the front, his hair still damp.

Ms. Pierce smiles. "You shine up like a new penny."

"I do feel better."

"Do you have time to eat a little something?"

Matt glances at the clock on the stove. "I think so."

"How about a glass of milk and a homemade granola bar?"

"That sounds good."

"Are you supposed to eat with Emily?"

"We were gonna have a picnic."

"Will this spoil your dinner?"

"I can eat twice. I haven't eaten much today."

Ms. Pierce grabs the granola bars from the pantry and milk from the fridge.

She glances at Matt. "Sit down," she says.

Matt sits at the kitchen table. Ms. Pierce sets a glass of milk in front of him and a plate with two homemade granola bars.

"I have leftover salad too, if you want some?" she says.

"That sounds good."

She fills two bowls with a salad of feta cheese, walnuts, and baby arugula.

"By the way, this arugula is the best I've ever had," she says. "I can't believe how fast it came in. It'll be nice when our tomatoes are ready."

"It'll probably be another six weeks or so for tomatoes. We can start harvesting lettuce and spinach soon. In a few weeks, we should get wax beans and peas."

"Plus we have bees now. When do you think we might be able to harvest honey?"

"Next spring, I don't like to take any honey the first year or before the winter. Most beekeepers take all the honey and feed their bees sugar water. But bees are supposed to eat honey, not sugar. I'll only take honey if they have a surplus going into the heavy nectar flow of the spring."

Ms. Pierce sets down her salad fork. "So you and Emily, how's that going?"

Matt blushes.

"That well, huh?" Ms. Pierce grins. "How long have you two been dating?"

"About a month, I guess, if you don't count a long time ago."

Ms. Pierce raises her eyebrows.

"We were … are best friends. We've known each other since we were twelve."

"I thought you two had history."

"What about you, Ms. Pierce? Do you have a boyfriend?"

She frowns. "I seem to be quite the magnet for jerks."

"What about Derrick? Was he a jerk?"

Ms. Pierce exhales and purses her lips.

"Too personal?"

"No. ... Derrick was the only really nice guy I ever went out with. He's just, I don't know, ... not that it matters anyway."

"I'd like to meet him."

"That doesn't surprise me." She glances at the red A on his chest. "You two would be like peas in a pod. Let's talk about something happier, like where you and Emily are going?"

"I wanna take her to this pond. Well, I guess she'd be taking me."

"So what's this pond like?"

"They have these benches at the edge. I thought we could have dinner there. The weather's been really warm. She likes ducks. They have some pretty mallards there. It sounded better in my mind. Do you think that sounds dumb?"

She shakes her head. "It sounds sweet. Did you get her a birthday present?"

"I was gonna buy the food for the picnic on the way."

"You probably want to have her present prepared ahead of time. You know what would impress me?"

Matt shrugs.

"If the guy made the dinner himself and packed it. It wouldn't have to be fancy or even that good. It's the thought and the effort that counts. How much time do you have?"

"About twenty minutes."

"Let's get to work then."

Matt adds baby arugula to the turkey sandwiches. Ms. Pierce cuts apple wedges and carrot sticks.

"You know I actually have a really cute picnic basket. It's made from real woven willow." Ms. Pierce rummages in the pantry. "Here it is," she says.

Matt and Ms. Pierce pack the food and silverware in the basket, with some tea and water in recycled glass bottles.

"Now you're ready," she says.

"Ms. Pierce?"

"Yes, honey?"

"I think you'd make a really good mother."

Matt reaches out and hugs her. Afterward she wipes the corners of her eyes with the back of her hand. The doorbell rings.

Ms. Pierce smiles at Matt, her eyes puffy. "You better get going, Romeo."

"Thank you, … for everything."

Matt opens the door. Emily stands in a knee-length floral sundress. Her blond hair is pinned up with wisps of hair dangling along her cheeks. She smiles wide at the sight of Matt holding a picnic basket. He steps out on the stoop.

"Happy birthday," he says.

"Thanks," she says, smiling. "You look … clean."

Ms. Pierce steps outside, holding a camera.

"Ms. Pierce," Emily says.

"Hi, Emily. You look so pretty," she says. "Do you mind if I take a few pictures? I'll make some for you to keep."

"Of course," Emily says.

Matt groans. "We're not going to the prom."

"Oh, don't be such a baby, Matt," Ms. Pierce says. "You guys look so cute together."

She snaps a few pictures, forces Matt to accept another envelope, and sends the couple on their way. Matt slides into the passenger seat of Emily's green Honda Civic.

"So where is this mystery place anyway?" Emily asks.

Matt and Emily drive down a country road, passing corn and soybean fields, flipping through radio stations.

"Pull over in front of that building," Matt says.

Emily pulls into the empty lot of Jacobs Land Development. She parks the car and looks at Matt dumbfounded.

"Why would you bring me here?" she asks. "Are you friends with him now?"

Matt shakes his head. "This isn't about him. It's about what's behind his building."

Matt and Emily walk behind the building. They stand on the hill, overlooking the pond, the late-day sun reflecting off the water, ducks swimming, and the splashing of the pond pump.

"It's really beautiful," she says. "And look at the mallards."

"I'm glad you like it. I thought we could have dinner on one of those benches and watch the ducks."

They walk down the hill and sit on a bench near the water's edge, secluded by the forest and the bluff. Matt places the picnic basket on the bench. Emily reaches over and grabs his hand, pulling him closer. Matt puts his hands on her hips. Her lips part; he leans in. They press their lips together, their tongues touching. He loses all sense of time and place. His heart beats faster; she tastes like strawberries and smells like fresh pears.

They open the picnic basket, spread out two cloth napkins, and set out their dinners of turkey sandwiches, apples, and carrots.

"Did you do this by yourself?" Emily asks.

"Ms. Pierce helped."

"Thank you. It's really nice." She smiles and pecks him on the lips.

"Ms. Pierce put this green tea with honey in here for you." Matt holds up a glass bottle. "She said you'd probably like it."

"She is so nice … and beautiful. I always think she should be a famous writer living in New York City, with a gorgeous husband. Not living in *this* town, teaching at *that* school."

"Selfishly I'm glad she's here."

"Me too."

The sun is orange and low on the horizon, as night settles over them, and the sunny day gives way to the cool night air. Matt puts their silverware and plates back into the basket. Emily sits on the bench with her legs pulled to her chest.

"Are you cold?" Matt asks.

Emily nods.

He retrieves a quilt from the picnic basket and wraps it around her.

"You need to get in," she says.

Matt sits down on the bench next to her. She sits across his lap, wrapping the blanket around them. He puts his arms around her. Emily puts her head in the crook of his neck.

She tilts her head up. "This is nice," she says in his ear.

He kisses her forehead.

"I love you," she says.

"I love you too," he says. "I always have."

She sits up. "Do you remember the first time we met?"

"Like it was yesterday. ... You offered to let me, a complete stranger, borrow your bike. When I told you that I had never learned to ride, you acted like it was no big deal and that you could teach me."

"It wasn't a big deal."

"And you did teach me," he says.

She smiles.

They sit, holding hands, enjoying the pond.

"I have some news," she says with a grin. "My parents are going on an anniversary excursion to the beach. They're leaving Thursday morning, won't be back until Sunday. You could sleep over."

Matt smiles.

"We could sleep together, like really sleep together. Do you think you could sneak out?"

"Grace is pretty oblivious, so definitely," he says. "I can't wait, ... but what about your brother?"

"He'll be in the basement with God-knows-who. He won't even notice."

The sky is clear, the stars brilliant. Outside, it's cool and brisk, but, under the blanket, in their cocoon, it's warm and soft and safe.

"I'm sorry I wasn't there for you after your uncle died. I wanted to be, but you were gone."

"I know."

"My mom said you were never coming back, that they'd put you in some other town, so you could have a fresh start. I feel so stupid for going out with Lucas. I just wanted to forget you, if I wasn't gonna see you again." She shakes her head. "I know that sounds terrible."

"It doesn't."

"I was embarrassed. I was afraid to talk to you, because I knew you were mad at me. And you were right to be mad."

"I wasn't mad at *you*."

Emily purses her lips. "But you are still mad, aren't you?"

Matt nods and takes a deep breath. "We just wanted to farm and be left alone. We weren't hurting anyone. It's always the powerless who take the beatings, and most people don't care. They would look at someone like Uncle and say he was breaking the law, and that's why it happened. People are too brainwashed to know the difference between the law and morality."

+++

Matt waltzes into the media room. Madison, Tariq, and Jared study the school roster, making updates to the master list.

"Good afternoon, everybody," Matt says in a singsong voice.

Madison looks up through thick black mascara. "Why are you so chipper?"

"No reason."

"I'm sure."

"I hate to kill the good vibes, my man, but we gotta problem," Jared says.

"Not *a* problem, many problems," Madison says.

"We're gonna have to make some hard choices. We're runnin' out of time," Tariq says.

"All right, give me the rundown," Matt says.

"Well, first of all, I got quotes on all the deliveries you wanted," Madison says. "With the out-of-town vendors, it's gonna be *ridiculously* expensive." She shakes her head and purses her lips. "The total is almost forty thousand dollars."

"That's fine. Let's wait until the Friday before to do the deals, but after school, so they can't call anyone to confirm. We'll have to pay these people up front, in cash. It's a lot of vendors, so we'll all have to help."

"I don't think you heard me. I said, forty grand."

"And I said it's fine. I'll have the cash."

"The second problem is that we only have e-mails for about 15 percent of the student body."

"We don't need to find something specific to everyone. Kids are gonna fall in line with their groups and their friends. We just need enough to light the match. Besides, I got another Saturday detention to dig up dirt."

"I gotta question," Jared says. "How do we get all these kids to do this, without anyone finding out? You could never keep something this big a secret."

"You're right, Jared," Matt says. "As of now, we're the only people who know about this. George doesn't even know yet."

"What about Emily?" Madison asks.

"She doesn't know."

"You better keep it that way."

Matt frowns. "She wouldn't tell her mother."

"You don't know that."

"I know for a fact she wouldn't. But don't worry, I'm not gonna say anything to her. If this goes bad, I don't want her implicated."

"That goes for anybody else outside this room," Madison says.

"I agree," Matt says. "The more people we tell, the likelihood of being found out increases dramatically. My thought is that we organize this like any good conspiracy. We only let people know what we need them to know to complete the mission. And we hold the information until the last possible second, so they don't have enough time to spread it."

"That's all well and good in theory," Tariq says, "but how do we actually do that?"

"Everybody in high school travels in a pack. And lots of times smaller packs are actually part of a larger pack. Between all of us, and especially George, we all know who the pack leaders are. So we set up a secret meeting with them on Sunday night as late as possible. At the meeting we give them the e-mails to distribute to their people, and we tell them where to meet on Monday morning. With the chaos of what's coming, and how pissed the kids are gonna be, we should have enough time to persuade the mob, before the SROs break it up."

"What happens if you can't convince the mob?" Tariq asks stroking his goatee.

"Then this thing blows up in my face."

"What if we tell the pack leaders the specifics on Sunday, to gauge whether or not they're gonna do it?"

"I thought about that, but, if we tell them on Sunday, the likelihood that someone in authority finds out goes up dramatically. If that happens, we're done. They'll bring in the police to stop it, and the kids will be too afraid. Plus people are selfish. If they think about it for too long, they'll realize that it's not in their best interest to participate. I'm hoping that the e-mails and my speech will piss them off enough to do what we want. I'm appealing to their emotions."

"These are some serious hurdles," Madison says, "but that's not even my main concern."

"Okay?" Matt says.

"I can't find anything on Hansen. I even tried talking to some of the parents of the juvie kids. Nothing, absolutely nothing. If we keep digging around, it's gonna get back to her, then we're screwed. I think we need to use the tape."

Matt shakes his head. "We already discussed this."

"She's right," Tariq says. "There's not enough to get Hansen, and she's the linchpin. What if we make a copy and threaten her with it, saying something like we'll release it on the Internet and send it to the school board if she doesn't resign. Nobody would find out. Emily would never even know."

"It's not a terrible idea," Matt says. "How would you get the tape and the threat *to* her?"

"We could go to her house early and put it in an envelope under her car wiper, with a typewritten threat."

"I'll think about it."

"What if they don't fire her?" Madison says. "What if they decide they can't use the evidence or the tape, because it was stolen? You do realize that everything points to you. You'd be arrested and put right back into juvie. You might actually be there long enough to go to real prison."

Matt looks at Madison. "It's gonna be fine."

Madison shakes her head with a frown. "Really? I think the love drugs you're high on are rotting your brain. Let me spell it out for you. If we don't put Hansen down, she'll make sure you get charged with computer hacking, disturbing the peace, inciting a riot, slander, breaking and entering, theft, and whatever else she can pin on you."

"This *is* a pretty insane idea," Tariq says. "Insanely cool, if we can pull it off, but pretty awful for you, if it doesn't work. We can always just not do it. Intellectually I can see how it could work, but it's just that there are too many moving parts. You know? Too many things that could go wrong. Are you sure you wanna do this?"

"I appreciate that, Tariq, I do, but we've come way too far to quit now. One way or another this place is going down."

[18]

Some People Can't Be Helped

Matt opens his locker, surrounded by raucous voices. He grabs his journalism textbook and his report. The previous tenant left a mirror on the door. He catches a glimpse of his pointed nose, tan skin, and sun-lightened brown hair. He slams the locker shut with a clang. He looks to his left. He sees Colton, gyrating and gesticulating. A handful of underclassmen are captivated. Matt sees cash exchange hands, with little baggies transferring from Colton to his clientele.

Matt strides into Mrs. Campbell's barren classroom. Madison sits in a corner desk, tapping a black boot.

"You ready for more Hero Worship 101?" Madison asks.

Matt grins. "Who'd you interview?"

"The old World War II guy who lives in our neighborhood. I shoulda wrote about what a freaking racist that guy is. All he wanted to talk about is how 'gays and coloreds' shouldn't be in the military. His words not mine. I guess white women are okay, provided they're nurses."

"That would be an interesting report. You could delve into the psychology of war. You know, like how all wars use racism as a way of dehumanizing the enemy."

Madison laughs. "I'd like to not have an F on my report card, thank you very much. We're supposed to be showing gratitude for their service, not criticizing. What about you? Who'd you interview?"

"I interviewed Herb. You know, the custodian."

"Are you crazy? She's gonna give you a zero."

"He used to work in the coal mines—"

"Class, sit down, *now*," Mrs. Campbell says. She sports an American flag pin on her sweater. "Let's continue with our oral reports from yesterday. Please raise your hand if you haven't presented yet." Seven people raise their hands, Matt and Madison included. "Okay, who would like to go first?" All seven hands drop. "Madison, I expect more eagerness from our student editor. Why don't you take the podium?"

Madison trudges to the podium, two typewritten papers in hand. She flips her jet-black hair off her shoulders. She wears a black T-shirt with homemade lettering that reads INGSOC. Matt smiles at the reference.

"I interviewed Corporal Frank Nance, who lives right here in Jefferson. He's a World War II veteran," Madison says.

"What a great find," Mrs. Campbell says. "There's not too many of those guys around anymore. They really are national treasures. Please continue."

"Mr. Nance is around eighty years old. I deduced that from some dates he gave me. I thought it was rude to ask an old man his age. I asked him what made him join the military. He said he was drafted. He didn't have a choice. He was a lumberjack in Washington before the war. He was stationed to Alaska in 1943. The Aleutian Islands of Kiska and Attu had been taken by the Japanese. He was part of the 7th Infantry Division.

"I asked him if he liked Alaska, and he said that he hated the weather, but he loved everything white." Madison cracks a tiny grin. "He took part in the Battle of Attu in May of 1943. He said the Japanese let them land on the beach, but they dug in positions on higher ground.

"The US casualties were pretty bad. Almost 4,000 dead or wounded. 1,200 of those casualties were cold-weather injuries. They had trouble getting supplies to the soldiers with the terrible Alaskan weather. He said that the Japanese eventually came out of their positions on a banzai charge. It was actually one of the biggest banzai charges in the Pacific theater. He was a supply clerk in the rear, but he saw close-up fighting, because some of the charge got past the front lines. He was wounded and got sent home. He said it was a 'million-dollar wound.' He also said that, to this day, he hates the cold because of the brutal conditions in Alaska during World War II."

"That was excellent," Mrs. Campbell says. "Class we should all take a moment to think about what these men sacrificed for us. They were freezing, hungry, injured, and dying at the hands of a determined enemy, one who would not surrender. I hope this winter, when you're sitting safe and sound in your warm home, you think about Corporal Nance. Thank you, Madison. Who would like to go next?" Nobody raises their hand. "Matt, you're next. Come on up."

Matt slides from his seat and slogs to the podium, holding a single handwritten page.

"I interviewed Herb Dickey, our head custodian," Matt says.

Mrs. Campbell glares at Matt. "Mr. Dickey is a fine man, but the assignment was to find someone who has or *is* serving our country and protecting our freedoms. Is Mr. Dickey a veteran?"

"No, but he did work in a Schuylkill County coal mine for twenty years."

"You'll have to find someone else to interview. This is clearly outside of the instructions for this project."

"Please explain your criteria for what we should consider *serving our country or protecting our freedom*?"

"Somebody who risks their life for our safety, like a soldier, a police officer, or even a firefighter. Now sit down."

"Being a coal miner is far more dangerous than being a cop or a soldier. In fact soldiers and police officers don't even crack the top ten for the most dangerous jobs in America."

Mrs. Campbell shakes her head; her eyes narrow. "I don't know where you're getting that information, but it's incorrect. Now sit down."

Matt stands still.

"I said sit down, or I'll call the SRO!"

"Stop," Madison says to Matt.

"Sit down," Tariq says.

Matt doesn't move from the podium. Mrs. Campbell stalks to the phone on the wall. She takes the phone off the hook and looks at Matt, as if to say, "Last chance." He stares back, blank-faced.

"This is Mrs. Campbell. I have a belligerent student. Can you please send an SRO?" she says into the phone.

"What about teachers? You allow teachers, and they certainly don't risk their lives." Matt's tone is manic.

"Teaching is a calling. We suffer low wages to teach children like *you*. Educating kids is certainly a sacrifice for this country."

Matt's classmates are a mixture of wide-eyed shock, suppressed grins, and glaring anger.

He pounds on the podium with both fists. "Teachers make twice the median income around here. You leave at three, have summers off, can never be fired, and you get a gold-plated pension with health benefits. I don't see a lot of sacrifice. Mr. Dickey risked his life to bring us something we need. Most of the people in this room would die without electricity. And for the rest of us, life would be pretty harsh."

"Are you finished?" Mrs. Campbell says with her arms crossed, the tip of her heel tapping the linoleum floor.

Officers Mullen and Blackman appear at the door. Mrs. Campbell turns to meet them. She points to Matt.

"Journalism without truth is propaganda!" Matt says and pushes over the podium, causing a loud crash.

Matt puts up his hands, facing the incoming officers. Officer Blackman turns him around and pushes him against the white board. Matt braces himself against the board, creating handprints in a sea of black marker.

"Put your hands behind your back," Blackman says.

Matt puts his hands behind his back. Blackman slaps on handcuffs. Officers Mullen and Blackman escort Matt, his hands secure. They take him to the main office. Blackman pushes him into the waiting room.

"Sit," Blackman says, forcing him into a chair.

Officer Mullen disappears into the corner office. After a moment she returns.

"She said we can take him back," Mullen says.

Matt trudges to the corner office, his hands bound behind his back, with Blackman poking him along, like he's walking the plank.

"Undo the cuffs, and leave us," Dr. Hansen says.

Officer Blackman removes the cuffs and shuts the door. Matt stands rubbing his wrists.

"Sit down."

Matt sits in front of Dr. Hansen, her white blouse cut low, a bit of lace showing. His mind drifts to her videotaped debauchery. Her blond bangs dangle over her wrinkled forehead, concealing the passage of time.

"You've been here five weeks, and, in that time, you've been in my office three times. You're already a Saturday-detention veteran, and you have three Fs. I know you're a troubled boy, but that doesn't mean you get to break the rules with impunity. I just got off the phone with Mrs. Campbell. She said you pushed over her podium and were insubordinate. Do you have anything to say for yourself?"

Matt shrugs.

She narrows her eyes. "I have the power to expel you."

"I don't care what you do."

She cackles. "Really? You don't care about being a high school dropout with no chance of a good job or a good career. I can ruin your future just like that." She snaps her fingers.

"That doesn't scare me."

She raises her eyebrows, her forehead erupting in wrinkles. "Excuse me?"

"Everything that I was afraid of already happened. That's the thing about fear. You get used to it. Don't bother trying to intimidate me, because I have nothing left to lose."

She marches around her desk and stands over Matt. She bends down, her face inches away from his. Her breath smells like coffee. She presses her index finger into his sternum. "You don't know a thing about fear, little boy. Maybe we find some drugs in your locker. Maybe you get two years in juvie. You'll be eighteen in a year, so you'll do part of that sentence upstate. What do you think happens to pretty little white boys in prison?" She pokes his chest again with her bony finger. He sits still, his face blank. "You still have plenty to lose. Do you know what it's like to have your rectum stitched up after you've been gang raped by a dozen inmates?"

Matt sits, blank-faced.

"If I so much as even hear a rumor about you causing trouble, I will ruin you. Do you understand?"

He nods.

She stands up straight, mercifully blowing her coffee breath elsewhere. "I'm suspending you for the rest of the week. I still expect you to attend your Saturday detention. I suggest you use your time to study, because if you do poorly on next week's finals, you will repeat the eleventh grade." She saunters back behind her desk. "The office has already called your foster mother. Officer Blackman will take you to your locker to collect your things. I hope when you come back next week, you'll come with an attitude adjustment. Do you understand me?"

Matt nods again.

+++

Matt focuses on the folds of Grace's pasty neck fat, as she marches in front of him, with Officers Mullen and Blackman still flanking him. Grace's white minivan is parked in the handicapped spot; a temporary placard hangs from her mirror. Officer Mullen glances at the placard, then back to Grace.

"It's my back," Grace says, touching her lower back and grimacing. "Hurts like the dickens. Thank you so much, officers. I really do appreciate what you do."

The officers nod. "You're welcome, ma'am," Blackman says.

Grace glowers at Matt. "Now get your little patootie into this car. Right now, mister."

Matt hops into the front seat of the Dodge Caravan. Grace groans as she hauls her girth into the driver's seat. She slams the door and drives out of the parking lot.

"I can't believe your behavior, young man." Grace looks over at Matt. "I've never been so embarrassed by one of my kids."

"I'm not your child. I think you know that." Matt stares at the road.

"I'm a good mother to all my kids, even pain-in-the-patootie ones like *you*. This suspension is not gonna be a vacation, no siree. You're gonna have chores in addition to your schoolwork, and you are *not* to leave the house under any circumstances."

Matt scowls at Grace. "What if the house accidentally caught on fire? Could I leave then, or would I have to stay in the house?"

"I don't like that tone, mister. Pastor Roberts said you were in crisis. I'm not sure it's safe to have you in my home anymore. I could make one phone call to Regina, and you'd be gone." Grace parks the minivan in the driveway. She turns to Matt glaring. "Is that what you wanna make me do? Send you to one of those state facilities with all those nasty kids? Maybe that's where you belong."

"Let's stop this charade, Grace."

"I beg your pardon?"

"How much money have you given me over the past six weeks?" Grace crosses her meaty arms.

"We both know that answer," Matt says. "You haven't bought anything for me, except food, and I bet the food bill hasn't changed, because I eat all the stuff no one else will. Come summer, I have a job lined up, so you can be more neglectful if you want."

Grace shakes her head. "Oh, no, you don't. You will not tell me that I do this for the money, because it is *certainly* not worth what I get."

"It's $671 per month—or $8,052 per year, if you prefer. What do you spend on me? A hundred bucks a month maybe? Seven grand net. That's not too bad. If you multiply that by five kids, $35,000 tax-free."

Grace's mouth and eyes are wide open. "This nice house, your room, it's expensive."

"I agree with you. I don't think you do it solely for the money. I think you get off on everyone thinking you're some kinda saint. All your self-esteem comes from this image, but, deep down, you're selfish. That's why you keep the money. It's your payment for your hardship, because it's all about you. Look, I get it. Don't worry. I'm not gonna say anything to DHS. But I can't have you caging me up, like I'm some kind of animal. That can't stand. I suggest you continue being neglectful, and I'll continue to pretend you're not."

Grace's eyes are wet. "I'm not gonna sit here and listen to this malarkey."

Grace gets out of the van and slams the door. Matt exits the vehicle. She points at Matt, her face a congealed mass of red splotches. "You are an evil, evil, evil boy! Pastor Roberts was right about you. Some people can't be helped."

+++

Matt lays on his bed, reading a tattered orange text, with a bespectacled Emma Goldman on the cover. He turns his head toward a knock at the door.

"Come in," he says.

Madison treads inside. She shuts the door behind her. Her mouth is turned down, her eyes bloodshot, and her face haggard.

"Can we talk?" she says.

"Of course." Matt sits up and pulls his legs in, cross-legged. Madison sits on the edge of the bed.

"I really wish you didn't make such a scene in Campbell's class today. It just makes you more of a target."

"That's the point, right? To make me the target."

"You did that on purpose?"

"No, but I'm glad I did. Hansen threatened me with planted drugs in my locker. It makes me feel a lot less guilty about the tape. Who's gonna drop it off?"

"Tariq's gonna do it at 3:00 a.m."

"Tell him no fingerprints on *anything*. And he should park down the block and sneak through the woods."

She smirks. "He knows."

"What else?"

She purses her black lips. "I'm thinking we should just let this go. It's not too late."

Matt raises his eyebrows. "Why?"

"I'm worried you're gonna go to jail, like real jail."

Matt shrugs. "Maybe."

"How can you be so nonchalant? I'm freaking out. Aren't you scared?"

He takes a deep breath. "Of course I am. Before I came here, I did what they wanted, *because* I was scared, and I still lost everything, including my self-respect. I didn't have the power to stop what happened. Most people go through life oblivious. They're brainwashed by their school, the media, their friends, their families. If they ever do wake up to the truth, they're alone and too powerless to do anything about it. This is our chance for just one small moment to wake people up and to give some power to the powerless. We can take something from those who've been taking for far too long. We can put an end to the high-school-to-juvie pipeline. We just have to cut off the heads."

"But you're on the hook."

Matt nods. "I know, but I'm one person. If we can take out a dozen or so corrupt school employees, the police chief, and Dr. Hansen, that's a pretty good trade, don't you think?"

She looks down. "It's a terrible trade. You're worth more than all of them." She looks up, her eyes wet.

Matt smiles. "Don't worry. I have a feeling I won't get charged. They'll be too embarrassed, especially once the press gets ahold of this."

"We met after school without you. Do you wanna hear the latest?"

Matt nods. "We should be about ready, right?"

"The website will go live one hour before school, and a link to the site will be e-mailed to the school board, the students, the parents, and the press, once school starts. The school's e-mail list that George hacked made this supereasy. Also we scanned the really bad e-mails and organized them on the site. We made a webpage for each offender. Mr. Dalton's page goes on forever. What a douchebag."

Matt nods.

"We put the autopsy on the front page, with your eyewitness account of what happened to your uncle. We decided on the domain name *JeffersonCountyCorruption.com*."

"What else?"

"When are you gonna get George on board?"

"I'll talk to him tonight."

"You think he'll do it?"

"He will. How many kids do we have specific e-mails for?"

"About eighty, plus whatever you and George can get on Saturday."

"Did you guys get addresses? We need to send hard copies to their parents too."

"They're already stamped and ready to go," Madison says. "The student directory had most of the addresses. The rest we got from the White Pages. I was gonna dump them in a mailbox on Saturday. They won't get them until probably Tuesday though."

"What if we mailed them Friday?"

"I thought about that, but, what if the mail is quick for once, and they get the letters on Saturday? I don't think we want those letters floating around any longer than they have to be. Parents would be more likely to contact the school and spoil the surprise."

Matt nods. "You're right. The kids will have them in hand on the day anyway."

"And the parents will get a link to the site Monday morning."

"That's true," Matt says.

"We need the money for the vendors on Friday."

"Don't worry. I'll get it Thursday. I'm gonna—"

"Stop." Madison puts up her hand. "I don't wanna know any specifics, other than you'll have it."

"I'll have it."

[19]

Going Down

George turns down the gravel road, passing the sign that reads Luxury Single-Family Homes Starting in the 200s. The late-day sun beats down on the homes in various stages of completion, some built two stories high, but awaiting vinyl siding and brick facing, while others are simply grassy lots marked with stakes. Yellow construction equipment sits idle. An excavator sits near the edge of a hole the size of a basement. A skid steer with forks is parked at the end of the cul-de-sac in front of pallets of lumber. George parks in the cul-de-sac behind Tony's pickup truck.

George and Matt step out of the Mustang. Matt carries a duffel bag. Tony steps out of his truck, the driver's side bouncing slightly as he moves his three hundred pounds off the shocks.

"What up, playas?" Tony says grinning, exposing his white teeth.

"Thanks for comin' out here on a Sunday," George says.

"What's this about? You got me all intrigued."

"We need you to show up at school an hour early and reserve eight spaces in the middle of the parking lot. Park your truck right in the middle."

Tony shakes his head. "You know I don't even show up until second period. I need my beauty sleep."

Matt unzips his duffel bag and hands Tony a Ziploc bag filled with an ounce of weed. "For your trouble," Matt says.

Tony grins and takes the bag with a hand that could double as a catcher's mitt. "I could make that happen. Ah-ite, playas, I'm outtie."

"There's one more thing," George says.

Matt grabs a stack of envelopes, held together with a rubber band, from his bag. He removes the top one from the stack. It's addressed to Tony. Matt hands it to him.

Tony looks down at the envelope with a frown.

"Open it," George says.

Tony tears the envelope and removes a single trifolded piece of paper. He reads.

From: Chris Dalton
To: Ben Richardson
Subject: Scholarship

Can you believe Tony got that scholarship to Rutgers? He's going to get his ass handed to him. He's got the size but he's too much of a punk to play at that level. The biggest shock is that the gorilla actually got a high enough SAT. Do you remember his sophomore year when he started crying during conditioning? Like I said. Punk.

"I'm gonna kick his ass." Tony gapes at Matt and George with a frown. "What the hell am I supposed to do with this?"

"What do you wanna do with it?" George asks.

"A whole bunch a shit that'd get me arrested. I'd lose my ride."

"What if I said you could get that piece of shit fired, and you wouldn't have to do anything illegal."

"I'm listenin'."

"You know most of the football players, right?"

"Yeah. I mean, I don't hang out with all of 'em."

"But they all wanna hang out with you," Matt says.

Tony grins. "What can I say? I got a dynamic personality."

"Can you give out these letters tonight?" Matt hands Tony the stack of bound envelopes. "Their names and addresses are on the front."

Tony flips through the letters. "These guys got e-mails like mine?"

Matt nods.

"I just give 'em these letters, and that's it?"

"With a message," Matt says. "Tell everyone that we're gonna make this right and that we're meeting in the middle of the school parking lot at 7:50 tomorrow morning. Oh, and make sure Tyler Hansen doesn't find out about this. I know he's your friend and all, but we can't trust him, because of his mother."

Tony nods, with a chuckle. "I like y'all crazy-ass white boys."

The shocks groan as he hops into his pickup truck with the grace of a ballerina. Matt waves as he drives away; Tony returns a crisp military salute and a broad grin.

"One down, eight more to go," George says.

"You think they'll all show?" Matt says.

"They'll show. The real question is, will they follow?"

A vomit-green and wood-paneled station wagon putters down the gravel road, parking behind the Mustang.

"Now that's a family truckster," George says with a grin.

A lanky teen boy with glasses and tight jeans steps from the car.

"It's Wyatt, king of the dipshits," George says to Matt.

"He has a lot of friends," Matt says, pulling the stack of envelopes from his duffel bag.

+++

Matt sits in the backseat of George's Mustang. His eyes are closed, his stomach rumbles, and his heart pounds. He breathes in and out, in and out, in and out, but his heart still races.

"I bet you feel like you're about to shit a brick," George says.

"Shut up," Madison says.

"Relax, I'm just tryin' to lighten the mood. Whatever happens, this is gonna be huge."

"What's happening?" Ryan leans forward, sticking his head between the front seats.

"It's nothing," Madison says.

"Matt looks sick. We should take him back home," Ryan says.

Matt opens his eyes. He pats Ryan on the leg. "I can't, buddy. I have a big test today."

George turns into Jefferson Elementary, and they let out Ryan. A couple of Ryan's classmates accost him.

"Cool car. Who's that?" a classmate says.

Ryan puffs out his chest. "That's my brother."

Jefferson High School appears on the left, sprawling as if the designers wanted to double park the structure.

"Can you pull over?" Matt asks.

George pulls over to the sidewalk. Madison hops out and pulls the seat forward. Matt staggers out, past the sidewalk to a chain link fence at the edge of the grass. He leans over and retches. Nothing comes out. He retches again, and warm yellow liquid spills onto the ground. He heaves again and again and again, until nothing's left. He spits and stands up. Madison hands him a bottle of water. He takes a swig and swishes it around in his mouth, spitting as if he were at the dentist. Madison pats him on the shoulder, her mouth turned down. She hands him a plastic container of white Tic Tacs.

"You all right?" she asks.

"I think so," Matt says.

"You should eat these."

Matt pops a handful of Tic Tacs in his mouth. "Thanks."

George leans over the passenger seat. "Come on, Matt. Don't be such a fag."

Madison glares at George.

Matt staggers back to the car, a bit steadier after releasing the sick. The trio pulls into the bustling school parking lot. They drive to the middle of the lot, where a three-hundred-pound black man guards a large cluster of empty spots, like an oasis in the desert. Tony steps aside, waving them in, his truck parked adjacent. The student lot is filled a bit earlier than usual. Students mill around the lot, many still sitting in their cars. Buses line the front entrance. Pizza delivery cars and trucks, with magnetic door signs, and roof-mounted signs displaying their pizzeria, queue up behind the buses. Interspersed are vans and trucks, with vinyl pictures of bouquets of flowers, dominated by the prototypical long-stemmed rose. Delivery men and women hustle along the sidewalk, carrying stacks of pizza boxes, and pushing carts of flower bouquets and large-leaved green houseplants. One delivery man pushes a cart with helium balloons tied to the handles that read Happy Retirement. Two dozen limousines line up on the curb just off-campus.

Madison and George step out of the Mustang. Students congregate around them, many holding printed e-mails. Voices are boisterous, some jovial, but many angry. A wave of students, like concert-goers at a mosh pit, push from the outside in. The crowd is turning into a mob. Madison and George hook up Grace's karaoke machine to George's car speakers, with power coming from an adapter hooked to his cigarette lighter.

Matt exits the car; the crowd cheers. Matt's heart pounds; his stomach churns. He takes a deep breath and hops onto the back tire of Tony's pickup. He steps over the side into the bed. George nods and hands Matt the wireless mic. From his new vantage point, he searches the endless sea of faces for Emily. The mob roars in approval. He starts as soon as they quiet.

"The hypocrisy in this place runs deep. It's systemic, endemic, and rotten to the core." The crowd cheers. "We don't go to school to learn. We go to school to learn how to follow directions, to obey orders, to be cogs in the machine, to respond to a bell, a whistle, or any order without *thought*." Matt looks around; the crowd is silent, ears hanging on every word. "Many of you now have very personal evidence of the corruption and the immorality of this place. You have every reason to feel anger, to desire revenge. Some of you, and even some of your parents, have been called terrible things. *Retarded, worthless, dumbass, white trash, hillbilly, and low class.*" Matt shakes his head. "Not my words ... theirs. They chide us. They lecture us. They hold us to standards they themselves fall short of. We have teachers like Mrs. Campbell, who flunks anyone with a dissenting opinion. We have Mr. Dalton and Mr. Richardson who sexually harass students and fellow teachers. Those two clowns watch porn on their school computers. They dehumanize the black athletes they coach by calling them 'gorillas' and making crude references to 'slave strength.' Of course this behavior—the general view that we are to be treated as cattle to herd and cage and poke with cattle prods—is at its most dangerous at the top. Dr. Hansen is the head of this beast. She is the one sending kids to juvenile detention on bullshit charges. She's the one profiting from your pain. She's the first one that must go." The crowd cheers.

Matt feels a tug on his pant leg. He looks down and sees George standing on the truck tire, reaching in to get his attention. "They're comin'," he says.

Matt nods and continues, his words spilling out faster.

"From the age of five, we're bullied, shamed, propagandized, and, most important, taught not to question. That curiosity that we're all born with is slowly degraded, until we simply accept whatever adults tell us. You have to ask yourself, why? Why are we force-fed biased and racist accounts of history? Why do teachers and administrators get so angry when you question them? Why are we treated like animals in a prison, with rules heaped on top of more rules?"

Matt sees Officers Blackman and Mullen pushing through the crowd. "They never take rules away. *Why?* Without the rules, without the mind control, we'd know how full of *shit* they really are. Divided and alone, we have no power, but together we can move mountains. We're not gonna take it anymore. At ten after eight, we're walking out of here together, and we're not coming back until our demands are met. For those of you who don't have transportation, the limousines"—Matt points to the queue of black cars—"are parked just off-campus and are paid up for the entire day. They'll take you anywhere you wanna go."

Officer Mullen heads for the speaker hooked up to the Mustang.

"Remember, they need us more than—" The sound is cut. The crowd boos. Matt drops the mic.

Officer Blackman lifts a thick leg and heaves himself onto the bumper of the pickup.

The crowd chants, "No more school, no more school, no more school!"

The bell rings; the crowd pushes on the truck. Officer Blackman steps onto the rocking truck bed. He reaches for his Taser. Matt pushes off with two short strides and dives off the sidewall of the truck. Officer Blackman shoots; the metal prongs stick to the rubber bed liner. Like Eddie Vedder at a Pearl Jam concert, Matt dives face-first into a sea of his classmates. Dozens of hands hold him up and transport him to the edge. The crowd cheers.

Two news vans and four township police cars arrive at the scene. They're blocked by bus and vendor traffic. Matt runs for the school; the crowd follows. Pandemonium ensues with students sprinting toward the school, screaming and yelling, like Scots in a Mel Gibson movie. Matt turns to look for his friends. He looks back at the Mustang. He sees George in handcuffs, and no sign of Madison or Emily. A brown hand grabs him by the arm.

"That was badass," Tariq says, beaming. "Let's finish this."

"You see Emily?" Matt asks.

Tariq shakes his head, his camera strapped to his neck.

"Madison?"

"I was with her before the crowd went crazy, but I lost her."

Matt and Tariq enter the building, surveying the scene. A few kids run, but most instinctually stop running once inside. A decade of conditioning can't be overcome with a single speech. Matt and Tariq jog by the main office and laugh. The smell of pizza and roses wafts into the hallway. Flowers and plants are stacked up on pizza boxes inside the office covering the windows. More flowers and pizza boxes sit outside in the hall in front of the office. Kids grab slices along the way to first period.

Matt and Tariq continue to class. Matt stops.

"What are you doing?" Tariq asks.

"You don't wanna walk in with me. Trust me."

"I know you don't wanna incriminate anyone, but I gotta know one thing."

"What's that?"

"Where'd you get the money?"

Matt smirks. "The good doctor had a stash."

"Had?"

Matt waltzes into Mrs. Campbell's classroom at 8:05 a.m. He sits in his seat, the room still half empty. Mrs. Campbell glares. The tardy bell rings. More raucous students spill in after the bell. Matt sees Madison among the tardy. He breathes a sigh of relief. Mrs. Campbell stalks toward Matt's desk in front.

"You're finished. The SROs will be here any minute," she says.

The loudspeaker clicks on. "This is Dr. Hansen, your principal. I have a brief announcement, and I strongly suggest that you heed my advice. Any student who walks out on their final exams today will fail for the year and will repeat *for the year*. Furthermore they will be arrested by the police for truancy. Jefferson Township Police Officers are waiting outside to secure arrests. If you resist, they will use tools at their disposal to make you comply. Be smart kids. I trust you will do the right thing."

The loudspeaker clicks off. Smiles turn down. Like a lit candle doused with a bucket of water, the excitement and fervor extinguishes. Kids stare at the clock, watching the minute hand pull back a half click, before clicking forward a notch and a half. The clock strikes 8:09 a.m. Mrs. Campbell grabs the final exams. She hands a stack to each student in the front row to hand back. She bypasses Matt and hands his stack to the kid behind him. The clock strikes 8:10 a.m. Matt stands up and flips over his desk. Mrs. Campbell whips her head around. Madison and Tariq stand up. The rest of the class remains seated.

"Come on, guys," Tariq says, looking around at his classmates.

"Go on. Get out of my sight!" Mrs. Campbell says.

Matt walks toward Mrs. Campbell. He stops and looks her in the eyes. She takes a step back, her eyes wide.

"The best slave is the one who thinks she's free," Matt says.

He marches toward the door; Tariq follows. Madison sits down. Tariq looks at Madison. She mouths *I'm sorry.* She looks down, her eyes wet.

Matt and Tariq spill into the hallway. Twelve kids cluster at the front door. The malcontents, the disaffected youth, the colored, the white trash, the mind altered, the suicidal, and one principal's daughter are all represented. Through the door windows, they see ten police officers with batons and Tasers drawn.

"I underestimated her," Matt says, "and I overestimated our classmates. Everybody's so afraid."

"At least Emily's here," Tariq says.

Emily runs over and smacks Matt across the face.

"Why didn't you tell me?" she says, her eyes red.

Tariq tiptoes away, joining the group of malcontents near the main entrance.

"I know. I'm sorry. I didn't want you to get in trouble," Matt says.

"Trouble?" She clenches her fists. "I don't care about getting into trouble. You used me."

His eyes widen. "I don't understand."

"The tape, asshole! That disgusting tape your friend put on my mom's car. You stole it from my house, didn't you? I know you did. It had to be you. Can you tell me the truth? Or are you really just full of shit like everyone else?"

Matt shakes his head; his eyes are downcast. "I took the tape." He blinks away the tears.

"I knew it."

"I didn't think you'd see it. I'm sorry."

"Your friend tripped the motion light at three in the morning. It shines right into my bedroom."

"Shit."

"I thought you loved me." Her face is flushed. "Were you just using me for some sick revenge plot?"

"I wasn't. The two things weren't connected, I swear. I stole the tape before we were even together."

"You're a liar. I know you stole something Thursday night. You were gone to the bathroom for a long time, and you took your bag with you."

"That wasn't the tape."

"It was something else then."

"It was—"

"It doesn't matter." Emily whips her blond hair around and storms toward her first period final exam.

Dr. Hansen exits her office, her mascara running. "Emily, come here right now!"

"Go to hell, Mom!"

Dr. Hansen glares at Matt across the wide hallway.

Matt wipes his eyes with his shirt sleeve and walks to the group.

"What's the plan, hoss?" a long-haired white boy says to Matt.

Matt takes a deep breath. "You guys have some serious brass balls, as my friend Tariq would say, especially after that announcement. Unfortunately this walkout, what's left of it, will fail. We don't have any leverage with a dozen people. Hansen's gonna fail us for the year. We'll probably get shocked by the Tasers and arrested. At this point our walking out is purely symbolic. We're doing what's right with the expectation that we will all pay dearly for this. I'm gonna make a run regardless, but it's not too late for all of you. You can walk back to class, and I don't think anyone will think less of you."

Two goth kids, friends of Madison, walk back toward class.

"Screw it. I'm failin' anyway," the long-haired white boy says.

The cluster of misfits nod to each other and smile.

"I'm in," Tariq says, "and I have straight As."

"Thank you," Matt says. "It probably doesn't mean much, but I have a lot of respect for everyone here."

"We should probably get moving," Tariq says. "What's the plan?"

"Maybe we should try another exit," Matt says.

"They're locked, dude," the stoner kid says, "with big-ass chains."

"They created a funnel to make it easy to scoop us all up," Tariq says.

"We're looking at the only way out then," Matt says with a frown. "If we run at the same time, they'll catch some of us, but they can't catch us all. If you have a car, get to it. You'll have to drive over the curb. They'll have the exits blocked. If you don't have a car, get to a limo. They're paid for. They'll take you anywhere you wanna go. Just be careful that a cop doesn't see you get in. If they do, you're done, because the limo driver's not gonna be a getaway driver. If you pick the farthest limo along the wood line, you might be able to slip inside without anyone seeing you. The key is, we all have to take as long as possible to get caught, to allow as many of us as possible to get away cleanly."

Officers Blackman and Mullen exit the main office behind Dr. Hansen. They stalk toward the group of students.

"Time to go," Tariq says, tightening his camera strap across his chest.

The kids grab the handles in unison.

"On three," Matt says. "One, two, THREE!"

The doors jerk open, and a motley crew of high school misfits stream out in a full sprint. The police officers converge, trying to create a bottleneck. Two cameramen and a handful of journalists stand behind, jockeying for good footage. Two police officers order the cameras to be shut off. The long-haired white boy yelps as he's pulled down by his wavy locks. The stoner kid twitches on the ground with Taser prongs in his chest. A black kid breaks free; three officers give chase. Matt and Tariq see an opening. They run through, past one of the cameramen. Tariq gives the peace sign. Matt sees Chief Campbell pull down a boy by the scruff of his Iron Maiden T-shirt.

Matt and Tariq run toward the parking lot, their shoes gripping the asphalt. Matt sprints ahead between the cars, high on adrenaline. He weaves in and out of the packed parking lot toward the wood line. He slips into the forest edge behind some briars. He turns to look for Tariq. He's gone. Police officers still track the runners. Matt sees an old pickup truck hop the curb, trying to make a getaway. A police car speeds behind, with its siren blaring and lights flashing. Matt continues through the woods, along the roadside, hiking toward the first limo in the queue. He sees a tall man with dark hair standing in front of a Lincoln Town Car. Matt walks from the woods to the front passenger door.

"Let's get going," Matt says, as he opens the door and slips inside.

The driver sits down behind the wheel. "What's goin' on here, kid?"

"I paid your company to take me anywhere I wanted to go today."

"There was a riot at the school, kids runnin' all over the place, cops. I don't wanna be involved in this."

"Then why are you still parked here?"

"Because I was paid a pile of money to sit here and pick up anyone who wanted a ride."

Matt shakes his head. "Am I not *anyone*?"

"If the cops pull me over, I don't know anything."

"Fine. Can we please get out of here?"

"Where to?"

"Philly."

[20]

Green Street

Matt scans the endless sea of forgetful redbrick row homes from the front seat of the town car.

"I think it's on Green Street, Chuck," Matt says.

"Do you have the house number?" Chuck asks.

"No."

"Well then, I don't know how you're gonna tell which one it is."

"It's the only one with a tree. It's a sickly eastern redbud, about the size of a man. It's the only thing green on Green Street."

"Like that one." Chuck points to the opposite side of the street.

"That's it. I thought it was on this side."

Chuck double-parks the black Lincoln in front of the row home. Matt opens the passenger door and steps from the vehicle. He turns around, his hand on the door.

"I'm not gonna find a space," Chuck says. "I'll just drive around the block, until you're done. How long do you think you'll be?"

"Not more than thirty minutes."

Matt stands on the stoop of the brownish-redbrick row home. Black burglar bars protect the windows and the door. Matt reaches his hand between the vertical bars and knocks. A curvy black woman opens, the barred door still shut. She smiles wide, a single gold tooth glistening among the ivory.

"George's little brother, right?" she asks.

"Yes, ma'am."

"You wanna get yer lil' cherry popped?" She laughs. "I gots some young white girls that I bet you be feenin' fo."

"I need to talk to Jimbo for a minute."

"Now, if you wanna work, you gotta go through George. Jimbo ain't gonna have nuttin' to do wich you. You best go on home now."

"It doesn't have anything to do with that. It's family stuff. Jimbo might be able to help me."

"You think Jimbo just help anyone, like he some kinda charity? Ain't nuttin' goin' on but the rent, sugar."

Matt retrieves an envelope from his pocket and hands it to her. She opens the envelope and smiles at the contents. She grabs a hundred-dollar bill and shoves it inside her bra.

"Well, come on then, sugar," she says, as she opens the barred door and steps aside.

Inside, the TV blares in the living room. Jimbo sits on the plastic-enclosed sectional, his hands propped up on his gut, mesmerized by the bickering guests on a talk show. The woman hands him the envelope. He ignores her, transfixed on the screen, where one woman pulls another by the hair. He laughs, his belly jiggling like a bowlful of jelly. The black woman smacks him across the face with the envelope.

"I know you see me standin' here," she says, with one hand on her hip. "I don't know why you be watchin' this trash anyway."

Jimbo looks at the envelope in her hand, then looks at Matt, standing behind her.

"Tell him to go through George," he says.

"It ain't about that." She hands him the envelope. Jimbo looks at the contents. "He said it's a family matter. He thinks you can help."

Jimbo looks up at Matt. "Have a seat, youngin."

Matt sits down on the sectional.

"Just so we're clear—I keep this money, whether I help you or not. Got it?" Jimbo says.

"I understand," Matt says.

"Is this about George?"

"No, it's about my parents. They used to live here. I lived with them until I was five. I remember seeing the eagle tattoo you have on your calf. I think you might have known my parents."

"George not your brother?"

"We're foster brothers."

Jimbo nods his head, stroking his beard. "A lotta guys in Philly got eagle tattoos."

"I know, but it's just you remind me of someone. I can't place it exactly, but I've seen you before."

Jimbo frowns. "So how long ago was this?"

"Twelve years."

"Well, twelve years ago, I was livin' in this here spot. Not a lotta white folks around. What did your parents do?"

"My dad was a civil rights attorney."

Jimbo chuckles, his massive belly moving up and down. "Not too many white attorneys in this neighborhood. I woulda certainly remembered that."

"He may not have been an attorney. That's just what I was told. Did you know anyone with the last name Moyer? My uncle's name was Jack, and my mom's, Ellen."

Jimbo shakes his head. "I definitely don't know any Moyers."

"My dad's last name was Byrd, with a Y."

"I don't get a lotta last names in my line a work."

"I keep remembering this gaunt young blond woman. In my memory she's pretty, but sad and sickly. I remember her saying something like, 'He never wants to see me again.' And then there's this big man with a green Eagles jacket. And this man sits next to her, like he's comforting her. Do you remember anything like that?"

"Listen, kid, the only white women I come into contact with are junkies. Do you know *anything* about what happened to your parents?"

"They died in a car accident." Matt frowns. "Well, at least that's what I was told."

"I don't wanna be disrespectful, but do you think it's possible your mom was a junkie?"

"I guess anything's possible. I don't even know if Ellen was her real name. I don't know what's real anymore."

"*Hmmph.*" Jimbo strokes his beard.

"What is it?"

"I do remember an Elle, but not an Ellen. I'm tryin' to think of the timeframe. It was probably late eighties, I think."

Matt sits up and scoots to the edge of the couch. "What did she look like?"

"Skinny white girl, blonde, … pretty, I think."

"Did she have a child?"

Jimbo nods. "A skinny little kid, always dirty from that nasty apartment."

"Was it a boy or a girl?"

"*Hmmmm* … you know, I'm not sure. I remember the kid had long hair."

"What about a husband or a boyfriend named Mike or Michael?"

"I don't remember anyone specific, but I do remember her havin' trouble with *someone*. Junkies act like I'm their bartender. I hear all sorts a sob stories. But I couldn't tell you about what. Then she was gone. I think she was arrested or she might've died."

"Are you sure?"

"No, but it's a good bet. You gotta understand, junkies up and disappear all the time. Sometimes they go to jail, sometimes they OD."

"What about the apartment? Do you remember where that is?"

"It was a row house. I know roughly where it is, but I doubt I could show you the exact one."

"Could you take me there?"

"You gotta car? I'm not about to lose my parkin' space."

+++

Jimbo groans as he sits in the back of the Lincoln.

"Go down five blocks and take a right," Jimbo says.

Chuck drives them into another section of row homes, much like Jimbo's neighborhood, but with the occasional boarded-up home to go along with the general blight of satellite dishes, concrete front yards, clashing brick colors, and mold growing on the north-facing homes.

"It's in this area here."

"Do you know which one?" Matt asks.

Jimbo shakes his head.

"Can you let me out here and give Jimbo a ride back?" Matt asks.

"Sure," Chuck says. "How much time do you need?"

"An hour or so."

"I'll pick you up then. I might have to circle the block again."

Matt watches the town car drive away. The row homes cast perpetual shade on the front sidewalk. Matt searches systematically from left to right. The first several homes yield nothing but doors slammed in his face or no answer. An older black woman steps out onto the sidewalk with a tied-up trash bag. She opens the lid on her metal can and dumps the bag inside, replacing the lid with a clang.

"Excuse me, ma'am?" Matt says.

The woman continues toward her front door. Matt moves closer.

"Excuse me, ma'am?"

The woman turns and squints.

"Can I ask you a question about someone who used to live here?"

"Whatever you sellin' child, I ain't buyin'," she says.

"I just wanted to know if you knew a young white woman who lived here named Elle, about twelve years ago."

"Elle ... Oh, yes, I remember. So sad what happened. She lived in that boarded-up house." The old woman points to the house, five units down.

"Do you know what happened to her?"

"It was so sad. She died right in that house. Someone choked her, and her little boy was in there too."

Matt leans against the railing of the stoop, the color drained from his face.

"You okay, child?"

Matt nods and pulls himself upright. "Did they catch the guy?"

She shakes her head. "Nope, and nobody lived in there since. Even the downstairs neighbors moved out. That place been boarded up this *whole* time. You oughta talk to the lady who lives over there, Mrs. Whitney. She knew her. I think her son used to date Elle." The old woman points to a house three doors down from her. "See that house there with the red door?"

"Yes, ma'am. Thank you."

Matt staggers toward the red door, each step an act of defiance against anxiety. He takes a deep breath and knocks. A cacophony of barking erupts. A diminutive, wrinkled shrew of a white woman answers the door, amid continuous barking. Her wig is curly and black and slightly off center. She wears a light blue frock of a nightgown at 1:30 in the afternoon. She talks through the screen door.

"What the hell you want?" she says.

"I wanted to ask you about Elle."

"I don't know nothin'. I never did like that little bitch." She slams the door.

Matt knocks again. The dogs bark with renewed vigor.

"Go away," she says.

"I think Elle's my mother."

"Shut up, stupid dogs." She opens the door and speaks through the storm door. "How old are you?"

"Almost seventeen."

She places the glasses hanging around her neck on the bridge of her nose.

"You might could pass for her son. But I ain't talkin' anymore unless you got a warrant."

Matt exhales. "I'm not the police. I can't get a warrant. I think what you mean is proof or evidence that I am who I say I am."

"Yeah, that."

"Did you know Jack Moyer? He was my uncle. He raised me."

"Yeah, I know that ole bastard. He put my son in the hospital. Whupped him real good, and the police didn't do nothin'."

"Why did he do that?"

"Don't know. My son was a good boy. I raised that boy right."

"Where is your son now?"

She shakes her head. "Upstate on some cockamamie charges. I told the cops, I raised my David right. One a them lawyer groups workin' on his case, tryin' to get him out. They don't do cases where the person done wrong."

"What about Elle? What happened to her?"

"She was choked to death. Never did catch the guy, but I know who done it. That ain't goin' be free."

Matt removes two hundred-dollar bills from his pocket and places them against the screen. She opens the storm door just enough to fit her boney fingers between the door and the jamb to snatch the bills. She looks at the money and grins.

"You got any more? If Elle *was* your mother, this is worth more than two hundred." Matt hands two more bills to the reverse ATM machine.

"It was the cop. The one busted my son. I seen him going up there all the time. She was supposed to be datin' my son, but that two-timin' bitch was seeing this cop at all hours. People around the neighborhood said that cop liked to strangle girls when they're ... you know ... in bed."

Matt rolls his eyes. "Do you happen to know the cop's name?"

"I'll never forget it, because his first name's the same as my son's. Detective David Campbell."

Matt clenches his fists. "Are you sure?"

"Course I'm sure. That bastard put my baby away."

"What about my father? Do you know who he is?"

She shrugs. "Hell if I know. Don't think your momma knew neither. I ain't tryin' to be rude, but your momma was loose."

"I gotta go."

Matt jogs down the street toward the boarded-up row home, his heart racing. A lower window has a loose board, wedged between two others. Matt pulls off the loose board and looks inside. It's dark and dingy. He sees broken bits of furniture, plaster and paint peeling off the walls, and exposed wood framing. A scorched brick fireplace sits just beyond the front door with brick and mortar bits sitting in front. He climbs through headfirst. He smells a concoction of dust, sweat, urine, and feces.

He brushes glass from the floor, before using his hands to support his weight. He pushes through and hears a glass vial crunch under his knee. He stands up and shakes the glass off his jeans. He wanders through the lower floor, hypnotized by the crumbling structure. An old refrigerator, stripped of its parts, is turned over in the kitchen, used as a makeshift table. Empty spaces exist between the counters, appliances long since gutted. Beyond the kitchen is a staircase without a railing leading to the second floor. He climbs the stairs using the crumbling wall for support.

At the top of the steps, a door lays in the hallway. Holes are still in the doorjamb for the handle and the two deadbolts. He remembers he wasn't strong enough to open the sticky lock. The bathroom is directly ahead. He sees pieces of broken porcelain and remnants of tile. A pile of hardened human shit sits where the toilet once sat. He remembers that the feet on the shattered bathtub looked like lion paws. He remembers his mother bathing him every day. Then the water went dry, and the baths stopped altogether. The tub became his hiding place and his bed.

He walks to the large room at the end of the hall. More paint chipping, plaster hanging, and exposed wood framing. Tiny bits of sunlight stream in between the boards on the windows. He squats down and remembers every inch of the room. He remembers exploring every crevice, every imperfection, every object, trying to find something of interest, something to keep his mind off his crumbling world.

He walks back down the dank hallway, toward the bedrooms. He staggers into the tiny room, with one window. He peers between the boards of the window. There's nothing green outside, only brick, concrete, asphalt, satellite dishes, and burglar bars. He remembers lying on an itchy mattress, before moving his bed to the tub. He remembers collecting toys out of Happy Meals. He rubs his temples to quell his headache.

He moves next door to the master bedroom. A stained double-size mattress sits naked in the middle of the room. He remembers his mother dancing around a canopy bed with a man. She's healthy and radiant, wearing a yellow dress with red flowers. The man is stocky, with curly blond hair, wide nostrils, and wide-set eyes.

Matt steps from the bedroom, shutting the door behind him. He sits on the floor and looks at the door. He shuts his eyes tight. He sees the man go into the bedroom and shut the door. Shadows move in the light underneath. He hears moaning and groaning, then gasping and elation. He hears banging and screaming, then silence. The man appears again, but his face and form are blurry, the moon and streetlamps providing dim light from the windows.

"You should get some sleep, little slugger," the man says. He winks and flashes a small grin.

Matt remembers falling asleep in the bathtub. In the morning, he feels hungry. He opens the master bedroom that doubles as the pantry. The canopy bed has been replaced by a dingy mattress, and his healthy, radiant mother has been replaced by a gaunt, sickly woman with a still expression, her blue eyes wide open. Her neck is red. Her face is pale. He shakes his mother, then searches for food. He finds none and shakes his mother some more, begging.

"I'm hungry, Mom. Wake up. I'm really hungry."

He remembers going back to the bathtub and trying to sleep. Sometimes food and soda came after he woke up. He waits as long as he can, checks for food, and tries to wake up his mother. He remembers thinking that she'll wake up if he just lets her sleep a little longer. He remembers feeling so thirsty and weak.

Matt opens his eyes; they're wet. He pulls his knees to his chest. His head sags; his tears drop on the dusty hallway floor, like raindrops in the desert.

[21]

Memories

Chuck guides the Lincoln down the gravel road. Matt rolls down the window. Gravel crunches under the tires. He feels warm humid air on his face.

"Slow down. It's right up here," Matt says.

Chuck slows the sedan to a crawl. A Ford F-150 pickup truck is parked alongside the stone cottage, almost concealed from the street.

"Shit, someone's there."

Chuck stops the car a hundred yards from the cottage.

"You want me to drop you somewhere else?" Chuck asks.

"I don't have anywhere else to go. Besides, even if I did, it's just postponing the inevitable." Matt extends his hand. "Thank you for helping me today."

Chuck shakes his hand. "It's been an adventure. I rarely get to say that at the end of the day. I hope you find what you're looking for."

Matt steps from the vehicle. He gives a quick wave. Chuck turns the car around and drives away. The afternoon sun is low in the sky. Matt walks on the grass alongside the road to the cottage. He crouches next to the bay window. Lights flicker from the television. He peers inside. He jerks back from the window, his heart racing, and his stomach churning. He marches to the front door, his jaw set tight, and his fists clenched. He yanks open the front door and steps inside the living room. Ms. Pierce jolts upright. Chief Campbell stands from the couch, his face red, and his wide nostrils flaring.

"What the *hell*, Ms. Pierce?" Matt says.

Ms. Pierce stands next to Chief Campbell. "It's complicated," she says.

"You know this degenerate?" the chief asks.

"He helps with the garden, Dave. He's my student."

"There's a warrant out for his arrest."

"There should be a warrant out for your arrest," Matt says to Chief Campbell.

Matt sprints toward the chief and launches himself at his midsection. Matt's shoulder jams into his thick stomach. The chief falls to the floor. Matt pops up and kicks him in the stomach. Chief Campbell lets out a groan. Matt kicks him in the face. The kick is partially shielded by the chief's meaty forearms. He lifts his leg to stomp the chief's skull. Matt feels a tight grip on his shoulder, tugging him off balance. His stomp misses the mark. He turns.

Ms. Pierce's neck is blotchy with red hives; her eyes are narrowed. "Matt, stop this right now!"

Matt feels a wallop on the side of his head. He's lying on his side, his head pounding, the room spinning.

"Don't you touch him, Dave!" Ms. Pierce says.

"Shut up, Olivia."

Matt feels a kick to his stomach. He struggles to breathe, the wind knocked out of him. The chief stands over him, casting a wide shadow.

"Stand up, you little shit. I'm right here," the chief says.

Matt wheezes; his ribs ache.

Matt hears a smack of a hand against skin. He looks up; Ms. Pierce's eyes are wild. Chief Campbell touches his face, glaring at her. She cowers, recognizing her error. The chief throws a right cross. There's a dead thud of knuckles against her soft cheek. Ms. Pierce kneels on the floor, holding her face. She rocks back and forth; her eyes dead. Matt tries to stand, but the pain in his ribs is excruciating. He pulls his knees to his chest and covers his head with his arms. He feels a flurry of punches to the back of his neck and head. His ears ring. The punches stop, only to be replaced by kicks to his back. He tries to wiggle away from the shots. The kicks stop. Chief Campbell steps toward Matt's head. His boot rears back; Matt puts his hands up. Everything goes black.

+++

Everything's bright, too bright to see. His eyes flutter; bright light overwhelms him. He shuts his eyes, content to stay in the darkness. He hears voices. His eyes flutter again. He tries to keep them open. He sees bright lights, and dark forms standing over him. He shuts his eyes, retreating into the darkness. He hears Ms. Pierce.

"Get the doctor! Get the doctor!"

There's bustling around him and unfamiliar voices talking about numbers, levels, and vital signs. He blinks again and again. The forms come into focus. A brown man with dark hair and a white coat stands over him. A woman in colorful loose-fitting clothing checks a monitor.

"Matt, can you hear me?" the man says.

Matt nods. "What happened?" he asks, his voice raspy.

"You had an accident. You're at the hospital."

"I need to get outta here. I need to get outta here!"

Matt thrashes about the bed, his body in pain.

"Sedate him," the man says.

+++

Matt lies with his head turned toward the window, tubes sticking out of his arm. A television sits quiet, hanging from a white wall.

There's a knock at the door. He ignores it. The door clicks.

"Your friends are here," Ms. Pierce says, entering the room. "They'd like to come in for a minute to see you. Do you feel up to it?"

"No."

"It's George and Tariq and Madison."

"No."

"Okay. Is there anything I can do? Do you want something to read?"

"No."

Ms. Pierce walks away, shutting the door behind her. After a few minutes, she returns.

"You should probably eat something. It's well past lunch," she says.

"I'm not hungry," Matt says, still staring at the blue sky.

"Madison thinks you're mad at her. She seems really sad. She thinks she let you down. You should talk to her."

Matt doesn't respond.

"Tariq said that he's not in trouble. Everyone was allowed to take their finals. He said that, even if he would've failed for the year, he still would've done it."

Matt is unresponsive.

Ms. Pierce puts her hand on top of his.

There's a knock at the door. A doctor enters the room.

"Dr. Patel, may I speak with you in the hall for a moment?" Ms. Pierce asks. "Matt, honey, I'll be right back."

He hears hushed voices in the hall.

"He's depressed, Doctor. He's barely eating. He won't see his friends. He won't read. He won't watch television. He just sleeps and stares out the window. Can you do something, please?"

"Ms. Pierce, you know I can only have these conversations with family. Ms. Grace Hart is the legal guardian, no?"

"That woman's been here once. She doesn't care about him. He doesn't have anyone. Will you please do something?"

"It is not uncommon for victims of serious head trauma to be depressed and disoriented when they first emerge from a coma. It is very positive that he was only out for a day. It may take a few months, but he should make a full recovery. His brain function is normal. His full memory should come back in time."

Dr. Patel and Ms. Pierce walk back into the room. Matt gazes out the window.

"How are you feeling today?" the doctor asks with a smile.

"I'm fine," Matt says, barely audible, not making eye contact.

"See?" Ms. Pierce whispers.

"I'll be back around in a few hours to check on you," Dr. Patel says, before he exits.

Ms. Pierce sits on the chair next to the bed. She puts her hand on his. "Is this okay?" she asks.

He nods, still looking out the window.

"Do you want me to read something to you?"

"You don't have to do this."

"Do what?"

"Be here." He blinks, two tears streak down his face.

"Look at me," she says. She places her hand under his chin, turning his head toward her. "There is no place I'd rather be. I'm not going anywhere."

"I remember my mother."

Her eyes widen.

"I found my old house," he says.

"When?"

"The day of the walkout, I went to Philly. I met a lady who knew her, and I went to the house, and I remembered." He turns back to the window, tears spilling down.

She squeezes his hand. "What, honey? What did you remember?"

"She loved me."

"Of course she did."

"She was an addict. It wasn't her fault." He turns to Ms. Pierce, his eyes wet, his face tear-streaked. "Chief Campbell killed her."

+++

Matt sits in the chair next to the window in jeans and a T-shirt. He watches birds flutter about the hospital courtyard. There's a knock, then the click of the door.

"I have good news," Ms. Pierce says, entering the room.

She smiles a small grin. A dim bruise appears as a smudge on the side of her face, the lone imperfection in her beauty.

"The police have finally decided not to charge anyone, including you."

Matt frowns. "Are they charging Campbell for murdering my mother?"

She sits next to him and takes his hand in both of hers. "I can't begin to tell you how sorry I am about what happened to your mother."

"Did you talk to the police?"

Ms. Pierce nods. "I did."

"What did they say?"

"They said that they need more evidence than a child's memory. I'm sorry."

"What about my uncle? Are they gonna charge him for that? I was there. I have the real autopsy."

"Well, it's not—"

"No surprise."

"There's something we need to talk about, about that night."

"No, I have to remember on my own. I have to be able to trust my own memory."

"Well, I have more news. The school board is up in arms about the website. They promised change."

Matt shakes his head. "Nothing's gonna change. As soon as Tariq compromised, it was over."

"He had to shut down the site. Why do you think they were willing to drop the charges? He did it for you."

Matt frowns. "I wish he wouldn't have. That's how it starts. We feel like we've won, because we aren't in trouble, but we didn't do anything wrong in the first place. Meanwhile the real wrongdoers never pay."

"Mr. Dalton and Mr. Richardson have been fired. That was a huge win right there. And Dr. Hansen resigned."

Matt frowns. "They always let the people in power resign, so they can go somewhere else and do the same thing all over again. They sacrifice low-level people, like Dalton, so we think the system can change. It can't."

Ms. Pierce purses her lips. "I think it would be best to let this go for now and concentrate on getting better. Are you ready to go?"

"I guess so."

Ms. Pierce pushes Matt out of the hospital in a wheelchair. She stops just outside of the sliding metal doors.

"This is stupid," Matt says, standing up.

"I think they make you do it for insurance reasons," Ms. Pierce replies. "I can go get the car, if you wanna wait on the bench."

"I'd rather walk."

They tread to the parking area. Ms. Pierce insists that he hold her arm for support.

She steers the Jeep Wagoneer down the gravel road. Matt sits quiet and listless, staring out the window, listening to the crunch of gravel beneath him. He remembers driving down the road in the Lincoln, and Chuck dropping him off near the cottage. She pulls into the driveway. The garden is lush. Cherry tomatoes adorn the trellised vines like lights on a Christmas tree. Squash, watermelon, and potatoes are halfway to maturity. Corn stands as tall as he is. Lettuce, spinach, peas, beans, radishes, and turnips are ready to pick. Matt staggers to the garden. Ms. Pierce follows.

"There's a lot to harvest," Matt says.

"We can make dinner from the garden, if you like."

"I would."

"I could invite Tariq, Madison, and George. They practically lived at the hospital."

"What about Emily?"

Ms. Pierce frowns. "She left last week."

Matt stares at the ground.

"I'm so sorry, honey."

"Where did she go?"

"California, I think. From what I heard, her mom got a job out there."

He shakes his head. "Pass the trash."

Ms. Pierce ignores his comment. "So what do you think? I know your

243

friends are really anxious to see you."

"I know. I just don't feel up to it. They're gonna want me to be happy. I don't have the energy to fake it."

"Whatever you want." Ms. Pierce grabs his hand and squeezes.

"How long can I stay with you?"

"Grace doesn't seem to care, as long as she still gets the checks. Don't worry. I worked it out with her. I made up the guest room for you."

"Thank you," he says, turning to her.

She smiles and gives his hand another squeeze. "Do you want to come in and get settled?"

He nods.

Matt follows Ms. Pierce past the bay window toward the front door, their hands still intertwined. He remembers the flickering lights of the television. He remembers looking inside and seeing her nestled with *him*. He snatches his hand back and stops.

"What's wrong?" she asks.

Matt is breathless. "I remember you … with *him*."

She stops and gazes at Matt, her mouth turned down. She blinks; her eyes fill with tears. He marches up the stoop, his mind racing.

"You were on the couch with *him*." Matt opens the front door and walks in. She follows. "You two were standing right there." Matt points in front of the couch. "He was angry. You told me it was complicated."

"I'm sorry. I was scared." Tears streak down her face.

He shakes his head. "This is so messed up."

"I'm so sorry." She tries to put her arms around him.

He pushes her away and steps back. "I wanted to kill him. I tried to kill him. You stopped me. Then he knocked me down, because I was focused on you. Why did you do that?"

"I loved him."

"You loved him? How could you?" His eyes are wet.

"Because I don't love myself."

"He hit you."

She nods, her eyes puffy, tears spilling down her cheeks.

"You were on the floor. I remember. You were scared. Then I was on the floor, and he was kicking me. Why did he stop? Why am I still alive?"

"I hit him."

Matt raises his eyebrows. "With your fists?"

"No, the coal."

Matt turns around and searches the mantel over the stone fireplace for the familiar lump of jagged anthracite coal. It's gone.

"They took it for evidence," she says.

Matt panics. "Are you in trouble?"

She shakes her head. "They're not going to prosecute. They ruled it as self-defense."

"He's gonna come back. We can't stay here."

"He's not coming back. ... He's dead."

Matt's eyes are wide. "You killed him?"

"I had to," she says, her voice shaky.

"To protect me?"

She nods.

[22]

The Family You Choose

His knees push into the earth. The sun beats down on the back of his neck. His breathing is labored, and his midsection aches, as he pulls grass from the garden. Matt glances up at the bay window. Ms. Pierce stands watching. She turns away, pretending she's not checking up on him. He stands with a groan and picks up two five-gallon buckets filled with grass, their roots, and some soil still attached.

He staggers around back and dumps the grass on top of the compost pile. He treads to the mulch pile and fills the buckets, using the fork stuck in the pile. He carries the mulch back to the garden, covering the soil unearthed by his weeding. He takes his rusty pruners from his side pocket and trims a few branches from the overgrown tomato vines.

"Hey, birthday boy, why don't you take a break?" Ms. Pierce says from the front stoop.

He turns around.

She stands with her brow furrowed, her blond hair in a ponytail and her ivory skin sun-kissed. "I made some meadow tea," she says.

"You think I'm overdoing it," he says.

"I'm just worried."

He locks shut his pruners and slides them into the side pocket of his canvas pants. He strides to the front stoop. He unlaces his worn boots and leaves them at the door. He follows her to the kitchen. A half-iced cake is on the counter. A glass pitcher and two glasses filled with ice cubes and meadow tea sit on the table.

"Are you hungry yet?" she asks.

He shakes his head, sitting down. "I usually don't feel like eating much when it's this hot."

"You need to drink something." She places a glass of tea in front of him and sits down. She purses her lips. "I'm worried that you're doing too much, too soon."

Matt takes a drink. He sets down the glass. "I'll be fine. I just need to *do* something. I can't sit around anymore."

She frowns.

"I'll be careful."

"It seems like a lot to me, and it's your birthday. If you tell me what to do, I can take care of everything, until you're fully healed."

"No, I told you that I'd take care of this for you. What does that say about me, if I can't keep my word?"

"You nearly died, Matt. I think circumstances trump your responsibilities."

"I'll spread the work out, just do a little each day."

She nods. "All right, but, if I see you in pain, I'm taking over the chores."

He nods. "The tea is good."

"Have you thought about what you'll do? The school board and the superintendent want me to give them an answer on Monday."

"I have. I'm not taking my finals. They can fail me."

Ms. Pierce frowns. "I know you're mad but don't ruin your life over this. You have a chance to put all this behind you. You and I both know you could ace your finals in half a day. It doesn't make sense to give up a whole year of school for half a day's work."

"Why do you think kids go to school?"

"You mean, apart from the fact that they have to?"

He nods.

"Well, a number of reasons, I suppose. To learn, to get good grades, to get into college, play sports, make friends, and I'm sure a bunch of other things I'm not thinking of."

He frowns. "I don't think they go to school to learn. What happens when you're teaching something, and someone asks if it's on the test?"

She purses her lips. "If I tell them it's on the test, they pay attention. If I tell them it's not, they tune out."

"And they cram for tests, immediately forgetting the information the moment they turn in the test. Everyone's so focused on getting the grade, getting into a good college, making more good grades, and for what? So they can work in some job that isn't really needed? So they don't have to get their hands dirty?"

"What's wrong with wanting a good job, getting good grades?"

"All those gold stars come with a price. From a very early age, kids are praised when they give the right answers. Praised with stickers or pluses or As, and chided for the wrong ones with poor marks. This encourages the smartest kids to continue to gobble up and regurgitate all the information fed by the adults and the teachers around them. But what if they're not taught the most important information and if sometimes they're taught outright lies?"

She furrows her brow. "Derrick used to tell me that the smartest are also usually the most indoctrinated."

"That's why, apart from Tariq, the only kids willing to participate in the walkout were the kids on the fringes, the kids who never get good grades, the outcasts, the kids who see no benefit in the system. Those were the only kids brave enough, because those were the only kids who had nothing to lose."

"God, you remind me of him." She takes a sip of tea. "I don't disagree with you, but, for better or worse, this is the system we have. I don't want you to end up like Derrick. This path you're on ..." She shakes her head. "It's a really hard road. I just want you to be happy."

"I have no intention of going to jail, but I plan to live my life as free as possible."

"And how do you plan to do that?"

"For starters, I'm dropping out of school."

She exhales and frowns. "I had a feeling this was coming."

"I'm gonna take that job working for Reggie doing tree work, and Mr. Clemens said I could work on his farm on the weekends. I can start paying you rent, if you'll let me stay. If not, I understand. I can be out of here next week. You've already done so much for me. I feel like I've turned your life upside down."

"You have."

"I'm sorry."

"Don't be. It's a *good* upside down. I'd like for you to stay, but I want to renegotiate our deal." She grins.

"Okay?"

"You still keep me in the produce that I've become accustomed to, but I will *not* accept a dime from you. I'm serious about this, Matt. You are not my tenant. You're …" She looks away, then to Matt, her eyes glassy. "You should get ready. Your friends will be here in an hour."

Matt smirks. "That means I can do fifty-five minutes more work."

She laughs. "I'm the one who needs to get ready then. I haven't even finished the cake."

"I can help."

She shakes her head with a smile. "You will *not* help ice your own birthday cake."

+++

Matt stands on the back patio, looking down at his new jeans, untucked polo shirt, and brown shoes. Ms. Pierce had insisted that he open one of his birthday presents before the party. She had beamed at the sight of him, telling him once more how he shines up like a new penny. He picks up the matchbook from the wooden picnic table and strikes a match. He lights the citronella candle.

He hears the low growl of a V-8 engine. He walks to the driveway. George exits his black coupe, his hair gelled, with a small wrapped box in hand. Madison steps from the passenger seat. Ryan climbs out of the back. Matt smiles at them. George hands him the box.

"Happy birthday, bro. This is from all of us."

Matt wipes the corner of his eye and clears his throat. "Thanks, guys."

"Don't get all weepy," George says. "It's not *that* good of a gift."

Madison frowns at George, and then reaches out and hugs Matt. "I'm sorry," she says in his ear.

Matt smiles at her. "It's fine." He puts his arm around Ryan. "Are you happy to have your room back?"

Ryan shakes his head. "It was more fun with you there. Can you come and visit?"

"I'll be working soon, and, when I get a truck, I'll pick you up anytime you want."

Ryan smiles.

A white Nissan Sentra parks behind George's Mustang. Tariq and Jared step out, each holding a wrapped gift. Jared struts toward the crowd.

"What up, party people?" Jared says, smacking Matt on the shoulder and handing him a box.

"Thanks, Jared. Thanks for coming," Matt says.

"Please tell me you invited some ladies up in here?"

"This is everyone."

"Damn, I'm gonna have to make some calls."

Tariq approaches, placing his keys into the front pocket of his jeans. He smiles wide, his goatee expanding.

"It's good to see you," Tariq says, holding out his hand.

Matt nods, shaking with one hand, while balancing his gifts with the other.

"Everything's in back," Matt says.

His friends and family walk to the back patio. Matt and Tariq linger behind.

"I wanted to thank you for what you did," Matt says. "You risked everything for me."

Tariq smiles. "No need to thank me. It was the most exciting thing I've ever done in my whole life."

"What happened to you in the parking lot? I thought you were right behind me, but, when I got to the woods and turned around, you were gone. Did they catch you?"

Tariq laughs. "Nah, I hid underneath Tyler's Jeep by a wheel. I gotta bunch of pictures of the cops roughing up kids. I stayed until the cops left. They agreed to drop the charges, partly because of the pictures, partly because of the website. I gave copies to the kids who walked out with us. It was like I gave them a million dollars. I think we all felt special in that moment, like we were standing up for what's right, when nobody else had the balls to. It felt good, you know?"

"Yeah, I do."

They walk to the backyard, joining the party. Everyone stands around the food and the presents, eating, talking, and laughing. Ms. Pierce steps out onto the patio holding a cake with burning candles. She's greeted by the guests. Matt sits at the head of the table. They sing "Happy Birthday." Jared and Ms. Pierce have angelic voices. Matt takes a deep breath, through aching ribs, and blows out all seventeen candles.

After eating cake, he opens his gifts. He slides on the rugged wristwatch.

"I know you like to tell time by the sun," George says with a smirk, "but this might work a bit better."

Jared and Tariq both give him a shirt. They say he should have some clothes without holes. In addition to the clothes on his back, Ms. Pierce gives him a new pair of boots. She tells him to look inside. He pulls a pair of Felco pruners from inside one of the boots.

+++

After the guests leave, Matt carries empty plates and glasses into the kitchen. Ms. Pierce stands at the sink, washing dishes, her sundress covered by an apron. He piles the dishes on the counter.

"Thank you for doing this," he says. "You were right. It was really good to see everyone."

She looks at Matt, her blond hair tied back, and her face flushed from the heat of the water. "You have really nice friends ... and family."

"Family?"

"Your foster siblings love you just as much as any blood-related siblings I've seen. And you have me, right?"

He nods; his eyes downcast.

"What's wrong?"

He shrugs. "Nothing. Everything was really great. I just wish Emily was here."

Ms. Pierce purses her lips and furrows her brow. "I know."

"I really messed things up. I never should've lied to her. It's like, by trying to protect her, I was insulting her strength as a person to handle the truth."

"Why don't you call her?"

"I have." He exhales. "Too many times. Her phone goes right to voice mail. I'm starting to feel like a stalker. I think I have to let her go."

"Maybe she'll come around. She probably just needs time."

"Maybe."

Ms. Pierce dunks a dirty dish into the soapy water, then into the clear water. Matt grabs the dish towel and dries the plate.

"So, when's your birthday?" he asks.

"Next month, and I'm not telling you how old I am." She grins.

"Twenty-four?"

She laughs. "This is why I keep you around. I need someone to boost my self-esteem."

"What do you usually do for your birthday? Does your mother make you a cake?"

She frowns. "I don't think *that'll* happen."

"I'm sorry. Did she die?" He looks down.

"No, she's alive. So is my dad."

"Do you have any brothers or sisters?"

"No." She turns off the water. Matt hands her a dish towel. She dries her hands.

"Where do your parents live?"

"Here, in Jefferson."

"That's great. I'd like to meet them."

She shakes her head. "I don't talk to them."

Matt raises his eyebrows. "Why? I'd give anything to know my parents."

She frowns and looks down.

Matt winces. "I'm sorry. That was insensitive."

"It's okay." She takes a deep breath. "I grew up in a pretty abusive household. I remember this time that Derrick and I were supposed to go over to my parents' house for Christmas, and I was complaining that I didn't want to go. He told me that we shouldn't go if I didn't want to. It was like a weight had been lifted. I had never even considered the fact that I could just stop seeing these people. They *are* my parents."

Matt dries dishes, stacking them next to the cupboard. "Why didn't you wanna see them? Because of the abuse?"

"What they did to me when I was a child was wrong. I confronted them as an adult. All I wanted was an apology, but they couldn't do it. They just told me that it never happened and that I needed to get over the past. And they were still abusive as adults in their own way. They borrowed money from me that they never paid back. They criticized me. They made fun of Derrick. They're just nasty people."

Ms. Pierce stacks dry plates in the cupboard.

"So you just stopped having contact with them?" Matt asks.

She stops and turns to Matt. "I did."

"How did that go over?"

She sighs. "It was pretty awful. They tried to manipulate me in every way possible, to get me to change my mind. Finally I stopped taking their calls. I don't want people in my life who don't make it better."

"That sounds like good advice."

"Its common sense, but it's so hard to do. I think I'm finally there."

"I'm glad," Matt says, drying the final glass.

"Me too."

"Do you remember how I told you about that woman I met in Philly who knew my mother?"

"Of course."

"She said her son used to date my mom. I was wondering if you'd go with me to see him?"

"Of course, honey."

"Before you agree so quickly, it's a little bit more complicated than just going for a visit."

"Okay?"

"He's in prison."

[23]

To Jack

Ms. Pierce steers the Jeep Wagoneer into the parking lot of the assisted-living high-rise. She finds an empty spot near the back of the lot. Matt and Ms. Pierce hop out of the Jeep. The stifling heat reverberates in a haze off the asphalt parking lot. A large wooden sign reads Manchester Lakes Assisted Living.

"I thought it would be cooler up here," Ms. Pierce says.

"I thought there'd be a lake," Matt says.

She smiles. "False advertising, huh?"

He grins.

"Are you ready?" she asks.

"Your friend's sure this is her?"

"You know I already spoke to her."

"Sorry, I'm just nervous."

"It'll be fine. She sounded really nice on the phone."

They walk through the automatic sliding doors. The cool air-conditioning feels too cold after coming in from the sweltering heat. Ms. Pierce struts toward the front desk, her light blue sundress billowing around her shapely figure. The middle-aged man at the counter smiles wide, his eyes up, but occasionally he glances down.

"May I help you?" he says, with a plastered smile.

"Hi, we're here to see Anne Thornton," Ms. Pierce says. "She's expecting us."

"I'll call and let her know you're here. What's your name, miss?"

"Olivia Pierce."

"And the young man?"

"Matt Moyer," she says.

The man calls Anne. He hangs up the phone. "You're welcome to go on up. She's in apartment 314. The elevators are right around the corner. I could take you up there, if you need help."

"We're fine. Thanks," Ms. Pierce says.

They step onto the elevator. She presses the number 3. She grabs Matt's hand and gives it a squeeze.

"Are you excited?" she asks.

He nods. "Thank you for doing this. I never would've found her without your help."

"You're welcome."

The elevator chimes, and the metal doors slide open. They step into the carpeted hallway and follow the sign that reads 300–320.

They arrive at apartment 314. Matt takes a deep breath. Ms. Pierce knocks on the door. A tall woman, with a broad smile and white curly hair, opens the door.

"Olivia, it's so nice to see you. And you must be Matthew. I'm Anne, but you already know that," she says, her words spilling out in rapid fire.

Matt smiles and offers his hand. She reaches out and wraps her arms around him.

"Come in, you two. I'm so glad you came. I can't believe I'm looking at Jack's grandnephew."

The apartment floor is covered in white carpet. A couch and two dark wooden chairs are arranged around a glass coffee table in the living room.

"Have a seat," she says. "Would you like something to drink? I made iced tea. It's hot as blazes out there."

"Tea sounds great," Ms. Pierce says. "Do you need some help?"

"Oh, heavens no."

Matt and Ms. Pierce sit on the couch. Anne disappears to the kitchen. Ms. Pierce looks over at Matt.

"I told you she was nice," she says in a hushed tone.

Anne returns and places a tray on the table, with a pitcher of tea and three glasses. She pours, while Matt squirms in his seat.

"You look like you have a lot of questions," Anne says to Matt.

"I do. … I never thought there would be anyone I could talk to who might know the answers."

"I might have a few questions for you too, if that's okay. I was deeply saddened when Olivia told me what happened. I'm so sorry, sweetheart."

Matt looks away. Ms. Pierce smiles at Anne.

"So, Olivia, you were Matt's English teacher, right?" Anne asks.

"For just a few months," Ms. Pierce replies.

"And now you're his guardian?"

"Technically, no, but I'd like to be."

Anne purses her lips. "What would you like to know?" she says to Matt.

He takes a deep breath. "Did you know my mother, Elle?"

"I did. Jack tried to look after her. His brother, Phillip, who would be your grandfather if he were alive today, died when she was a teenager. It was some sort of cancer, if my memory serves me correct. Your grandmother, Ruth, suffered from bipolar disorder. After Phillip died, Ruth fell apart. He was the glue that held everything together. Your mom moved out at sixteen. Your uncle looked after her, not like a father, mind you, but more like a friend.

"Your mother had a mind of her own. Jack gave her money when she needed it or a place to stay occasionally. He tried to give her advice, but she was so strong-willed. Not too much different than you, I gather. She was a very beautiful girl and smart too. Her biggest mistake was in the company she kept. Jack and I often had to go places and physically remove her from some of the people she got involved with. She'd get in over her head, then she'd call Jack."

"Did my mom have any brothers or sisters?"

Anne shakes her head. "She was an only child."

"What happened to Ruth?"

"She committed suicide shortly after your mother moved out. It was a lot for your mother to handle, the death of both her parents at such a young age. I wish Jack and I could've been a better stabilizer for her."

"Do you know who my father is?"

Anne shakes her head. "I wish I did. Jack and I lost contact in 1982, before you were born."

"Is there anything *you* wanna know?" Matt asks Anne.

She forces a smile. "Did he talk about me much?"

Matt shakes his head.

Anne looks down.

"I think it was too painful for him. ... but I did get him to talk once."

Anne looks up.

"He said you were smart as a whip and the most unselfish person he had ever met. He also said you helped him get clean. He told me the biggest mistake he ever made was walking out on you. He said he did it because he felt like he was a burden."

Anne wipes her eyes with a cloth napkin. She smudges some mascara. "I waited forever for that old kook. I was sure he'd come back. I guess I was right. I just didn't think it'd be twenty years later, beyond the grave."

"My uncle told me that he had two regrets in his life. One of them was walking out on you. He wouldn't tell me the other. Do you know what he might've been talking about?"

Anne nods her head. She takes a sip of tea and wipes again at the corners of her eyes with her napkin. "It's your mother. Jack was hooked on heroin, and your mother got her first taste of the stuff at his apartment. One of his stockbroker buddies gave it to her. Those guys were a bunch of creeps, if you ask me.

"I always told him that she would've gotten into drugs somehow anyway. I've seen thousands of addicts as clients. I know the common personalities and family backgrounds of addicts. Your mother, bless her heart, had it in spades. He always blamed himself. Your uncle got clean, but your mother got worse. He wouldn't see her for months at a time, until she needed money. He eventually had to cut her off. He didn't want to fund her killing herself. I know it haunted him that he didn't help her. I imagine having you was the closest he could come to making it up to her."

Matt takes a deep breath and looks away.

"I'm sorry, sweetheart. Is this too much?"

Matt turns back toward Anne. "No, I already knew that she was into drugs. I guess I didn't realize how hard her life must've been. Thank you for telling me. Is there anything else you'd like to know?"

"Since Olivia called and I found out about you, I've tried to imagine Jack taking care of you all these years. What was he like as a father figure?"

Matt offers a small smile, looks away for a moment, then back to Anne. "I'm not sure I really appreciated what he did for me, until he was gone. When I was twelve, he got sick. He slowly deteriorated after that. I resented him for not being able to help as much with the farm chores. He told me that he was sorry he was a broken old man. What I didn't realize is that he took me as a broken five-year-old and brought me back to life. It couldn't have been easy. I really don't remember the early years.

"I do remember that he encouraged me to think for myself. Actually a better way to put it is he *challenged* me to think for myself. We had philosophical discussions that lasted hours sometimes. He taught me to read and write. He taught me math. By the time I was twelve, I had to teach him. I learned so much preparing lessons for him. He was the worst student too." Matt laughs. Anne and Olivia join in. "He'd ask me so many questions, like he was one of those students trying to show up the teacher."

"Sound familiar?" Ms. Pierce says with a grin.

"I was good in your class," Matt says. "But I had to be ultraprepared for my lessons with Uncle, or he'd be that annoying kid. And, if I didn't connect with him, like if I tried to read directly out of a book too long, he'd act bored or pretend he wasn't paying attention. It was actually pretty funny, but it also forced me to learn things so well, that I never forgot them."

"He sure was ornery," Anne says, laughing. "What do you think was the most important thing you learned from Jack?"

"He taught me about nature. It wasn't just about farming or beekeeping or animal husbandry. He taught me to really watch and listen. I spent so much time on our farm that I knew every inch of it. Before all the problems, I was working on a design that would mimic the natural systems and would provide for all our needs plus the needs of the plants and animals. It was a closed loop that had zero waste, required zero inputs, and produced an abundance of food, medicine, and fuel, with less labor than a traditional organic farm.

"Uncle was always trying to look at what I was doing. I told him to stay away, that it was a surprise. I was gonna give him the design for his birthday. I thought it would turn the farm around. He died a month before his seventy-ninth birthday."

Ms. Pierce grabs Matt's hand and squeezes.

"That must've been so hard," Anne says.

Matt nods. His eyes are downcast.

Anne raises her glass of iced tea. "I'd like to make a toast to Jack Moyer, the love of my life, and a great father to a wonderful son."

Glasses clink; smiles, laughter, and fond memories follow.

+++

"Do you want to stop before it gets dark?" Ms. Pierce says. "There's a rest stop coming up."

"Okay," Matt says.

She enters the turn lane for the interstate rest area and parks in front of a brick building with signs for bathrooms and vending machines. A concrete walkway snakes its way under and around large shade trees, with empty picnic tables scattered throughout. She puts the Jeep in Park and cuts the engine.

"I'm going to run to the bathroom. Do you want to find a table?" she asks.

"Sure."

Ms. Pierce strides into the brick building. Matt opens the rear hatch and takes the picnic basket from the Jeep. He meanders down the concrete path to the table farthest from the road noise. He spreads a blue tablecloth on the table. He sets up Ms. Pierce's tea, his water, and pulls out the salad container, along with two sandwiches. He sets up the silverware and folds the cloth napkins underneath. He sits, listening to the sounds of the squirrels rummaging through the trees and the birds singing their songs. Ms. Pierce strides down the sidewalk toward him.

"What a beautiful spot," she says, as she sits across from him. "You didn't have to wait for me. You must be starving."

"It's okay."

"No Whole Organics this week. All the veggies are out of *our* garden." Ms. Pierce smiles and takes a bite of her salad.

Matt grins and bites into a cherry tomato.

After the main course, they place the containers back into the willow picnic basket.

"I brought that yellow watermelon for dessert, the one you picked and cut yesterday. It's really sweet," she says.

Matt and Ms. Pierce sit in the shade of the oak tree eating cut pieces of watermelon. Matt swallows the seeds whole. Ms. Pierce picks them out with her fork.

"So what did you think of Anne?" she asks.

"I can see why Uncle loved her," he says. "It's sad though."

"What's sad?"

"They loved each other. They're both nice people, but they ended up alone."

"Sometimes we're our own worst enemies."

"I agree," he says, placing his empty bowl back into the basket.

Ms. Pierce gazes at Matt. "I want to ask you something, but I want you to know that it's okay to say no."

Matt folds his hands on the table and leans toward Ms. Pierce. "Okay."

She takes a deep breath. "I know you'll be eighteen in less than a year, but I want to adopt you." Her eyes water; her speech is strained. "I want to be your mother. I've never wanted anything more in my life. I already think of you as my son. I love you very much."

Matt stands up.

She wipes the corners of her eyes. "You can say no. I know you probably don't need a mother at this point. You're more mature than most men I know."

Matt moves around the table. She stands. Matt hugs her tightly for a moment. He steps back and looks into her puffy eyes.

"I'd really like that," he says.

[24]

Visiting Day

Matt unscrews the gas cap and plunges the nozzle into the hole. He holds down the trigger and clicks the latch to hold it in place. He leans against the Jeep, watching the numbers march higher. Ms. Pierce walks across the parking lot, with tea and a bag of barbecue potato chips. Despite the heat wave, she wears a conservative billowy dress that hides her figure.

"You sure you don't want something?" she asks.

Matt shakes his head, glancing at the potato chips.

"I know they're bad for me, but they're *so* good."

The nozzle clicks, and the gas pump stops. He resets the nozzle and returns her credit card.

Ms. Pierce drives the Jeep down a country road, surrounded by soybean fields. A massive concrete wall, reminiscent of the Great Wall of China, emerges in the distance. Towers on the corners of the octagon-shaped building look like part of a medieval English castle. Ms. Pierce turns into a spacious parking lot, only half full. She parks the car and shuts off the engine. She grabs a white sweater from her bag. She puts it on over her dress, further covering her chest.

"Are you ready?" she asks, her face red.

Matt nods. "You look nervous."

"Don't you worry about me. I'll be fine. You have your passport?"

"It's right here." He holds up the blue booklet.

They stride across the hazy asphalt parking lot to a concrete building, built into the massive walls. Matt opens the glass door, holding it for Ms. Pierce. They walk into the lobby. A handful of frazzled women, who are probably younger than they look, try to entertain their children. An older couple holds hands and whispers to themselves. A sign greets Matt and Ms. Pierce, just beyond the glass doors.

YOU MUST HAVE IDENTIFICATION: Adult visitors must have a current state-issued ID, driver's license, or passport. Visitors under the age of 18 must be accompanied by a parent or legal guardian during the entire visit. Minors between 15 and 18 years old must also have a current state-issued ID or passport.

VISITORS MUST BE DRESSED PROPERLY: Clothing cannot be suggestive or lewd. The visitor will be refused, if the receiving officer deems it so. Do not wear tight-fitting clothing, tube tops, tank tops, halter tops, skirts above the knees, spandex of any kind, low-cut tops of any kind, and see-through fabrics. Individuals wearing these unapproved items will be refused entry. Any person wearing clothing, visible tattoos, hairstyles, or other items associated with a drug or gang lifestyle will be refused entry.

VISITORS MUST ACT PROPERLY: Anyone caught exposing or flashing one's genitals or other sexually explicit parts or engaging in any behavior deemed to be of a sexual nature will be escorted from the premises and barred from visiting this facility in the future.

THE METAL DETECTOR MUST BE CLEARED BEFORE ENTRY: Pockets must be emptied before going through the metal detector. The following items are prohibited:
Tobacco products and paraphernalia

Electronic devices, including but not limited to:
    cell phones, pagers, computers
Sharp objects, including but not limited to:
    scissors, toenail clippers, knives
WEAPONS OF ANY KIND
Food or drink
Pornographic materials of any kind

"This place isn't much fun," Ms. Pierce says, after skimming the sign.

They walk up to the bulletproof glass. A uniformed middle-aged white man with a crew cut sits behind the glass, browsing a hunting magazine. Matt and Ms. Pierce stand in front of the officer. After a minute, she taps on the glass. The man looks up, his brow furrowed, his eyes wild.

"Step back from the glass," he says.

He returns to his magazine.

"We're here to visit someone," Ms. Pierce says.

The man exhales and slaps his magazine shut. "Did you sign in?"

"I don't know where to do that."

He shakes his head. "On the wall, where it says Visitor Registration. Then slide it in the slot here and *wait*, like everyone else."

He turns away from Ms. Pierce and reopens his magazine.

They walk to the wall with the Visitor Registration sign. Matt pulls out the paperwork and attaches it to a clipboard with a pen attached. They sit in a lonely corner.

"That guy's a jerk," Matt says.

"Do me a favor. Don't ever get yourself put in a place like this," Ms. Pierce says. "I shudder to think we both could've been put away."

"Some people think that crime statistics are massively underreported because it doesn't include prison crime, where rape, assault, and murder occur regularly, but nobody seems to care. In fact prison populations are growing. We have more prisoners than China, with a fraction of its total population."

"Another excellent reason why I absolutely do not want you in a place like this. Do you understand me?"

Matt nods.

Ms. Pierce slides the form and their IDs through the slot next to the glass window. The officer ignores them. Matt and Ms. Pierce sit, alternately chatting and scanning the waiting room.

A door opens next to the reception desk. A young uniformed white man with a brown crew cut enters the waiting room.

"Olivia Pierce, Matt Moyer," he says. They approach the officer, who guards the door. "I'm Officer Reeves. I'll be your receiving officer for your visit. First I'm gonna take you to the screening room with Officer Tubbs."

The officer leads them to a room, where they're given a seat in front of another officer, a middle-aged black man, with a gold name plate that reads Tubbs.

"I'm not sure I should allow this visit," Officer Tubbs says. "Let me ask you a few questions. The paperwork you gave us states you've been Matt's legal guardian for about two weeks. Is that correct?"

"Yes, Officer," Ms. Pierce says.

"And, Matt, can you tell me about your relationship with David Whitney?" Officer Tubbs asks.

"He was an old boyfriend of my mother's," Matt replies.

"Are you sure about that?"

"That's what his mother told me."

"What do you hope to get outta this visit?"

"I'd like to learn a little bit more about my mother."

Officer Tubbs turns toward Ms. Pierce. "Ms. Pierce, you seem like a fine woman. And Matt seems like a fine young man. I'm just worried that this visit might not turn out like he hopes. Do you two know why Mr. Whitney's here?"

"We are aware, Officer," Ms. Pierce says.

"Then you can understand why I'd be concerned about a kid and a pretty young woman seeing this man."

"I understand," she says.

"You can imagine that, as a kid without biological parents, I've seen some things that a kid shouldn't have to see," Matt says to Tubbs. "I can assure you that I can handle talking to Mr. Whitney. If he says something that I can't handle, I'll walk away."

Officer Tubbs smiles and shakes his head. "I can appreciate that, Matt. I'll grant the visit, but, if he gets unruly in any way, we will shut down the visit. Understood?"

"I understand."

"Officer Reeves will take you through the metal detector. Then he'll take you to the visiting room. Any questions?"

"No," Ms. Pierce says.

Matt shakes his head.

Officer Reeves leads them down a corridor with white walls and a gray linoleum floor. Two officers stand by the doorway-size metal detector. Ms. Pierce and Matt walk through without any beeping. Officer Reeves opens the door to the visitors' room. The walls are painted a dull yellow. The floor is still gray linoleum. Plastic chairs face a battery of partitioned counter spaces, facing thick glass, with a single telephone hanging from each space. Black numbered placards are attached to the front of each counter.

"He's at number 6," Officer Reeves says.

Matt and Ms. Pierce sit down at the number six counter, the phone next to Matt. A man in an orange jumpsuit sits on the other side of the glass. He's forty-two, but he looks closer to thirty. His nose is pointy, his hair light brown and wavy. He has a thin but muscular build. He's handsome. The color drains from Ms. Pierce's face. Her eyes are wide. Matt stares at the man's facial features, searching for an answer to a question he never considered. David Whitney picks up the phone and taps on the glass with the receiver. Matt awakes from his daze and picks up the phone.

"Let me talk to the lady," he says.

David stares at Ms. Pierce. His eyes move around her face, around her body, searching for something to hold on to, something profane. Matt hands the phone to Ms. Pierce. She listens for a moment. Her face turns red.

"You will talk to this young man, or I'm walking away *right now*," she says.

She hands the phone to Matt. He puts it to his ear. David still stares at Ms. Pierce, licking his lips.

"What the hell you want?" David says.

"I wanna talk to you about Elle Moyer from Philadelphia, my mother."

"Elle," he says, as if he's savoring a thought. "She had nice tits." He gazes at Ms. Pierce's chest.

She covers up with her arms.

"Hey, dumbass, look at me," Matt says, tapping on the glass with his knuckles. "I can't believe I'm related to you."

David looks at Matt dumbfounded. "What you mean, *related*?"

"Don't you think we look alike?"

David studies Matt's face.

"Well, would you look at that? You can thank me now for them good looks. I bet you be gettin' a lotta action with them little high school girls."

"Do you think I could be your son?"

"Could be. I screwed a lot without no rubber. Me and your mama was back and forth for damn near eight years. We was practically married."

"She didn't tell you that I was your son?"

"She was a wild one, your mama. I wasn't the only man she was seein'. We would be so hot for each other, then shit'd blow up, and I couldn't take it, so I'd leave. I remember comin' back, and she was big as a house. I done axed her if it were mine, but she said no. I thought it might be, but, if she ain't gonna shake me down, I ain't gonna make it easy."

Matt rubs his temples. "Detective Campbell, ... do you remember him?"

David chuckles. "'Course. Why you think I'm here?"

Matt takes a deep breath. "Did Campbell kill my mother?"

"I seen him comin' outta her house at two in the mornin'. I was gonna go see her, but I don't do sloppy seconds. A couple days later, when she started to smell, there was police cars everywhere. Campbell tried to pin it on me but ain't no evidence."

"What about the other girls? There *was* evidence. I looked it up."

David frowns. "Campbell had it out for me. Pinned them rapes on me, so nobody looks at *him*."

"So you're innocent?"

"That's what I said, didn't I? Damn, boy, listen up. Now I got them lawyers at Amnesty Philadelphia. They don't take cases for anybody. Gotta be innocent, or they won't touch you."

"I'm not buyin' it."

"Ain't nuthin' to buy. It's just what is."

"They found your semen. Are you saying they somehow took semen from you and put it inside these women, and they all went along with it?"

"Don't know how they done it, but they done it."

"I'll be calling Amnesty Philadelphia to let them know they're wasting their time."

Matt starts to hang up the phone. He hears, "Wait, wait, little slug—"

Matt puts the phone back to his ear. "What did you call me?"

"Little slugger. ... Ain't nuthin' bad."

Matt slams the phone on the receiver, shoots out of his chair, and bolts for the exit. Ms. Pierce fast-walks behind him.

"Hold on," Officer Reeves says, as Matt blows past him.

Reeves jogs down the hall, past Ms. Pierce, catching up to Matt. He grabs Matt's upper arm.

"Let go of him *right now*," Ms. Pierce says. "You will *not* touch him."

Officer Reeves blushes and releases his grip. Matt stares ahead, blank-faced.

"I'm sorry, ma'am, I just need you guys to sign out. I could get into trouble if you don't."

"Oh, ... sorry," Ms. Pierce says.

They sign and date the sign-out sheet. Officer Reeves leads them to the exit. Outside, in the fresh air, Matt puts his hands on his knees, sucking in oxygen. Ms. Pierce rubs his upper back. Matt stands, his eyes glassy. He closes his eyes, and tears drip down his cheeks. Ms. Pierce reaches forward, holding him. A mother and two small children walk by.

"Why is that man sad?" the young girl asks.

"Because this place is sad," the mother says.

Matt pulls back; Ms. Pierce lets go.

"I remember him," Matt says. "He was the one …"

"What do you mean, *the one*?"

"Campbell didn't kill my mother. My father did."

[25]

Take a Chance

Matt presses in the clutch and shifts into third gear, the dirt road spewing dust behind them, with wind whipping through the cab of the old Ford pickup truck. Endless rows of ankle-length corn seedlings wave in the breeze. He places his hand in the wind, letting his fingers play with the pressure. He glances across the bench seat. His mother leans against a young-looking man with an athletic build, dark wavy hair, and a trimmed beard. Their fingers are intertwined.

"I thought the honeymoon was over," Matt says with a grin. "You two are worse than a couple of teenagers."

Olivia Pierce turns to Matt with a smile. "You're *still* a teenager."

Matt smirks. "I guess, technically, but only for a few more months."

He stops his truck, at the end of the road, parking behind Mr. Clemens's dusty old pickup. The old man stands in a straw hat, suspenders, and his mustache-free white beard. Matt hops out of his truck and greets Mr. Clemens with a strong handshake. Derrick and Olivia step from the truck.

Mr. Clemens tips his cap. "How was that honeymoon?"

"It flew by," Derrick says.

"It's so nice to see you, Elam," Olivia says, giving the old man a hug. "I'm really sorry about Doris."

He steps back and waves his hand. "It was a long time comin'. I'm lookin' to join her soon. I guess God has a few loose ends for me to tie up before I do. Speakin' of loose ends, you wanna walk the property awhile?"

They walk the hundred-acre cornfield. Mr. Clemens points out boundaries and features.

"This road you came in on is an easement," the old man says, "so you'll always have access by truck."

They walk down the road to the edge of the property, then across the cornfield to the top of the hill, adjacent a two-lane highway. Cars and trucks motor by.

"And you have six hundred feet of good road frontage. I know Matt's been wantin' to put up a market." Mr. Clemens smiles at Matt. "He tried to convince me to do it, but I'm too damn old. A new business is a young man's game. I think he's right though. This would be a good spot for it."

They walk down the hill.

"It's a south-facing hill too," Matt says. "Perfect for growing fruit trees or anything else that likes the sun."

They stop in front of Mr. Clemens's truck.

Mr. Clemens looks at Matt. "Son, it would make me mighty happy to see you buy this land. The goin' rate these days for ag land that can't be subdivided is twelve thousand an acre. This tract is 104 acres. We'll call it a hundred for the sake of argument."

"One point two million," Matt says.

Derrick lets out a low whistle.

"There's just no way," Olivia says.

"I'll tell you what," Mr. Clemens says. "I'll sell you this tract for eight thousand an acre."

Matt smiles.

"If it weren't for my damn kids, I'd give you the land. They've been bankin' on this payday for thirty years."

"Thank you, Mr. Clemens. Can I get back to you tomorrow?" Matt extends his hand.

Mr. Clemens shakes it. "You're a hard worker, you know that? I got four boys, and not one of 'em put in a hard day's work here. You've done it every weekend and holiday for two and a half years, without a single complaint."

They wave good-bye as Mr. Clemens drives away in his truck.

Olivia turns to Matt. "Eight hundred thousand dollars is a lot of money, and I didn't want to be rude to Mr. Clemens, but it doesn't look like much. I mean, there's nothing here. There's no barn or house or even any trees."

"I'm sorry, Matt, but I'm inclined to agree," Derrick says.

"You guys aren't seeing the potential," Matt says. "We'd get tons of customers, just having the market along the road. And we could put in swales and productive trees and shrubs to heal the land from all the abuse it's taken over the years. We could run livestock between the swales. At least three places would make good, cheap valley dam sites, where we could have fish and water plants. We could put in a native wildflower meadow and raise bees for honey and wax."

"That infrastructure sounds expensive," Derrick says. "I mean, you'd have to build a market, and, correct me if I'm wrong, but wouldn't those trees take a while to produce?"

"We don't have to do everything right away. We can grow annuals for cash flow to build the farm."

"How much do you need?"

"About two hundred thousand for the down payment, plus infrastructure, equipment, and seed money."

Olivia frowns. "I don't have that kind of money. I have maybe ten thousand in savings and, if I liquidate my retirement, maybe another forty."

"I have about twenty thousand saved," Derrick says. "You can have it."

"I don't think you understand," Matt says. "I'm not asking you to give me any money. I'm asking you to be my partners in this business."

"Honey, I don't know anything about farming," Olivia says.

"Neither do I," Derrick says.

"I could teach you," Matt says.

"We still don't have near enough money," Olivia says, "and I already have a job."

"But we do. I've saved almost $150,000 over the past three years."

Olivia's and Derrick's mouths hang open.

"How?" Olivia asks.

"I've been living with you rent-free. I work eighty hours a week, and I don't buy anything."

Derrick shakes his head with a grin. "Unbelievable."

"I still have my job," Olivia says.

"Keep your job," Matt says. "I'll build the farm. You can help on weekends and in the summer, if you want. I can't get the loan without you. You have the type of steady job that banks like. And, if it doesn't work out, we can sell the land, and you can have your money back plus 10 percent interest. Either way you win."

"I don't care about winning," Olivia says. "How about I cosign and lend you the money? And you pay me back when you can?"

"I can't ask you to do that," Matt says. "If you loan me money, I'll make you a partner based on how much money you invest. If you want me to buy you out when I have the money, I'll do that with interest."

"I'm in," Derrick says with a grin.

Olivia's eyes widen. "What about *your* job?"

"I hate my job. Seriously, Liv, what are we doing with our lives? Didn't you say that you didn't want to be a part of state-run education anymore?"

"I know, but my *state job* pays the bills. Plus we need it to get the loan initially."

"How many twenty-year-olds do you know who've saved 150K in three years? I wanna do something good. What could be better than feeding people healthy food? This farm is gonna be successful, and I'd like to be part of it."

Olivia smiles at Matt. "It's a lot of work, isn't it?"

"It's not work if you love it."

[26]

Abundance

M att picks up a handful of subsoil from the mountainous pile in front of an equally cavernous hole. He takes the soil in his hands and makes a baseball. He squeezes it. The ball holds its form but does not shed any water. He rubs the ball back and forth between his hands, creating a snake. Two young men stare at him, one bearded and burly, the other skinny and baby-faced. A massive loader and a twenty-ton tracked excavator loom large in the background.

"This seam is mostly clay, and the moisture content is right," Matt says. "If we don't leave it out too long, it'll compact and seal nicely."

"Can we start buildin' the wall with this clay?" the bearded man asks.

"This clay is good for the dam wall, but we gotta have a keyway, or the wall could fail. I'd like for you to dig down six feet, then compact the layers six inches at a time. We should end up with a wall height just below where the state would get involved, seven feet from the original grade. Give me a call on the radio, if you run into any problems."

Matt sits down on the driver's side of the repurposed electric golf cart with knobby tires, a small cargo bed, and bamboo sides. He drives along the graveled access track away from the future fish pond. As he continues, the property is more developed. Long open ditches snake across the hill, forming wavy contour lines with berms in front. The swales overflow into the occasional fish pond. Mostly fruit and nut trees grow on the berms, with large-leaf comfrey, berries, and nitrogen-fixing shrubs in the understory. Behind are nitrogen-fixing trees, such as black locust and mimosa, to provide fertility and nectar for the bees. In the pasture between the swales, chickens and cattle graze behind electric fencing.

He stops next to a long narrow structure with a metal roof, similar to an open carport, except its six hundred feet long and only ten feet deep. Lattice windbreaks are fastened to the north side to shield the inhabitants from cold northerly winds. Matt walks toward the structure. He hears the collective hum of busy bees. A hundred Warre beehives sit facing southeast. The hives are protected from wind, rain, and snow.

Matt kneels next to the entrance of a hive. He watches the bees coming and going, like an overcrowded airport runway. He sees them land gracefully on the platform, with orange pollen attached to their legs. A honeybee lands on his finger. He watches the bee search for nectar, then take flight. He gazes down the line of hives that appear endless from his vantage point. He scans the natural beauty of the trees, shrubs, vines, herbs, weeds, and flowers that bloom every color in the spectrum. He smiles to himself as he thinks of the short five years it's taken to turn a degraded corn and soy field into natural abundance.

He hops back on the golf cart and continues up the path. Near the top of the property, a colossal bamboo grove provides a windbreak, building materials, and food from the new shoots. The giant canes stand fifty feet tall, with thick trunks. Two men hack with machetes at the base of a couple of canes. An older man saws small limbs off the harvested stalks. A green Ford F-350, with faded vinyl lettering on the doors that reads Reggie's Tree Service, is loaded down with canes. Matt approaches.

"How are you doing, Reggie?" Matt asks.

"Matthew, my man, we got ourselves quite a harvest comin'." Reggie looks up from his saw and grins, exposing two toothless holes. "You sure we ain't cut too much?"

"We're good. It'll grow back in no time."

Matt continues on the path to the expansive wooden building along the main road. The quiet sounds of the farm ecosystem begin to merge with the street sounds of the outside world. A handful of workers harvest produce from the terrace garden behind the building. They carry willow baskets, overflowing with vegetables, fruits, and herbs. He parks the electric cart and strides to the front of the single-story building.

The gravel parking lot is full, with a few cars double-parked and three cars in the wildflower meadow. He glances up at the sign—Moyer & Pierce Natural Foods. He steps inside the market. Customers bustle about, pushing bamboo carts filled with produce or filling up willow baskets. He scans the shelves, taking note of inventory and the varying popularity of the products. Honeycomb, gooseberries, eggs, fish, crystal apple cucumbers, and purple asparagus are running low.

"Excuse me, sir?"

Matt turns to see an elderly woman. "Yes, ma'am. How can I help you?"

"My friend told me that you have these little green things that are like kiwi, except it doesn't have that fuzzy brown stuff I don't like. She said that they are so sweet, but I can't find 'em."

"I agree with your friend. *Those* are really sweet. The fruit is the Hardy Arctic Kiwi, and unfortunately they don't store too well, so we only have them in the fall for a month. If you check back in October, we'll be overflowing with them."

"Thank you so much, young man. Please tell your boss that I just love this place. Everyone here is so knowledgeable, and the food is so unique and wonderful. You know, I haven't seen gooseberries since I was a little girl."

"I really appreciate that, ma'am. I'll pass that along."

Matt strides toward the counter. A hanging bamboo sign overhead reads Fresh-Cut Herbs. An attractive young woman—with wavy brown hair, a round face, khaki pants, and a green polo shirt embroidered with Pierce & Moyer—explains the fresh-cut herb service to a pregnant woman.

"These are the pictures of everything that's in season, and their uses are underneath. Here's the form. You just check off what you want and the amount, and one of the girls will pick it for you, while you finish shopping. It usually only takes ten minutes, depending on how much you need. This gives you the freshest herbs possible."

"Thank you," the pregnant woman says, as she hands over her order.

Matt walks over to the attractive woman. "How are we doing on the herbs, Madison?" he asks.

"The plants are holding up. Thankfully they grow as fast as we cut 'em. I think we should plant more rosemary and basil. They're the most popular."

"This was a fantastic idea, by the way."

Madison smiles, her lips pink.

"Did you hear from Tariq last night?"

"I did." She places her left hand over her heart, exposing her wedding band. "I was really freaking out. It had been almost a week. He was in a remote area outside of Fallujah. He didn't have Internet service. He's fine. He said he got a lot of footage. I just really miss him, you know?"

"Yeah, I know. How's Ryan?"

Madison smirks. "It's nice having him home from college, especially with Tariq gone, but it's also really annoying. He's so messy. By the way, he wants to work here this summer. Do we have anything he can do?"

"He can help customers, stock shelves, work the register. We're a little shorthanded inside, with Olivia out of commission."

"He said he wanted to work outside, get a tan."

"I love Ryan, but I don't think he'd last long out in the field. Video games don't exactly prepare you for that. The guys outside work hard. They're not gonna be happy, if Ryan can't pull his weight. They'll think I'm playing favorites."

"You're right. It'd be a disaster. I'll break the news gently. He'll be happy to be in here anyway. The customers will love him. By the way, Derrick was looking for you. He's in his office."

"Thanks."

Matt strides past the raw milk and cheeses, and the sprouted breads to the back of the store. He opens a door that leads down a corridor. He passes the bathrooms, and stops at an office door with a placard that reads Derrick Pierce, General Manager. Matt taps on the door.

"Come in," Derrick says.

Matt opens the door. Derrick sits behind a computer. He looks like a lumberjack with dark wavy hair, a trimmed beard, and an athletic build. Derrick looks up, his brow furrowed.

"I was calling you," Derrick says.

Matt feels his belt. "I'm sorry. I left my radio on the cart. What's wrong? You look stressed."

"It's George. He keeps sending all these orders from the road, and this website he set up is blowing up. Who knew people would want to order our honey from all over the country?"

"That sounds like a good problem."

"Come take a look at the orders from the last few weeks."

Matt walks to the computer screen and looks over Derrick's shoulder. "Whoa."

"Exactly. At this rate we'll be out of honey by next month. And we can't harvest more until next spring."

"The hives are actually doing better than I thought they would with the shelters and all the bee forage. I think we can do another harvest, as long as it's soon. Also we need to build more shelters, because the bees keep swarming, and I'm running out of space for new hives."

"Maybe we should bring George home," Derrick says. "Let him do the website and marketing, until the big fall harvest."

"That's a good idea." Matt smiles. "And here I thought we had a problem."

"Sorry, Matt. I'm really anxious these days. I just want everything to work out. Could you talk to her? She's doing way too much. You know how she is."

Matt laughs. "She doesn't listen to me either. Is she in her office?"

Derrick nods.

Matt crosses the hall and knocks on the shut door.

"Come in," she says in a singsong voice.

Matt steps into the office. "I'm sorry to interrupt. I know, technically, it's still writing time."

"I'm actually finished," Olivia says.

"For the day?"

"No, it's done," she says with a wide grin. "I hope it's actually good. I can't wait for you to read it."

Olivia hands Matt a stack of double-spaced pages fastened with a clip.

Matt reads the title page. "*People Farm*, I love it."

"It's an allegory for our exploitative state-run system, using high school as the setting. I hope you don't mind, but I based the main character on you."

Matt laughs. "I hope you use a pen name. Big Brother might come looking for you."

Olivia laughs.

"I'm flattered that you'd use me in your novel," Matt says. "I'll start on this as soon as I get home tonight. I'm really excited to read it. On another note, Derrick told me that you've been doing too much."

Olivia exhales. "I do love that man, but he's such a worrier." She stands up, her arm supporting her back. Matt braces her other arm. Her stomach is round and swollen.

"Congratulations."

"I haven't given birth yet," she says.

Matt grins. "On the book."

"I knew what you meant. Thank you, honey."

Matt gives her a brief hug. She kisses him on the cheek.

"Do you think I'll be a good mother?" she asks.

"You already are."

She starts to cry. "You've gotta be careful around your mother these days. I cry about everything." She laughs through the tears.

"One more thing, … you're fired for the next few months. I don't wanna see you stocking shelves or even working at the register."

Olivia nods and smiles with tear streaks on her cheeks.

Matt walks to his office and drops the manuscript on his desk. An old wooden desk, a dusty computer, and a metal filing cabinet complete the Spartan furnishings. He marches back to the store floor.

The lunchtime rush dies down, but two dozen shoppers still linger, mostly elderly women. A familiar face looks over the last of the root-cellar apples. His heart beats faster. Her blond hair is cut shorter now, to chin length. She wears a sundress that tugs in all the right places. She still looks young for her age, her porcelain skin showing no signs of cracking. She stands out among the sweatpants clientele, like a single rose in a field of wheat. Her movements are haphazard, like she's not sure what to do with her arms or how she's supposed to stand.

Matt walks across the floor, his gaze following her every movement. He catches her eye. She glances up and sees Matt walking in her direction. She smiles and blushes. She looks down at the apples. He's only a few feet away. She looks up again, still blushing.

"How much are the apples?" Emily says.

"The price is whatever they're worth to you."

Dear Reader,

I'm thrilled that you took precious time out of your life to read my novel. Thank you! I hope you found it entertaining, engaging, and thought-provoking. If so, please consider writing a positive review on Amazon and Goodreads. Five-star reviews have a huge impact on future sales. The review doesn't need to be long and detailed, if you're more of a reader than a writer. As an author and a small businessman, competing against the big publishers, every reader, every review, and every referral is greatly appreciated.

If you're interested in reading my other titles for free or discounted, go to the following link: http://www.PhilWBooks.com. You're probably thinking, *What's the catch?* There is no catch.

If you want to contact me, don't be bashful. I can be found at Phil@PhilWBooks.com. I do my best to respond to all emails.

Sincerely,
Phil M. Williams

Made in the USA
San Bernardino, CA
27 August 2018